THE BEAUTY IN SCARS

USA TODAY BESTSELLING AUTHOR

M.L. PHILPITT

AUTHOR'S NOTE

The Beauty in Scars is book 3 of The Fractured Ever Afters series. While his can be read as a standalone, there is an overarching plot which starts in The Hunt in Elusion.

There is a part at the end, second half in chapter 47, that is a time jump and implies a lot within those three days. I did not skip over such a huge part of the series' overarching plot. It's coming in book 4. Just a note so you don't feel like something major has been missed. It's the next characters' story, not Isabelle and Rafael's.

This book has content some people may find triggering. You can read the content warning list on the last page.

This book uses Canadian spelling. This means words will have U's in them, "re", or double LL's. (colour vs color, centre vs center, signalling vs signaling, etc.) These are not typos.

PLAYLIST

"Heathens" by Twenty One Pilots
"Hypnotic" by Zella Day
"Not Strong Enough" by Apocalyptica & Brent Smith
"Roses and Gold" by Bryce Savage
"Fallen Angel" by Three Days Grace
"Dangerous State of Mind" by Chri$tian Gate$
"Empty" by Letdown.
"Bring Me To Life" by Evanescence
"Paralyzed" by NF
"Control" by Halsey
"Ricochet" by Catch Your Breath
"Something There" by Emma Watson & Dan Stevens
"What Makes You Beautiful" by One Direction
"Addicted" by Saving Abel
"Not Meant to Be" by Theory of a Deadman
"Love The Way You Lie" by Eminem & Rihanna
"Under Your Scars" by Godsmack
"I Want You Here" by Plumb

"Beauty and the Beast" by Angela Lansbury
"How Does a Moment Last Forever?" by Celine Dion
"Evermore" bu Josh Groban
"Every Breath You Take" by Chase Holfelder

For those who want a real-life book boyfriend

Well...sorry, I might have given you another one.

BUT enjoy watching one of our own find her book boyfriend come to life.

1
RAFAEL

What a fucking day.

And it's only noon.

When my phone pings with a message, a gut feeling says it's about to get worse. I abandon the stack of paperwork I'm working through to retrieve my cell, buried beneath a few contracts. Even with the bullshit Stefano De Falco has dropped on my family's lives, Eden can't run itself; therefore, I manage to get work done when I can.

The cat-and-mouse game we're playing with him is one thing. The fact that my twenty-year-old baby sister, Aurora, is lying in a hospital bed, in a coma, because of the fucker is an entirely different thing. We've barely gotten her back in our lives, and already, assholes are trying to take her from us.

Helping to hunt Rozelyn De Falco, Stefano's daughter, gave me purpose for a few days, but with her found, the feeling of being in limbo, not knowing when Aurora will awaken, has returned. Which has made Eden an ideal place to spend my time while Flynn, our enforcer, is torturing information from Rozelyn. My older brother, Nico, is keeping everything afloat in the meantime, while our parents, his new wife, Della, her sister, and our older, estranged brother, Hawke and his girlfriend, sit by Aurora's bedside.

The message on my phone reads:

MAURICE

Capo, can we talk?

An odd message to receive from the soldier who's old enough to be my father. For one, he rarely reaches out in general, and two, he typically comes out and states what he needs.

ME

About?

MAURICE

Trust me. You'll want to hear this. Come to this location please.

He shares a pin on a map, which I click, and it opens the app, providing directions from Eden to Mount Royal.

What does he think I'll want to hear? And why can't it be said over the phone? Caution flares up inside me because Maurice's behaviour is moving to a new level of strange, but there's an urgency I must respond to.

I abandon my work and snatch my car keys, opening a text thread to the man who, besides recent developments, I trust as much as I do Nico.

ME

Meet me at the pin.

I attach the same pin Maurice sent me to Rosen, and then a screenshot of Maurice's message, so he knows why I'm asking him to tagalong.

ROSEN

On my way.

I drive to the pinned location, arriving at the base of Mount Royale. The openness of this spot is disconcerting, and my gaze constantly wanders, scanning for danger. Within minutes of parking, Rosen arrives, parking his car beside mine.

"I'm surprised you want me here," he says as he approaches.

I roll my neck to look at him, amused. He should think that. After all, when learning that a highly respected and trusted bodyguard *and* friend is fucking the woman he's meant to be protecting, one has the right to be pissed. But he's proven himself over the past few days, remaining awake to scour the city for Rozelyn, all in vengeance for her drugging Aurora, so I'm over any anger I felt when learning about their secret relationship. He clearly loves her, even if he doesn't realize it yet.

Still, I joke, "What, because of recent revelations? I mean, sure, you're scum and all," I grin, easing the weight of my statement, "but you're still one of the best. And a friend. Nico won't kill you, you know."

He would have done it already.

"Wanna bet?"

I can bet my sports car on that fact, and while I'm about to tell him that, an older Toyota Corolla stops beside Rosen's car, and Maurice gets out, his gaze darting over the open vastness.

My stomach flips with anxiety, even though I tell myself his inspection is simply his training. He stops in front of us, standing a few feet away, but his studying doesn't end. I glance at Rosen, checking if he shares my confusion.

"You wanted to talk, Maurice," I start, breaking the soldier's attention. "Very strange circumstances, I must say."

He jerks his head into a nod and shifts his feet, rolling his lips around. Maurice is typically good at holding in his emotions. Given his experience, in the past, he's often helping train the younger inductees—me and my brothers included.

"The entire family has been hunting for De Falco."

The mention of that asshole's name has me pushing off my car door where I was slouching. "You have news?"

Maurice rubs a hand down his face, highlighting what I haven't noticed. The crazed, red-rimmed eyes, cracked lips, and blatant fear as he continues glancing around.

"I-I do. I know where he is. But..."

But? There's no time for *buts*.

"But?" I prompt, my feet bringing me nearer. "But what, Maurice? Where is he? What do you know?" The demand for his response grows, and my hands curl by my sides, fighting to prevent from strangling the truth out of him.

The man I've known my entire life and the one standing in front of me are not the same. This one, with his shoulders hunched, his breathing heavy, his eyes puffy, is not the man who helped train me. Is not the one who fought by my father's side for many years.

"I-I'm sorry, Capo. I-I h-had to protect her and—"

"Who?" Rosen demands.

"My daughter."

His daughter? Maurice doesn't have a daughter. All our men are extensively background checked before they take their oaths. Maurice has always been a single guy, quieter than some, sticking to himself.

Father would know about this. No one can hide a family from us, even one that was created during his employment.

"Stefano De Falco is—" Maurice stops, swallowing. "You must help me protect her. De Falco is—"

His words cut off into a gurgle, his eyes bulging, hands flying to cover the spurt of blood coming from his neck. He stumbles toward us, and Rosen lunges, catching Maurice's body before he hits the ground. But the moment Rosen has him, Maurice takes his final breath.

"Get down!"

Reaching for Rosen, I yank on his sleeve until he drops the dead soldier and I'm able to drag him toward my car, using it as a shield. The shot came from somewhere behind Maurice, so that's the direction to avoid.

"We can't leave him!" Rosen argues, positioning his feet as though he's about to stand again.

I wish we didn't have to but retrieving his body means being in the open again, and a dead man's body isn't worth our very much alive ones. Empathy for the man who's been around my entire life can't be felt until later, when we're safe. Sometimes, grief must be set aside.

"We need to get out of here," I counter. "Standing could mean death. We'll come back for his body, but our lives matter more." I reach up and pull on the driver's side door, slipping inside quickly. No further shots have come at us, but that's not to say they won't.

Once Rosen climbs in the back seat, I peel out of the lot, abandoning Rosen's car and Maurice's body.

~

"Rosen and Aurora, huh? Our family doesn't do simple."

If it wasn't for Hawke's use of "our," I'd laugh. Rather, it comes out as a huff because I'm too stuck on his acknowledgement of what he is to us.

Family.

Hawke. My other sibling, older than Nico by barely a year, should be underboss right now. When he was fourteen, he was kidnapped and raped over a series of days before our father rescued him. Already, he held a tentative hatred for the mob life, and it gave him an out.

Until a few months ago, when he reached out to Nico for assistance in saving the woman, who's presently occupying the back seat of my sports car, as I drive them both to the private airfield the Corsetti jet is waiting on.

That single contact started a domino effect. When Nico told Della about Hawke, she suggested inviting him to their wedding. Shocking enough, Hawke agreed to come, and even brought his girlfriend, Willow, who he's fiercely protective of. They remained in the city long past what they agreed to due to Aurora's unforeseen drugging. Since she woke earlier today, they're headed home.

"I think it's sweet," Willow speaks up from the back seat. "He's her bodyguard, but clearly being around each other so much sparked something between them."

"It'll be weird," I comment, pulling up to the airfield and stopping a short distance from the plane. "My entire life, I've seen Rosen in one light. Once Aurora's out of the hospital, we won't hear the end of this. Which means, soon, I'll be adjusting to the idea of them together."

Hawke laughs. "Would now be the time to admit I encouraged it? First at the reception and then today when I said goodbye. She doesn't deserve to be forced into an engagement to Erico Rossi, who'll only make her miserable." He narrows his eyes as though daring me to disagree.

Shutting off the car, I shrug, uncaring what my siblings do. "I agree. I've been saying to Nico from the beginning that she'll hate him for the engagement, but he was insistent she'd fall in line. Guess I was right."

Hawke isn't listening any longer though. He's staring at the jet, a wistful expression consuming him. His body posture changes subtly, his spine curling with his slump.

"You don't have to leave." My neutral tone hides hope. Having Hawke remain in Montreal and rejoin the family is a dream. "We all like having you home."

He doesn't face me, but the corner of his mouth lifts, his lip ring becoming more obvious in the setting sun's glow. He couldn't look more different than Nico and me with his gothic style and multiple facial piercings, but we'd all take him back instantly.

Especially our parents, who he hasn't spoken to, right up to leaving.

"You sound like Aurora. She asked me the same."

"What'd you tell her?"

"Same thing I'll tell you. I might be going home, but there's a reason I came in the first place, Rafael. I won't allow another fourteen years to pass without visiting."

As though he hasn't just dropped great news, he slides from my car and helps Willow out. After a moment, I trail behind them, not bothering to hide my grin as I come around the other side of my vehicle.

"Thanks for the ride," Willow says with her typical small smile. "At the hospital, it seemed like you were headed elsewhere when Aurora kicked everyone out."

I was, but I simply shrug off her comment. "Like I'd leave you guys to take a cab. Or worse, ask for a ride from our parents." Hawke would probably walk before doing that.

Hawke reaches his hand out toward me, and I take it in a shake, but in the action, he pushes a piece of paper into my hand. "My number," he explains. "I also gave it to Aurora. Only you two and Nico have it. Don't give it to our parents."

I unfold the paper, reciting the digits in my head. For all the shit that's gone down with Aurora and De Falco in the past few days, there's been one major positive in this and that's been having my brother back.

"Thanks, Hawke."

He stands there for a beat, as though thinking about doing something, but changes his mind and reaches for Willow's hand, pulling her toward the plane.

She waves before turning around and walking up the staircase first, disappearing into the body of the plane. At the top of the stairs, Hawke stops, turning around to face me again. He's too far to see his expression, but he lifts his hand in a final wave and then disappears into the plane.

Originally, once seeing Aurora awake and well, I was going to head for Maurice's house, but Hawke requesting a ride to the airport is much more important. De Falco and the hidden truths swirling around my family can wait until tomorrow because today was about family. Aurora's health and Hawke's reconnection.

The pilot gets to work prepping the plane for takeoff, but I don't budge. Not as the jets whirl, blasting loud and blustering winds around me, or as the plane moves. Not even when it turns down the runway, getting farther and farther away, speed eventually lifting it into the sky.

When it's finally out of sight, I push off from my car and unfold the note with Hawke's number on it again, reading it over and over before inputting it into my phone's contacts.

Love you, big bro.

More than anything, I want him back and to never leave again, but he has friends and a successful law firm where he's made home. I should be proud of him for doing what he wants, for chasing his dream, but it's difficult to feel pride when my own selfish desires continue to take over.

I get it, though. He has his life and I have mine.

Life of a capo.

2

ISABELLE

His fangs glinted in the low light of the candles lining the room as he stalked closer.

"Little prey," he cooed, his lips curling, making his fangs more prominent. I always should have feared how easily he could kill me, but my betraying body reacted in other ways instead, and I only felt lust at the sight of his teeth.

He side-stepped me. His shoulder brushed mine, a barely-there touch I felt in the bottom of my stomach. I turned my head to follow his trajectory, keeping him in sight.

"You're not supposed to smell as delicious as you do," he murmured, his lips dangerously close to my ear, causing me to shiver.

I stopped breathing when strands of his hair skated over my neck, reminding me how close he was. How easy it was for him to sink his teeth into me.

How much I wanted him to.

"What am I supposed to smell like then?" I find myself asking.

"My enemy," he purred, shifting closer. His chest aligned with *my back and his hands came up, cupping my shoulders and locking my feet in place. "My enemy, instead of my downfall."*

His teeth plunged into—

"How can you read that shit? There's no pictures."

I've never hated a person more than I do right now.

Slamming my Kindle down, I remind myself to breathe deeply before I risk getting fired from a job I should technically not even have yet based on the education requirements.

The deep breaths calm my mind enough to respond to who's become the bane of my existence the past couple weeks. I find him patiently watching me, his chin propped up on his fist from where he leans against the counter, acting as though he's innocent and hasn't just insulted my reading preferences.

With his free hand, he gestures toward my e-reader. "You were totally into that scene, but from what I read—and I did read over your shoulder to see what you were so engrossed in— it's not that exciting. Some vampire dude's about to bite a chick, right?"

Every syllable out of this guy's mouth sets my teeth on edge.

No amount of breathing will make Gage more tolerable, so I turn away from him, opting not to respond. Over his past two weeks here at Bibliothèque de Côte-des-Neiges, I've come to terms with the fact that he's just someone I can't stand.

I play nice because my manager told me to, but I certainly don't need to like the douche. And a douche he is. An idiotic douche, to be exact. Anyone else would have learned their lesson the three—yes, *three*—times they were caught and fined for illegal hunting. But not Gage. Instead, he aimed for a fourth, pissed off the courts, and not only was fined again, but sentenced to community service. Something about "giving back," though I find it difficult to imagine what they think working in a library will do, considering he murders innocent animals for fun.

How and why do I know all this? Because Gage talks about it all the time. All. The. Fucking. Time. Like he's proud and views it as an accomplishment. Sometimes I imagine he has dead animal furs and other trophy-like items scattered over his house, and then I despise him more.

Putting aside his unsavoury murderous hobbies, he's a douche in general. Insults everything I read, reluctantly follows my instructions, rolls his eyes when patrons enter, and acts like books will burn him alive every time he has to touch them.

Maybe they will. If I'm lucky.

To top it all off, he doesn't exactly understand the word "no." It makes sense coming from the guy who repeatedly went behind the court's back and continued doing what they caught him for.

"If you're getting turned on by the idea of biting, I could make that a thing." Gage leans closer, stretching his arm across the counter. His large hand rests over my Kindle and he tries to tug it free from my hand, but I hold firm, glaring, fucking *daring* him to steal it. "If you'd finally accept my offer to hang out, that is."

"Thanks," I tighten my grip, ripping it from under his hand and tucking it beneath the counter, where I typically store it when I'm working, "but no thanks."

He trails behind me as I walk away, first to a nearby shelf, then to the cart of books I abandoned earlier that need to be shelved. "You're not seeing someone. Obviously."

Obviously. I know why he says that, why he assumes. It's why everyone assumes. I've lived the experiences enough to know I'm not what guys want, but it doesn't mean morons like Gage get a free pass because they think I'm desperate.

I'll *never* be desperate enough for him.

I'll happily die my virgin, spinster self before remotely considering his offer.

I sort the recently returned books, stacking them into piles based on genre. The mystery stack is the largest, so I grab that and shove it roughly toward him, doing more damage to my fingers than his chest.

"Here. Put these away."

He takes the stack, his fingers brushing mine as he moves away, his lip lifting in what he thinks is a sexy smirk, but he'll *never* be like the men I read about. No one will.

"You got it, Isabelle."

I've never hated hearing my name more than when he says it.

After Gage walks away, I put the remainder of the books away, taking my time as I walk through the empty young adult and youth floor of the library. It's the middle of the day, so with most children and teenagers in school right now, patrons are much fewer.

Which makes my job very simple and provides a lot of extra reading time, which is a perk. Plus, with Gage as my involuntary helper, I have an extra set of hands.

When I finish shelving the books, I do a quick clean-up of the counter, ensuring everything is orderly and in its place. When all is done, I get my Kindle again and unlock it, opening to the scene Gage interrupted earlier.

After what ends up becoming a gruelling, long shift with Gage continuously interrupting me and me having to give him various tasks to keep him busy, I'm pleased to be heading home.

The four o'clock sun shines in my face as I walk toward my apartment complex. Once I cross a street, I glance behind me, taking a quick survey of my surroundings. I turn down my music, ensuring I'd be able to hear footsteps come up behind me. Half a block down, I check behind me again.

It's wise to be vigilant in a city, but the obsessive checking Dad drilled into me is a pattern I'm trying to break. There's vigilance and then there's psychotic.

Dad's a bit...paranoid. That'd be the best word to describe him. He's been like that for as long as I can remember. He's always feared something, choosing to homeschool me instead of allowing me to attend a public school. Even living alone now, he's always reminding me to triple-check the lock on my door before bed, to constantly scan my surroundings as I walk, to keep my keys in my grip for an easy weapon.

I maintain quick strides, thankful the library isn't too far away from where I live. When I get to my apartment, I turn the deadbolt as well as the door chain. Little behaviours I *could* and maybe should change, but they remind me of living with Dad.

Moving out last year meant him allowing me to be a regular adult and doing something with my English Literature degree— which I completed on an expedited path because home-schooling meant graduating high school before everyone else when there's nothing else to do but study.

He agreed since he spent so much of my childhood not present. Like, he was there but not truly and mentally *there*, which makes his obsession with safety even more irritating. I don't have it in my heart to suggest he go get his mental health checked, but I want to because his paranoia is stifling.

Thinking about him reminds me of the date. We should be having our weekly dinner tomorrow night at his house. I glance at my phone, thinking how he's typically habitual in his confir-mation messages the day before. I haven't gotten one yet, which is strange, but I have noticed his job as a security officer for some downtown office has been keeping him busier than usual these past couple of weeks.

If I hear nothing by tomorrow, I'll head over there regardless.

I wander through my apartment, shutting curtains as I go, heading for the bathroom to clean up. Washing my face at the end of the day is probably the best part. Being able to take the makeup wipe and reveal the redness I try so hard to hide when I'm at work.

Well, not hide. It'd be impossible to completely conceal the ugly scars on my face. One that starts on my forehead and skates down my cheek, with the other on the opposite cheek, ending at my chin. They're always *there*, impossible to ignore, but my foundation does a decent job of managing to reduce the redness.

As I wash my face, my fingers brush over the raised skin. I have no recollection of receiving them, but it must have happened when I was young, since any photos of me as a child already has me with them. Dad claims it was an accident. No matter how many times I've asked for details, he brushes me aside and claims it's for the best.

But I've always wondered: what kind of accident turns a child into a monster?

3
RAFAEL

There's a common joke that the youngest child—or, in my case, son—has it easier. They're the least anxious, having less worries of all the siblings. By the time they're born, their parents are so exhausted from raising their older siblings, there's fewer restrictions placed on them.

It's completely true.

I've grown up with a lot of freedoms. When Hawke left, Nico slid into the place of Father's heir, eventually becoming underboss and me, the son next in line, capo. And after what happened with Hawke, Father spent extra efforts training Nico, which left me to certain liberties.

When Nico took his position of underboss, I also became mine, which is why I find myself parking my custom-painted Audi R8 in the Ville-Marie neighbourhood, outside a small, picturesque house.

Seriously?

Definitely imagined Maurice's home more bachelor-like, rather than a two-storey house in a residential neighbourhood.

It seems too large for the man I've known my entire life, but then again, apparently he has a hidden child, so this is starting to make more and more sense.

I glance at my phone again, rereading the address found in Maurice Dupont's file and matching it to the house number and street sign in front of me.

This seems to be it.

I slide from the car, not bothering to lock the doors as I stride away. Anyone can take two seconds to peek at the car and then me and determine I'm someone they don't want to fuck with.

Once I'm in the shadows provided by the house, I push my sunglasses up and onto my head, fixing my features to be sympathetic. Maurice isn't the first man I've seen killed in front of me. We've lost plenty of good guys over the years, and while each of their deaths make me feel bad, they get easier. Expected. When one deals and witnesses death so much, it's easier to switch off the grief.

Striding up to the door, I steel a breath. No matter how many deaths I've seen, this part, informing the family, is the hardest. These men opt to work for us, so it's only proper to do their families the graciousness of delivering the news directly.

I lift a fist to the white door and knock in three rapid successions, and then wait. Eventually, I hear feet approaching the door. It opens a crack, a woman's deep brown eyes peering through. The colour is so dark, so soft, I'm momentarily distracted.

They quickly flick down my body before she opens the door a few more inches, revealing more of her. Dressed in a simple tank and jean shorts, her shapely legs momentarily steal my attention. I love a woman's legs. I love them peeking out from a dress. I love watching them be spread for others, or even parting them myself. The feel of plump skin beneath my hands; the perfect handle to grip onto as I push into her.

"Who are you?"

Her rough, rude tone forces my attention upwards, stunned to be spoken to like this. Clearly, this woman hasn't been taught manners.

She shuts the door a fraction, blocking more of her body from view. I can appreciate her fear. Makes her wise.

My gaze travels back to her face; her chestnut hair is wrapped up in a messy bun, clearing the way for me to notice what I hadn't before.

Scars. Two of them.

One long one, etched along the edge of her face, starting on her forehead, inches above her right eye, and curving down her cheek. The other one is on the left side of her face, from her cheek to her chin. Raised and pink, but obviously not new.

I don't know what to think or say. Scars like that, like they were etched, permanently marking up otherwise smooth skin makes me wonder who hurt her. *Why* they hurt her. What their names are so I can hunt them down and disfigure them.

"Who are you?" she repeats warily.

The scar beginning at her forehead wrinkles as her face pinches into a sneer. The door closes another inch, but I throw my hand into it, stopping it from being shut any farther.

This woman can't be his daughter because, based on her appearance, she must be in her twenties, and there's no way Maurice hid a child from my father for over *twenty years*. Perhaps she's a girlfriend or a babysitter to the child.

"My name is Rafael Corsetti. I'm an associate of Maurice Dupont. I need to speak with his daughter."

It's a barely noticeable change, but her expression smooths a fraction, which I only notice because I'm so intently watching her. Her gaze drops before quickly flicking upwards again, but there's a new strain behind her eyes. Her hand on the door tightens.

"What do you want with her?"

"I have news about her father."

"What about my father?" She crosses her arms, cocking her hip to lean against the door. Through her façade, fear filters in, her skin growing paler with each passing second.

Her father?

I scan the tiny, scarred woman again. *Oh, fuck.* Not a babysitter then. This could be beneficial though. If there's a possibility of Maurice's child overhearing something useful, an adult makes this even more likely.

"*You're* his daughter?"

"Glad to find someone with such a pretty face doesn't need his hearing checked. Yes, that's what I said."

Spunky. She's the opposite of Maurice's quiet demeanor. He's always been reserved, but his behaviours don't seem to have duplicated into her.

"Where is my father?" she demands, her voice getting harder, her words quickening. "Why hasn't he answered my messages? W-where is he?" The stutter does it for her, and every muscle in her body slumps as the realization dawns on her face. "No."

Not the way I wished to announce it, but with her own understanding, she's opened the pathway for me to finish. "I'm sorry. This morning, there was an acci—"

"*No!*" She screeches, stumbling back from the door, her hand blindly reaching for it, for something to hold onto.

I don't know why, but I stretch my hand for her. Stepping over the threshold, I complete a quick scan of the small, domesticated living room, finding the couch against the closest wall, and lead her toward it. She allows me, not fighting my hold. The moment her ass touches the cushions, her tears begin to drip down her face, sliding right over those scars.

"No. No, I won't believe it. No!" She yanks her hand from mine, placing it with her other on her lap, tightening them into fists as she continues denying the facts. "No. My father works security in a downtown office. I don't know who you are or how you're *associated* with him, but he's fine."

Security. So, she doesn't know the truth of her father. Seems like he was hiding from us and his daughter.

I take a knee, positioning my arms on either side of her lap. Her head tips down to her chest, the tears continuing to pour as she mumbles her denials. She rocks lightly, her legs coming up to her chest.

She's not allowed to hide from me though, or from the truth. A shit part of this life, no matter one's role in it, is the pain. With two fingers under her chin, I tilt her head because regardless of her assumptions, she needs to hear the facts.

Instead, she rips her head away with a snarl and, like a flipped switch, she shoves me, trying to make me stumble, but my stance holds firm.

"I don't know who you are but leave. My father is fine. He's fine. He's running late at work, that's it." She swipes at another fallen tear, rage quickly replacing her sadness.

Denial. It's a common emotion when faced with grief.

She shoves me again, but before she can knock me over, I stand. She instantly stands too, her hands ramming into my side, my back, anywhere she can reach.

"Get out of here. Go! Leave! Never come back."

I back up, palms up, indicating I don't mean any harm, regardless of the news. "I'm sorry, Miss Dupont. I hate—"

"*Leave!*"

I hadn't realized a woman could master the look of death, but this one does.

With a final tip of my head, I conform to her request. The moment I pass the threshold to the outdoors, she slams the door shut. I head back to my car, promising to see her soon because I'm not finished with her yet.

4
ISABELLE

Impossible.

He's a creep.

My father works security for a downtown company, which means no one would be interested in harming him. He checks goddamn ID badges to ensure only staff are the ones entering.

Whoever the guy was, he was lying. An *associate* of my father. Bullshit. This is some trick, because if anything were to happen to Dad, his company would reach out to me. HR, or someone. The police. And that man clearly was not someone from Human Resources because he barely identified himself.

So, why am I crying? Why are tears dripping down my face as if, somehow, deep down, I *know*? Dad's religious with his check-ins. Lifting my phone, I reread the last message from him, early yesterday morning when he wished me a good day.

I'm crying because of the tingling feeling in the base of my gut telling me I'm wrong to believe everything is fine.

Easy way to solve this.

He'll answer. Of course, he'll respond.

I lay my phone on the coffee table and scoot to the edge of the couch, propping my elbows onto my knees to watch and wait.

And wait.

After ten seconds, I tap the screen, hoping it froze and that his reply had already come through.

It was only ten seconds, relax.

I stare at the time change in the top right corner of the phone. I wait until a full five minutes pass before worry begins to creep up again.

It's only been five minutes, relax.

My hands rub on my thighs, a slight rocking motion controlling my body as I wait. Dad's answer will appear. He'll text he's on his way and then he'll show up and that's how this will go. He'll come through the door, and I'll brush that stranger's visit off as a prank.

Maybe I've inherited Dad's paranoia and that's all this is.

Besides, who shows up at someone's door to give such news? The entire situation was peculiar, and that's putting it politely.

What did he say his name was again? Rafael. Rafael Corsetti.

I lift my phone and open the search engine app, typing his name into the bar and watching as dozens of results flash over my screen.

Rafael Corsetti: Mafia Playboy.

Eden, a new adults-only club, opens its doors downtown. The owner, Rafael Corseti...

Corsetti or Criminal?

Illegal drug handling linked to the Corsettis…

With every mention of his last name, of him and his family, there's a clear theme in the results. Crime. Mafia. That's a *thing?* I know my fair share about the mafia through romance books. Arranged marriages, guns, crime, drug trades, and sexy, dangerous male main characters, but that's all they are—fictional.

The man at my door certainly fit the bill. Who walks around in a suit in broad daylight? And a suit that's seen better days, being rumpled, like he plucked it from a pile on his floor. His messy hair didn't say straightlaced, but the look in his eyes certainly did. Who else could speak about a parent's alleged death and not blink an eye, not show any compassion?

But wait, getting back to the point in my research—if the man who was at my door is Rafael Corsetti, crime lord, then how is Dad associated with him? Maybe Dad is security for one of their legal businesses?

Even as the thought crosses my mind, my scoff immediately follows. People often acquaint homeschooling with being dumber than other kids my age, but in fact, I've always been more advanced. When other teenagers were still in high school, I was beginning my Bachelors. When high school graduates were moving away to attend college, I was ending my degree and applying for my Masters in Library Science, which I'll be completing my final semester this fall.

Therefore, I'm not dumb. And believing Dad is associated with Rafael Corsetti, simply because the security company he works for oversees the Corsetti's buildings, would make me completely inept. Given the illegal stuff they do, it'd make sense they want their own staff to monitor their buildings. People they trust to check properly. Which means…

My phone slips through my hand to the floor when the thought officially formulates. A thought, deep down, I must have known the moment I researched Rafael Corsetti, but one I hadn't allowed to form because I don't want to consider the truth.

Dad works for the mafia.

How though? Every single night, he was vigilant to return home in the evening, dismissing the nanny who'd care for me during the day. Mafia life doesn't exactly scream nine-to-five career options.

And how have I never noticed? Is a little kid's ignorance that strong? Is that where his paranoia comes from: trained to be vigilant and wary of his surroundings?

What the fuck is happening? No, this is impossible. Dad is *not* mafia. It's impossible...

Right?

I stand, brushing my hands against my bare legs, and wander toward the kitchen. After retrieving a clean glass from the cupboard, I fill it with cold water. I'm not thirsty, but it keeps my hands busy while awaiting Dad's response.

I chug the water in large gulps and place the glass on the counter, treading back into the living room, but maintaining a distance from my cellphone. It'll vibrate with his message; I don't need to check it.

It'll happen.

Even if minutes have already passed. It'll happen.

Dad isn't part of the mafia and he's coming home soon. Work is running late, that's all.

Walking by the living room, I head for the carpeted staircase, ascending the stairs. Directly across from them is the room I grew up in, still decorated from when I lived here, although sparsely filled, since I took most of my belongings with me.

Beside my old room is Dad's. I open his door and enter. He'd be annoyed to find me here, and rightly so, since he has strict rules about being in his private space. In fact, as I walk slowly through, I don't think I've *ever* been in this room without him.

I scan the tidy space, from the made bed, to the single nightstand on the right side. A phone's charging cord waits for its partner to come back. The lamp is off, but the mystery novel he's reading waits for his next session, a bookmark in the middle of it. It was one I gave him after I horrifyingly observed him fold a page's corner. It was the best item I've ever donated, saving hundreds of books over the years.

Across from the bed is the double-doored closet and I grab a hold of the metal handles, pausing as I take a deep breath. I have no clue what I'm doing in his room, let alone what I'm looking for—if anything. Or why I'm about to open his closet. Or what I'm about to find, but—

I yank them open before I can think on it longer, studying the row of hung attire. Flicking through them mindlessly, I find nothing. The shelf above the hangers is bare, and the floor has two boxes. Rifling through, I find only clothing. Probably items that no longer fit him.

There's nothing here.

It's like my subconscious seeks for ways to contradict the fact that a mafia man recently showed up at my door, alleging my father works for him. But it's difficult to find evidence against such a claim when Dad keeps an empty room.

I wonder if it's always been this empty, because if so, why was he always scared of me in here without him? There's nothing interesting to discover here.

I exit his room and shut his door before he knows I've entered and then return downstairs, heading for my phone, positive he'll have responded by now. It's been so long since I've sent him the message and he never forgets our supper plans. His nine-to-five job means he's consistently around in the evenings.

When I lift my phone, only my blank lock screen reflects—

no text message. Weight drops into my stomach, dragging my body to the couch. I still can't believe this. I don't *want* to believe it.

Dad isn't dead. He. Is. Not. Dead.

That's what I repeat to myself all evening. Eventually, I curl up on the couch, staring at the door with my phone clutched in my hand, waiting for the moment it opens and Dad enters like nothing's amiss. Then we'll eat a late dinner and I'll forget all about Rafael Corsetti's prank visit.

And I won't admit to myself that I'm in denial.

5

RAFAEL

The elevator doors to my condo can't open fast enough before I'm pushing out of the elevator, shedding my suit's outer coat in the doorway. After kicking off my shoes, I head straight for the bathroom, stripping the rest of my clothes as I go.

Today needs a redo, and it starts by returning to Maurice's house and finding his secret *adult* daughter again. My gut says hiding her was obviously purposeful on his part. I need to call Nico and should have on the drive from Maurice's house to my condo, but I continued to replay the interaction instead.

Once the shower is steaming and coating the glass walls, I enter, letting the scalding water penetrate my exhausted muscles. Beneath the rainfall showerhead, I think about how I didn't even get her name.

Maurice knows something about De Falco, which means his daughter is my only connection to that truth. No matter how much she denies her father's death, she's now valuable to me.

Once I finish showering, I wrap a fluffy towel around my

waist and pad out of the bathroom and head next door, to my room, unlocking my phone as I go.

I can't put into a text how strange it was, so when Nico calls, I recount everything that happened, including who I found, with only slight grunts and murmurs as my brother's responses.

Once I finish speaking, he agrees, "Return tomorrow. Don't let her push you out this time. There's more to her, and I want to know what it is. She could very well know what Maurice does, which means she's our connection to De Falco."

"Agreed. How's Rozelyn coming along?"

"Flynn hasn't updated me yet, so I assume there's nothing."

"And Aurora?" Now that she's been awake for a complete day.

"Rosen's with her," my brother replies, a slight bite in his tone. "She snuck out of the hospital last night to come here and stayed the night with him. This morning, she bombarded my office, shouting about how she deserves her happiness and not to be used."

"I mean..." He knows me well enough to recognize my tone, which says I agree with her. I've been on Aurora's side since the beginning. Regardless of Rosen, she should never be forced into a wedding she doesn't want.

"Fuck off, brother." He grunts, amusement weaving between the harsh words. "I know, I know, and believe me, she does too."

"I take it she won?"

"Yes. Now, we need to figure out how to break this news to

the New York *Famiglia*. Ending this engagement means losing the union, but also pissing off our biggest North American rival for a second time. They could declare war over this."

He's referring to when Mother was engaged to one of the Rossis, before Father killed him and kidnapped her for himself. Nico has been trying to renegotiate a union with the *Famiglia*, considering both sides' leadership has changed hands, and pasts can be forgiven. Once, not twice.

"That sounds like a *you* problem. I have other shit to deal with. Has someone gone to retrieve Maurice's body?"

Nico pauses. "I sent a few men to the location earlier. His body's no longer there."

"Fuckers. So the shooters took his corpse." *Fuck.* Now, not only is his daughter in denial, but I have no proof he's even gone. Just my word, which will likely mean nothing to her.

"Learning about his daughter creates more questions than answers," he mutters, sighing heavily, the sound of a man with too much on his shoulders. At least I can deal with her, so he can focus on his new wife, Aurora's health, and De Falco.

"Don't worry about her. She's my issue. I'll visit her again tomorrow morning now that she's had some time to hopefully process the news. I'll figure out how much she knows about her father."

"And if she knows nothing?"

"I'll work with that. There's a reason Maurice asked us to protect her, and that's exactly what I'll do. Like you said, Nic, too many questions to be satisfied with her claiming to know nothing."

"Thanks, Raf. Get some sleep. I suspect this is the beginning of more."

When Nico hangs up, I return my phone back to the nightstand and all but throw myself into bed, remaining on top of the covers, my towel loosely coming undone with my movements.

I don't even have the girl's name, but I want to know it. I want to know about her, aside from the secrets her father apparently holds. First off, those fascinating scars. They weren't from an accident. In this world, I've seen a lot. I've seen wounds and injuries bad enough that they scar when healing. But two lines down the sides of her face isn't an accident. They're too perfectly drawn, avoiding her eyes and other features, but still present enough to be noticeable.

What is she doing right now? She seemed convinced I was lying, but at this time of night, she must realize her father isn't coming home. Her father, who was fearful for *her* life. So scared, he couldn't get out what he tried to tell us before he was murdered.

I imagine her wandering the house, staring out the windows, waiting for his car to pull into the driveway. I imagine her awake all night, waiting anxiously for someone who'll never come.

It's those pictures in my mind that has me rolling from bed and going to my closet to find fresh clothing. I dress in jeans and a Henley shirt, snatch my keys off the counter from where I tossed them earlier, and head for my private elevator, taking it all the way to the ground floor, past my adult-only club, Eden, and right to the basement parking garage.

With my car, I retrace the path I drove only hours ago, toward the quiet neighbourhood, this time parking a few houses down, not to alert her to my presence if she is looking outside.

Scanning the street, most of the houses are dark. I imagine many of the residents have gone to bed in preparation for their jobs and schools tomorrow. I wonder if they'd know anything about Maurice's habits or about his daughter especially.

For now, I slink between Maurice's house and his neighbour's, heading to the backyard. Sticking to the shadows, I position myself between two trees, remaining in the dark in case she peeks out the window. Propping myself against the bark, I cross my arms and wait for movement.

I've never stalked a woman before—or anyone, for that matter.

Although, the act of waiting and watching this woman through her windows reminds me of being in Eden. My personal favourite area is the voyeur and exhibitionism wing, made up of a set of rooms with windows that allow those on the other side to witness the sexual acts within them.

There's nothing like dominating a woman in front of others. The act of being watched, but unavailable for them to touch. The knowledge my partner and I are turning others on by simply sharing our bodies. It's thrilling, a sense of power like none other, to control someone else's pleasure, including who gets to witness it and who doesn't.

Similarly, I enjoy being the voyeur too, watching people as they move together, touch one another, being so open and vulnerable. To see fingers, tongues, cocks, or even toys enter the most intimate parts of someone's body and to be involved in their pleasure from afar.

Movement tugs me from my thoughts. A figure steps by the kitchen window, stopping to peer out. I lean back into the tree; certain she can't see me but not willing to risk the chance.

The light is on, so I'm able to clearly see her as the sigh wracks her form and her head drops low, her arms propping her body on the counter. Misery overtakes her and though I can't tell if she's crying from this distance, I can almost sense it.

Maybe she's done denying the truth.

One hand lifts from the counter and she swipes it over her face, pausing with her fists in her eyes, rubbing roughly.

Stop harming yourself. I want to burst through that back door and wipe her tears away, though I have no idea where that sudden thought came from. She looks so...*broken.*

She turns away from the counter. The kitchen goes dark after a moment, and then so does the room beyond. My eyes drift up the side of the house, waiting for one of those rooms' lights to switch on, since I assume she's going to bed.

No light turns on though.

A few seconds pass, and I step a couple feet closer to the house, hoping to see a dim light somewhere through the windows, but there's nothing.

Did she leave?

Sticking to the bushes again, I press close, ignoring the pokes and prods of the branches as I slowly walk the side of the house, planning to check the front in case she's slipped out.

"Fuck, ow."

I freeze, my hand flying to my holster for my Glock. Someone is here. I hope it's a neighbour nearby, except there's been no additional sounds, such as other houses' doors opening.

I scan the small backyard, eyes studying every bush and short tree, searching for movement as I bring my gun up, removing the safety. A gentle rustle from the other side of the backyard drifts toward me. It could very well be the wind making the leaves dance, but no, I don't think it is. Instinct deems otherwise.

Sticking to the shadows still, I slink through the yard. There's no way to hide from whoever is here, but it's now a matter of speed, of who shoots first. I won't shoot blindly into the night, not here in a neighbourhood with so many civilians around.

Keeping my pace slow and careful, I lean down and take a

blade from my boot. Father trained Nico and me to carry multiple weapons, so we have defensive options.

I'm only a few feet away from where I first saw the movement when a body lunges from the bush, throwing his weight into me. I see him coming, mostly, and side-step him, rolling to a crouch, my knife lifted and waiting for one more wrong move.

I can't identify the guy with how quick he jumps around and from the hoodie covering his face, but he aims for me again. The shadows shift at the right moment, and I spot the knife in his hand.

He came to fight.

Stupidly, I glance toward the house, the reminder of where we are. Of whose property we're on. Something tells me, this guy knows Maurice is already dead and isn't here for him, which means—

I spin, avoiding his knife, as my arm comes up and stabs the guy's heart with mine. His body jerks as the blade makes its mark and he drops to the ground, instantly dead.

"Shit." If I thought this through better, I could have only injured him, and he could be another person for Flynn to facts from. "Fuck."

Scanning the backyard, I check the nearby houses to make sure no one is peering out their windows, before tucking my gun away and leaning down to grasp under the guy's shoulders. I drag him over the grass and deeper into the shadows.

Once I have him hidden, I pull out my phone and tap the second name on the list. "Hey," I start once my call is answered, "we have a problem."

6

ISABELLE

My eyes feel as though I've stared into the sun for hours and the heat rays burned my retinas. This might be because I've been awake all night, curled up in the corner of Dad's living room, staring at the front door, willing, with every ounce of my energy, for it to open and for Dad to enter.

Or my eyes hurt because every hour that passed without a response, my mind let go of its denial, and more tears fell.

I don't remember much of the night. Only my arms wrapped around my legs and the slight rock that kept my body awake. Hours passed quickly, or slow—I don't know. I might have dozed off at some point because I recall my face being dry for a brief time, but then, I might have also just stopped crying. I don't know anymore.

What I do know is that Dad never came home.

My cell phone remains abandoned on the floor a few feet away from me. I've stopped checking it, stopped opening the messages to Dad, despising every letter typed because they taunt me with a reminder that they will never be responded to.

Dad's not coming home.

I'm not sure when I finally allow my brain to think it, finally allow myself to accept what it knows, what it's been denying. I'm finally allowing reality to seep in and take over what I refuse to believe...but what I think is true.

He's not coming home. He'll never walk through that front door again. He'll never wrap his large arms around me, lifting me off the ground in his bearhug. He'll never scold me for not triple checking my door when I leave my apartment.

He's not coming home. He's not...here. He's de—

That part I won't allow my mind to admit. No, even Rafael Corsetti didn't say those precise words yesterday. It's not true until the words are said, so until then, my denial remains firm. His absence is unexplainable, but it's not *that*. I won't accept that.

Even if I already know the truth.

Knock, knock! Two rapid bangs sound from the front door, but I can't move.

I don't think I can anyway, and I don't want to try, if I'm being honest. The thought of getting off this floor, even if my ass is so far beyond numb right now, sounds like death itself. The requirement to find that kind of energy, to answer the door and then to interact with whoever's at the door...No. I'd much prefer to avoid reality right here than do anything else. At least down here, I can pretend it's Dad coming home.

But Dad wouldn't knock on his own front door, which means whoever is there, can fuck right off.

Knock, knock!

"Miss Dupont."

I recognize that voice. The smooth tone from the equally sexy man who was here yesterday. Rafael Corsetti, or as my research claimed him being: the mafia. A criminal. A person who shouldn't be around me.

A person who could be responsible for Dad's disappearance.

"Miss Dupont, open the door."

No. Fuck off. That's what I want to yell, but to speak also takes energy my broken body doesn't have. If I say nothing, he'll go away and let me live right here on the floor, where I'll wait for the afterlife to come claim me.

The doorknob jiggles again, which I find stupid for him to bother attempting. Of course, I'd lock it. He clearly doesn't know my father, if he thinks any door around me would be unlocked, especially overnight.

The jiggling continues until the door falls open and a burst of fresh air enters alongside a figure.

A screech flies from my throat and my hands feel around for the wall at my back, trying to use it to lift myself up, to run away from whatever death and danger Rafael Corsetti enters my father's house with, but exhaustion quickly snips away the modicum of adrenaline that was created, my body falling right back into its position.

"Oh, Miss Dupont." Feet come into my view, his form towering over me. He pauses there before crouching. His arm reaches out and with two fingers, he tips my chin up.

Stop. I try to pull away—or I tell myself to try, but all that happens is my neck muscles give up and I remain a limp doll in his hands, helpless, like so many of the heroines often found in romance novels.

Green eyes clash with mine and he looks almost angry. Angry at me? I didn't do anything. If anything, I should be pissed at him. His lips curl, pinching, as his eyes continue studying me.

"Did you sleep at all?"

"I was waiting for Dad." I don't know why I'm admitting this to a stranger, but I am. Because although the guy screams death and pain and agony—and so far has yet to bring anything else to my life—there's another feeling he brings. Another feeling I can't make sense of, but it's there. For some reason, somehow, it's present.

Safety.

His expression shatters for the briefest of seconds; a second in which I see a kind countenance. His other hand comes up to the side of my face and he cups my cheek, making me hum instinctively. Instinct? Not sure where such an reflex has come from, but again, it's there.

I'm way too tired to be rational. That's all this is. Exhaustion creating irrationality.

"Miss Dupont."

The way his full lips say my surname makes me want more of that.

"Isabelle," I admit. "My name is Isabelle."

"Isabelle," he repeats, granting me the very thing I sought; the very purpose in giving the deadly man my name. "Belle."

Dad calls me Isa. Never Belle. There's no one else in my life to give me a nickname, but the stranger does almost immediately, and I don't know how to feel about it.

His hand shifts to my neck as the one holding my chin turns my face to the right and then the left. I can't even imagine what I look like right now, but he probably finds a mess. I wonder if my face is stained with tears or if they've dried by now, and if my eyes look like I was crying.

"Leave," I murmur with no conviction behind the demand. Worse, because then I find myself asking, "Why are you here?"

"I came back for you, to make sure you're all right."

Joke's on you. I snort, or I try to anyway. I don't know what I'm doing anymore.

"You're not all right," he finishes, dropping my chin.

"No shit."

His lips twitch. "Sorry for how I broke the news yesterday."

News. Is he talking about the supposed death of my father? Dad's not dead. He'll be home soon.

Denial again.

When Rafael's hand touches my leg, I flinch, my body finally wakening. I curl myself away, into the wall behind me as one hand pushes against a hard frame, doing my best to ignore the abs beneath my palm.

"No, he'll be home. He'll...be..."

I don't know why now of all times. Perhaps being awake for over twenty-four hours finally hits my system or crying for the past eight has dragged me on long enough. Maybe it's because, at this rate, if Rafael's come to grant me my death, I'll happily accept it.

But my vision fills with blackness, my consciousness drops, and the last thing I hear is an angel's voice.

What a strange fucking dream. First, a *mafia man* shows up at Dad's door to announce he's dead. It's laughable that Dad—sweet, cautious Dad— would work for people who participate in criminal, illegal activity.

Mind, you're creative.

I read too much. I need a palate cleanser. Something like a sweet romance, or a smutty office romance. Nothing dark. Nothing with suspense and certainly nothing involving the mafia or any crime-related trope. No morally grey, dangerous heroes who enjoy kidnapping their women and claiming them. Gentle. Sweet. That's what I require.

Because aside from Dad's supposed death, my dream got

better. That same hot mafia guy found me in Dad's house and tried to comfort me.

Me.

Unless the guy's name is Gage, I've had zero interactions with men. Men who cupped my face and controlled my body, like I was some doll.

Chuckling aloud, I think, *Mind, you're a bit whacked sometimes*, as I open my eyes, staring at the familiar white ceiling, trimmed with pink.

Trimmed with pink.

A heavy weight drops in my body. The ceiling in my apartment doesn't have pink on it, but the one in my old room, at Dad's house, does.

Why am I at Dad's?

With my hands pushing into the mattress, I sit up, eyes rapidly blinking to clear away the sleep, scanning the familiar room I've lived in most of my life, somehow knowing what—*who*—I'll find by the door before I see him.

7
RAFAEL

The second Isabelle woke up, I knew. It's all in her breathing. How it went from slow and paced, almost-sighs, to quicker and shallower when realizing where she is.

I don't look at her, granting her the time to make that first move. Instead, I continue reading the book, one of many, I found. There's a whole stack of them in the corner of the room and after hours of being here, waiting for her to wake, they started to look appealing. Then again, death also began to look appealing given how bored I was, and after getting into this novel, I'm realizing the two hobbies are one and the same.

The Corsetti mansion may be outfitted with a huge library, but I don't think I've spent longer than a few minutes in there my entire life. Once, when I was younger, and my buddies and I were hiding from Mother, we used that room, but that was it.

I carried Isabelle to her room this morning when she passed out after mumbling her denials, and we're nearing nine at night —almost a full twelve hours of her passed out. In that time, I've hit the end of every social media platform a dozen times over, have spoken with Nico regarding next steps, and answered two business calls for Eden, but once all that passed, I had nothing else to do. It was succumb to painful fictional teen drama or stare at a wall and let myself slowly go insane.

Though, reading this book is pretty much the same.

Isabelle sits up, breathing heavier. "Wh-what?" Even though I'm staring at the strips of scripted trees in my hand, my peripheral vision catches her legs swinging toward the floor as she rights herself, standing, swaying. "Y-you..."

"Articulate," I drawl, leisurely dragging my eyes away from the book in favour of something much more appealing—the sexy brunette glaring at me through sleep-filled eyes. Gesturing to the book in my hand, I add, "I must say, this whole love triangle between the ghost and the vampire is useless. I mean, polyamorous relationships are a thing, and speaking from experience, threesomes are fun, so this whole battling each other for the girl is stupid." I pause to shake the book, pulling her sleepy attention to it, smirking as it shifts into frazzled confusion. "You actually enjoy these things?"

She blinks again and shakes her head, managing a step toward me. Her gaze darts out the window and back, her head-shakes growing quicker with every pass. Her sleep-frazzled hair flies around her face and I suddenly long to push it away. Panic widens her eyes, followed by a string of curses—colourful words I hadn't pictured emerging from this woman's full lips.

"No. No, no, no." Her finger comes up in the air, gesturing to me, but then lowering again. "No," she repeats again, staggering a step. One step back, and then two forward. "No."

I rest the book aside, not bothering to save my place since, hopefully, I'll never be subjected to that horror again, and using the wall at my back, push to stand.

"No," she repeats, bringing her hand to her face. Her chipped nail slips between her teeth and she nibbles on it for the briefest of seconds. Mumbles continue to seep from her lips, but I can't make any of them out.

"Is that the only word you know?"

Speaking breaks the spell over her, and her hand drops. Her next words are whispered. Spoken so low I barely catch them.

"It...it wasn't a dream?"

"Which part?"

"You. Dad. All of it. Any of it." Her words quicken, her gaze becoming lost as tears line the bottom of her eyes. Her hands rub at her cheeks, stroking over them once, removing the tears, but they're quickly replaced. "Holy fuck. No. No, it can't be. This isn't...no. Mafia? No." She falls back, landing on her bed, but I'm not even sure she's noticed she did so.

So, she Googled me. A weird sense of pride creeps up, pleased to find she's smart enough to research the stranger who appeared at her door yesterday.

"I thought...No. I thought you were a dream."

I approach Isabelle, lowering myself to one knee in front of her, lining our faces up, exactly how I had yesterday when entering her house and finding her balled on the floor. Placing my arms around her body, I cage her in, ensuring she realizes I'm not a dream.

Her dark irises expand as she takes me in, first my face, and then she allows her gaze to travel my body. They pause at my neck, right on the spot where I know one of my tattoos peeks out from my shirt. Her study ends at my hands, resting on either side of her hips, inches from touching her.

She doesn't pull away. If she's Googled my name, she must know what to expect.

"I'm not a dream," I murmur. "I wish I could be, to save you from this pain."

Her expression cracks and more of those tears fall. Her lips roll together, and her head moves back and forth, once again denying what she obviously realizes.

"I'm sorry."

"Dad...you..."

I've never been good at this—yesterday being evidence of that—so I push out the next part. Life only moves on once bad news is conveyed, and this girl needs it. Needs to understand it, and then has to come with me. I had planned on lying to her, claiming she's unsafe as a method to keep an eye on her until I learn what she does or doesn't know, but after the man last night creeping outside her house, I'm starting to think she's truly not safe. Which is why, to be certain, I've positioned two men around the house, one at the front and one at the back.

I tuck back strands of hair that have curtained her face. My fingers accidentally brush against one of the harsh scars on her cheek and she flinches, but doesn't move away, instead continues watching me like a rabbit observes the wolf approaching—with a mix of caution, fear, and a brewing plan. This isn't the fiery girl who answered the door yesterday, and I curse Maurice for everything he's done in the past forty-eight hours. Not from hiding a daughter from us, or even his secrets about De Falco, but hiding himself from his daughter. For dying and making me the bad guy having to deliver the news. To be the villain about to lock her up, for both my family's safety and her own.

With my words, her life will change. The acceptance of what happened with her father, and the next stages. Nico and I agreed on one thing last night when I called him about the stranger I killed: that Isabelle can't be out of our sight until we know what Maurice has on De Falco.

"There's no easy way to say this," I start, not moving my hand away from her face, stroking a small patch of skin, "so I just have to, and I'm sorry. I met with your father yesterday, and there was an accident." Maybe less of an accident. "He was shot."

For a moment, it seems like she hasn't heard me. A lone tear slides down her cheek, pausing at the scar on her chin. With my thumb, I capture it as the lowering sun peeks through her white curtains and catches on it, making it shine.

"Leave." The single word is covered with ice, nothing like the soft-spoken woman who was here moments ago.

"Belle," I start, using the nickname I unconsciously gave her this morning. I don't budge, and I won't be leaving this time.

"Leave!" she shouts, shoving her palms into my chest.

With a slight reposition of my feet, I manage to remain steady and unmoving as she continues to push me. With every bit of force, more of her tough farce plunges, her breathing getting weightier and more shallow, her throat moving with her every swallow.

"You did this." Her hands lower from my chest and instead of fighting, she stands. "You and your fucking world did this."

I stand too, easily towering over her. Her head comes to my chest, and with two fingers, I crook her head up to force her to look at me, like I had this morning when returning. Surprisingly, she doesn't fight my hold.

"Yes," I admit. "Yes, this life does do it. I'm not sure why he hid us from you, or you from us, but he did, and now we both need to deal with it. Your father took oaths of loyalty to my family, and sometimes the price of that is death. If you've Googled my name, you know the kinds of things that have come up." I lean in slightly closer, our mouths inches from each other, ensuring she listens to what I'm saying—reads it from my goddamn lips if she must. "It's not a gentle job. It's not a cushy nine-to-five office job, where we come home at the end of the day. We have enemies. Every single day, my family knows I might not return to them. Soldiers are aware that to serve us is to protect us, to be whatever we need them to be, and that is what your father knew when he was inducted. So, if you're looking for someone to blame, look closer. *He* did this to you."

For fucking once, she doesn't fight. Instead, her eyes shut and she becomes limp again. Lifeless. A shudder passes through her body, and I release her chin, noticing she's lost her fight.

When she does speak finally, it's to ask, "Why are you here?"

"Because I couldn't sleep yesterday after you kicked me out, so I came here to check on you."

Her eyes shift to the side, and I spot the mental calculation. "But you didn't come until this morning. You..." Realization breaks in her expression, her head tilting slightly to the right. "You *stalked* my house all night?"

"You should be lucky I did." From my pocket, I pull out my phone, readying to show her the image of who could have been here instead of me.

But she bends to the side, peeking around me at the spot I occupied for the past few hours. "You sat there all day?"

"You were asleep," I reply in a tone implying the obviousness in my reasoning.

"You entered my home uninvited, watched me freak out, then passed out, and what—carried me to my room?"

"That's precisely what happened."

"But why come back? You did your job; you informed me of the news. Why are you still fucking *here*? In my life. Rafael Corsetti," she snarls my name, "has better things to do than hang around here with me. You can go now."

"Do you watch crime shows?"

She blinks, taken aback by my seemingly random question. "What?"

"Do you watch crime shows?" I repeat. "You know, dead bodies, blood, gore, and all that."

"Um," one brow dips, "sometimes."

I turn my phone to face her. On the screen is a picture of the man from last night after I killed him. Blood seeps from the wound on his chest, his face partially hidden in the dark from the number of shadows that made taking this photo challenging. Still, it's clear he is dead.

"You're lucky I, as you claim, 'stalked' you last night because he was too. I found him slinking around your backyard, and I promise, he wasn't there to keep you safe."

Her eyes narrow, still studying the image. "I'm sure he'd say the same about you."

Smart girl. "Yes, yet, he's the one dead and I'm the one standing in your bedroom."

"Which isn't doing you any favours," she shoots back. "Good to know I'm inches from a killer."

I don't deny the truth but remove the phone from her line of sight. "Either way, I promise I will not hurt you, but I'm sure he wouldn't have made the same promises. So, before you point fingers, think about the facts, because it's no coincidence that people targeted you last night, only a day after your father was killed."

Her jaw falls slack. "Excuse me?"

"You are in danger, Isabelle. That's why I'm here."

8

ISABELLE

I'm still not entirely positive I'm *not* dreaming. The facts indicate otherwise.

One: I'm not the kind of woman who has hot guys, supposedly from the mafia, show up at my door.

Two: mafia? Enough said.

Three: Dad being a part of the mafia? Right, okay.

Four: the same guy carries me to my bedroom, after appearing in my house again, camps here all day *and* reads one of my young adult romance books that I've never boxed up to take with me.

Five: Dad being shot.

Six: apparently, I was stalked by another man, who this one murdered last night. My stalker murdered another stalker. Ironic.

Seven: yesterday, I kicked said guy out of my father's house, but today, he's around, which means the dream gods want him around.

Eight: he's touched me. Not just once. But a few times. Caged me in with his arms. Towered over me. Stroked my cheek, caught my tears, and tucked my bangs back. All actions of a dream because I've certainly never been touched like that. Or touched, period.

Nine: Not sure, but there's probably a ninth fact in all this somewhere that I'm missing.

And when Rafael speaks again, he lists number ten.

"You are in danger, Isabelle. That's why I'm here."

Ten: so now, apparently, I'm in "danger."

Uh, huh, right. And how's this not *everything found in fiction?*

I. Am. Dreaming.

I must be.

I must be...

Hands cup my face, shocking my system once more, and I jerk to pull away from the warm, inviting touch. He seemingly doesn't care about my ugly scars. They're not smooth; they ruin the planes of my face, but it's never mattered before, since no one's touched me like this.

Why am I even thinking about this?

"Look at me," he gently commands, and my betraying eyes meet his, even as my mind is telling me to push him away again.

Because what he says is insanity. In-san-i-ty.

He sighs, and warm, minty breath blows over my face, reminding me, once again, how strange it is to have someone close to me. How uncertain I am about this.

"Listen to me. I know you're still processing everything, and I realize what I'm saying is upending your life, but it's the truth. It might be a lot to learn that the mafia is a real entity, but it is. We are. *I* am." His thumbs stroke the skin at the base of my chin. "If someone had been sent last night, what's to say more won't come?"

"I don't even know how to respond to that," I murmur. I must be in shock. Having barely understood that my father is—

nope. I don't think the words. Thinking it makes it real, which means I'll cry. Again.

Rafael drops his hands, backing up a few inches. "My point. So, get a bag. Grab whatever you need," he scans my childhood bedroom, "and then we'll go."

Go.

"You're kidding me? You're a fucking *stranger*. I hear you. I-I—" I despise the words I'm about to say. "I believe you. That Dad was part of your whole thing, but *I'm* not. Danger or otherwise, I can't alter my life and what—?"

"You'll be living with me."

I bark out a rough laugh, shoving away from him, moving to the other side of the room, stepping near the book he was reading earlier. "You can leave now," I demand for what feels like the millionth time. "This is fucking weird. I'm going home and I'll be grieving my father in peace, so if you'll excuse me..." I turn for the door, opting to leave instead. If Rafael won't go, then I will. I'll return to my downtown apartment where I can deal with my denial in peace.

I barely make it to the doorway before a large hand is there, shoving through the air until he pins the door shut. Heavy breaths coast along my neck as his body comes nearer.

I don't budge, instead taking deep breaths to calm myself, focusing on the hand in front of my face. The rose tattoo on the back of his hand with thorns wrapping around his fingers. The two rings that glint in the room's lighting.

Even his fucking hand screams danger. There's no possible way I'll be doing what he's commanding—moving into this deadly stranger's house.

"You seem to think I was asking, Belle."

His use of the nickname halts my argument. That's the third time now he's called me it. "My name's Isabelle."

"Belle. Isabelle. *Belle.* French for *beautiful.*"

Beautiful. I've never been called that. There's been no chances for me to become beautiful and done-up either. No proms. No school events.

This is a trick. Deception. The heroes in romance books are good at luring the woman in with pretty words.

I whirl on him, my back against the door. "Stop with the mind games and let me go. Or leave. Those are your options, Rafael, but I'm not going with you."

Rafael doesn't do anything but watch me. His lids lower in the slowest blink I've ever seen someone take and when he opens them, it's like I'm with a new man. His bright, playful eyes get duskier, daring, and for once, I can imagine this guy killing the stalker from last night. Imagine this guy pushing his way into my bedroom as he reminds me of all the ways he's a villain.

"I wanted to be nice. I leave the bad cop job to my older brother, but you're pissing me off. I've shown you the proof, and if you don't come with me willingly, then I'm sure you can refer to your books as a manual for what happens next. I'll have you hogtied in my car until I can lock you in a basement to keep you safe, if I must."

I forget how to breathe.

"Why?" is the only word I manage. "Before yesterday, we didn't even know each other, so what makes you so interested in my safety?"

Rafael leans back a fraction, but he doesn't drop his hand, so really, it feels like no extra space has been gained. "Your father asked me to, and while you may not believe this, I take my men's lives very seriously. As their leader, it's my job to inform the families. To help them however they need. That's what I came here yesterday to do. Someone lurking in your backyard is grounds for extra precautions."

Dad, what have you gotten yourself into?

The better question though: what has he gotten *me* into? The same paranoid man who wants me to check my surroundings as I walk home is no longer here, leaving me in the hands of a mafia capo.

Yeah, Dad, because that's so much safer.

His paranoia makes sense now, I suppose.

Still, what Rafael is demanding is pure craziness. I have a life; one that isn't wrapped up in whatever criminal bullshit Rafael's is. He might be pulling all that alpha male authoritative energy, but he'll have to do more than *command* me to make me—

Bang! Bang! Bang!

"Shit!" Rafael finally drops my hand, but it's only to retrieve something at his hip, beneath his leather jacket. In horror, he removes something metallic, black, weighted—an item I've only seen in movies. A gun. My legs feel weak at the sight of the weapon.

"What the fuck?"

Rafael ignores my question as he nudges me aside and pulls open my bedroom door, peering out slowly. He glances back, his jaw tightening. His eyes flick to the window, to the door again, and back to me.

"We need to get out of here."

"Capo!" another voice shouts from downstairs.

Rafael releases a sharp exhale and grasps my hand, keeping his gun angled up. He tugs me out of my bedroom, keeping me behind him.

"Listen to everything I tell you, Isabelle. This isn't some joke, so before you make a snide comment, just fucking trust me."

Of course, I'll listen. I didn't invent the sounds of gunshots, and I'd prefer to remain alive. I think about the picture he showed me, the mentions of my life being in danger.

Obviously, they're connected. Even if I don't want to believe it.

Trepidation courses through me as I trail closely behind Rafael, glancing at my childhood bedroom as we leave it behind. Then Dad's room as we pass it. The bathroom, the hallway closet—all the elements of my childhood. The realization that those gun shots mean more than danger.

They mean change.

They mean following Rafael through my house as he leads me to, hopefully, safety.

He treads slowly down the stairs, his arms positioned halfway upright, ready to shoot if necessary. To *shoot*. Rafael doesn't look much older than I am, but I get the sense our life experiences are worlds apart.

His other arm comes up to the side, bending toward me. "If I say run, you'll run upstairs and shut your door. You will not open it until I come for you. Understand?"

"Y-yeah."

Suddenly, all fear regarding Rafael is gone. All the stress over this insanity he's brought into my life. Every fight I was ready to have with him in my room, gone. This is *real*. This is happening. I'm not sure how to make sense of it all or why it's even happening, but it is. And if he says, run, then I'll fucking run, to survive. Something tells me he's a better judge of danger than I am.

At the bottom of the stairs, a figure rushes from the front. A screech works its way up my throat, my feet stumbling backwards, but Rafael waves his hand.

"It's fine. Just one of my soldiers." Rafael lowers his gun, signalling all is well, as he focuses on the very large man coming toward us. "What the fuck was that?"

The man says nothing but angles his head toward the front

entrance and to another guy, slumped against the doorframe, blood coming through his clothing by his shoulder.

Blood! Like, actual blood! Somehow, it's more terrifying than the dead body in the picture. I could pretend he was sleeping, but this...this is a man literally in front of me.

Rafael breaks away to crouch by him, but he swats Rafael's hand away, his eyes jerking into the house, toward me. He nudges his chin in my direction and through wheezes manages, "Go. Capo, go. Take her...away."

The other man joins them, his fingers flying over his phone's screen. I hope he's calling for help because I'm useless, feet stuck as I blankly watch on.

Dad, what did you do to my life?

"We didn't see who, but the gun shot came out of nowhere. I tried to chase, but no luck."

Rafael grunts and lifts to his feet. "Get him home. Call Dr. Shappo to come patch him up. I'll be with Isabelle." He waves me forward, and for all my talk of not blindly listening, this time, I do, instantly going to his side.

Rafael lifts his gun again and leads me past his bleeding man out the front door. I peek behind them, but Rafael yanks on my wrist, jerking me to his side. My body heats when he presses against me, wrapping an arm around my waist as he walks us forward. A simple touch I'm sure other women wouldn't think twice about, but I've never been this close to a man.

Even though he's a dangerous criminal leading me away from my father's house after breaking the news of his death, Rafael still feels nice.

Once we make it across the front path, Rafael shoves his gun in his waistband, muttering, "Not smart to be in public with a weapon. Raises questions."

Despite everything, his comment makes me giggle because apparently rational responses are too far gone for my brain to manage as I lose my shit bit by bit. "Yes, I suppose so. Where are we going?"

Rafael stops by a black sports car only a few spots away and unlocks the door, scanning the nearby houses as he angles his body around mine, while nudging me into the vehicle. I sit, swinging my legs inside and once I seated, he slams the door shut and jogs to the front of the car, sliding into the driver's seat.

My eyes sweep the dash—a giant screen. Numerous lights and buttons turn on when he starts the car, and the engine purrs beneath us. Holy shit, this is an expensive car. Hell, it even smells expensive.

Almost as good as he does. Because in the middle of everything happening, *that's* what my brain—which I'm sure is traumatized by now—latches onto. Mint. Mint and something else.

He punches the gas pedal with his foot and we fly through the quiet neighbourhood. Once we make it onto one of the main roads, he asks, "Now do you believe me?"

"Yes," I reply in a small voice. At this point, unless Rafael is an absolute psycho and got his own man shot, simply to make his claims realistic, there's no choice in the matter. If I was alone and the shooter entered my father's house, or even the man from last night, I also wouldn't be alive right now.

Oh my god.

"I'll send someone later to get your stuff."

Because he's assuming I live there. "That's not my house. I moved out a couple months ago. I have an apartment."

"Really?" he checks in a tone I should find downright insulting. Instead, he reaches into his pocket and tosses his cellphone into my lap. "Input the address then. That's where we're headed."

9
RAFAEL

One of the most concerning parts in all of this is how well she's holding up. The fiery bookworm who argues with me at every turn—and rightly so. I'd be equally concerned if she blindly went along with everything I told her. Submissiveness is more Nico's thing than mine.

I wait for her to put in the address to where she apparently lives, noting how she isn't living with Maurice. Which means yesterday when showing up at his house, there was a real possibility she would have been at her apartment and I'd have had to track her down.

The address listed brings me to an apartment complex with a large side parking lot. I don't bother taking a spot, instead stopping the car in front of the main entrance. Silently, I get out and meet Isabelle on the other side.

Her eyes glance up the side of the building, her hands knotting. There's bound to be a snide or nervous comment on the tip of her tongue, but she remains silent, instead leading me toward the main entrance, where she types in a code, angling her body like she's trying to block my view. Except with my height, I'm able to see right over her shoulder and take a mental note of the digits, should I ever need to return. *5-8-9-4.*

The moment the low buzzer grants her entry, I reach around her and open the door, gesturing for her to go first. She barely pays me any attention as she skitters to the elevator.

She motions toward the couple of padded chairs off to the side. "You can wait here. I'll get my things."

I tip my head, wondering if she really thinks I'm that dense. "You were almost attacked. Twice. Do you realize how easy it'd be for them to trace you here? No, I'll be coming up with you." That's not even counting the fact that if she goes up alone, she'll likely never come down.

Her nostrils do this cute, little flaring thing, but the elevator pings with its arrival, and before she can argue that point too, I slide by her, tapping my finger playfully against the tip of her nose.

"Coming?"

She huffs so loudly, I'm sure I'll hear about it for hours to come. She follows, a cloud of annoyance filling the small elevator. She hits the button to take us to the fifth floor before positioning herself in the farthest corner, away from me.

Smirking, I let her have the space, leaning by the door, knowing for all her bravado, she'll need to walk by me to exit.

When the elevator arrives on her floor, she shoves away from the wall with another huff and moves by me and into the hallway, walking a short length before stopping in front of a door marked 511, which I also memorize.

Unbeknownst to her, my men will come by at some point to search her apartment right after searching Maurice's place. If she lives separately from him, there's likely nothing of value here, but experiences have taught me to never trust someone's word. Women aren't always as innocent as they might initially seem. Della lied to Nico about her true identity, so what's to say Isabelle isn't doing the same.

She thinks I'll be protecting her, and there's truth to that. But until we have De Falco in our grip, Isabelle Dupont seems too important to release. She'll lead us to her father's secrets hopefully, while solving why she's also a target.

"You can wait out here," she states in a firm voice, believing I'll be obeying that command too.

Instead, I nudge her out of the way and enter first, my hand floating toward my hip, where my gun is hidden beneath my jacket. Not that I think they've found her location already, but I'd rather not risk it.

"Come in," I say after completing a sweep of the room.

Once I hear the door shut and know she's inside, I wander through the tiny apartment. Its size is a fraction of mine. There's barely even a hallway separating the main area from her bedroom.

There's not a lot of personal items, as though she's recently moved in. Mismatched furniture in her living room, a moderately-sized TV, and books. Literally, books everywhere. If there's a shelf, it's hosting at least a stack.

"You really enjoy reading," I mumble, passing the small bathroom before finding the single bedroom. My eyes sweep the space, ensuring no one's hiding before I back away and allow her through.

Turning back toward the living room, I find Isabelle poised in the centre, her lips pursed and arms crossed. Her attitude is cute. "You done inspecting my apartment?"

"Sorry for wanting to make sure you're safe and no one's hiding." I snap my fingers, flicking my hand toward the bedroom. "Ten minutes. Pack whatever you think you'll need and then we're leaving. If you've forgotten anything, I'll send someone to get it another time."

For a brief second, she doesn't budge, her eyes narrowing with every beat of my heart. Finally, she does, stepping past me. "I'm not one of your men, Rafael. You can't order me around."

"You're right because if you were, you'd fucking listen better. Still not comprehending the danger you're in, I see." I trail behind, not letting my point go—not letting her out of my sight until I see her packing her shit. "*My* soldier getting shot at wasn't enough for you? Your father's death? This isn't some game."

She halts walking so fast, and I nearly bump into her. Her shoulders tighten as she whirls on me, jabbing her finger into my abs. Her nose flares again, her eyes hardening into dark chocolate, which doesn't have the effect than she's going for when my dick twitches in my pants.

"*My* father's death," she repeats. "I understand I'm in danger—apparently. I saw that much at the house, but you need to give me a fucking second to catch up and realize how strange the last twenty-four hours have been. Before you decide my fate, take a fucking breather and step back."

I slap her hand away, stepping closer until she's forced to tip her head. My hands remain by my side because the need to grasp her hips and pin her down grows with every passing second; every time she opens her mouth.

"Life and death, Belle. Just remember that. Ten minutes."

Her full lips part and close. Then open and close again. Until she gives me her back and wanders to her closet, reaching for a small suitcase. Still silently fuming, she tosses it on the bed, opens it, and returns to her closet, pulling clothes from hangers.

I study the small space. The queen-size bed. The dresser with stacks of books. I wander over to one, expecting to find another romance like the one I was reading earlier, but this one seems different. More plain. A black cover with dark roses and a skull make up the cover.

Intrigued, I lift it. "What's this one about?"

"Awfully interested in what I read," she comments instead of answering.

I shrug. "Pretty sure I've never read a book in my life, so what you saw earlier was no less than a miracle. Call me intrigued because I've never known someone to have so many books. Have you read everything you own?"

She pauses from rolling up a pair of jeans, peeking up at me. "Most, but not all. Some have been on my to-read list for years."

"Years? You buy books and keep them unread for *years*?"

"Judgemental for a guy who claims to have only read his first book this morning."

Touché. "And this one." I wiggle the paperback in my hand. "Have you read it?"

"Yeah. It's about a vampire who kidnapped a woman in revenge. Then they fell in love."

"Dark," I comment, setting the book back on the pile. Dark, but intriguing. Because as I study the mousy, scarred woman in front of me, she seems like someone who'll stick to her made-up fantasy worlds, rather than be involved in the obscurity of real life.

She strides around me, reaching for a pile of cords on her bedside table. When she bends over to unplug her chargers from the power bar, my gaze lingers on her ass, only sliding away when she straightens, taking the items to her bag.

While she packs, I flop on her bed, reclining with one arm as a pillow. Her mattress is soft, like mine, and I make a show of lazily stretching.

Her icy glare finds me instantly as she stomps back to her bedside table, lifting a small tablet-like thing. It looks like a tablet that would have existed many years ago, before technology improved. The screen's not much wider than my phone's, the black borders so thick it's easy to imagine this device is from the 90s.

"You can get off my bed now," she snarls as she takes the device to her bag.

Ignoring her suggestion—if we can call it that, I jerk my chin to the age-old device in her hand. "What's that?"

"My Kindle."

"Your what?"

With a huff, she drops the "Kindle" into her suitcase with more force than I assume she means to. An annoyed gaze pins me again. "My Kindle. It's where I read e-books." She pauses, her eyes flicking to the stack of books I looked through before explaining, "Electronic books."

"Got it." I don't, not completely.

"Before we go anywhere, you need to give me more details."

10

ISABELLE

The fact he invited himself to lounge on my bed is annoying. I mean, who does that? We're *strangers*, but okay. Then to watch me pack with that intense, probing gaze, like he's trying to figure me out, is also irksome. A lot of effort was spent in pretending to ignore him.

I get the sense that Rafael Corsetti is not a man easily ignored.

For one, inquiring about my books and my Kindle shows some level of curiosity. If he wasn't interested, he wouldn't care about the answer, which is more than I can say for others in my life, like Gage.

Once I'm done packing, I'm sure he'll expect me to blindly follow along. I might have been raised as a recluse, without the influences of society, but Dad always taught me to protect myself—physically and emotionally.

My throat feels thicker just imagining the number of times Dad instilled random lessons in me. Stuff I barely understood the meaning of at the time, and maybe still don't.

Don't let people close to you. It only hurts more.

Don't talk to strangers and if anyone inquiries about your childhood, run away.

Don't trust anyone besides me. I'm the only one who has your best interests at heart.

And here I am, somehow finding myself having to trust a stranger. Worse—a stranger who's a part of the life my father hid from me. Not sure if that says something bad about me or him. He *did* kill a person in my backyard and protected me from whoever was shooting at the house, but that doesn't necessarily indicate trustworthiness.

But for those very things, I've followed Rafael's commands so far, using his physical protection, but now I need to know what to expect from him.

"Before we go anywhere, you need to give me more details," I start, fighting to ignore how *good* he looks sprawled on my bed.

Rafael rolls his neck, stretching out the silence until finally muttering, "Such as?"

"How long until I can come home?"

He shrugs. "When it's safe."

"Which is?"

"When we have your father's killer in our grasp. Assuming that's who's after you."

"Who's that?"

"Wish I knew. Anything else, Belle?"

My stomach flips in a pleasant way at the use of that nickname, but I push through it, seriously hating that I have any sort of reaction whatsoever to him and demand, "How do I know I'm safe with *you*?"

One perfectly-shaped brow arches upwards. "Have I hurt you?"

"Well," *fuck him for making that point because I have nothing to counter it,* "no."

His face shifts into a cocky expression before responding with, "Exactly. I won't hurt you."

"You said I'm coming home with you."

"Yes."

I'll have to be around Rafael Corsetti for an undetermined length of time? Other than Dad and my old nanny, I haven't been around people full-time. Blood rushes through my ears, my heartbeat thrumming, but not in a good way. Fear. Anxiety. My throat feels thick.

"With you," I repeat.

"That's what I said." His fingers fiddle with my pink comforter as he speaks, which only makes me bristle. "You'll be safe at my condo."

"So we'll be around each other all the time?"

He shoots a wolfish grin my way. "I can see how much that bothers you."

It does. "I have work."

"You still want to go to work after everything you've seen today?"

No. Yes. My life can't stop, and Dad wouldn't expect it to. Whenever I got sad as a child, one thing he always taught me was to keep it inside until I was alone. Bad shit happens every day, he once told me, but the world can't stop spinning, nor should others assume I want it to. Sitting around and doing nothing gives my brain time to focus—to grieve. And for how long would I be doing that? At what point does grieving become less acceptable and returning to life is necessary? At least this way, there is no question of it. In the daytime, I continue living—*for him.*

"I do," I finally answer.

"Okay. Where do you work?"

"At Bibliothèque de Côte-des-Neiges."

"Let me know your work schedule and we'll go together."

I jerk back, his response unexpected. "*You'll* come with me to work?"

Rafael...at work with me. Watching me with those inquisitive, deep eyes as I assist patrons, shelve books, and walk the aisles. I shiver, despising how much that appeals to a miniscule part of me.

What is wrong? My attraction to the stranger is a trauma response, I'm certain.

He pushes into a sitting position, leaning on the arm that was previously propping him up. "What, you don't think I'm good enough to protect you?"

I scan his form, the obvious muscles beneath his jacket. His sheer size. The way his complete persona shifted when leading me from my childhood room out Dad's front door. "Oh, no, it's not that. Just, *you're* going to sit around a library for eight hours a day? Don't you have anything better to be doing?"

"Not when you're my priority."

Priority. Such an interesting choice of words. "What about after work?"

"Then you'll come to mine."

"Yours?" I scan my room, as though that'll have the answer before pointedly staring at his hip, where I know his gun to be. "You have another job?"

"I run a club called Eden downtown. My condo's in the same building so we'll be a few floors above it. Ever heard of it?"

I haven't heard of much in this city, despite living here my entire, sheltered life, especially a club. I shake my head.

Rafael lifts to his feet with a grunt and comes around toward the end of the bed, stopping just shy of walking into me. His head hangs over mine, his lips coming dangerously close to my skin.

"Anything else you're demanding to know?"

So much, and yet, my mind is blank, all those questions

stolen away by his minty scent and inviting form inches from me. Even while wondering what's wrong with me, it's impossible to think clearly, leaving me to mutely shake my head.

"That's what I thought. We need to be going."

That's what he thought? For some reason, his blasé statement pisses me off. The same man who just questioned me about even going to work is now assuming I'm okay with everything he's throwing at me?

"Can you just not be...uh, not be..." An appropriate, rude nickname for him evades me. Frustrated, I grunt, my teeth pressing together. "Um. Not be a...fucking beast for three-point-one seconds and let me to catch up?" Not the most menacing name I could have come up with, but it works.

Somehow, he gets bigger with his next inhale. He becomes *more*, in how his shoulders seem to widen, his body moving a fraction closer. Only a fraction, but he robs me of breath, of thought, as he towers over me, looking every bit his last name suggests him to be. His cheek passes over mine as he leans over me, but I don't dare look away from his captivating gaze to see what he's reaching for.

"Give me a chance and I'll show you how *beastly* I can be, Belle."

The words are growled softly in my ear, but loud enough my pussy hears them, causing heat to course through me.

Then he lifts my suitcase, straightens, and spins on his heel, walking away. Before he completely turns around, I spot the hint of a smirk, which quickly zaps away any previous good feeling I had moments ago.

I fell for his fucking charms when I should have been continuing to hold my position. Growling under my breath, more at myself than him, I trail him out to my living room, my eyes doing a sweep of the small, intimate space, realizing I have no clue when I'll be returning. Rafael gave no timeline, so it could be days from now, or weeks. Months? Hopefully not that long, right?

He doesn't slow his steps, heading right to my door, uncaring about the fact he's about to destroy my life more than he already has. *Beastly asshole.*

Before following, there's one more thing I need. I pass my couch, which Dad had bought me the day we found the apartment. It was the first piece of furniture that was *mine* and walking away from it today hits differently. Like, I'm leaving a piece of Dad behind.

Dad…Dad, who isn't here anym—

I cut the thought off, shaking my head of those thoughts until later, and continue heading for the side table, reaching for my laptop and its charger.

"Laptop, huh," Rafael states when I return to his side.

"Wow, you're smart," I remark sarcastically, rolling my eyes. "Yeah, just because you've come to kidnap me doesn't mean the other parts of my life end. I'm on break between semesters, but since you've given me no timeline of when I get to return home, I need this in case I'm not back in time."

"University?"

A concept seemingly strange to him based on that tone. I suppose when your family is filled with crime lords, one doesn't need a post-secondary education. I wonder if he's even graduated high school, or they paid his way to a diploma.

"Master's degree."

"At your age? You're, like, what…?" He trails off, leaving me to fill in the gap.

"Twenty-one. But I was homeschooled. When you have no life and nothing better to do than study, I finished high school when I was seventeen. Then I did my Bachelor's degree in three years, and began my MA in Library Science earlier this year. I shouldn't be able to work in a library without it, but special circumstances were made while I finish the degree."

After all that, he repeats a single word: "Homeschooled. Huh."

When he doesn't continue, I probe with a jerk of my hand, motioning for him to continue. "Huh...?"

"Nothing," he responds, gruffer than earlier.

Rafael opens my door and gestures for me to exit first. Without asking, he reaches into my jeans pocket and pulls out my keys, locking the door behind us, while my insides try to ignore his blistering touch.

Scowling, I despise my body's reactions. Not only is he a near-stranger, but lust shouldn't be overshadowing the grief of what this day has revealed.

Rafael doesn't say more, and I follow him back to his car, which I'm almost surprised wasn't robbed in the twenty minutes we were inside. I don't live in a *bad* area of the city by any means—Dad would have had a coronary. He only allowed me to live here after doing extensive research on the area, the building, and the distance to him. But still, we're in Montreal, so you never know what kind of creeps wander into the area and would be interested in the expensive vehicle.

Rafael loads my suitcase and I rest my laptop in the space beside it, pressing it against the side of the car to hold it in place. When we're seated again, Rafael starts the vehicle and takes it back onto the busy roads.

Instead of heading downtown though, he takes another exit, which prompts me to wonder, "Where are we going?"

"Corsetti mansion. My brother wishes to speak with you."

11

RAFAEL

After telling Isabelle where we're heading, she gets extremely quiet, which should be worrisome, but I appreciate the silence. From now on, I go where she goes, and she comes with me. Moments of quiet might be far and few between.

The moment I turn down the single road, which is actually the stretch of my family's driveway, she gets more attentive, leaning forward in her seat and scanning the massive stretch of land on either side of us.

I take the car around the circular driveway and park in front of the mansion, only a few feet from the staircase leading up to the large, double doors. Gaping, she immediately unlocks her seat belt and opens her door, her eyes devouring every inch of my family's home.

"My father worked here," she murmurs when I come around to her side.

Not sure if she's speaking to me or herself, but regardless, I answer, "Yes. Not every day, as sometimes he'd be downtown, like he told you, but this is where we're based out of." I don't know why I'm rambling about him. Maybe because Isabelle deserves a fraction of the truth. "He was well-respected," I tell her, gauging her reaction. "Experienced. Eventually helped train some of the new inductees. Including me."

My words don't seem to register as she continues looking to the side, toward the sprawling land, catching the side of the small patch of woods behind the house, where Nico and I used to play hide-and-seek as kids.

"This is beautiful."

I suppose. I prefer my downtown condo because it's smaller. More me. A place that is mine, away from what my family name decides I am. After a day's chaos, I've learned it's best to have some distance.

"Let's go in." I turn for the doors, expecting her to follow, and partially surprised when she does. Her feet echo behind mine, up the stone steps. I tug open the massive doors and step aside. "You first."

"Holy shit." She passes through the doorway, almost tripping over her feet as her gaze remains upwards, scanning the open foyer. "This is some rich people shit."

Is now the time to inform her my family's worth? There's a reason we own this mansion.

"The property has been in the family for many generations. Long before I was born."

"Why did you move out?"

"Distance." Tipping my head, I indicate for her to follow me down the hallway, toward Nico's office. "When you meet my brother, you'll get it. They're intense. Moving out gives me a bit of freedom from the chaos."

"I get that. Also why I moved out." Her gaze gets unfocused, probably thinking about her father again.

It's interesting a man so protective over his daughter allowed her to move out on her own, but I wonder if it speaks to her tenacity. At some point, kids become harder to control. She could be an example of that.

"This is...wow." The marvel in her tone brings a smile to my face as I lead her down the main hallway. We pass the ballroom, where so many of our events are held, when she curses. "Holy fuck, you have a *literal ballroom*. Who are you people?"

Her voice is further away, so I turn, noticing she's stopped following me to stare at the space. She wanders through the archway, her dirt-smudged shoes bringing her toward the centre. No one dressed so casually has stood where she is, but I find myself appreciating it.

She spins slowly, scanning the walls, her grin growing every second. All considerations of why we're here, of what's happened today—gone in her smile. I long to know what's in her head.

Having seen so much death, I recognize when people compartmentalize, and I suspect that's exactly what she's doing. Her sadness is hiding beneath an appreciation of her surroundings.

After a moment, she stops, focusing on me again. "*This* is where you grew up? Where my father worked? This is...wow." She repeats her earlier sentiment. "This is insane."

"Insane is one way to put it," I reply dryly, thinking of the past two events held here. A party to find Nico a wife, which worked, I suppose, when Della snuck her way in for villainous reasons and they fell in love despite that. And then their engagement-slash-Aurora's re-entry-into-society party. I got wasted that night to tune out the numerous people in attendance because I had no interest in speaking with any of them, to avoid my parents who'll likely start hunting a bride for me soon, and to ignore the obvious misery on Aurora's face as she met the man she would have been shackled to.

Belle returns to my side. "It's like a fairy tale."

"Maybe a bloody fairy tale."

That seems to snap her out of her daze. Meeting my eyes warily, she nods and continues down the hallway by my side, her attention only in the direction we head, and not the ballroom behind us.

"You think I've forgotten the mafia isn't a good thing?" she murmurs. "I'm here with you, now fatherless because of it."

"Sorry." We stop in front of Nico's office door, and I comment, "If my brother's a dick, ignore him. He's intense, but harmless."

Without knocking, I push open the door, holding it open as we both enter. She trails closely behind, stepping closer once we're inside. Already viewing me as the safer option in a house full of killers.

Not that Nico's exactly helping his case from where he sits at his desk, arms crossed, hard gaze observing. Della stands beside him, her smile an attempt to ease the tension. They remind me of our parents, of when I'd come in here as a kid and would find Mother and Father in a similar position. Scary sometimes when I witness how effortlessly Nico has become our father.

"Hello," Nico starts, gesturing to the two chairs in front of him, as though he expects her to sit rather than stand stoically by my side. Gone is the smile as she stood in the ballroom; reality has returned, smashing into her.

I stride forward, plastering a lazy grin, so Isabelle sees Nico doesn't require formality. "Hey, bro, if this can go quick, that'd be great."

Isabelle trails behind me, stopping where I am, right behind the set of chairs.

"You can sit," Nico offers.

Isabelle doesn't move, causing a smirk from Nico.

"Very well then. No, this won't take long. I wanted to show

my support for what you're going through and give you my sincere apologies for what happened. Your father was a loyal and trusted soldier."

Was being key in that statement. *Was* loyal and trusted. Now, perhaps not so much after recent discoveries.

"Thanks," she replies curtly, her back stiffening.

"If there's anything we can do for you, we'll make it happen, Miss Dupont."

"My father's body. Where is it? I want to see him."

Nico's mouth opens and shuts, and his gaze flicks to me, wary for the first time since we've entered. I hadn't told her that we were unable to retrieve his body. She barely accepted his death; I couldn't admit we fucked up.

"We're in the process of retrieving him," Nico responds carefully.

Isabelle understands the underlying meaning of his words and the stiffness in her form evaporates as a redness creeps up her neck. "You *lost* his body? How do you even fucking know he's dead then?"

"I saw it," I murmur.

She turns her snarl onto me, her lips flattening, a complete one-eighty from who she was even five minutes ago. "You're who I should be blaming then for losing his body?"

In my peripheral vision, I catch Nico smirking, rocking back in his chair as he observes her anger rightfully shifting to me. I won't apologize for how yesterday went down.

"If I went for his body, I'd be dead too."

Her nose lifts and she turns away, making how she feels about my possible death apparent.

"We're trying," Nico continues smoothly. "It'll be a challenging attempt because if whoever killed him went back for his body, we might never see it again."

"Thanks," Isabelle says in a tone implying no gratitude.

"Well," I shove away from the chair, "if that's all, brother, then we'll be—"

"Stay," Nico interrupts, "I need to speak with you alone."

Will this day ever end? With a huff, I gesture toward the door behind us. "Isabelle, you can wait in the hall. I won't be long."

Della breaks away from Nico's side, speaking for the first time. "I'll come with you, Isabelle."

With a wary look toward Della, Isabelle follows her out, realizing she has no other option. Once they're gone, I drop into one of the chairs, stretching my legs out and propping up my arms on the chair's side.

Nico glances at the door. "You sure about this?"

I shrug. "What other choice do we have? You hear about what went down at Maurice's house?"

He nods, rubbing his thumb across his lip in a seemingly-mindless motion. "Yeah. Fucking weird. We could keep her here if you want. No need to have her in your condo."

That's one option, but one I wouldn't prefer. Not after meeting her. I'm intrigued by her personality. She gives me the sense there's a lot beneath the surface once she allows someone inside.

"She's already starting to trust me." Trust might be a stretch, but we're heading in that direction. At the very least, she reacts differently to me than Nico, if this meeting's any indication to go by. "The body in her backyard, the shooting at her house, it's all waking her up."

"Figure out if she knows anything yet?"

I blow out a breath, shaking my head. "Not entirely sure there's anything there. She didn't even know her father worked for us. Thought he was security at a firm downtown. Yet another reason I don't think it's best for her to stay here. One-on-one, she might come to trust me and open up."

He grunts. "She might be a dead-end then."

"Yeah, but I think there's too much going on with that family to ignore her. Keeping her from us for one thing," I hold up a finger, and then a second when I add, "Nic, she was home-schooled. He didn't just hide her from us, but from the world."

Nico curses softly. "That's noteworthy. He took a lot of steps to keep her locked away. Dupont, what secrets are you keeping?" He slides his laptop over, which is shut. "I'm escalating her name to the federal level. I'll call on our RCMP contacts and see what they can dig up."

"Good idea. Notice her scars?"

His eyes flash to me, his fingers paused on the laptop's keys. "They don't look natural."

I nod in agreement. "Peculiar scars to have for a woman who's been hidden from the world, fathered by a man keeping secrets. Coincidental?"

"Coincidences don't exist," he comments, repeating a statement he lives by. It's how he knew something was *off* about his wife. Regarding Isabelle, I agree, coincidences might not exist, and the mystery is too great to ignore.

"She won't trust easily," I muse. "Not now. Not when she's blaming us for her father's death. She's somewhere between shock and denial, which I can work with. I'll make her trust me. See if she'll talk about her childhood. There might be more there too."

"I agree."

"We done here?" I slap my palms on the chair, moving to get up when he speaks again.

"Not yet. I figured out how to solve our New York issue."

"Other than just not telling them?"

"Basically. Now isn't the time to start a war. Both sides want the connection, but without Aurora..." He trails off, his brows lifting as he locks his gaze on me.

"Whoa," I lift my hands, palms out, "no. Pretty sure Erico Rossi isn't gay based on what I've heard of the guy."

"No, I looked into their family lines in more depth. Erico has no sisters...but he has female cousins."

Fuck that. I stand, ending this conversation. "Like you said, De Falco is our priority. Then we'll worry about New York."

Nico's chuckle follows me to the door. "Nice try, Raf. I know what you did there. In either case, enjoy your new roommate."

"Fuck off," I call over my shoulder, yanking open the office doors, suddenly wanting to get Isabelle out of here. If only to get away from my brother before he invents more unwanted plans.

I find her leaning against a wall, staring at her feet, while Della rocks on her heels nearby. Neither talking to the other.

"I'm ready to go if you are," I announce.

Isabelle pushes off the wall, her expression breaking in relief, already heading back down the hallway in the direction we came from earlier. After a head tip to Della in goodbye, I follow her, jogging lightly to catch up.

"What'd you guys talk about?"

"She gave her condolences. Offered a ceremony in his memory, but I'd rather have a body first for that."

Another jab at what she believes is an error on my part. Still, I respond, "Got it. Let's go home."

12

ISABELLE

Today has shown me how not rich I am. Dad's always been able to provide, and our house is in an upper middle-class area of the city, but now I understand where his money came from. After witnessing the sheer size and grandness of the Corsetti mansion, it's obvious they're rich. Beyond rich, actually. Knowing what I know of the mafia from fiction, I suspect I don't want to ask how they make their money either.

Then, if the mansion wasn't enough, Rafael's gorgeous penthouse condo makes my own apartment look like a bedroom. I've made it no farther than the doorway, stunned. The whitest walls known to man, with a black trim around the doorways, gives it an elite appearance. The table in the entrance-way, where Rafael drops his car keys into, is so shiny, I catch my own reflection in it.

Without kicking off his shoes, he leads me down the wide hallway, my suitcase in his grip. Mutely, gaping in the most unattractive manner, I trail behind after removing my shoes. He might keep his on, but I'm not an asshole; I'll respect the hard-working staff he no doubt has clean for him.

The short hallway opens into a *massive* apartment. Bachelor-style, despite the size of this place being able to suit multiple bedrooms. Individual elements are on different split levels. The kitchen to my right is three steps up, the attached dining room —more like, platform, I guess—one down from it, and then two from the main living room area. Straight to my left is another hallway, which Rafael heads down.

"You hungry?"

Food. The mention has my stomach twisting. After sleeping most of the day, and receiving the initial news yesterday, I can't recall the last time I ate. Breakfast yesterday, before work? I think I am, but the concept of eating seems so foreign. Especially eating *with him*?

I don't respond. At this point, I'd rather starve than ask him for anything. I pause to study the living room as Rafael disappears into a room at the end of the hall.

Black, leather couches—three of them are positioned in a U-shape around a glass coffee table. Because, apparently, one couch isn't enough. A huge TV takes up most of the wall across from them, and I imagine him reclined back on the middle one, watching sports or something.

"Isabelle?"

I pull away from the living room, walking the length of the hallway, passing a bathroom I don't look in, too curious to see where he's brought me to. At the doorway, anything I debated saying catches in my throat.

Dark, like much of his other furniture, but beautiful too. The far wall is entirely made of glass, and given we're on the top floor, we're able to see right over other downtown buildings, making the scenery breathtaking. Given it's nighttime and the outside is black, the buildings across from us only show a scattering of white lights.

The huge bed is the next thing I notice. Black, metal posts, black bedspread, black everything. And my suitcase rests on top of it, which means—

"Oh, no," I move into the room, waving my hand, "that's fine. I'll take the couch." Considering he has *three* of them, I have options.

Rafael pays me no attention and treads over the dark grey, thick carpet that my feet sink into like I'm walking on a constant cloud. He disappears through a single door across from the bed, and I wander closer, wondering where he's gone to. Another room, which is easily the size of my own bedroom. Difference is, this isn't a room. It's a fucking closet.

"Here's how this will be, Belle," Rafael calls from deeper in the closet. "Make yourself at home. Help yourself to anything. Like I said, you can continue to go to work, and I'll guard you, and then you'll come to mine. We'll spend evenings here."

So I'm a prisoner. He really wasn't kidding when he said we'd be together all the time. A notion that causes my stomach to flip in ways I don't understand yet.

"This will take a hit on your social life. Dating, and all that."

He doesn't respond, which suggests I'm right, but when he comes back into the bedroom, any other thoughts I had are gone. Stolen. Removed by the sight of Rafael's bare chest and grey sweatpants that do ungodly things to my insides.

Holy. Fuck.

"Um."

My mind shuts down, unable to even look away from his body. I certainly shouldn't be studying him how I am, appreciating the very man who's so far only brought despair to my life. Guilt has me lowering my eyes but interest forces me to look again.

Chiseled abs marked up with all sorts of black tattoos. Roses and vines connecting them to one another. I wonder the significance. Over his heart, a different tattoo stands out from the rest, this one with script. He's *hard* everywhere. His arms. His chest.

Everything about Rafael Corsetti is something only found in a romance book. His appearance, his job, his house. Men aren't supposed to look as good as this; that's just not how it works in real life.

It's so *much*.

He breaks my stare by walking by, a smirk dancing on the edge of his lips. "Get changed. Shower if you want. Or in the morning—whenever. You're not trapped, Belle. I'll go find us some food. Unpack."

The last command reminds me of what we were arguing about before he exited his closet and stole every one of my brain cells.

"About that, like I said, I'll sleep on one of the couches. No need to give up your bed."

He throws a smirk over his shoulder, soon followed by a low, gruff, and sexy laugh. "I'm not giving up my bed and you're not sleeping on a couch. We're sharing the bed."

Share. He wants us to *share*? "The floor then." It comes out weaker than I mean it to.

His grin expands. "Won't hear of it. The bed, Belle. Deal with it."

Then he exits the bedroom, leaving me to *deal with it*, as he put it. To...unpack. To move in for an undetermined time while I try not to imagine him finding me food.

What.

The.

Fuck.

What the fuck is happening in my life? *Who* am I right now? Nothing makes sense.

Dad, what did you do?

Feeling suddenly heavy, I shut the door, needing the small reprieve of being alone, since I suspect there will be few opportunities. Dad's been there for me every step of the way, but now he's not and I'm expected to move on. What does moving on even look like? How do I make sense of all the fuckery in life right now?

My hands end up knotting in my hair, and I slide down the door, bringing my legs up into a scrunch, a scream working up my throat. I hold in the pain, so Rafael doesn't hear me, biting down on the fear.

Dad's gone. Killed. Killed by the same kind of people I'm expected to now live with. *Live* with, as if Rafael and I are some domesticated couple. There's not even a guarantee of me being safe with him, but for now, he's my best option. My *only* option, until I make sense of what's happening.

"Isabelle, I have a snack for you."

Right. He was getting food. I totally forgot about that, and despite the hunger pangs, the thought of eating seems unimaginable. Food holds no interest for me. Is eating after the chaos, the heartbreak, even possible? I get to eat when Dad—

Lifting my head from my lap, I project my mumble. "I'm not hungry."

There's a moment of silence and I almost expected him to have left, but then he speaks, in that low and dangerous tone I've heard only once so far. "Bullshit, Belle. Open the door or I'll break it down."

"Like you'd do that to your own door."

"Don't be difficult. I know you're starving because I heard your stomach on the trip over."

"I don't want to eat."

Again, a pause. And then the door pushes into my back, throwing me away from it with the force. I scramble away, to avoid injury, as he stalks in, a plate in one hand.

"I'm not the person who'll walk away when I know what you need. Deal with it."

Without questioning why I'm on the floor, he drops to his knees beside me and rests the plate on the floor. What I'm sure is fancy, expansive cheese is sliced, alongside meat and crackers.

"I went small," he explains, gesturing the spread. "Figured you might not want something heavy right now."

"I don't want food at all. But thanks."

Pressing his lips together, he holds up a cracker, tapping it against my lips. "You feed yourself, or I will, but I want to see you eat something before bed."

I'm not so pathetic he needs to feed me, so I take the cracker, nibbling on the edge. The second the flavour hits my tongue, my body's instincts kick in; the need for energy overtaking grief and I slip the rest in my mouth.

"Better," he says with a pleased grin.

After another cracker, and two slices of cheese and meat, I mumble, "You don't need to sit here with me."

"Maybe I want to. To make sure you continue to eat."

"I'm getting full." The plate is hardly half eaten, but I've certainly eaten more than I thought I would.

He shrugs and reaches over for a block of meat, popping it in his mouth. "You're eating. It's all that matters. I won't have you withering in front of me."

Unlike my father, who you watched die.

Rafael never mentioned that part before visiting his brother, and I'm unsure how I feel about it. He saw Dad's death. Was *there* with him. And now he's with me...

Rafael suddenly stands, his movements making those perfect abs of his more noticeable. "I'm going to shower. Take your time. Leave the plate whenever you're done with it. I'll put it away."

He leaves the bedroom, and within a moment, I hear the shower from next room switch on. Once I think he's safely beneath the water—the warm steaming water where he's... naked—a vision I try *not* to think about—I take the plate and walk it to the kitchen myself. He might have said to leave it, but I'm not totally useless.

The bathroom door is shut, which is good. Back in his bedroom, I unzip my suitcase, suddenly eager to end this day. Too much has occurred; so much of it like a nightmare. Rafael's about to come to bed, probably smelling like fresh mint and everything pleasant, while I have no idea the last time I showered.

Rifling through the suitcase is the first time I realize how much I've already fucked up. My usual sleep shorts and tank top are *not* appropriate to sleep beside a total stranger in. But there's nothing else in here that will be comfortable.

How many boundaries will I need to set? I stare at the bed. It's larger than anything I've ever slept in, but I'll still be sleeping in it with him. *With him.* Everything Rafael's done so far has been decently respectable, but I don't know him. Not really. Everything I've seen so far could be a façade and the real monster emerges at night when we're alone.

There's always his clothing, I think, glancing at the closet. Given our size difference, he's bound to have a shirt that'll cover more of my body, but that means I'll be wearing *his* clothing.

You know what, no, fuck it. He's changing *my* life. I refuse to also switch up my sleep attire.

Moving the suitcase to the floor, I shove it in the corner and wait until I hear the water shut off, keeping my clothing and toiletry bag in a pile until it's my turn for the bathroom. This kind of reminds me of living at home with Dad, of having to share communal parts of the house.

The bed behind me is still extremely tempting to slide into but scrubbing two-day-old sweat and grime from my body sounds more appealing.

By the time Rafael appears in the doorway, my aggravation feels like it's climbing to the max degree but holding onto the items in my arms is keeping me grounded. Of course, the mere sight of him causes my stomach to flip and my irritation to momentarily dissipate.

He enters in only a towel, his sweatpants draped over one arm. His dark hair is plastered against his forehead. Water droplets decorate his chest, making his dark tattoos more prominent. My eyes strain not to look down, not to show how I'm affected by his presence.

He pauses in the entrance, his eyes flicking to the things I'm holding. Wordlessly, I slide by him and out the door, ignoring that when my arm brushes his, it feels like my skin ignites in a fire I need to extinguish.

Cold shower it is.

Escaping to the gleaming bathroom I passed before, I drop my items on the counter, secretly thrilled they consume so much of his space. Serves him right.

I brush my teeth and wash my face, using the large mirror over the sink. Then I get into the massive, glass shower with multiple heads. *Multiple* heads. Who the fuck needs more than one? That's what I'm thinking anyway, until I switch on the water and the different heads mean all my muscles get hit at the same time.

Despite wanting to wash my body and get to bed, my muscles stop working and it has nothing to do with the steaming water, which slowly feels more cool to my skin. The water swirls around my feet before escaping down the drain, and damn, I wish it could take me with it.

Dad's dead.

Dad. Is. *Dead.*

And that's when the day crashes around me. When everything I've been holding up thus far falls. Crumbles. Shatters. Pieces land around my feet. Pieces of my heart, of my mind, of my sanity. Of my life.

Dad's gone.

The man who, until I was ten, tucked me in every night, who read me books, who brought me to the library whenever I asked him to. Who frequently surprised me with treats when he came home from work at the end of the day. Who held me when I had a bad dream. Who was there every step of the way as I grew up.

How do I continue to survive after the only person I've known my entire life is no longer here? Just gone.

When the shower's water pounds on my head, I wonder when I sat down. When had my legs given up standing? I'm seated on the shower's base, hunched, my arms wrapped around my legs, which are drawn up to my chest, making myself as small as possible.

Dad's dead. I'll never share another meal with him. Never see him smile. Never get to annoy him talking about my books. I'll never be able to do anything. Anything and nothing. There is *nothing* more I can do with Dad.

When salty drops of water seep between my lips, I realize I'm crying. And like this realization was *it*; the barrier comes crashing down and the tears come in waves. Messy waves, sobs that I try to bite my lip through. How much sound carries through to Rafael's room? How much of this is he able to hear and at what point will he come dragging me from the shower and force me to face my future without Dad?

Or, given who he is, maybe he'll leave me alone. Perhaps I can hide away in here all night and by morning, I'll have cried everything out and can be who I have to be. To do what I must. Live.

I don't know how long I cry for. How many memories of Dad invade my mind, which only bring on fresh waves of sobs. Or how I can stop these feelings for the night, but somehow, I do. Somehow, my body runs out of tears and finds the strength to stand again.

I manage to wash my body, but everything feels mechanical. Like I'm on the outside witnessing it and not actually feeling anything. Finally, I switch off the water before Rafael comes searching for me, but I don't leave the steaming glass room yet. Once I do, this ends. Once I do, I return to feeling nothing. I can't or else I'll have these breakdowns all the time and I can't survive crying every five minutes.

Nor would Dad want me to.

I manage to push open the glass door, and with a towel from the shelf beside me, I pat myself dry, and dress in the tank and shorts I chose to sleep in.

The reflection in the mirror shows a woman who looked like she just cried. My cheeks a deeper shade, my eyes red-rimmed and puffy. My wet hair falling in scraggly strands around my face. I look like a mess about to climb into bed with a man for the first time ever.

Given the length of time I've spent showering, I'm positive he's already pieced together my breakdown, but still, I run the tap and splash my face with cold water, trying to ease the puffi-ness. It'll be a while until it looks like I haven't been crying, but I wait out a few minutes until it becomes slightly less obvious.

My fingers float to my face, lightly tracing over the scars I've had for so long that I've gotten used to them. They look bolder; the redness in my face making them brighter. When Rafael first came to Dad's door the other day, he, like everyone else, noticed them right away. Not that I blame him. They'd be impossible to ignore, taking up so much of my face.

Then I chuckle. Has Rafael ever had a woman enter his room in such a mess? I imagine most are dressed in lingerie, their hair brushed, their makeup flawless. They walk toward him with a grin rather than holding in their grief.

With a heavy sigh, I shove away from the counter, exit the bathroom and stalk straight into the bedroom without a second thought to avoid spiking my anxiety again.

But what I see throws my determined stride into a standstill, my stomach somersaulting. Rafael reclined in bed, his phone in hand. He has one knee propped up, his arm dangling over it. His damp hair falls into his face, blocking his eyes from view. With his reclined position, his abs look more prominent, more rippling.

Oh my fucking—

He turns his face toward me, bangs flicked aside, a slow smile spreading on his cocky lips. I feel the moment his gaze passes my legs, starting at my toes, taking in every inch of my body. Over my stomach, over my breasts. Every inch, with only an appreciative expression until he reaches my face. The smirk falters a little, sympathy, or something close to it, seeping in.

Despite the nerves he ignites, I shouldn't be feeling like this. Not for him and not now, especially. Not after everything I felt inside the shower. The conflicting emotions battling within me are exactly that—a battle of grief and desire. Of betrayal and lust.

Glancing at his closet, I debate once again about using his clothing, but almost figure that'll be worse, especially since he's already seen me. Once I'm safely beneath blankets, I'll be fine.

Huffing, I push past his stare and stomp toward the bed, stopping shy of the side he's apparently deemed I'm sleeping on.

"I can take the floor." A last-ditch effort.

"I won't have a woman sleeping on the floor while I'm in the bed. Get in."

"Sexist. Then you sleep there."

His crooked grin sets my nerves on fire, burning every one of them. "I'm not sleeping on the floor." He gestures to my side, to the large chunk of mattress between where he lays and I stand. "In case you haven't noticed, the bed is large. We'll each stick to our sides. Relax."

Relax. Does he realize how fucking aggravating it is to be told to *relax*?

"What's your fascination with me sleeping in the bed?"

Eyes blazing, he rests his phone down to give me his complete, undivided—dominant—attention, which makes me wish he'd send it elsewhere. "You don't want to know the answer to that. Now, get in the bed, Belle, before I put you here myself."

He thinks so? With a slight arch of my brow, I purse my lips. "You won't touch me. Not like that."

His chin tilts a fraction, his guise becoming both deadly and sexy. "You don't know what I'll do, so before testing me, you may want to remember who you're dealing with." Then he moves, dropping his arm to the side, threatening me with his approach.

I slide beneath the blankets before he has a chance to act on his threat.

"Better."

Grumbling below my breath, I take one of the two pillows at my back and place it between us. Stabbing my nail into it, I growl. "This stays here, Rafael. This is our wall. In fact, if there's more pillows somewhere in this place, I'd appreciate a row of them."

Shaking his head, he smirks. "There isn't, and they're not

needed because I won't touch you. You'll come to trust me soon."

Narrowing my eyes, I push myself down the bed until my head is on my remaining pillow. Before I roll over, I mutter, "Don't make promises you'll never be able to keep."

"We'll see, *ma belle,* we'll see."

My beautiful. That's a new nickname.

13
RAFAEL

In the middle of the night, during the most restless sleep I've ever had, the whimpers sound so much louder. It starts with a hitch of her breath. Then a sniffle. Finally, a sob.

Peering through the dark, I wait until my eyes adjust to the nighttime, catching her form over the pillow she's determinedly stuck between us. A shudder travels her body, making her twitch.

Her next sob is stilted, and I imagine her biting her lip, trying to ensure I don't hear. I almost pretend I didn't and give her the space to grieve properly. The days I cried myself to sleep were when Hawke left us. Nico came to my room to comfort me, both of us stuck in our shared hatred over the events. He consoled me, allowed me to cry away from our Father's unforgiving, emotionless attitude and continued to tell me that we'd see him again.

And what do you know? Guess Nico was right.

I understand concealing sadness. For those days following Hawke's exit, I'd wake up and go down for breakfast, sharing a secret glance with Nico; the look only siblings can have that say we wouldn't rat each other out to our parents.

At least I had Nico to share in my grief. Isabelle has no one. Based on the little I know of her, I believe Maurice was her entire life, so she's truly alone now. She has no one to help shoulder her grief. To walk her through it. To be there when things get hard.

At first, I thought her tough exterior was a guise, but with every passing moment with her, I get the sense that it's *her*. She's tough, forced to be alone in so many of her emotions. Anything she didn't want her father to see, she would hold in.

She's not only grieving him, though. She's grieving the life she's come to know. The safe life, where her father is a security guard—mentally, I scoff—the life in which they see each other for dinners and she goes to work and then home.

Which is why slowly, I shift over, reaching for her pillow wall. Comical, but whatever makes her feel more comfortable. I toss it to my side of the bed, and slide closer, knowing by now, she'd feel my movements.

For a moment, I remain still, my chest an inch from her back, letting her control the direction this takes. That she's not alone. She doesn't hold back her next sob, and I'm proud of her for letting me hear her emotions.

Tentatively, I lay my hand on her hip, right on the bare patch of skin between her tank and those tiny shorts. My fingers first, as a test, and then my whole hand, giving her physical reassurance.

She sniffles through her cries, her noises increasing, and without warning, she flips over, burying her head in my chest. Her hands come between us, covering her face as she curls into my body.

One arm goes around the back of her neck, holding her there while gently stroking her hair. My hand on her hip remains still, my fingers lightly stroking the patch of her skin, needing her to know it's *me* caring for her.

"Y-you're t-t-touching me. You said you wouldn't."

"That was before you were crying, *ma belle.*" A nickname that slips out so easily again that I'm left wondering why it feels suitable. "I'm not so much of a beast I'll ignore your grief."

I think she murmurs, "I know," but it's buried between her hands and my chest, so I can't be certain.

Instead, I continue petting her head, making the soothing noises I once found helpful. She shifts closer to me, her hips aligning with mine. Slowly, I move my hand from her hip to her back, hugging her tightly.

"Let it out. It's okay. It's natural to feel like this."

"To feel lost?" She manages a staggering breath I feel against my chest. "He is—*was*—" She pauses, the weight of the word robbing the air. "He *was* all I knew. He's been my entire life. I never...I never knew my mom. It's only been him."

She opens the door for me to ask about her childhood and family, but now isn't the time. There will be other chances to probe, especially with her having already mentioned the subject.

I stroke my hand up and down her back, dipping low to her hip. Eventually, her hands move away from her face, lying limply between us instead. I loosen my hold in case she wants to roll away.

"No, don't." She grabs onto my abs, halting my movements. "Please. This feels...I don't know. Just don't move. Please."

Into her hair, in the secret of the dark, I smile.

"I won't," I promise. "I'll hold you for as long as you'd like."

She falls silent again, the dampness of her tears against my skin the only sign she's still awake. Even those, after a few minutes, seem to dry up with no more replacing them. Her breaths become even, so tightening my hold on her, dipping my face into her hair, and breathing in her sweet scent, I shut my eyes, knowing for now, she's okay.

Okay to sleep, at least.

I sabelle and I are still tangled up together when I wake. The wise thing to do would be to release her, but she feels too good, so I keep her locked in my arms and shut my eyes, faking sleep until she wakes up.

About twenty minutes later, she wakes. She stretches her limbs as much as my hold allows for, and tips her head back.

I've never seen a woman look so *normal* in the morning. The ones I seem to find think I want perfection all the time, so they wake before I do and get ready, as though it's believable women wake up like that. They never realize I'm a light sleeper and catch them every time. Part of my training is not to sleep too deeply, as that's when enemies can creep up.

Isabelle in the daytime is beautiful, but in the morning, she's downright gorgeous. Her eyes lined with sleep, unfocused as she wakes. Her skin is flushed, her face natural and dewy.

Unable to stop myself and needing to feel her for myself, I stroke my thumb down her cheek, flicking stray hairs to the side as I examine her face, her eyes, seeking any sign of anger. More of that guardedness enters her expression, but she doesn't pull away.

"Never again," she starts. "Last night was—never again. It wasn't an invitation. This isn't me."

Telling me or yourself, ma belle? "Of course," I reply in a smooth, soothing tone. "I know, Isabelle, but I was also serious. I'm not gonna let you cry yourself to sleep when I can help shoulder a bit of that pain."

She nods, seeming to take my words seriously. Her eyes get

distracted, and she whispers, "How did life change so drastically in the last twenty-four hours? I mean, I shouldn't be *here*. Being held by you. Being held for the first time ev—" Her lips clamp shut, her skin growing a deeper shade of red with what she's nearly admitted.

But she said enough for me to finish the sentence. First time being held, which is a damn shame, although unsurprising. The homeschooled, scarred, quiet woman hidden from the world, including me and my family, doesn't exactly scream experienced. I wouldn't assume, of course, but can guess. Considering I manage a sex-positive club, it's easy to pick out virgins.

I let her retain her self-esteem and answer with, "Life's funny that way. No one's ever safe. It's how it is."

"Maybe in *your* life." She tips her head to better see me, pulling from my hold. The time has come where her walls build back up and she becomes guarded again. As she pushes into an upright position, she adds, "And in Dad's life, I guess."

When she doesn't get off the bed, I do, coming around to her side until I can see her face again. Like yesterday, I tip her head up, gaining her complete attention as I lean closer.

Before I can speak, she does. "I feel like I should hate you and your family for his death."

Should. "But?"

"I don't," she whispers, her lips barely forming the words. "I think I'm more mad at Dad for lying to me."

Belle, I am too.

I'm getting the sense, his job is merely one of many facts he's hidden from her.

Something passes in her chocolate gaze, hardening the colour to near-black. Jerking from my hold, she pushes to her feet and heads for her suitcase. "I work in two hours. If you're done trying to sympathize with me, I have a life to return to."

And you're about to make mine very interesting.

14

ISABELLE

Breakfast was weird. Rafael left the room long before I did because I struggled to follow. Once getting dressed, reality hit *hard*. Exiting the bedroom meant sharing a meal with a stranger, the day after my entire life fell apart.

Dad used to cook me breakfast every weekend, since he didn't get the chance to on the weekdays. He was often gone shortly after I woke which meant my nanny would prepare food, until I got old enough to do it myself. Pancakes were his specialty.

And based on the sounds that were coming from the kitchen, Rafael's cooking. No staff, which is a pleasant surprise. When I finally left his bedroom—and thoughts of Dad behind for the day—I found him shirtless, flipping eggs and frying bacon.

When I pointed out that he was preparing food, he shrugged and explained, "Which is why I often go to the mansion for breakfast, so I don't have to do this. The chefs there know what they're doing."

Now, we're pulling up in front of the library. My shift always begins the half-hour after opening, so luckily, I don't have to switch on the computers or complete all the opening tasks.

He parks in one of the staff spots I indicate, and I lead him inside, sensing he's only two steps behind me.

"No one will attack me here," I mutter, rolling my eyes.

"We don't know that."

"Whatever makes you feel better."

I stride through the small lobby, instantly heading for the staircase to the right, which leads to the bottom floor, where the children and young adult section is. A mother and two children stand by the counter, getting their books checked out by one of my co-workers, Emma. She begins the day down here until I arrive, and then will head up to the adult section, where they need more help during the daytime.

As I round the counter, she glances from her task, to me, to Rafael, who wanders toward a far corner. When eager, small faces peer over the counter toward her again, lifting onto their toes to watch, she quickly finishes with the family and waves goodbye.

The moment they're gone, she whirls on me, whisper-yelling and jerking her head not-so-subtly to the side. "Who the hell is *that*? I mean, go you, Isabelle."

"It's not like that. It's—" I stop, unsure how to explain the situation.

"Well," she taps the counter with her fingers twice before stepping away from the counter, "whatever it's like, you have fun. I'll be going now." She rounds the counter, heading for the back staircase that allows staff an easier way to get between floors. Foot on the bottom step, she pauses. "Oh, Gage is already here. Guess he has something to do later so he showed up at opening to leave sooner. He's in the back corner, hanging new posters that were delivered."

Fuck. Gage is here when Rafael is. It sets butterflies off in my stomach. As irritating and unwelcoming as Gage's flirting is —if we can call it that—I can handle him. It's easy to give him tasks and keep him occupied, but with Rafael here, it feels like *more.*

The return cart is already full of books that were returned post-closing yesterday and before opening today. Another benefit of not doing the opening is I arrive to the books already down here, rather than having to retrieve them from the return chute and separate mine from the adult books.

Sorting them by section, I almost miss when heavy steps come up to the other side of the counter, his inquiring gaze making my back prickle.

"Yes?" I growl without turning around.

"Nothing. Just watching. You know, I've never been inside a library before."

The horror of never visiting a place as wondrous as this one is, is ridiculous. Even with Dad's overly-protective behaviours, in which he didn't allow me to attend a public school, or play outside for too long, this was one place he always allowed me to be free in. Maybe because it's small, or because it brought me so much joy.

When I turn, my heart leaps in my throat at finding him so close, leaning over the counter, peering intently as I work.

"You've never been inside a library before," I recap, needing him to repeat it, to ensure I heard correctly.

His lips pull up on one side as he glances at the two young adult fantasy books I'm holding. "Ironic, considering we have one inside the mansion."

The books begin slipping from my hand and my knees feel weak, so I latch onto the counter. "Y-you have a library inside your house?" I was fascinated with the ballroom when there's a *library*.

One shoulder lifts in an offhanded shrug because he clearly doesn't comprehend the dream home he has. "I'm not sure it has the kind of books you like."

"Still though," I murmur. "A home library is every reader's dream."

Step one: find his library.

Step two: read.

"I'll bring you back to the mansion at some point and you can explore it to your heart's content."

Despite all the shit, all the weirdness, all the negative emotions I should be feeling, his words bring me joy. Rafael and I are strangers, but granting me one tiny desire, something so minor...

Stop going there.

Rafael tugs one of the books from my hand and rests it beside him and starts flipping through the pages. "Do you know what this one's about?"

He's asking me to talk about a book when I'm still trying to wrap my head around a home library.

"You live in a house with its own library, but you've never read a book?" He stated the book he was reading in my room yesterday morning was the most he's ever read of one.

He chuckles, shutting the book. It's one I've read in the past and can answer his question. "Books don't interest me. Maybe I need someone to teach me otherwise."

Is it me or did his bright gaze twinkle beneath the florescent lighting?

"Then you *are* a beast," I joke, returning to the moniker I coined him. "Books are life. That one," I flick my fingers toward the one he has, "is a young adult fantasy novel. There's a small romantic subplot, which I usually prefer to be more of the focus in a book, which is likely why I felt very iffy about that one. But romance aside, the characters were good. I really liked how the main character didn't just roll over when the king threatened her family. She started an entire uprising, gathering all the half-fae he once banished, and together they—"

The more I ramble, the greater his grin expands.

I stop, my lips clamping shut, and rock back on my heels, needing to release the built-up excitement elsewhere than rambling about a book. A book I barely even enjoyed. Imagine if he gets me talking about one I do.

"Why'd you stop?" he asks. "That was cute. To be so animated about your hobby."

I shrug. No one's ever wanted to hear about what I read. Dad either. When he asked what my book was about, he was being polite and looking for a one-sentence summary, not a review.

"I don't know. Because I was going on a tangent."

Rafael lays the book aside and leans closer, the counter digging into his stomach as he stretches. "I think it's amazing to have so much love for something. Never apologize for being you, Belle."

"Never apologize for being you, Belle."

But isn't that what I've always done? Been myself. Stayed in my room and observed the outdoors as groups of teenagers passed by in small hoards. Their laughs and commentary drifted to me, where I'd sit in my room studying while Dad was at work, and Marie, my nanny, was downstairs. When Dad came home, he was only interested in staying inside, watching movies, and talking about my school work. He may have taken me to the library when I begged him to, but he never asked about what I was reading. When I rambled about a book, I immediately followed up with an apology before keeping the story and my love of the characters to myself.

That seemed to be his personality so I stopped pushing my hobby onto him.

"Yeah, well, maybe I need to learn to shut up sometimes." Taking the book from the counter, I add it to the other in my hand, murmuring another, "Sorry," before turning to the cart again.

His arm darts across the way, grasping my elbow, which makes me stop with a low gasp. "Again, do not apologize, Belle. I like you talking about this stuff. You become a different person."

"Different, or one you don't know."

"Does anyone know you, other than your father?"

Barely even him. But his point resonates deep in my chest, lodging itself at the base of my heart until breathing becomes difficult and I can do nothing but give him an expression even I can't identify.

"Maybe one day you can read to me."

Read to the hot mafia guy? Right, that sounds like some made-up fantasy. Something he's saying to be polite.

"Yeah," I swallow through the impending dryness zipping up my throat, "that'd be good."

When steps approach, I yank from Rafael's hold right as Gage comes into view. My cheeks heat, though I'm not sure why, and I return to busying myself with the returns.

"Hi," Gage rumbles, coming up beside me, closer than normal. Certainly closer than I'd prefer and I take a small step away. "Need help, Isabelle?" He pointedly glares at Rafael, who's since straightened.

"I'm good," I reply. "Posters hung?"

Cold eyes remain locked on the mobster behind me. Gage might be working off a sentence, but I suspect his crimes are nothing compared to what Rafael and his family have done.

"Who's this?" he asks.

"A friend."

"Rafael Corsetti," Rafael interjects. His attention shifts a fraction to the tiny bit of space I've managed to gain between Gage and me.

"C-Corsetti." Gage swallows. "The Corsetti family."

Rafael smiles, but it's nothing like the flirty one he gives me. Rather, this one is cold, malicious. A grin of a killer. "You've heard of us then. Good. It'll save some energy."

"Energy?" Gage echoes.

"The energy of explaining who I am before I drag a blade along your throat if you don't back the fuck up and give Belle more space."

Holy fuck, what kind of showdown did I get into? What Rafael's saying is *nothing* close to how he talks to me.

"Belle," Gage repeats another one of Rafael's words, this one heavier and weighted. He glances at me, a question in his depths, but Rafael's low growl—a fucking *growl—People do that in real life?*—pulls Gage's attention back to him.

"Now, don't you have a fucking job to do? And if you don't, find something before I decide to entertain myself with your bones."

Whoa! That's...whoa! Rafael's getting next level. I quickly scan up and down the length of the library floor, thankful no one's here.

Taking the stack of unorganized children's books, I shove them into Gage's arms. The children's section is on the other side of the floor, which will keep him away from Rafael for a while.

"Here. Put these away please."

Gage takes them, shooting a death stare at Rafael before stalking away, grumbling something I don't catch beneath his breath.

The moment he's gone from sight, Rafael returns to the

man I know. He drops back onto the counter, leaning with an easy grin, swapping personalities quickly.

Before I scold him, he jerks his head in the direction Gage left. "Who the fuck is he?"

"Volunteer."

"Name?"

Why, so you can search him up?

"It doesn't matter. He's no one. Volunteers here to work off his community service requirements."

"Community service," he repeats in a deadly tone. "What'd he do?"

"Illegal hunting. Nothing super dangerous. Toward me, at least. Besides, like you're one to talk!"

"It starts with hunting. His name, Isabelle. And before you say no, knowing he volunteers here will make it easy to figure out every staff member working here, volunteers too. So, to save my men the twenty minutes of work, I'd appreciate his name."

I level my stare, still trying to catch up to the fact I'm having this conversation with a self-proclaimed criminal. "Why? I should make you do the work. It's nothing less than you all deserve."

Rafael doesn't blink. One brow hikes a fraction, and keeping his stare on me, he removes his phone from his back pocket. "I don't see why you care," he comments as he types. "You clearly don't like the guy. Anyone paying attention could see how fast you moved away from him."

"He's a dick," I agree. "Constantly asks me out. Doesn't like taking no for an answer."

Emerald eyes flash up. "Has he ever touched you?"

I shake my head, which seems to instantly ease him. My heart squeezes, making breathing impossible. Attention from a man like him is refreshing, to have someone so protective, even if I'm not a fan of him threatening people. Even someone like Gage.

Just then, a patron enters, pushing a stroller, and I've never been more thankful to be interrupted. I shift into work mode, greeting the woman with a large smile as Rafael pushes off the counter and returns to the corner of the room, where he stood earlier. He crosses his arms and leans against the wall, his probing gaze locked on me as I work.

For the rest of the afternoon, he doesn't move. I'd say it's downright creepy if I didn't feel my back tingle every time I peek at him.

Whenever Gage comes around, they end up in some stare down. Rafael threatening death with his eyes and Gage replying with hatred before disappearing to complete whatever task I give him. When Gage's shift finally ends, hours before my own, and he leaves, I monitor Rafael to ensure he doesn't follow him. He doesn't, which makes me feel a bit better about the earlier interaction.

Actually, I don't know how to feel about that interaction. It reminds me of one thing: that no matter how friendly Rafael is, regardless of comforting the crying, grieving person as she sleeps, or protecting her during the daytime, he's dangerous. Hints of that emerged today.

He's a part of the same family my father worked for.

The same family my father got killed for working for.

Which poses the question: am I safe with Rafael Corsetti?

15

RAFAEL

Normally, I would work during the club's open hours. I prefer to be around in case there's an issue with any patrons, since I strive for such an open and welcoming environment. Today, I've informed my staff I'll be dropping by earlier in the evening to complete paperwork, before any of their shifts, and leaving before opening.

Truth being, I could do it anywhere, but I need to start getting facts from Isabelle and an interview-like conversation isn't the best way to go about it. If I can strike up conversation as I work, it'll seem more casual.

I park in the underground garage of my condo building and instead of taking the private elevator straight to the top, I take it only one level up, to Eden.

Isabelle glances at the number panel and then the opening elevator doors as I lead her out, her question silent but very present.

"The club is in the same building. I own the whole thing. Club on the bottom, condos on the top." With the entire top floor being mine. I told her this in the beginning, but she was probably lost in her head at the time.

As I approach the interior staff door, the one only I use, since most enter through the back entrance, she studies the smoked glass, her eyes narrowing. "What kind of club is this?"

Right, I never told her. I wait for her to enter first, flicking on the hallway light, which we usually keep dimmed. I'll let her figure it out for herself. Let's see if those books have taught her anything.

Instead of taking the path to my office, I lead her forward, to the end of the hallway, by the registration stand and main entrance. The wall beside the main desk will indicate how much she knows.

The giant map is difficult to miss, and she immediately approaches, even standing on her tiptoes to peer closer, which I find fucking adorable.

"Voyeur & exhibitionism hall," she reads the labels, murmuring low. "Private rooms. Group..." She whirls, her mouth in an O. "This is a sex club."

Red blooms immediately down her arms, up her chest, peeking out of her shirt, and straight to her neck. I long to learn where else she's turning red. Little Miss Virgin is about to walk into another world simply by being here, and now, I'm pleased to have brought her before opening, without other staff here. Or worse, patrons.

She glances at the map again, hooking her thumb toward it. "Why's there a directory?"

"Because as much as I like to promote openness, some people are shy, and we're not pushy. I'd rather guests have the visual to direct themselves than be too embarrassed to ask and end up in an area that'll make them uncomfortable."

She tilts her head and only replies with, "Huh."

"Huh what?"

"Thoughtful. Not something I imagined."

"From me?" I smirk, enjoying her reaction. "You seem to have this preconceived notion about me, which is entirely false."

"So you're not a killer?"

"Oh, I am." And I'd love to be one again. Specifically, that asshole Gage Roche—*yeah, I got his name*—who stood way too close for my comfort. For *her* comfort. I know what he wanted and what I won't allow him to take.

Has there ever been a time I've been possessive over a woman? Bodies—men and women—are meant to be shared. To be explored. I've had a healthy history of mutual pleasure, but I won't share the small scrap of a woman in front of me. Who could be the key to De Falco. I won't share her laughs or *her*. A discerning fact bringing forth an unfamiliar feeling.

Turning away from Isabelle, I swipe a hand over my hair while I command her to follow me to my office, opening the door and gesturing for her to enter.

"It's so...plain. Depressing," she comments, stepping farther in the space.

"No point in decorating. I'm the only one who comes in here."

"By that belief, I should never have decorated my bedroom because no one ever came over when I was a kid. I did it for me, to have a space I enjoyed." She gestures to the walls, spreading her hands dramatically in the air. "Imagine if there was something here to remove the blandness of the wall."

I chuckle, dropping into my leather desk chair as I pull it closer. She's amusing to watch, but for different reasons than I'd normally enjoy. Isabelle talking about books, watching her work, and simply *being* is oddly enjoyable. She's intriguing in every boring way she shouldn't be. An image of her in one of my voyeur rooms, her fingers sliding through her pink pussy as she brings herself to the edge for me, just for me, bombards my mind.

Coughing, I force my head to clear of that thought before I throw her over my shoulder and go make it a reality. Gesturing to the chair across from me, I say, "You can sit. I don't plan on being here for long."

"Take your time." She pulls that small black tablet from her purse. "You're with a reader. We're good at being alone." She throws her feet over the armrest and reclines in a way that wouldn't be comfortable for anyone who isn't her size.

I wait until she unlocks the device before pulling out the stack of paperwork I need to go through before the month ends. Mentioning being alone provides an opening, so I wait a full ten seconds, counting each one, before commenting, "Good at being alone. Did that often?"

Dark eyes peek up from long lashes. "Still do, you can say. But yeah. It was only me and my nanny growing up while Dad was at work. With your family, I guess."

A nanny. Pressing my lips together, I fake reading over a contract, trying to rein in my excitement. Grow her trust and learn the little details she'd believe to be minute. Isabelle might not know what Maurice was hiding, but her memory could.

"She helped you with schooling, I assume." Small talk helps ease people and hides my true intentions.

"Yeah. She'd been around from the very beginning." Her brows scrunch together, gaze lifting to the far wall she spoke about decorating. "In fact, I don't recall a time she wasn't around."

"Did you like her?"

"Oh yeah," Isabelle glances at me, her eyes still unfocused, confused, lost, "she's lovely. I still get Christmas and birthday cards from her every year."

"Positive relationship. She was the only nanny you ever had?" One trusted person Maurice brought into the fold.

"Yes."

"What's her name?"

"Marie Potts."

I tuck that tidbit away so the moment she isn't paying any attention, I'll text it to some of my soldiers to gain an address. Ms. Marie Potts will be receiving a visit soon.

"No friends, then?" I ask, returning to the previous topic about being alone.

She scoffs, staring down at the Kindle in her hand, but not reading. "That would require going out. Which we didn't do for very long. I can probably count on one hand how many times I'd visit a park, and never when other people were there."

My heart hurts for her. Fuck, Maurice, what were you into you couldn't give your daughter a normal childhood?

"Wow," I murmur, having nothing else to respond with. Empathy isn't exactly my strong suit. "That's unfortunate, Belle. Lonely."

"You could say that again."

Now's an ideal time to stop probing. To not continue when I've already brought her mood down, but it's difficult when she's opened up so easily. Perhaps connecting with her on this emotional level is exactly what's needed.

"Only you and your dad growing up then. And a nanny," I summarize. "Where's your mother?"

Isabelle is silent and after counting to ten again, I glance up from the form I was fake reading, worried I might have taken this too far. Maurice never mentioned a spouse, but he also never mentioned a daughter. What if she died? A million reasons for her absence and—

"She chose herself over being a mother," Isabelle finally whispers. "I never knew her. Only what Dad mentioned."

"Which is?" I ask carefully, treading in territory I certainly don't deserve being.

She shrugs a shoulder. "She was beautiful. Brunette. Short. Dad claims I look exactly like her. I think that's what made it hard on him, knowing I was a daily reminder of her."

My grip gets tight around the pen. "Did he tell you that?" I push out through a tight jaw, thinking of any possible thing he could have said that'd make her feel shitty.

She shakes her head. "Just a feeling. When he spoke about her, it was only positive things."

Maurice spoke fondly about a mother who ran out on them. That's...odd. An act like that would typically entice a lot of negative feelings from the spouse. And why continue talking to his daughter about a woman who, as Isabelle put it, chose herself over motherhood?

I drum my fingers along my thigh as I tuck more facts away. We still have people looking into the accident regarding Della's mother, and I feel like another one needs to be done on Isabelle. Father trained Nico and me to always listen to our gut instincts and mine says Isabelle is being lied to.

Something's *off* about this.

For now, I drop the subject. So much more to know. So many loose ends, but we've untied enough for now. Forcing the new data aside, I focus on the document in my hand, since it is one of many reasons we're here right now, and she returns to reading.

At one point when I glance up, she's staring at the wall past her Kindle, and not her book.

Every five minutes, I check on her, and she never looks away from that one spot.

〜

An hour before my staff is slated to arrive, we escape Eden and return to the private elevator that brings us straight to my penthouse.

"Surprised you didn't have the elevator connect to your office," she comments when the doors *ding* with its arrival.

"Brilliant. Never thought of that. Guess I'll have to redo the building to make that possible." I'm joking, of course, but the laugh that bursts from Isabelle makes it worth it. The first giggle I've managed to get from her since mentioning her mother and she spent the hour in a daze, clearly lost in her head.

The smile quickly fades and she enters the elevator and tucks herself in the far corner, crossing her arms.

Feeling at a complete loss, I stand against the other side, watching her, trying to figure out what to say. I wet my lips twice and still nothing comes. Not until the elevator drops us off at my condo.

"Supper?" I offer, noting she's turned down every offer of food throughout the day. It's obvious why, but I will see her eat before bed. "I can cook or order in."

"Whichever." She follows me down the hallway, kicking off her shoes at the doorway, but stopping at the end of the hall, while I continue forward into the living room, finding the iPad I keep on the table.

"Pizza?"

"Sure. Whatever."

"You good with meat lovers?"

"Yep," she replies.

I glance up from the app, watching as she rocks on her feet, her lip curling beneath her teeth and her hands linking behind her back. She's staring into the living room, then the large windows across the room, showing Montreal's skyline, then toward the couches.

"When I said make yourself comfortable, I meant it."

"Comfortable for me isn't what you're used to."

I rest the iPad on the table, the sound it makes against the glass echoes through the split-level space. "Pray tell, what am I used to then?"

"I read. Like, that's my entire evening. I lose myself in books. I'm not exciting."

This girl is an enigma with two different personalities that emerge at random times. There are moments where she's fiery and feisty and willing to throw a verbal punch and then there's times it seems like she questions herself and gets shy and apologetic about her habits.

Which makes me wonder more about her childhood. What kind of environment did Maurice create that had her think her hobbies and personality aren't enough or "normal?"

"I lose myself in TV," I counter with the truth. Well, half-truth. Normally, I'm at work until late in the night and then I go straight to bed, but I've been known to binge on TV, same as anyone else. "Belle, like I said, making yourself at home means doing all your regular activities. If that's reading all night on the couch, do that."

Her expression turns quizzical, and then like a switch, she blinks and shrugs and begins heading down the hallway. "So be it then."

I watch as she heads toward my bedroom before placing the pizza order. I prop the iPad up to watch for the delivery notice.

Within moments, Isabelle returns, dressed in yoga pants and an oversized hoodie with the slogan *Smut Whore* stretched across the front. She gives me the sense of being everything opposite of a whore, but to wear a slogan like that makes me wonder more about what she's reading.

What's most enjoyable about her outfit is its casualness. There's never been a woman here not dressed to the nines. Even Mother, growing up, always looked put together. Simple clothing and mob life don't go hand in hand. Isabelle's obvious comfort, or lack of care, is pleasing.

She drops on the couch opposite of me and pulls her feet up, tugging her hood over her head, and unlocks her Kindle. "This is me," she mumbles without looking away from her book. "This how I dress. What I do. I'll probably be ignoring you for the next few hours, just a warning."

She's validating herself. Looking for an argument or an agreement? Kicking my feet up onto the glass coffee table, I recline backwards. "Enjoy. Will this be a book I get read to me?"

For that question, I do garner her attention. So fast, her head whips up, her eyes wide, skin growing pale. "Um, no. I don't think—No. This isn't something you'd be interested in." Her cheeks flash red immediately, telling me it's indeed something I'd enjoy. Something that's likely indicative of the hoodie she's wearing.

"Try me," I challenge, hiking my brow. Glancing at the time listed on the delivery notice, I tell her, "Twenty minutes until food's here. Perfect time to get a chapter in."

"But you don't know where I am in the story. How about the next book I start, I'll read to you."

"Twenty minutes, Belle. That's all I'm asking for. Humour me."

Her mouth opens and I expect an argument, but she quickly shuts it and repositions her hood, somehow hiding more of her face.

Then she begins reading:

"'Sit,' he ordered, gesturing to his lap. 'Sit, so we can show everyone how you've become my whore.'"

Hm, I think I like this book. I sit up, positioning my elbows on my knees and glancing at the time on the iPad, hoping the driver hits traffic to slow his arrival.

Isabelle continues: *"Gritting my teeth, the bite on my neck compelled me to obey. I sat on the edge of his knee, trying my best to avoid touching him at all, but he didn't allow me to maintain the distance. He clamped down on my thigh, fingers curling painfully into my skin, causing me to flinch.*

The crowd observed, waiting and watching. Every vampire—all hundred of them—had their fangs out, lust coating the room, as their leader brushed his thumb along the bite on my neck.

A mating bite I hadn't realized I was getting when I fucked him. When he tricked me into this.

My enemy had become my adversary."

This seems a bit rape-y, but still intrigued, I let Isabelle's book take me to a place I certainly hope it goes: with these characters fucking on the throne in front of everyone.

"My adversary made my body his when he yanked me to his chest. Lips dragged over my neck, his fangs teasing where he had already bitten.

'I hate you,' I mumbled.

'Tell yourself that. It'll make you taste even sweeter. Every human emotion changes the flavour of their blood and there's nothing better than a mix of hate and lust.'"

It's there, though barely, but the mention of lust has Isabelle's body flushing. Embarrassment consumes her, even her hands gripping her Kindle gets tighter.

She continues, reading past her own emotions, *"I scoffed. 'Lust? In your fucking dreams.'*

He made a purring noise which I felt right down to my core. Hoping he didn't notice, my thighs pressed together, trying to hold back the desire that did indeed begin taking over.

Of course, he noticed. Fingers crawled up my thigh, flicking the slitted dress aside. With my legs draped over his, he forced mine wide. Forced my bare pussy to be seen by all.

'Mm," he moaned in my ear. 'Even without touching you, I

can smell your desire, little one. I'm a king, which means I must share everything with my subjects.'

My eyes flashed up to the observing crowd that had been easy to pretend wasn't present. Trepidation took over and my hands stupidly gripped onto the throne's armrests, wonder coursing through my mind: is he going to allow every one of them to fuck me?

'No, no,' he replies, although he can't hear my thoughts. Perhaps our connection made it so he can read my fear though. 'No one's touching you. You're all for me. But they'll be allowed to watch you fall apart in my arms.' His finger travelled up my leg, pausing right in the heated space between them and—"

Isabelle stops talking, her gaze flashing to me. She tries to tug the hood over her face more, but she's run out of material. She glances at the tablet on the table, licking the corner of her dry lips. "Pizza almost here?"

"No."

When her expression falters, I bite down on my smirk. "Continue." I nod to her Kindle. "Please, this is very enjoyable."

16

ISABELLE

Continue. He wants me to continue through the most embarrassing moment I've probably ever had in my life. There's acting interested in what I'm reading, and then there's *this*. When he asked me to read out loud, I've never hated being in a sexy scene more than I was at that second. *Any* other scene would have been fine, but the one where the vampire king fingers his human captive in front of everyone is a bit much.

"Liar," I mutter, hoping to get Rafael off the trail of wanting me to continue reading.

"On the contrary." He smirks, his bright gaze darkening as it dances down the length of my body. "Continue."

I don't know what he's searching for, considering I'm hiding in an oversized hoodie. When I came out earlier in this, Rafael's expression was something I still can't decipher. I expected humour or even distaste. After all, I'm sure the women in his life are a lot more scantily clad. Getting comfortable to them would mean removing clothing, not adding on layers.

Instead, he seemed curious. Like he couldn't figure out his own thoughts.

I begin reading again, wanting to end this mortification as quickly as possible: "*His finger travelled up my leg, pausing right in the heated space between my thighs. His finger stroked between my pussy, gathering my juices.*

Hundreds of vampires hissed as the scent of my pleasure reached their senses, but with his hand wrapping around my neck and pulling me tighter against him, it was easy to ignore them.

'Ask me for more, little one.'

'More,' I pleaded immediately, cursing my stupid, lust-riddled brain.

'Gladly.'

His finger sunk inside me, going as deep as he could before adding another. I moaned. My throat proved to him what my words wouldn't. His lips dragged against my neck, and I felt him smile, felt as his teeth pressed against my skin, right over his previous bite marks."

Rafael stands, moving from his couch to mine, sitting inches from me. I keep reading, lowering my head, using my hood to block his view, while pretending he isn't right beside me.

"*I rocked my hips, lost to what I should not be. My body arched into his touch, silently begging him to bite me again.*

'Look at everyone watching you come undone on my lap, little one. Look at them witnessing you become my pet.' Firm hands grasped the base of my head, and he forced it straight and onto the crowd. Onto the multiple vampires who looked seconds away from joining in.

'We could ask any of them,' he murmured. 'Any one of them to lick up your desire as it drips all over my lap. Would you like that?'"

In the corner of my eye, I catch Rafael lift his hand. In a

blink, he has my hood pulled down, revealing my very warm face. I flinch. Isn't reading the book enough horror for one day? He doesn't need to witness my face during this humiliation.

With a smirk way too sexy, he says, "I'm starting to think there's something to this reading thing."

Then he leans closer, using the grip he has on my hoodie to ensure I can't escape. I should be frightened, but instead, I feel something I refuse to admit to myself. Something I shouldn't be feeling amidst the chaos of my life.

"If every book is vampire porn involving exhibitionism, I might have to take up the hobby."

My thighs press together, and I hope he doesn't notice. I'm not entirely sure I'm breathing anymore.

"I suppose," he continues, his voice soft and seductive, "the act of reading itself is like a form of exhibitionism. Made-up people fuck on page, and you picture it in your head."

Huh. I glance to the side, mentally going through the endless romance books I've read. The endless pornographic-level intimate scenes I've visualized and how my body reacted to them.

"I think you're right."

Rafael releases my hoodie, but even with the freedom, I don't shy away. How can I when his intense gaze dares me to remain? He leans in closer, his lips an inch from my ear. The power he exudes wraps around me, restraining me.

"Have you ever imagined yourself in a character's place?"

"Um." *Why does he want to know?* I swallow, taking a long blink, praying when I open my eyes again, he'll be gone. Except, he isn't. He's very much there. "Yeah, I guess so," I admit, giving him the unbridled truth.

Sure, I mean, who hasn't when they read?

"And tell me, Belle," he whispers, the nickname making my stomach flip happily, "what kinds of things have you pictured?"

Ha ha, no, I'm not admitting that. I press my hand into his hard chest, trying to shove him away, even as I slide myself backwards. He doesn't follow, but his gaze flicks down to my hand and back up, his lips curling in a devious grin that makes my core clench.

"You won't tell me? Shame." He pauses, his eyes searching my face, skirting over my scars, which make me want to hide from him again. "If you won't tell me, then I hope for your sake, you've gotten to at least work some of them out."

I look away, realizing this isn't a flirty game anymore. My mood plummets the moment Rafael says it, and when I look at him, my mood drops lower, somehow, because he doesn't seem surprised by my avoidance. He knew. He runs a fucking sex club; of course, he knew. He probably smelled my virginity or some shit, but he was testing me.

I should be angry. Annoyed. Instead, I'm ashamed. A new emotion I don't understand. When one spends a lot of time alone, these things matter less. Will I ever lose it? Who knows. Even when Dad was alive and I first moved out, I realized ten minutes into my job that my social skills suck. Meaning, I don't have any. I don't know how to use whatever meager amount I have. To go out to a nightclub, dance and party with people, get drunk and meet guys—it's incomprehensible.

"Hey," his eyes soften, his hand sliding against the couch, lightly touching the side of my leg, "it's natural. Nothing to be embarrassed of."

"At my age?" I counter.

"Sure." He shrugs. "Not unheard of. With your situation, it's understandable."

When I say nothing more, he slides two inches closer, his hand reaching toward my chin, tipping my face to his. He does this often, but I'm coming to realize the momentary lack of control is gratifying.

"Isabelle," he starts, my name like soft velvet in his mouth, "when you give it away, it'll be of your own choosing. Never let anyone talk you into anything you don't want. You're fucking strong, *ma belle,* and—"

"You say without knowing me," I interrupt.

"I know enough. You're the girl who kicked me out of your house. Who literally took their house getting shot at before accepting what I've told you. You hold your emotions, your grief for your father, for your old life, like they're a lifeline. You don't take shit from anyone, not even me. I have mad respect for you, Isabelle, even though we barely know one another. You're beautiful, but I wonder if you realize how much exactly. You will shine one day, and I hope you have someone worthy by your side when you do. Someone deserving to see this light that your life has forced you to bottle up."

How do I respond to that? The first half was believable, maybe, but then he started spewing shit about beauty, and I don't know...

My mouth opens and shuts three times and when I think I'm about to manage words, the spell between us is shattered by a shrill piercing sound.

The doorbell.

For the remainder of the night, Rafael watches TV from his couch, while I munch on pizza and finish my book. It's not the same now; not after the conversation Rafael and I had. Something's changed in the room. Something's become electrified, even if I can't put words to it.

It makes focusing on my book difficult, which allows thoughts of *why* I'm struggling to focus come to light. Rafael's fault, but why's Rafael in my life? Because Dad is—*No. Shut it down for now.*

Hours later, long after I've finished eating, I stand and grab my Kindle, clutching it to my chest like a lifeline. "I'm going to bed."

Rafael glances away from the TV, where he's watching a crime show. He nods, but there's a wrinkle in his forehead, like he's thinking about something else entirely.

"I'll be a bit. I have something to do first."

Something illegal, no doubt. It doesn't matter because if his criminal acts mean finding my father's killer and letting me go home, it's all that matters. In which case, he can spend hours doing felonious stuff.

"Good night," I mumble, walking down the hall, where, after a quick visit to the bathroom and getting changed, I crawl into bed, re-placing the pillow barrier from last night, and shut my eyes, trying my fucking hardest to hold in the pain blooming across my sternum.

17
RAFAEL

I enter my penthouse, untying the cloth I've looped around my hand now that I can properly clean the drying blood off. Cogs, one of my men, stands from the couch he was seated on, and passes by me toward the elevator, knowing my arrival means he can leave now.

"She's been crying on and off all night," he comments.

"Have you gone to her?" My blood boils with the thought of someone else comforting her when they don't know the full story.

He holds his arms up just as the elevator doors begin sliding shut. "I ain't that dumb, Capo."

With him gone, I head straight for the bathroom to quickly shower and wash the blood from my knuckles. The cuts hardly throb, not more than my need to return to Isabelle's side. I had debated sending a soldier in my place and remaining with her, but as I watch the red stain the water before being sucked down the drain, I decide this is better. Much more gratifying.

When I exit the shower, I find a text from my brother.

It's one in the morning and it doesn't surprise me that Nico is still awake. With a sigh, I tap his name, placing the phone between my shoulder and ear as I finish up in the bathroom.

"What, Nico?" I bark into the phone. "Why aren't you in bed fucking your wife?"

"Careful," he responds in a warning tone. "What has you so testy?"

"Long day."

He grunts, but I know my brother well enough to recognize it's a sound of disbelief. More like a roughened snort than a grunt, really, but he continues, "Yeah, well, I heard back from our contacts at the RCMP about Maurice's file."

"And?" I demand, leaning against the counter when he says nothing further. "It's late, Nic, say what you got to."

"Well, for starters, Maurice Dupont didn't exist before seventeen years ago."

"That's ridiculous. Our files go back to his own childh—"

"No, Raf," my brother interrupts, enforcing his next words, "there is nothing on Maurice Dupont before seventeen years ago. Our files are incorrect."

"That's..." *Ridiculous*, I want to repeat. "That's...how? Seventeen years ago..." Mentally, I calculate, using Isabelle's age of twenty-one. "Isabelle would have been four."

"I had them run a check on her too. They managed to get her results quicker, but what would you know? There's nothing on her before she was four. No birth certificate."

"Fuck." I slide against the counter, continuing until my ass is on the floor. Staring through the wall, I imagine her in my bed. A girl without a past, apparently. A girl who, I fucking pray for her own well-being and life, isn't lying to me.

Then my brother tacks on another fact: "Maurice began working for us sixteen years ago."

"A year, maybe even only months, later." I pause, mind racing, finally reaching the finish line. "He was using us to hide."

"Hide him and Isabelle is my guess," Nico agrees. "Before age four, it's unlikely Isabelle would recall memories, which means the timing was either a coincidence or planned. My other guess is Maurice Dupont is an alias. That's why there's nothing on him. No one can wipe away an entire life, not even us, which tells me, he found another way to rid himself of it."

Holy fuck. I wipe a hand over my face, reminded by the slight throb in my knuckles. Tonight's activities are nothing compared to this conversation.

"Which means Isabelle might be an alias too," I conclude. "We need to figure out who went missing seventeen years ago. Middle-aged man and female child. That's a national search. Maybe even international. Goddamn it!" By my sides, my hands form fists, wishing I hit the fucker a little harder, pre-releasing pent-up anger I hadn't known I'd be feeling right now. "Nico, this is bigger than we thought. Why was Maurice, or whoever he is, using us to hide?"

"From De Falco, you think?"

"Why remain in the same city? I don't think it's Stefano." Grunting through my frustration, I lightly punch the floor with my fist. "Fuck. Fuck, fuck, fuck. Where do we begin, Nico? How the hell do I tell Isabelle?" I've already destroyed her life by announcing her father's death, and now to tell her that the man she knows has an alternate past?

"You don't. We don't know for certain she isn't in on it."

"She was *four* at the time," I counter. But he's not wrong. Until there's certainty, we don't *know*. Except, I feel it in my gut. Isabelle doesn't seem like someone who's an expert liar. My gut could be wrong, but she seems as lost and as confused as any of us. I blow out a long breath, tipping my head back against the sink's cupboards. "Remember how you *knew* something was off about Della but couldn't put your finger on it? That's how I feel with Isabelle. I don't believe she's lying."

"I trust you, Raf," he says with absolute conviction. "Have you gotten any details from her yet to back up your claims?"

"All she knows is life with her father and a nanny. If you can get me an address on a Marie Potts, I'll meet with her. Same nanny her entire life, apparently. Isabelle was home-schooled by the woman. Maurice kept strict rules on them. Grew up with no social life. And," I pause, "everything you've learned is peculiar, but I have one more thing to add to that growing list. She was told her mother ran out on her as a child, but Maurice apparently mentioned her a lot. With fondness, not hatred."

"Hm." My brother grunts, and I know his thoughts are where my own are. "Woman abandons her child and husband but is still spoken nicely about. Those aren't behaviours of a love-scorned man turned single father."

"My thoughts exactly. This is *weird*, Nic. I feel like we're in a game we don't know the rules of."

"As long as we win, I don't fucking care. Keep digging. Anything she might know, any small fact, could lead us to her father's true identity. In the meantime, I'll get you that address."

Long after he hangs up, I don't move. The weight of reality is getting heavy, but when a faint sob comes from the bedroom, it sparks energy into my limbs and I lift myself to my feet, quickly returning to my bedroom, into my closet first, where I throw on shorts.

Then I join her in bed. Isabelle's curled in a ball, her head buried in her pillow in such a way, I'm surprised she's not suffo-cating. Her body quakes beneath her tears. I sidle closer, removing her weak barrier, and take her into my arms, recreating the position we woke up in this morning.

"Why does it hurt so much?" she mumbles into my chest.

Everything with Nico, everything about her father and her dissipates until the only thing left, the only thing I care about, is making her feel better.

"Because you lost your father."

"It's easy to forget during the day when I'm busy. But at night…"

"It creeps up," I finish. "You need time, *ma belle*. Going back to work so soon is draining."

"But I want to. I can ignore the misery until nighttime." She finishes speaking, and when I'm about to counter her point, she adds, "When you're able to hold me and make all the bad shit go away. Make me feel less alone."

"You're not alone," I murmur into her hair, tightening my hold, ignoring how my heart seems to beat faster with her against my body. "I have you, Belle. I'll always have you."

We wake in a similar manner than what we did yesterday. She pulls from my arms with a deep, apologetic look, which I don't comment on. I wonder if she remembers the three times she woke in the middle of the night, whimpering through her nightmares. I held her tighter and made soft noises until she quieted and passed out again.

When she begins rooting through her suitcase, preparing for the day, I suggest once again, what I had last night. "Why don't you take the day? A few days off. It'll be good for you."

Gone is the blushing woman who read to me. Gone is the crying, grief-stricken one from last night. When Isabelle looks at me, it's as though a demon took over, changing her eyes from a soft brown to a hardened place of hell.

"Are you suddenly a fucking therapist? Have a psychology degree I don't know about? Mind your business." She swipes the pile of clothing she was gathering and begins stomping toward the door, heading for the bathroom to shower.

"Not a therapist," I call out. "But I've witnessed my fair share of death, and I know how hard it can—"

"You *don't* know! You don't know what it's like to lose a parent, so until you do, just don't, Rafael." She stops at the door, her shoulders lifting and falling with a deep breath. In a gentler tone, she whispers, "I know you're trying, but stop."

I do know though. Not a parent, but a sibling.

Difference is, mine came back. Hers won't.

Fuck, hers wasn't even real.

18

ISABELLE

We're halfway to the library when I notice the new marking on his knuckles. Unlike the black art otherwise etched on his skin, this is red and rough, like he hit something.

"What happened to your hand?"

Rafael glances down, and then shrugs. "Business," is all he replies, and I wonder if it has to do with his "something" from last night. He drops his hand to his lap, positioning it until his injury isn't in sight. "Sorry for this morning. Words, I rarely say unless I mean them." His gaze cuts to me. "I've seen enough grief to know how it fucks with your mind. Seems like you're holding so much of it back, and then your body tells you otherwise at nighttime. All I was suggesting was that you take time for yourself."

"I know." I hadn't meant to snap at him, but how else do I release this pent-up feeling inside me? This *rage* I can't quite understand. The sense of hopelessness.

"Also," he continues, "I might not have had a parent die, but I did experience a loss that certainly felt like he did. I'm not trying to devalue your loss, but the notion that you won't have your father to speak with, that he won't be around any longer to spend time with, that you'll never see him smile or even get angry again, I can relate to." The skin around his eyes gets tighter.

"Who'd you lose?"

"My brother." After a beat, he adds, "Nico and I, we're two of four. You haven't met my younger sister, Aurora, yet, but she's here. We also have an older brother."

"Older than Nico?"

He nods. "My parents had them back-to-back. Hawke left when he was a teenager after breaking all ties with us. To me, a ten-year-old at the time, it was heartbreaking. One day, my brother was there, and the next, he was gone. Nico got it, but I was still a kid, you know. A kid who'd seen more shit than other people my age, but a child nonetheless. My parents hadn't exposed me to everything at that point. My training was in the early stages. I understood crime life as a conceptual idea. So, for Hawke to up and leave, for my parents to try to reach out to him, but him never calling home again…" At the next red light, he takes a moment to relax his arms, dropping them off the steering wheel, his expression one of extreme pain. "It hurt like hell. Yes, he's still alive, so this is where our pain differs and I'm not trying to invalidate yours, just show you how I can relate to a point."

For sure. On one hand, at least as an adult, I understand what happened. Even if it's vague because Dad's job was a lie and had he told me the truth, perhaps I could have better prepared for such instances, but that's beside the point. For Rafael to be a child and lose an older sibling; someone he loves and looks up to, admires and views as a role-model, is difficult.

"What happened to him?"

The car glides forward at the green light and Rafael answers with a small smile, "Family business, sorry. No outsider knows."

It's a casual comment and certainly one that makes sense. After all, Rafael hardly knows me. But a familiar pain blooms across my chest regardless, shooting up to my eyes, making them burn. I turn my head away, focusing on the outdoors passing us by instead of responding.

Always on the outside. Always looking in on other people's lives. Never involved in anything. Not growing up, and not now.

Getting to the library is no less than a relief and I escape from the vehicle, having to chide myself for rushing off. Rafael doesn't need to see the self-hate our conversation, which he was only hoping to ease my own emotions, brought on.

I manage to get us inside, down the stairs, and into the children's section. Like yesterday, Emma waves and disappears upstairs right away with a wink while I get settled.

"Need help?" Rafael asks from his spot against the wall.

"Nope." Goodness knows what would happen if my boss came down and saw Rafael working. Not that I fear for Rafael in any manner, but as I glance at the man who exudes pure menace, even in how he's casually leaning against the wall, his phone in his hand, his intense gaze stalking me, I have no doubts Rafael would be the one to win that fight.

Minutes later, Gage strolls in, dressed in baggy jeans and a hoodie with the hood drawn up, covering his face. He comes around the side of the counter, mumbling a "Morning," as he checks himself in on the volunteer clip board.

"Gage?" I follow him. He's nowhere close to the top of my list of favourite people, but his odd behaviour throws me off. "Is everything okay?"

"Fine." But when he turns around, I catch a flash of what he's trying to cover.

A swollen cheek, a cut eye. A face that was clearly hit a few times.

I gasp, but he continues ignoring me. Movement in the corner makes us both look up and Gage immediately jerks in response at the sight of Rafael, slipping away before I can make sense of the interaction.

Rafael approaches, casually leaning on the counter, his lips pulling into a smirk, but his eyes are locked on the spot Gage last disappeared. He rests his phone down, the movement drawing my attention to his right hand, realization dawning on me.

"Oh my god," I breathe. How did I miss this? Rafael's "something" from last night, Gage's fear, Rafael's injured hand. "What did you do?"

"Made sure he won't go the fuck near you," he answers without a beat. No denial of his actions.

"He's harmless, Rafael. He might be horrid, but that didn't call for abuse."

When I try to turn away, disgusted at the man I'm becoming attracted to, he reaches for my blouse, gripping tight and making it so even as I try to pull myself free, he maintains his hold. Huffing, I cross my arms, granting him a look of unamused attitude that is demanding he make his point quickly.

"Were you comfortable having him around?"

Well. No. Not completely. But I don't think he'll do anything. Shifting from foot to foot, I mutter, "Not really."

With his grip, he tugs me closer, until only the counter separates us. Counter or not, we're in the same small bubble.

"You're welcome then."

"Was that necessary?"

"Very much so." He lifts a hand, an action that might have once caused me to jerk away but now has me going still. He tucks strands of hair that were freed from my bun behind my ear. "It would have been a very quick phone call to the police to have his sentence transferred to another library. Maybe one on the other side of the city to make his transportation a bit shittier each day."

Of course, he has the police in his pocket. I get the sense Rafael and his family have a lot of control in this city. "Why didn't you?"

"Because having to see me every day, a reminder of what not to do when he's here, sounded much more fun." He grins, a look of pure deviousness that I shouldn't appreciate as much as I do. "He won't look at you anymore if he knows what's good for him."

I'm disgusted still, but for different reasons now. It's not directed at him anymore, but at myself. I'm repulsed with myself for feeling anything positive about this conversation—for his actions. In his own fucked-up way, Rafael was defending me. I shouldn't be condoning the abuse that moments ago I was irritated about.

Is this what men do to a logical mind? Makes them into mush.

When Rafael cups my cheek, I realize how close we are. I have every reason to back away, but don't.

"Thank you," I murmur.

Green eyes flick to my lips, and I know immediately what he wants. What I could give him.

But that's not the kind of relationship between us. He's a stranger in my life, meant to protect me. I don't know him. He's tied to my father's death and someone I shouldn't have *any* positive feelings toward.

I pull back, and this time, he releases me, his own eyes clouding with a question. But he doesn't get it. Why would he? He, who I'm sure has been with many women. I mean, he owns a fucking sex club! I've never been touched. Never been kissed. Those opportunities never came up. And doing so with one of my father's ex-employers who is the reason he's dead feels wrong.

Even if Rafael feels right.

Instead of heading toward his condo and Eden, Rafael turns off into some ritzy neighbourhood. Houses I could only dream of living in line the streets. Much smaller than his family's mansion, but still million-dollar homes, I'm certain.

"What are we doing here?"

Rafael doesn't respond; instead of turning the corner, he stops in front of an expanse of land that consumes half the block. A play structure surrounded by sand sits in the centre.

"A park?"

Rafael gets out of the car, still without answering, and comes around to my side. He opens the door and reaches for my hand. Keeping my eyes on his, I give it, and he helps me to my feet, shutting the car door behind us. Heat travels up my arm and down my body. His hand is so much larger than mine, making me feel small.

He leads me to the edge of the sand before leaning down to untie his shiny shoes.

"W-what are you doing, you weirdo?"

Silently, he kicks off his shoes, rolls up his pant legs a few inches, and then leans over and lifts my feet one by one, pulling off my Toms. I use his shoulders to remain steady when his lack of warning makes me stumble, unprepared to lose my balance.

"Again, Rafael, what are you doing?"

He takes my hand and walks me off the edge of the grass,

right into the sand. My feet sink into the soft grains as he leads me closer to the play structure.

I peek around, wondering how many people are glancing out their windows, snooping on the two adults who are using a child's play area.

He tugs me over toward the swings and positions me in front of one, briefly meeting my eyes. Then he moves behind me and his arm becomes a band around my middle. He pulls me backward, his knee holding the swing seat steady as he positions me on it, and then places my hands around the metal chains.

"You mentioned not getting much of an opportunity to visit a park growing up."

Oh. How can a man I've known for such a short time have brought so much light and darkness to my life?

"Which I find extremely depressing, if I'm honest," he continues. "Even Nico and I were allowed to visit parks. I mean, our parents had a private one installed on Corsetti lands, but we were very insistent to go where the other kids were." He pauses, gesturing between two houses across from us. "Behind them, drive for ten minutes, and you hit Corsetti property. This is the nearest neighbourhood to us, so this is where my mother took us."

Even those who were trained to kill had a happier childhood than me. My heart decompresses, sorrow for only myself robbing my energy.

Rafael's large, warm hands rest over my own and he pushes the chains forward, and then back, before releasing me into a slow rocking motion. His hands shift to my lower back and with every swing back, he pushes harder, ensuring my every swoop slowly becomes larger. Instinctively, I pump my legs, using momentum to get me a bit higher.

"This is silly," I tell him, thankful he can't see the huge smile taking over my expression. It feels so wrong to be happy in this fucked-up situation we're both a part of. "Plus, don't you have to work?"

"Silly, but fun, and no. This matters more than the club. My family's brought a lot of pain into your life, and I want to see you smile, Belle. I don't want you to look back on your father with negative memories. With everything going on, whether he deserves it or not, you love him."

Deserves. A very particular word. I glance behind me, trying to catch his eye but the swing causes too much movement to focus properly. "Strange statement."

He's silent for two more pushes before responding with, "You're holding back your grief, Isabelle, but I want this to be a place you can come to and remember him."

A nice park in a neighbourhood I can't even afford to breathe in? I highly doubt once Rafael returns me home, I'll ever be seeing this place again. Or him.

Another thought dragging down what should be a good time.

"Thank you," I murmur. "I won't lie, I hadn't thought when you took me away from my home, this is what it would consist of. Having a friend."

Oh my god, did I just admit that? Rafael and I aren't friends. I should hate him for not protecting Dad, for altering my life. I shouldn't enjoy the fact that he beat up a guy for me or takes me to the park simply because I hadn't been to one often as a child. None of this should be happening. He and I *aren't* friends.

"Sorry," I immediately throw into the evening air. "I know we're not—Sorry."

"No," he counters, his hand sweeping over my neck as I sway toward him. "I think you titled us appropriately. I've had more fun with you in the past two days than I have with anyone."

I drop a leg into the sand, dragging my foot until I've slowed the swing enough that I'm able to turn around, positioning my knee against the chain so I can better look at him.

"Seriously?" I hike a brow, thinking of his mansion, his siblings, his parents, his club—his *life*. This man is *not* lonely. *I* grew up lonely. He doesn't understand the meaning.

Rafael grasps the chains above my head and uses them to lean in as he peers down at me, thoughts coursing through his eyes. "I've never been like Nico. I suppose I was more like Hawke, in that this life holds less meaning than it should."

"You don't like it?"

"I don't love it," he counters. "Being a capo, third in command after my father and brother, and having that responsibility is fine. Life is good. I'm not about to whine, but there's a loneliness factor. I'm always around people who want to humour me, to serve me, or to be me. It's exhausting. So, yes, finding the quiet girl who's happy to read has been welcoming."

Rafael's has brought a little bit of good into my life, so I'm pleased to do the same for him. But I have to know if his world has the same pressures as what fiction shows.

"Are arranged marriages really a thing?"

He laughs, a loud melody that mixes with the evening air around us. "Unfortunately, yes. My brother was slated to be in one, but chose Della, who was kinda an outsider. My sister is in one, but we're in the process of breaking that off since she fell in love with Rosen, her bodyguard. My mother was in one, but my father kidnapped her for himself."

This time, I laugh. "So no one in your family has *actually* been in an arranged marriage. Not one that had gone through."

He smirks. "Guess so. I'll probably be the one to change that."

Oh. I don't know why I'm upset. Once I go home, Rafael will return to his regular life, and that means one day being wed to a woman his family will choose for him. One with connections. One who's beautiful and enjoys the spotlight; who's been raised to manage it and not hide away inside a house.

Rafael's hand lowering to my face wipes away those thoughts, bringing me back to the present. His thumb strokes the top of my scar, while his eyes search mine. Finally, he asks the question I've been expecting since day one. "Where'd you get these scars, Isabelle?"

"I don't know."

"They look drawn."

I think they are.

I truly don't know where I got them from. Dad doesn't have baby pictures of me—said Mom stole them all—so I have nothing to look at from when I was younger. I just remember growing up with them. My earliest childhood memories involved looking into the mirror and tracing them with my finger.

"They'll protect you, Isa," Dad had said. Words I've never understood.

"Isabelle." Rafael growls in that protective tone.

I tug away from his hold, even if it costs my heart to shatter to do so. "I told you: I don't know."

"Were they always there?"

I shrug. "For as long as I can remember. I don't know how old I was. Four? Five? Whenever people start retaining memories."

He glances away, toward the direction he said his house was in. His expression ripples with confusion, which he quickly shakes off. "Four, huh. An interesting time in one's life."

19
RAFAEL

Nico expects me to tell Isabelle about her father and his identify, but a part of me is waiting for Nico to return with a definitive name for both of them. How can I rip yet another part of her life away?

I've never hesitated in my role. Being capo means responsibility, even if I don't always want it, but I suck it up and get what I must completed. Always.

But not with Isabelle. Nothing's gone how I planned since meeting her. I should have had her father's secrets by now, rather than spending so much enjoyable time with her. And not because I think she needs someone, but because I *want* to.

With my hands still on her face, I don't stop touching her. I'm not sure I could if I wanted to. Her skin is soft, other than where the scars are.

I've asked her about the origins of her scars because I feel it's linked. Everything connects to when she was four and she and Maurice acquired new identities, and her some scars. Very convenient time in a person's life: right when childhood memories begin to stick.

But now I want to know for other reasons. I want to know so I can hunt the bastard who dared mark her skin and make him pay with my own knives. I want a repeat of last night, what I did to that asshole, Gage. It was too easy to find his address, but even luckier to find him smoking in the back of his apartment building. By using only my fists, the interaction was friendlier than I could have made it. The person who harmed Isabelle won't be so lucky.

With a heavy sigh, I release her swing and back away, dropping my hand entirely, even though it aches to do so. At the last second, she snatches it back, holding it in hers, looking up at me with the roundest set of eyes I've ever seen.

"I feel," she starts, her voice so soft I have to strain to hear her properly, "so many emotions I don't understand, Rafael. Gratitude, for one. For you, even when that's silly."

"Is it silly?"

She shrugs one shoulder, her smile downturned. "We barely know each other. I've slept in a bed with a stranger. He's held me both nights as I cried all over him. He beat up a guy for me. I'm only in your life because of what happened to my father. This isn't exactly stuff people who've known each for mere days do. I shouldn't be enjoying myself at all after what's happened."

Maybe. Maybe not. It's hard to say because neither of our lives are average. Isabelle's been sheltered, and my own is far from typical. I might not have had the same restrictions as she did, but things work quicker in my world. Friendships, unions, marriages, business dealings. At any moment, a bullet can wipe us out, an enemy can encroach; there is no time for gradual.

"Do you feel like we're stepping over lines?" I ask, curling one hand by my side, hoping for a particular answer.

She shakes her head, granting me the response I wanted, but then says, "What are the lines anymore?"

"They're what we make them."

She seems to think about that for a minute, her gaze lost amidst the ocean of grains of sand. "Can I break one line then? One neither of us should probably be crossing."

What is she asking?

"I cross many lines in my work, *ma belle,* so I'm sure this will be no different." I plaster on an easy grin, meant to calm her visible nerves as she lifts to her feet.

Her slim fingers wind into my jacket, her head coming up to the middle of my chest. It's easy to forget how small she is until she stands close to me. She tips her head back, her eyes latching onto my lips. I'd be an idiot not to know what she desires.

But this is the same woman who looked at me with absolute fear when I asked her about her virginity. A woman who deserves someone who isn't a criminal. Who isn't essentially lying to her by hiding the truth of her own background.

A woman who needs to dominate for once, rather than be dominated. A fucking gorgeous sight that'll be.

She lifts onto her toes, moving slowly, and my hands can't help but grip her hips.

"Is this stupid?" she murmurs. "I shouldn't even *like* you, but this attraction..."

With one hand, I cup her nape, easing her tight muscles by stroking the patch of skin there. I long to start this, to take her mouth, to show her all the ways I also think she's beautiful, but she needs to be the one to initiate.

Her lips brush mine, tentative, soft. So fucking soft, I bite back my moan.

I let her start, let her take us deeper, until I can't hold back any longer. My own urges consume me—want to consume *her* too, and I walk us away from the swing, bending until I'm able to lift her off the ground. My arms wrap around her waist as her legs fold around my hips, the two of us locking ourselves together.

I walk us away from the swings and toward the play structure. My kisses get harder, more ravenous, and my little book worm matches my energy.

At the structure, I rest her on the edge of a stair, releasing her when she's seated and stepping between her spread legs. My cock jumps to attention, even when I know we won't go that far.

Not yet.

My hands weave into her bun, yanking the elastic free, so I can tangle my hands between her strands. Our tongues battle, her back arches into me, losing herself completely.

"Rafael," she mumbles against my mouth. "Rafael, we're outside."

I trail my lips down to her neck, needing to taste her everywhere. To lick her pulse and feel her come alive. My teeth lightly nip her skin, nothing to cause harm, but it makes her shiver regardless.

"I know," I murmur. "Imagine all the people who could be watching us right now."

"Watching a million dreams come true. You're my first kiss."

I knew that. Or, at least I guessed it based on everything else I know of her. Same reason she's still a virgin, I'd assume; she's never been close enough to anyone to have her first kiss.

Unfortunately, being aware is one thing. Being reminded is another. And her words are like a fucking cold shower to my body. A primal, insatiable part of me is so fucking ecstatic to be her first and dreaming of all the other firsts I can give her. The other part gets shadowed with a heavy layer of doubt. A horrible emotion that has my lips pulling away from her skin.

I'm lying to her. There are facts I should tell her here and now, to grant me the freedom to be able to continue, but I can't destroy her life that way. What if I get information from her nanny, or if Flynn's torture of Rozelyn begins getting us results? What if I can release Isabelle back to her life without her having to ever know the dark mark on her past?

I might be a dick. But I'm not a villain. I won't hurt her like this.

Breaking the spell encompassing us, I drop my hand and back away, subtly trying to rearrange my hard-on. Taking her hand, I help her back to her feet, immediately stepping away when she's right way up.

If there's one thing that hurts more than ending this, it's the look of complete brokenness that flashes over her expression. Gutted. A look of pain reminding me of her grief. As usual, she's good at hiding it, and bites back the emotion so quickly, but I saw it; it was there.

One thing I won't do though is allow her to believe she's at fault.

"Hey," I tip her chin up, dropping my hand the moment I feel she won't look away, "this isn't about you."

"It's not you, it's me, right?" She rolls her eyes, jerking away and stomping toward where we left our shoes. "Can you be any more of a cliché?" she grumbles, in a tone I'm certain isn't meant for me. Louder, she adds, "You stopped the moment I mentioned you being my first kiss. I'm sorry to have put such a burden on you."

Without stopping, she swipes her shoes from the grass and continues stalking toward my car, parked by the curb. I rush after her, grabbing my shoes, running barefoot over the grass. For the first time ever, I'm chasing a woman. Nico would be on the ground rolling in laughter if he saw me.

"Belle." I reach for her elbow, but she leaps away, throwing a look resembling death over her shoulder.

"It's *Isabelle*. Get it right."

She lobs open my door rougher than a sports car should be handled, but for once, my focus isn't on my precious vehicle but rather the person who's shattering before my eyes. This was supposed to be a pleasant trip, a way to show her I'm listening to her struggles.

"Dick," is what she mumbles the moment she slams the door, leaving me standing barefoot on the other side.

For the first time ever, I feel at a loss.

I don't join her in bed for hours until after she's gone there. This time, she's filched one of my two pillows as well and added to her wall. It'd be easy to remove them and take their place, but I wait for her to cry, using the urge to comfort her as an excuse to hold her.

She doesn't cry though.

So I don't hold her.

20

ISABELLE

I'm a fucking joke. Time and time again, I've told myself I'd never lose myself to a man and look at what fucking happened. Last night was the epitome of me not following my own advice.

Halfway through the day, I found positivity in his rejection, even if my heart claims otherwise. I shouldn't have kissed him. *Him*—the man who was present for my father's death. It's so fucked up beyond words.

I manage to go through the entire day without hardly looking at him. Every time he's about to speak, he wisely shuts his mouth and doesn't. After the library, we return to his condo where he cooks pasta for dinner. I eat silently and stare out the living room windows, thinking about everything until he says we have to go downstairs to the club for a few hours.

I curl up in the same chair I occupied the other day, except this time, I drag it across the room to the farthest corner. His gaze penetrates my back while I get comfortable, but I don't pay him any attention. When I'm sitting and pretending to read—pretending because focusing on the small words on my screen becomes difficult with my mind going in multiple directions—his sigh breaks the silence we've managed to maintain.

"We're really doing this, Belle?"

That nickname is for non-assholes. "Isabelle. And yeah, we are. We're going to be what we should have always been. I'm your captive until you deem it safe enough for me to go home." Looking up from my Kindle, granting him a small fraction of my attention so he can see me rolling my eyes, I snarl, "Is anyone even after me or was all that some ploy? Because so far, there's been no one. So..."

"There's been no one because you've been with me," he counters. His expression seems passive, but the tick in his jaw tells me I'm affecting him. "And you're not my captive."

I make a show of standing. "Oh, I hadn't realized I was free to go then. Well, in that case—"

"Sit your ass down, *Belle*. What is wrong with you today?"

Did he seriously ask that? I drop into the chair again, levelling my glare with his. "From the beginning, I never wanted this, but I stupidly let myself get relaxed around you, even when everything in me said I shouldn't. Grief, guilt, logic—pick one. That was a mistake and one I won't be doing again. Fucking beast."

Rafael lifts to his feet, an air of pure calm. So opposite from the radiating anger coursing through my own nerves. His steps are light as he comes toward me and I stand again, resting my Kindle on the chair, prepared to fight him any way I'll need to.

"Again, calling me a beast. I'm sure after last night, that's exactly what you think I am." He reaches for me, pulling me limply to his chest, even as my arms come between us, fighting back. "Let's look at the facts, Belle. You're not upset with me. You're upset with yourself."

"Oh, your job as capo certainly has taught you a lot about people's emotions." I lift my chin, trying to make it not look like he's intimidating me. "If you're so wise, please tell me why I'm upset with myself."

He steps to the side, taking me with him, pressing my back to the wall by the door, his minty scent strong. His arms come up beside me and it's then I realize I've been playing the wrong game. The innocent game. But Rafael Corsetti isn't innocent by any means.

"You're upset with yourself," he murmurs in a low, seductive tone, "because you've come to like me. But don't worry," he backtracks the second I open my mouth to deny his claims, "because I like you too. Believe me, *ma belle*, I *really* fucking like you, even when there's a pile of reasons I shouldn't. A similar list to the one you have. You and I are no more than strangers, tossed together because of a stray gun shot. Because you need my protection." His thumb strokes a patch of skin between my ear and my scar, his gaze not leaving me. "Believe me when I tell you, last night wasn't because you're a virgin or any of the other very incorrect things you're assuming. In fact," he lowers his tone to a near growl that makes my knees weak, "I wanted nothing more than to peel off your clothing and kiss every inch of your skin. To lay you back in the sand and make you see the stars, even hours before they've emerged from the sky. It'd be a fucking honour to be the first man to show you such pleasures."

Words that sound pleasant but could be complete bullshit.

"So why didn't you? Tell me the truth, Rafael. Why did you stop?"

By my head, his hand curls and uncurls into a fist. The brief flash of body language telling me it's something I won't want to know and something he doesn't want to admit to.

"Guilt."

"Guilt?" I echo, somewhat glad we were feeling the same. "Why?"

"Why indeed, *ma belle*." He takes strands of my hair between two fingers, rubbing it together thoughtfully. Today, I've left my hair down and free, and I'm thankful I had. "Maybe because your first kiss deserves to be with someone better than me."

A conscience. That goes against everything I expected from Rafael's laidback personality.

"Except I made the first move. I wanted you to."

He lowers his head, his lips lightly brushing mine, robbing me of breath, of life, of everything that allows my mind to retain its sanity to control our interactions. When he pulls back, he murmurs, "I know you did, but it's not always that simple."

I open my mouth to respond with something—I barely know what—when the vibration of his phone yanks both our attentions away. Groaning, he releases me and backs away, swiping the phone off his desk and immediately placing it by his ear.

"Yeah," he says, as he answers. As the voice comes through the other end, which I can't hear, Rafael slowly nods, his gaze making its way back to me. "Got it," he comments after a moment, already inching toward the door. To me, he whispers, "Be right back," and then he's gone from his office, leaving me to wonder what's so important he'd have to take the call elsewhere.

Away from me.

When the door opens and shuts, noises from far away drift toward me. When we arrived, the club was still closed, but it sounds like it's in full swing now. If they're anything like what I've read in fiction, I'm kind of curious. Call it comparable research to know how factual authors write.

I grasp the knob before I can think twice and pull open his office's door, slipping out into the dim hallway, hardly recognizing my own behaviours at this point. With every step, I question myself. At the end of the hall, it breaks into two directions: right, where the main entrance is, and left, where the main play-room is.

Glancing to the right, to ensure Rafael isn't hanging around, I go left. It's a short hall before breaking off into a large room. Which by the time I get there, I wonder what on this earth compelled me to leave the safety of Rafael's office.

People in couples or small groups mingle, in all varying states of dress. Rafael had said everything takes place in the rooms and nothing out in public, to ensure all who attend feel comfortable. I spare a quick glance toward Rafael's staff working the bar, hoping none of them recognize me as the quiet girl seething in the corner of his office earlier, when they all popped in to say hello.

The room is circular, with each hallway having a different theme. I know which one I want, and I recall where it's located, from when I studied it on the map the other day. I want to determine if his opinion about reading being similar to voyeurism is correct.

Skirting through the room of people, I duck my head to avoid anyone's gazes or interest. Not that I think they would take interest in me, but just in case.

By the time I make it to the other side of the main room and into the darkened hallway, lit only by coloured LEDs, I'm breathing heavy. But pleased, because the lit-up sign on the wall informs me I'm exactly where I planned on being.

Voyeur & Exhibitionism Hall

Glancing behind me, once I'm sure no one's paying me any attention, I venture farther into the darkness, passing one door lit up with a red X in the middle. I pass another with the same, and then finally find one with a green checkmark.

Unoccupied is my assumption. Glancing behind me a final time, I open the door, ready to lose myself in a world I only know from my books. A world I've been kept away from.

What I see isn't what I expect. A dark room with a few cushioned benches and couches, all facing one way: toward the wall-sized window across from me. Light shines through, illuminating the room. More so, it's what's in that other room that has me gasping.

People.

Sex.

People having sex.

I realized where in the club I was entering, so sure, a part of me knew what to expect but to actually *see* such a thing...

To see a man's cock entering a woman's body. His hands gripping the fleshy part of her thighs, driving into her from behind so they're both facing the window. Both with similar expressions of hunger, of pleasure sweeping their very form.

Going against everything I should be doing, for the first time ever, I do what I want and enter the room, shutting the door behind me. It dings and I assume the other side is now lit with a red X.

I venture farther in the room, my whole attention locked on the scene playing out in front of me. Of the man gripping the woman's short hair, yanking it backwards until he's able to bend over her, taking her mouth in a messy kiss. It looks like she can't reciprocate properly, for every thrust into her body, her mouth opens, a silent moan escaping, breaking their kiss.

What I wouldn't do to hear them.

My thighs press together, body flushing with the live-action sex playing out. Of the man's hands sweeping over her body, reaching beneath her to pinch her clit. Of her body quivering, nearly dropping onto the floor, muscles giving way as the orgasm ravages her.

I glance at the couch behind me, wondering if I should sit.

It seems strange to lounge and watch people get off, but my feet are stuck, unable to move.

My hands drift down the front of my body, pausing right over my jeans, over the spot I ache. I want...I need relief. This couple's in here to be watched, and I want to make their show worth it.

The man taps the woman's ass, silently commanding her to change positions as he lies down on the bed in the centre of the room, his thick cock erect and straight. The woman throws a leg around his hips, giving her back to him and facing me. She sinks down on him and—*holy fuck!* It's one thing to enter when they were already fucking but another to watch her stretch and take him. Observe the mindless bliss taking over her expression as her head falls backward and her hands come up, pinching her own nipples.

I want...

Somewhere far away, I hear a beep. I pay it no attention, assuming it's from another room, as I'm unable to even *think* about looking away from the scene.

"*Ma belle,* this is the last place I would have thought to look for you."

21

RAFAEL

Nico passed on Marie Potts's home address, but I didn't take the conversation in my office, on the chance Isabelle would overhear. Leaving her in my office allowed her to do things I never thought she would, which is why when one of my staff reported spotting her slink down the exhibitionism hallway, I just *had* to follow. Thankfully, my staff are loyal as fuck and were able to tell me which room she entered.

With the master code, I open the door and peek inside, finding her standing in the centre, stiff with surprise as she observes the couple through the glass. The air is stifling with the electricity that pours from her as her eyes eagerly devour the couple.

I barely spare the woman fucking the man reverse cowboy style any attention because my focus is on the mousy woman who consumes so many of my thoughts. The way her breaths stall every second, her thighs pressing together, turned on by the couple.

She's so attuned to them, she doesn't pay my entrance any

attention, or when I shut the door. I don't think she hears as I step across the room, coming up right behind her, leaning down to whisper in her ear.

"*Ma belle,* this is the last place I would have thought to look for you."

She gasps, finally glancing away from the couple, her wide eyes becoming rounder when they land on me. "Rafael! I—"

"Went exploring," I fill in.

In truth, I didn't think this shy woman would *want* to explore Eden, but I'm unable to ignore what's right in front of me. Guilt might have hindered me yesterday. Isabelle—or whoever she is—is either an accomplice to something greater and I'm falling right in her trap, the same way Nico had for Della once. Or she's not.

I can't ignore the other signs. That history and deception aside, Isabelle left my office with one goal in mind: to explore. And I want to be the one who helps her uncover who she is in every sense of the manner.

"It's okay," I murmur, taking her chin in my grip and turning her face again until she's focused on the couple. "Is this like what you've read in your books? What you imagine?"

"Sex club and all," she replies, a little breathy, a little humoured.

"Tell me what this makes you feel."

"Um." She bites into her bottom lip, not answering.

She needs coaxing, and I will be the one to help her. "When you watch his thick cock drive into her, what do you feel?"

"Warm."

"And?"

"Tingly."

"Where?"

"My—my..."

I smile into the darkness, dragging my nose up the side of

her neck, breathing in her natural aphrodisiac. Normally, I too would be lulled by the voyeurism of the act before our eyes, but Isabelle's breathy reactions, her focus, *her*, has me compelled instead.

"Your what? Say the words, *ma belle*. I won't know how to help you if you don't tell me."

With my hands on her hips, I nudge her shirt up, trailing my fingers up her sides, until reaching her bra's edge. I trace it, following the curve of her breasts. She arches into my touch.

"Where do you want my hands now? Where does it tingle?"

"My...my pussy," she murmurs low.

When I move my hands slowly down her stomach, her head falls back against my shoulder. Without realizing it, we've slowly gravitated to one another, her back to my front.

"Keep watching them," I command. "That's why you snuck away. To watch people fuck. To feel it *here*." I press my palm into her jeans, right over her core, causing her to whimper and arch into my touch.

"Yes."

I fiddle with the button of her jeans, easily unsnapping them, my touch dragging along the edging of her cotton panties. "Say the word, Isabelle, and I stop." I pause, waiting for her rebuttal, but when none comes, I slide a finger beneath the material of her panties. "Your silence is your consent, baby."

She whimpers again, but this time, it has nothing to do with my touch. The couple have finished, and they clean up, gather their items, and leave the room hand-in-hand.

"Where are they..." Her question trails off as the door immediately opens again. I've learned since opening the club, a fair amount of people enjoy being watched. It's the kink people pretend they don't have until they get to play it out.

This time, a group of three enters. Of two men and a woman, who almost instantly latches onto the one closest to her, while the other sidles up behind her, stripping the bustier from her body.

I couldn't have asked for better.

Isabelle looks completely shell-shocked. "There's three people."

"You can't tell me this doesn't happen in those books of yours."

Her cheeks turn red, obvious even in the dark room, tell me everything. I chuckle, dragging my tongue up and down her neck, pausing on her pulse point. "Watch them, Belle. Watch how they take her together. How they *own* her pleasure."

As the guys begin playing with the woman, stripping her and then each other, the three swapping kisses and touches, I stop paying attention. Like the couple, normally, yes, I'd be down to observe the threesome, but Isabelle's breathy noises have me completely enamoured.

I dip my fingers into her pants, moving slower than I normally would, not wanting to spook her. The need to finish this means the world can burn for all I care, but the night will not end until I have her orgasm.

"Rafael." She clutches my hand and I pause my movements, mentally cursing.

"Yeah?"

"Just...don't stop." Her nails unhook from my arm, but she doesn't release me, not completely, as though battling herself.

"Are you watching them?" I murmur into her skin, my fingers drifting toward her heat. My other trails up her stomach, painting small circles on her skin. "Describe what they're doing to her."

"Uh, she's on her knees. Between them. Taking turns."

"Doing what?" I ask when she doesn't expand.

"Sucking on them."

"Their what?"

She huffs. "Cocks, Rafael. She's sucking on their cocks."

"Atta girl." My fingers slide over her pussy lips, lightly teasing her, though I don't need to. She's drenched already, which will make what's next easier.

Shifting my hand the best I can in her tight jeans, which I'm seconds from ripping off, I slide my finger between her, finding her clit. She gasps, hips jerking into my touch, while her nails sink into my skin again. Her response, her heat, her everything, has my cock making my pants tighter, but right now's all about her.

I hum into her skin, showing her how pleased I am with her reaction. "You're drenched, *ma belle*. I should be jealous because I know this isn't all for me. It's from watching a woman get fucked, and another about to be by two men."

"And you," she argues. "You make me..."

"Make you what?" I demand, tampering down the urgency swelling inside me.

"Tingle," she replies, her voice momentarily hiking with humour as she uses her same term as earlier.

"I make you tingle," I repeat, smiling into her skin. "Tingles are nice and all, but what I really want is to make you quiver. To make you tremble until your senses only know one thing—*me*. My scent, my touch."

"*Yes*. I want that too."

Movement in my peripheral vision causes my eyes to flick over her shoulder as one of the guys lifts the woman up, impaling her on his cock with little preparation. She throws her head back, her scream—silent to us—filling the room next door. The second guy lowers to his knees and begins eating her cunt, his tongue dragging over his partner's cock as well.

"Watch her expression as she gets fucked by both a cock and a mouth."

Isabelle makes a sound in the back of her throat when I dip

the tip of my finger inside her core. Just the tip, allowing her to get used to the feeling. She's so wet though, and I need to see how far I can take her.

"Tell me if this hurts." I add a second, letting her pussy stretch to accommodate me.

Her head falls back against my shoulder, and I allow it for a moment. Give her a chance to get her mind to where it needs to be and for there to be no pain.

With my other hand, I lower the cups of her bra, lightly flicking her budded nipples. Her body moves, shoulders rolling to push her breasts into my hand, while her hips rock lightly too, silently begging for more.

"Look at how they're using her. Watch how she comes from a mere few licks of his tongue."

My cock, now raging stiff in my pants, cries to be for Isabelle what both those men are to the woman. To be the one on his knees, eating her out until completion. To be the one slamming her down on my cock, cum coating her insides.

My fingers sink in a fraction deeper with every light thrust. I curl them, pressing them right on the spot I know she won't be able to resist. A low moan bursts from her lips and her hips rock into my hand, taking me deeper, milking her own pleasure from my touch.

I wonder how she'd feel if I used the tablet on the far wall and switched on our side. The rooms are designed to be two-way, so you can either be a voyeur or an exhibitionist—or both. How would she handle me fucking her in front of three other people? All of us sharing our pleasure with one another.

I nearly offer it too. She's come this far and I long to tease her with more; to drag her down and see how far into debauchery I can take her. But for now, Isabelle's orgasms are *mine* and mine alone. She's made it very clear, another man hasn't touched her yet, so her first climax will be only for me. Cherished and soaked up.

"R-Rafael." She whimpers. My name has never sounded so fucking perfect from a woman's mouth, and I pinch her nipple at the same time I tap the button on the inside of her pussy, making her sounds louder, her pants heady, her nails sinking almost painfully into my arm. "Rafael. I'm..."

"Do it, Belle." The speed of my thrusts increases, my lips trailing up her neck, lightly stroking over the sensitive parts of her, flicking against the multitude of nerves back there, which cause her to twitch. "Give me this."

She lifts onto her toes and sinks down on my fingers, fucking herself, my own speed too slow for her. I'd be concerned she'll be hurt, considering how new she is to this, but my little wanton *belle* knows what she wants, what she needs, so who am I to stop her?

Across from us, movement causes my eyes to lift over her shoulder, watching as the man crouching stands and takes his cock in his grip, lining up with the woman's dripping cunt. Her other partner removes his cock from her pussy and shifts it an inch. Her eyes go wide for a moment, her breaths picking up. She slams her eyes shut to focus as he slowly enters her asshole.

"Look at them," I command. "Watch how they take her next."

"I never stopped," she murmurs, her head rolling against my chest, as the man's cock enters the woman's cunt, both men now inside her. "Holy fuck," Isabelle curses.

My responding chuckle is muffled against Isabelle's skin. "You like that? Watch her face. How she looks at both of them. They own her. Control her." Isabelle's hips rock, almost bouncing on my fingers. Based on her noises and the way her pussy clenches around my fingers, it'll be very soon.

There are so many things I want to do with her, considering

after yesterday, it seemed like I spooked her. I want her drenching my hand, but I also long to carry her to the couches behind us and spread her cunt with my fingers, to sink my tongue inside her until her thighs clench around my head, ensuring I'll never leave. Then I want to flip her over and fuck her in every single position imaginable. To turn on the window and let other men watch as I claim her pussy for myself.

"I'm...I'm—" Whatever she was attempting to tell me is cut off by a long, dragged-out moan. She lifts onto her toes a final time, her legs going rigid, her spine arching into my touch. Her pussy ripples around my fingers, milking them, but the only thing I think about is what it'd feel like on my cock.

Isabelle moves, lowering back to her feet as her pants subside. My fingers slip from her slowly, not quite ready to leave their newfound favourite place. Until they're forced to when she spins around, giving her back to the trio and practically climbs my body, her hands grasping the sides of my face as she yanks me down into a heady kiss.

My own need for control takes over the second our lips touch, and I lift her into my arms, walking us backwards until the back of my knees hit the couch and I drop down, dragging her over my lap, one leg on either side of my thighs. She lowers herself onto my cock as our tongues tangle, her fingers gripping onto my hair like there's nowhere she'd rather be.

I rock my hips, letting her feel me—all of me—and I feel victorious when she moans into my mouth and meets me thrust for thrust. If she were any other woman, I'd already have her naked and my cock so deep inside her, but I'm worried I'd traumatize her.

A strange feeling for me. Women are so easily attainable; they're almost boring. Sex is for a good time, and it's simple to find others who feel the same way. I hardly have to search for a partner because there's always someone willing.

With Isabelle, I don't want to rush. As much as I'd love to be buried deep inside her for hours, I'm happy with playing this at her level—to leave this as a heated kiss and an orgasm and be finished for the night.

Her hands travel up and down my chest. I want her to explore. To see where she'll take this, but I also can't get over the feeling of *her*, and sitting up, I propel her to my chest, ensuring there's no space between our bodies. Nowhere she can't feel me.

With my hand knotted in her hair, I angle her head, kissing her how I'd love to fuck her, until she breaks away, resting her forehead against mine, her heavy breaths filling the small gap between our mouths.

"Rafael." She fists my shirt, curling it in her grip. "Rafael, I want...I want..." She never finishes though, her eyes flashing down.

My stomach leaps. I think I know what she's about to ask, but I need to fucking hear her say it. I *need* it more than I've desired anything, so holding her jaw, I force her gaze back up, pinning her with my eyes.

"Tell me what you want, *ma belle*, so I can make your wishes come true."

She bites her bottom lip, still uncertain, so with my thumb, I pull it free.

"Isabelle," I prompt, voice a near-whisper. "Say what you want to. I *want* you to tell me. I know you're used to observing the world pass you by while you hide inside, but that's the past. Take your future. Control your present. And that starts when these pretty little lips of yours," I stroke my thumb over her bottom one, "tell me what I can give you."

Her hand trails up my chest again, indecision still in her eyes until she blinks, swallows my words, and licks her lips. "You. I-I want...you. You to take it. My virginity. Um, I know—"

Smashing my finger against her mouth, I stop her painful

rambles, knowing they're only doing her more harm than good. She's adorable, but has said what I needed her to, and before she second-guesses herself and believes her virginity will be held against her, like she assumed last night, she must know it isn't the case. I'll cherish every moment. Pulling back last night, letting guilt creep up, was an eerie, new sensation. I don't get guilty with women; it's not in my nature. When I'm with a woman, it's because we both want it, and last night was no different, except it felt more deceptive.

But the second I found her in here, all bets are off. She's made it this far, wandered through a sex club, and never pushed me away. My demure, shy little book nerd knows what she wants.

And I'm gonna give it.

By the end of the night, she'll know only me.

22

ISABELLE

My entire life has been lived voraciously through the fictional characters in my books and the real-life people I observed from my window.

The moment Rafael touched me, the moment he discovered where I had snuck off to and placed his hands on me, was the second I decided to start living. From the very first gentle murmur that coasted along my neck, last night dissipated. Rafael might have pulled back then, but he wouldn't have touched me now if he didn't want to.

I wouldn't be perched on his lap, grinding on his extremely hard erection, if he doesn't want me to be.

My life is a mess. Days ago, I had a father and an apartment I escaped to each night, scared to leave the house and explore, even away from Dad's watchfulness. But with Rafael in my life, I need to take it. Take hold of the reins and do what I want.

And I want *him*.

Whyever I'm in his life doesn't matter as his mouth is fused to mine. My inexperience is easily forgotten when his touch wipes it away. Everything besides him and me and this moment don't exist. Even the fact that eventually, he won't be in my future; he'll return to his crime life, and I'll figure out how to survive in my boring, quiet world again, doesn't matter.

That doesn't mean I can't make this worth it. One day, when I look back on this time in my life, it won't be with regret.

For all my bravado, asking is something else entirely. His intense, bright gaze makes me feel so naked, so open, regardless that he had his fingers buried inside me minutes ago, fucking me in tandem with the woman in the room beside us, taking two men.

Giving me something else to focus on, I fiddle with his shirt, sliding my hand up and down his chest, obsessed with the feel of his abs. My swallow feels rough, and I lick my lips to rid myself of the dry feeling as I finally manage to push out, "You. I-I want...you. You to take it. My virginity. Um, I know—"

How can a person fuck up a question as badly as this? It's like my nerves and mind haven't caught up to my bravado.

Rafael pushes a finger against my mouth, cutting off my rambles. No doubt, he's about to deny me. If my uncertainty in asking is any indication of his response, that is.

He drops his hand once I don't fight him and shifts the same one to my backside, cupping my neck as he brings my face close to his again. He growls his response, his lips painting mine with it, ensuring they're words I'll feel the rest of the night.

"Fuck yes."

In one swift movement, he's on his feet, taking me with him, his large hands cupping my ass. The change in elevation shocks me, and I let out a partial squeak that has my legs wrapping around his waist, my arms around his neck, clinging tightly.

"Where are we going?" I glance toward the forgotten trio, but they too seem to be finishing up, taking turns wiping the woman's body.

"You think I'm fucking you on a goddamn couch? Think again."

With his hold, I can only watch over his shoulder, see the direction we've come from rather than the one we're headed in. The couch we recently occupied, which, in my opinion, seems perfectly acceptable to me.

"I was fine in there."

"The fact you were, Isabelle, makes it almost impossible not to fuck you right here in the hallway." He shuts the door to the room we occupied and strides away, down the hall and toward the main exit.

I lean back to look him in the face, catching his determination in the dim, erotic lighting. "I think I'd enjoy that." My admittance is a whisper, packed with a certainty only he's been able to pull from me.

Rafael growling in my ear is the sexiest thing I've ever heard in my life, I'm certain of it. I've read about the noise in books but hearing it only has me realizing it's a sound I've never mentally mastered.

"One day," he says with promise. "But for your first time, I'd be worthy of that beast title you've been giving me if I were to take you on a couch or against a wall. I want you in a bed, just for me." His nose skates my jawline, breathing me in. "For your first time, I don't want anyone else to see or hear you. Your noises are for me and me alone. If at any time, you wish to stop, I don't want you to feel pressured."

Oh. That's...sweet.

Still, I gesture to the hall he's about to exit. "Because there's not beds in here?"

"Patience," he replies with a chuckle, nipping my collarbone with his teeth. "I guess I wasn't clear enough. I want you in *my* bed."

"Look at you being romantic."

Rafael carries me through the main room, and despite the numerous groups, some in varying stages of dress and intimacy, a few do glance toward us. We arrive at his elevator and he walks inside, his arm smacking to the side, slapping the door close button. As the doors slide shut, he presses me against the far wall, angling my head to steal my lips again.

"I never believed I'd love a woman's lips as much as I do yours," he mumbles against my mouth. "Your kisses are fucking addictive."

Says the man who's making my head swim.

"I really want my mouth on you." He glances over his shoulder, toward the number panel. We're still on the ground floor since he hasn't indicated a floor. "Let's see if I can make you come before we reach my apartment."

What? He slaps the highest number before dropping my legs to the floor and immediately yanking down my jeans. I help, eagerness coursing through me. If anyone ever told me I'd be getting eaten out in an elevator, I would have laughed.

I suppose it's a good thing the elevator is his private one, but also the thought of possibly being interrupted at a stop seems...exciting.

Lost in my head of what-ifs, I almost miss when Rafael lowers to his knees, and raises one of my legs, balancing me on one foot. He wraps it over his shoulder, baring my pussy to him. Something I *should* be more nervous about than I am.

This isn't kissing. This isn't even him putting his fingers inside me in a nearly pitch-black room. The lights in the elevator are bright and unforgiving and there is no hiding from his devious gaze.

My hands clutch the railing behind me, fingers wrapping around the edge tightly as his other hand climbs my leg, fingers pausing by the heat of my core.

This is happening. I suck in a deep breath.

Rafael peers up the side of my body, his eyes sparkling and he jerks his head back, indicating the doors behind him. "Watch the numbers, *ma belle*. Count the floors."

Count? He wants me to *count* while I live through this brand-new experience of somehow maintaining my balance while—

His mouth covers me and the noise that leaves my throat is ungodly and inhumane but so fucking good. Wild and free. Something I never thought I'd be for a long time.

His tongue lavishes over my clit, dipping inside my core, his open mouth moving over me in ways I've only ever read about. It doesn't feel enough though. Like it'll never be enough. That even as my hips seem to move on their own, the feeling is too great to ever let him go.

My eyes flash up. The fifth floor.

"You're so fucking wet," he growls into my thigh, "there are no words to describe how delectable you taste."

Hopefully he doesn't need a response because words evade me.

My other leg is suddenly hoisted over his shoulder, lifting both off the floor. Only my back keeps me balanced. My hands fly to his head, grabbing onto his hair to keep me steady.

"I have you," he reassures me. "Believe me, war will have to break out before I let you go."

His tongue drags up my centre, pausing at my clit. He nips it with his teeth, but not in a painful way, but rather one that has a moan climbing my throat again.

"Floor," he reminds me.

Tenth.

He pulls my clit between his teeth, sucking in air, suctioning the little nub of nerves that make fireworks go off in my mind. And that's all without coming. I can't imagine the pleasure he's about to bring me.

"This feels..." Words stop working, my sentence trailing off into a long moan as Rafael drags his tongue to my core again and fucks me with it. His hands knead my thighs, seemingly relaxing the tightly wound nerves there, but it doesn't completely work.

As the heat pools in my stomach, my eyes flash up. Fifteenth floor. There are still so many floors, yet it feels like not enough time. Like I'm caught halfway between about to explode and unable to come in time.

His hands work the flesh of my ass, moulding it into his touch, holding firm as he nips me again. His hands splay, shifting until his fingers can pull my lips apart. He blows, the flash of cool air doing indescribable things.

Twentieth floor. Ten more.

My hand pushes down on his head, urging him to return to sucking. I liked the pressure he used, but I don't know how to tell him that. And if he makes me talk, it'll shatter everything.

Thankfully, he understands my silent request and takes my clit into his mouth, his tongue flicking rapidly.

"*Yes,*" I hiss, my hand pushing down on him again. "I feel it, Rafael."

The burst inside me. The tingles that erupt over my form, wiping away everything logical, everything right and wrong in my life, leaving only one thing remaining. The *craving*—the undetermined, undying feeling of needing this. Needing *him*.

Twenty-fifth floor.

I might make it. So as long he doesn't pull back or change any part of what he's doing, I will.

"I'm..." Trying to tell him, but words continue snapping, my brain unable to form anything concrete.

Somehow sensing what I crave, his pressure on my clit intensifies, increasing my body's heat. The warmth that feels like I'm about to explode. The fervour that will consume me.

"I'm…" My teeth sink into my lip, cutting off my speech, trying to lower my tone when I come because it feels like I can't hold it all in. I'll be too loud and—

The pressure disappears for a second, but the intensity in me doesn't dissipate at all when he growls. "Fucking scream, Isabelle. Don't hold back. I want to hear you."

My teeth scrape my skin as I release my lip and the moment he puts his mouth back on me, that explosion occurs. The bubble bursts in my stomach, every nerve in my body hardwired to recognize one thing only—his touch.

His licking increases as I come, embarrassingly wetting his face, but he doesn't pull back. He doesn't stop, and it's incredibly hot.

Ding! Amidst the heavy breathing and slowing moans, I laugh as the metal elevator doors slide open, revealing Rafael's apartment. I did it.

Rafael lowers my feet to the ground again and stands, not backing away when he takes my hand between his two palms, holding me in a way that can be considered almost tender, except his kiss is anything but.

Rough, claiming, and *different*. Tinged with me. it's unexplainable, but it turns me on immensely. For only tonight, I'm the one who has his attention.

Without a word, he lifts me again and my legs wind around his waist. He carries me from the elevator in the same way we entered, walking the straight hall and heading right through the living room.

"I'm not sure I can get enough of you, Isabelle," he says when he enters his bedroom, and he's lowering me onto the bed.

It might be his words or the look in his eyes, but that very statement makes my insides twist in desire. Desire and nerves as the two battle it out.

This is silly. It's only sex.

When his hands leave my body, he takes my shirt with him, pulling it over my head. I move to help, until I'm seated on the edge of his bed with only my bra on. The remainder of my clothing has been abandoned in the elevator.

He towers over me, still dressed, which is quite unfair. With his gaze stalking my every move, I stand, pressing my nearly naked form against his fully clothed one as I push his shirt up his chest.

He takes the edge and pulls it over his head, dropping it to the floor by our feet. He doesn't touch me, but looms over me, his arms hanging by his side. My hands hover over the immensely sexy curves of his abs. Living with him, seeing him work at his club, it's easy to forget that, in the end, he's a killer, exactly like his family. Trained to fight, skilled at shooting, and lives his life in the dark lane. His body is a contradiction to the man I've come to know.

His head tilts a fraction, giving me permission to touch. I can't look at him as I do, because for all my nerves down in the club, they're quickly disappearing beneath the intensity in his watchful gaze.

Bringing my hand toward his body, I set my palm on his abs, softly trailing my touch up to his chest, over the tattoos covering his sides, his arms, his heart. He feels good beneath my hand as he stands unmoving, staring.

My hand continues up to his shoulders, feeling the muscle there. Rafael dressed and undressed are two different experiences. He doesn't look this filled out when he's in his leather jacket or even his suit.

There's still a part of him I have yet to see, and my hand returns down his body, pausing at his waistband. Realization crashes down on me that I don't know how to do *this*, and while I might have been the girl getting fingered in a sex club, I have no idea how to properly initiate this next part.

Rafael steps back at the same time he grasps my wrists and moves them away from him. Disappointment weighs down my shoulders. No doubt, he's used to women who don't hesitate.

"Go sit on the bed."

That's not a no, and Rafael gives me the sense of needing control in his sexual encounters, so I listen, sliding myself onto the bed until I'm in the centre. Only when I look at him again, does he move.

He first undoes his pants, and I swear, my mouth goes dry. His fingers hook inside his waistband, removing his pants and boxers in one go. If I believed my mouth was dry before, it just learned the true meaning of that word because *oh my fucking god.*

That's what he is. A motherfucking *god* stands there, all power and muscle. His tattoos continue over his hip and wrap one leg. And his cock stands erect.

"You're already..."

He smirks. "Not even ten minutes ago, my fingers were inside your cunt. Then I had you riding my mouth. And finally, your soft hands were stroking my body. Believe me, Belle," he approaches the bed, every word, every step, laced with dominance that makes my own legs curl up, "I've had a hard-on for you the second I stepped into that room and found my every desire."

I scoff. For all his pretty words, I'm no one's desire. There's in-the-moment, sure, and that's what's consuming Rafael and me, but to claim his *every* desire was to find me in his sex club is pushing the believability scale too far.

Rafael hears my noise and leans over the bed, his hand wrapping around my ankle as he jerks me closer. His other arm balances him over me, his chest inches from my breasts.

"It's no laughing matter. Why is it so unbelievable?"

"Have you seen me?" I gesture to my face, so far from self-depreciating because it's the truth. I've never been insecure about my scars because I've never had anyone to be self-conscious around. No one I've wanted to *like* as much as Rafael.

"Yes," he answers. He advances, his face so close to mine, I can see the different shades of green specks in his eyes. "I have seen you. And I'm *seeing* you now. You're fucking gorgeous, Isabelle. *Ma belle.* And if you still don't believe me, I'll tie you to this bed and keep you here until you do. Don't test me."

My face heats. All of me heats, even parts I hadn't known could do so. Being tied to his bed doesn't sound like such a bad idea if I get a repeat of earlier.

When I don't counter him, he takes me in another intense kiss. His hand holds my face tenderly, even when his kiss is everything but. His hips lower to mine, his hard erection between us. He rocks his hips, pushing his cock through my slit, and blinding pleasure consumes my every sense. By the time he pulls back, I'm panting, trying to catch my breath and my pussy feels like it's on fire.

He smirks again and rolls over me, landing on his back, one arm perched above his head. He looks like a model. I glance at his face, and then his cock, rolling my lips together, trying to determine what he wants from me. Guys like him seem like they'd rather take charge.

"You were on top of me, and you didn't..." Words escape me once again.

His other hand reaches out and he strokes my leg until I look at him. "Believe me, Belle, after tasting you and having my fingers inside you, I want nothing more to shove my cock in you, but it's your first time, so we're going to prepare you properly."

Prepare me? I feel like I already have been.

"You look upset," he comments, a question in his tone.

I shrug, not quite certain how to organize my thoughts into words.

"Just for your first time," he says. "I suspect, once I get inside you, I won't want to leave. Which means, caring about your initial time and not taking you roughly. Preparing you starts with," he moves his hand to my face, tapping my temple, "your mind. I want you to touch me first with your hands, so when I'm buried inside you, you know *every* inch of the man claiming you."

23
RAFAEL

Growing up in the mafia taught me many things. A few of which involve people's faked bravado. Not that I think Isabelle was faking any of it, but once the lights came on and the moment approached, reality crashed down and my reclusive bookworm, who's only known intimacy through the screen of her reading device, got spooked.

I might have my asshole, beastly—to use the term Isabelle would—moments, but I won't do this to her. Fucking her with the deception swirling around, the truths I have yet to tell her, is one thing. Traumatizing her by fucking her on a couch, against a wall, in front of others, or slamming into her now isn't how I'll allow this to happen.

Even if every single suggestion she's thrown at me down-stairs made it more and more difficult to back away and do the right thing, rather than what I craved. Did I want to fuck her right there in that room, with the trio in the next room watching us? Fuck yes. Do I want her first sexual experience to be shared with strangers? Not really. She'll look back on tonight remembering only one face—mine.

Once we got to my apartment, I realized what a right deci-sion I had made. I can smell a person's fear as easy as I can see it, and for all her previous excitement, Isabelle is scared.

"Explore me," I suggest again, propping my arm behind my head so I can watch her as she does. "Get used to the feel of my body."

She nods, biting her lip in the sexiest manner possible, and shifts onto her knees, shuffling closer. Just like when we were standing, she starts at my abs, trailing her fingers upwards, stroking over the tattoo covering my heart—my family's insignia and the script of my vows.

There's nothing sexier than watching a woman explore, and I want to study her every expression, a voyeur on my own expe-rience, but her hands are so fucking soft and tentative, her touch uncertain and addicting, and my lids slide shut, revelling in the gentle sensation too much to remain focused.

Her hands lower toward my waist, which is where she had stopped last time when hindered by my pants. But I'm not wearing any now, and without hesitation, her touch continues. With every inch of my skin she passes over, it feels like more of her confidence from earlier returns, telling me, this was the best course of action.

My eyes won't allow me to keep them shut when my mind quickly gets taken from ease and soft pleasure to an intense thrumming in my nerves as her nails pass over my thighs, pausing for the briefest second before trailing up my cock.

I jerk. My hands fist the bed. A hiss escapes my lips.

Most women grasp me and try to fuck me with their hands right away, but Isabelle's gentle touch is new and welcoming, an exploration of sorts.

"Feels good," I tell her before she can get in her head.

Her fingers circle my head, brushing right over the sensitive spot. She traces my shaft once before wrapping her hand around me, stroking me with confidence.

Her hair falls over her face and I reach up to drape it over her shoulder, revealing her smirk. "You really don't give me enough credit, if you think I would need to be prepared for your body. You're sweet, but it's not required." She roughly jerks me, her tongue flicking out the corner of her lip in a sly, devious smirk. Fucking girl knows what she's doing.

She continues stroking me, maintaining an effortless, self-assured pace. My balls draw up in my body, once again, being teased with her nearness. My dick's still screaming at me for not fucking her on the couch downstairs when she was riding me.

"Oh yeah?" I challenge, pushing into a sitting position. I clasp her hips, yanking her over my lap. My cock brushes her heat and it'd be so easy to shove her down and have her ride me right here, right now, and fuck, I want to. Even if she doesn't believe she needs to be used to my body, I want her pussy prepared.

Reclining backwards, I take her with me, shuffling her knees until she has to grasp the headboard for balance. Peering down, she cocks a brow.

"Once again, I was right on top of you, and you didn't..." Those pesky nerves creep up again, and she can't say the words.

"Fuck you? I told you; you're being prepared in every way possible, *ma belle.* Whether you like it or not, because the taste I got of you in the elevator wasn't enough." With her ass in my palms, I nudge her farther up, right on top of my face. "Sit, Belle."

"O-on you? I'll—"

"Suffocate me? I'm begging you to. Now, fucking *sit.*"

With my strength, I shove her down, spearing her with my tongue, right in her tight hole. No number of orgasms will ease the pain completely, but the wetter she is, the more orgasms her insides experience, I can make it a tad easier on her.

Besides, I'm a selfish man. Today has certainly been proof of that. And I want more of her on my tongue.

She makes a whimpering sound that only increases the lust in my veins. Massaging her inner thigh, I ensure she's comfortable and isn't in her head as I flick my tongue over her clit, returning to the pace I learned earlier that she enjoys.

My tongue rotates by fucking and licking her pussy. With every cry she fills my bedroom with, every sound the walls will reverberate back to me when she's no longer here, her thighs clench around my head. I fucking love of it. The feel of her release, even before her actual release. The release on her nerves; her tightly wound personality as she lets go.

When she begins shaking and quivering, her body revealing her impending orgasm, I don't let up. I refuse to when she's so close. Her hips rock, her control taking her over.

"Rafael." Her hands smack the headboard, and I massage her ass, encouraging what she's warning me of. "Raf—" Her moan interrupts my name; I've never heard it spoken so sexy. She cries into the room, her rocking increasing for a second before her legs tighten unforgivingly around my head, stiffening as she goes still, her orgasm bringing her the ultimate pleasure.

I don't let up, drinking in all her body releases, and even as her cries subside, I continue flicking my tongue over her.

"Rafael, what—"

Lifting her up a fraction, only so she can hear me speak, I mumble into her thigh, "Told you. We're gonna make this pussy a nice, sloppy mess before I fuck it."

I push her right down on my tongue again, but this time, I don't move her hips. My hands slide forward, thumbs pulling her lips apart.

"Fuck my face, Belle. Take what you need."

For once, she doesn't fight, hips lowering as she finds a pace she enjoys and rides. Her greedy little pussy only takes a moment before she's releasing again, her cries getting louder and louder with each one.

This time when she finishes, her weight falls onto my face, but I don't mind. I give her a second to catch her breath before flipping her over onto her back. She releases a surprised squeak that turns into a moan when I sink two fingers inside her.

"Again?"

"Always," I promise. I can't get enough of her moans. Of her body giving me ultimate control, even though she is nearly ready to take me.

I curl my digits and she instantly makes a noise in her throat. With my fingers pumping inside her, I lower my head, taking one of her budded nipples into my mouth, biting lightly. Her hands fly to my shoulders, but not to push me away. More to hold onto me as she arches into my chest.

"You taste good everywhere," I mumble into her skin as I trail my lips over her chest to her other nipple, licking that one too. "And you feel fucking glorious." I pump harder, pulling a long moan from her.

I enjoy that sound. So much, I shift my face to her neck, licking and nipping as my pace increases. Her pussy clenches around my fingers, her breathing more shallow. I trace her pulse with my tongue, feeling her pants. She's seconds from coming.

"Raf—" She cries into the room, her feet jamming into the mattress as she pushes her hips into my fingers, her head thrown back into the pillow.

I kiss down her chest, circling each nipple as I pull my fingers from her, placing them at my lips. With a long lick, I savour each one under her watchful, heated gaze.

"A taste I won't tire of, Belle. I'm warning you now. No

surface will be safe because I'll have your legs spread everywhere so I can devour this pussy."

I roll off her toward my side of the bed, heading for my nightstand, where I reach inside and return with a condom. Before putting it on, I offer, "Need water? Hydration."

She shakes her head with a sexy smirk, so I lie on the bed.

As I roll the condom over my cock, Isabelle's head tips to the side. "What are you doing?"

"What does it look like I'm doing?"

"I mean, you're lying down. You're not, like," she rolls her lips together at the same time her hands fuse together, "on top? Alphaness and all that?"

Alphaness? Laughter bubbles in my throat, but I do my hardest to hold it in, in case she thinks I'm laughing at her. More like, at her term.

"Believe me, *ma belle,* that will come in time. Only a true alpha understands what their woman needs, and you'll need the control."

My woman. Words that flowed entirely too easy from my lips.

Once the condom is on correctly—a shame because I'd fucking love nothing more than to be inside her bare, but I'm certain she's not on any form of birth control—I reach for her. Grasping her hips, I pull her body on top of mine, instantly taking her lips.

Her legs naturally fall around my waist and with my cock against her pussy, she rubs against me. Taking her hands, I position them on my shoulders, giving her a place to hold.

"When you're ready, put me inside you. It might hurt a bit. Could sting. But being on top will give you control over the pace and depth. If you need to pull back and take a break, do it."

Isabelle isn't the only one having a first, but I don't admit that to her. I've never taken a woman's virginity. The women who find themselves beneath me are because they've used their body and seduction to get there.

Isabelle nods, and I'm proud as fuck, there's no fear in her expression. She shifts on her knees, and lines herself up with my cock, which I grasp and hold steady for her.

Then she lowers herself.

In the course of an hour, I've had my fingers and tongue inside her, but there's *nothing* like the feel of her heat, of her tight cunt as my cock is swallowed inch by inch. First the head, and then the shaft. She pauses, a hiss slithering between her teeth. Her legs tighten around my hips and her head lowers, her eyes scrunching as she breathes through the pain.

I wish I could take this from her. Stroking her face, I wait until she's inhaled at least five deep breaths before I speak. "Eyes on me."

She listens immediately and after a long, shaky breath, lowers herself another half-inch.

Training for the mafia meant learning a lot of self-control, but *nothing* prepared me for the feeling of Isabelle. She moves slowly, teasing, and my dick wants nothing more to bury deep inside her.

Soon. Soon, but she needs this first.

"Lift up and down. It'll make it smoother and easier."

She does, lifting on her knees before lowering again, this time managing to take me deeper as her juices coat my cock and provide lubrication. Her nails dig lightly in my shoulders, where I've placed them and I stroke her thighs, comforting her as she slowly takes another half-inch.

"You're doing so good, *ma belle*. So fucking good." *So* good, but I resist from telling her exactly how much. How many of my nerves are compelling me to grip her hips and yank her all the way down, to flip her over and pound into her. To take her roughly before returning to the club and fucking her in front of others so they see who owns this beautiful woman's pussy.

In time, of course.

She hisses again, dropping another inch. She's nearly there, so I lightly rest my hands on her hips, still letting her lead.

"You're almost there."

She finishes the last bit easily, a low moan filling the room as her head falls back, her back arching and her breasts angled to the ceiling. She's a fucking goddess, and one I'll happily and with honour, bleed for.

"I didn't know," she murmurs, rolling her head to the side to look at me. "I feel so—I didn't know."

"Does it hurt?"

"It did."

"And now?"

"No. It feels *different*. Nothing like I imagined. I'm stretched but not in pain anymore."

"Guess those books haven't taught you everything." I smirk. "And Belle, hold on, because I can't wait to be the one to."

24

ISABELLE

I get it now. I understand the feeling of complete mindlessness because my brain can process one thing only—Rafael.

Rafael inside me.

Rafael telling me he'll be the one to teach me everything my books haven't, and I certainly fucking hope so.

He pushes into a sitting position, angling my legs around his waist. With one arm around my waist, he keeps me on his lap, his cock buried deep inside me.

"What are you—"

His teeth take one of my nipples in his mouth again, stealing my words, as he rocks into me, gently at first.

Whoa. I hadn't thought...It's the only thing I *can* think. That this isn't anything like I imagined. Experiencing bliss and paradise is something no words can accurately describe.

His free hand grasps strands of my hair and he lightly pulls my head back, arching my back in a way that should be painful, if it wasn't for the angle it puts me at. I roll my hips into his motions, trying to meet his thrusts.

"Pain?" he checks, his lips shaping the word against my breast.

"None," I manage through a whispered, strained tone.

"Good." With his word, his hips move faster, slapping up into mine. His arm around my waist works in tandem with my own movements, bringing me down on top of him.

Can there be anything better than this? First time or not, it's difficult to imagine. What I can't imagine is orgasming *again*, but somehow, and thankfully, the heat and pressure builds in my core.

I try to straighten my head, but Rafael holds firm. His thrusts get harder, and I'm seeing the real Rafael Corsetti now. The gentle, caring one here moments ago was for me, for my experience, and I appreciate him for it. Getting through the pain, I realized after he urged me on top, was better like that. Being able to control how fast and how much I took of him.

But now is a different manner.

"I'm...I'm..." I can't finish, but he can figure it out.

Rafael doesn't let up, his teeth sinking lightly into my breast and it's that bite that does it for me. As pleasure consumes me, I go still, my legs unable to move, even as the pulsing inside urges me to take him deeper somehow and never release him.

He growls into my chest. "You will become my addiction, Belle. How are you so fucking perfect?"

Rafael's arm tightens around my waist and in a quick movement, he has me on my back, him looming over me. My head's on the pillow where his was. My knees come up, wrapping around his waist, and keeping him inside me.

His green eyes travel the length of my body, toward where we're fused together. With a slight smirk I find way too sexy, he comments, "I'm glad we're still on the same page because I'm not quite done with you."

He takes my hands in his, his fingers weaving in between

mine and he raises them above my head. His eyes lock on mine, and he moves, rocking into me at an unforgiving pace. One that should be painful, but instead, it's easy not to think about, considering the pleasure he's creating.

I try to meet his thrusts, but he moves too quickly. Too explosive. Too fiery.

So I hang on for the ride. My hands tighten in his, gripping to ensure he doesn't think about going anywhere. This one's quicker, blinding, and overcomes me nearly instantly.

I scream. *Scream.* And not in pain, but in hedonism. My body produces noises I hadn't thought possible.

Rafael doesn't let up, even as my orgasm takes me down. He releases one of my hands to hike my leg off his hip, lifting it at a different angle as he hammers inside me faster, in a pace I didn't know possible. He takes my mouth in a rough, claiming kiss. His teeth nip at my bottom lip, and he groans into my mouth.

"I can't hold back, *ma belle*. You feel too fucking good."

My other leg clenches tighter around his waist, my silent demand for him not to.

I feel his orgasm everywhere. Through his kiss, inside my core, in every single nerve inside my body as he electrocutes me with his own release. The condom blocks the heat of his cum, but I have a new curiosity—to feel it.

He releases my mouth with a heavy pant. He drops my leg and I lower both to the bed. For a long second, he remains on top of me, his face in my neck, his arms around me, his hot pants canvassing my naked breasts.

This is the part of sex I always was most curious about. The intimacy that accompanies it, especially afterwards.

I trail a finger up his spine. "Well," I start, but don't finish.

"Well." He lifts his head to look at me. "Well, that was intense."

"Very much so."

Rafael slowly lifts to his knees, his cock slipping from me. A sting of something close to pain flashes through my core, like now that it's empty, I realize how much he truly stretched me. No doubt, I'll feel it tomorrow, but I'm okay with the sensation.

He removes the condom quickly and rests it on the side table, out of sight. His finger traces over my wet pussy, and an appreciative noise quickly follows.

"You'll have to keep me away from you. Let you heal before I fuck you again."

Again. He's talking of this happening again. I should be frightened, considering why I'm even in his life, but just like agreeing to do this, I'm enjoying the concept of my vacation from harsh realities.

I giggle, reaching for him again. "Not necessary."

His chuckle is dark and does dangerous things to my insides. "You say that now." He slides to the end of the bed and reaches for me, pulling me along.

He wants me to stand? After my...who knows how many orgasms, I can't even *think* about standing. Sleepiness is quickly creeping up and as much as I'd love to follow him, my body won't allow it.

"Why?" The word ends on a whine to emphasize how much I do not want to get up.

"You will thank me in the morning when we get you cleaned up properly."

"Eh. That sounds like a morning problem."

I drop on the bed, playfully grinning at him. Rafael gives up for a moment and retrieves his clothing from where he dropped them by the foot of the bed. He removes his phone from his pants, plugs it into the charger on his bedside table, before tossing the clothes to the side and focusing his attention on me again.

"Fine, but I'm going to get you a warm cloth. I'll clean you up, but before you pass out, you really do need to go to the bathroom to—"

"I know the mechanics, Rafael."

He chuckles and walks by the bed, his shapely ass holding my entire focus as he exits the bedroom, giving me a couple moments of much-needed silence.

Holy fuck, what has my life become? Where has it gone? I'm not myself anymore because I don't do things like *this*. Crazy, insane fun things. I should be at home mourning my father, hiding beneath blankets because that's what I know how to do.

Because it's what Dad trained me to do. Frightened of even my own shadow, while Rafael's shadow is consuming mine, taking the frights away, making it so *he's* the only one I fear. Except I don't. Mafia family aside, Rafael's *normal*. As normal as he can be in his life, I guess.

Rafael's phone vibrating on the table draws my attention to it, but only for a second. He'll see the text when he returns. Not even ten seconds later, it rings. This time, I sit up, peering at the screen to see the name calling him. If it's the same person texting, they're persistent.

The call eventually goes to voicemail and the screen flashes with the missed call notification. It drops back to the lock screen, where the text message notification also resides and that's when wintery chills consume my nerves.

Where, even though his phone is certainly not my business, I slide to the edge of the bed, reaching for the device, unable to stop myself from rereading the message he received over and over. And over. And over again, until it imprints in my head and makes any sort of sense whatsoever.

NICO

Did you tell her yet? Stop thinking with your
dick. If she knows something, every second
you're fucking around is a second longer De
Falco wins.

So many questions flit through my mind. The most pressing: who the fuck is De Falco? I've never heard of that name.
Then, what do I supposedly know?

But the worst is the feeling that quickly accompanies it—
betrayal.

The icy, merciless grasp of treachery that yanks my heart out
and grounds it beneath its firm fist.

Every instinct I've had about Rafael comes true in that
second. Worse, because I'm the fool who slept with him,
viewing this experience as a vacation. That was probably his
ploy too—get the naïve girl to emotionally open up by first
spreading her legs.

I've been so wrapped up in him, I've completely lost sight of
the fact that he's still the *mafia*. Rafael's been my villain from
the beginning.

I drop the phone, uncaring as it lands by the floor, dangling
only by the charging cord.

I need to get away from here. From him. From *this*. I glance
at the phone. From whatever that means. From whatever lies
Rafael's keeping from me.

I roll to my feet, disgust casting my gaze away from the bed.
Talk about a fucking mistake. I stomp to the other side of the
bed where my bag is, and begin pulling out whatever clothing I
can. Pain flashes through my core, my body demanding rest
after the intense night but I push through it.

His steps bring him into the room. "What are you doing,
ma belle?"

Ma belle. It means my beautiful. *My* beautiful. Yet another level of treachery, no doubt.

I drop the clothes and straighten, whirling on him, unable to fully look at him though. His very face, his skin, his body the reminder of what we did.

"Why am I here, Rafael? And no more fucking lies."

25
RAFAEL

When I return with a warm cloth in hand, a glass of water, and a pill to prevent the possible aches she'll gain throughout the night, I expect to find her already passed out.

What I don't expect is to find her crouching by her suitcase, rifling through it.

"What are you doing, *ma belle*?" I ask as I enter the room. *Why are you not in bed?*

Isabelle straightens right away and turns. Her expression is devoid of emotion. Broken almost, a stark difference from what I left her as.

"Why am I here, Rafael? And no more fucking lies."

"Why do you ask?" I immediately toss back. There's nothing of tonight that should have revealed anything, so where have these questions come from, now of all times?

Her hand gestures toward my bedside table. "Check your messages and figure it out the fuck yourself."

Fuck. I curse my brother. It'd be no one else. Resting the glass of water, pill, and cloth on her bedside table, I walk toward

185

my side of the bed, lifting the phone, which dangles from the nightstand by its cord, somehow already sure at what I'll find.

A missed call, and a text message that was sent seconds prior. As usual, my impatient brother couldn't wait five fucking minutes.

"What aren't you telling me, Rafael?" Isabelle's wrath-filled voice comes right up beside me. She stands there, pulling on leggings, her breasts already covered with a shirt she's thrown on. "What do I supposedly know?"

If she thinks she's leaving, that's not happening. Tossing the phone on the bed, I turn toward her, my hands clenching her upper arms to keep her still.

She reacts right away, throwing her body away, twisting her shoulders to loosen my hold. I grip firmer, rotating her until her knees hit the bed, and using a bit of strength, I push down until she drops to the mattress.

When she doesn't fight, I release her, backing away an inch as uncertainty rolls through me. It seems like my time is up. I need to tell her what we've learned about her identity, but I don't want to.

The second there's a few inches of space between us, she's on her feet, throwing herself toward the other side of the room, her back to the windows. Her hand comes up, stopping me in my tracks. Normally I wouldn't, but something in her devoid expression tells me I should.

"Rafael," she starts, "what the fuck was your brother talking about? What aren't you telling me?"

"It's not so easy, Belle."

"Isabelle," she snarls, reminding me so much of this morning, when she was pissed at me. "And it's pretty fucking easy. You're not protecting me, are you?" She gestures to the other side of the window, toward the dark outdoors. "No one's coming after me. This is some ploy to keep me here, isn't it?

Because you're certain I," her fingers come up in quotes, *"know something."* She drops her arms with a scoff and pushes off the glass, taking a few steps forward. "You know what's funny? I was starting to enjoy my time with you. So much, I've been forgetting who *I* am. No longer."

She makes it three steps before I pitch myself in her way, my hands coming up to stop her. She's playing with fire, forgetting what my last name means. I might be considered the kinder one of my family, but in the end, I'm still a Corsetti.

"Isabelle, stop. Listen to me."

"No!" She throws her hands out, shoving into my chest, but my legs lock me into place, so she makes no headway. "I'm fucking done listening to your lies. You spew all about needing to protect me. That someone killed my father and might be after me. *You* murdered him, didn't you?" Her fists fly again, hitting my chest in no way that is painful. "Who *are* you people? What the fuck do you want with me?"

With her next hit, I move, my arm darting so quick, reflexes stopping her next punch. Keeping her hand in mine, I slowly lower it to her side as I erase the space between us, towering over her.

"You are in danger. Trust me on that."

"*Trust* you?" She yanks out of my hold, turning her body to shield herself. "I'm done trusting you. Unless you tell me the fucking truth right this second—"

"I can't," I interrupt, feeding her half a lie. Can I? Certainly. But I'd prefer to discuss things with her old nanny, to see what she knows before admitting anything to Isabelle. This won't be an easy conversation, so any extra information I gain will be better.

"*Can't,*" she repeats, her voice rising in disbelief. Shaking her head, she sidesteps me, shoving into my arm on the way by. I turn, stalking her every step to the door. "Well, Rafael, I *can't* stay here. Thanks for disrupting my life. Thanks for the lies. It's been fun. See ya." At the doorway, I hear her grumble, "Fucking beast."

Fucking beast. No. She hasn't seen me be a beast. That's not who I am, but it's certainly who I *can* be.

Snatching my jeans from the floor, I shove one leg into them, then the other as I stumble toward the doorway. Fucking Christ, when did my life become *this*?

"Isabelle, don't fucking walk away when we're talking," I holler down the hallway.

She's made it into the living room now and right before turning toward the elevator, she peeks behind her. "Talking? Is that what we're doing?"

I rush down the hallway when she disappears, my legs eating up the space of my condo as much as I can until reaching the end. Hooking my hand on the wall, I turn toward the elevator just as the doors open and she steps inside.

"Belle."

She slaps the button, igniting the doors to immediately shut. "Good bye, Rafael."

I rush toward the elevator, but the doors have shut. My fingers jam between them, trying to pry them open, but they're secured. The ding on the other side tells me it's moving already. I punch the button, even aware it's set to drop her off first before returning all the way up.

"Fuck!" My hands fly to my hair, yanking on the strands, needing something to release anger on before I punch a hole in my wall.

I have to go after her. For everything that just happened, we still don't know anything about Isabelle, or who's after her father—and her. Who showed up at her house.

And I don't want her to go.

Shoving feet into my shoes, I head for a locked cabinet,

retrieving a gun and a knife, thrusting both in a holster. In my room, I quickly yank on a shirt and grab my cell before returning to the elevator, which has now dinged again with its arrival.

Pushing the button, I'm anxious as it slowly travels the length of the building. Memories of a mere hour ago, when I had her pinned against the wall, my mouth on her delicious cunt drive me to find her.

She and I are *far* from done—Nico's plan aside. Today started something.

An obsession I hadn't realized was building until I witnessed her rush away from me.

Never run from a beast.

I'll find her. And I'll make her sorry she ever thought to leave me.

26

ISABELLE

Leaving at this time of night is easily the dumbest decision I've made to date. Even more stupid than fucking my captor. The urgency of escape meant leaving my wallet, my clothing, and all other items behind, even my beloved Kindle.

It doesn't slow my steps though as the elevator finally arrives on the main floor of Rafael's building. Without a glance behind me, I quickly exit the private elevator, striding through the lobby, and into the downtown Montreal streets.

I'll buy a new Kindle at this point. My books will sync. Everything else in his house is replaceable. Anything to avoid having to see him again. My laptop is backed up in the Cloud. When I get a new one, I'll sign in and download all my files. My ID's the main issue; that'll be a pain to get replaced but not impossible.

I take a sharp turn, walking down the connected street when panic begins to set in. When my heartbeat quickens along with my steps and my neck tingles in awareness. I have nothing but my cellphone on me, so with the maps app, I input my apartment's address and figure out how to get from here to there. My stomach drops when the walking time is recorded at twenty-seven minutes. At midnight. Downtown Montreal. No money or anything useful on me.

Fuck.

I glance toward Rafael's building, wondering if he's watching me from his place above, or if he's coming after me. Maybe he's given up entirely and will search for me tomorrow. There's little doubt, I will unfortunately see him again because if his brother's text message is any indication, he's not done with me.

Dad, what did you do? What did you get me into?

Either way, being there was about *his* needs, not my safety. Those men at my house were probably fake. I mean, he's the damn mafia leader's brother; of course, they have means. The bullet wound the one soldier on my front step—staged.

Fictional. I should have known. Everything about Rafael is fictional.

Ducking my head, I aim to make myself shrink into the shadows, even while my eyes survey every inch of the sidewalk in front of me, the street to my left, and the sidewalk across the way. And again. Gaze continuously sweeping the area, checking behind me. Not only for Rafael, but anyone.

Dad's voice creeps into my mind again, instructing me to always be observant, putting aside the grief that accompanies hearing him comes with.

A figure steps out from the shadows of a building, stepping right in front of me. Clasping my lips together, I try my best not to make a noise. Keeping my head low, I move around the figure, hoping this person too is simply someone walking by.

I make it around him, so focused on escape, another figure steps in front of me, my feet halting before I accidentally bump into the person.

"Sorry," I mumble, moving to step aside them too.

The first one approaches, and the one I've nearly walked into throws his arms out, blocking my way. "Nuh uh, girlie. Our boss wants to see you."

Fear jams into my throat. Finally, I look up at the two, large figures. Their shadows consume mine.

No! This can't be happening.

Sweat blooms on my neck, in my palms, my anxiety making even breathing a challenge. It's impossible to be calm as I whirl around, to escape the opposite way, when a third person comes up on my other side. And then a fourth. I'm encircled by a crowd of wolves that make me feel like I'm the prey they've come to consume.

"No." It comes out weaker than I want, but I shove my shoulder into the nearest one. His mass simply pushes me back into the circle as another one grasps my hips, another one my wrists.

My mind isn't even processing what's happening. The flurry of movement my body goes through. I try to drop to the ground, only to be yanked back to my feet. I throw elbow after elbow into their firm bodies. I kick, but one snatches my ankle, growling in my ear.

"Feisty, aren't you. Just like your father."

His words free my nerves. I think...I think these are my father's killers.

"Fuckin' carry her," a deep voice commands. "Tie her hands if we need to. Put her in the trunk."

The trunk! Hands tied!

"No!" I scream, twisting my body everywhere, trying to break their holds as one lifts me by my chest, and another reaches for my legs, likely with the intent of carrying me off.

Amidst downtown Montreal, there's not a peep of anyone

nearby. In a city of a population of half a million people *no one is watching this?*

"Stop making this difficult."

A large, sharp knife enters my vision, and I comprehend the threat. Be silent or pay the price. It should be enough for the fear to dissipate and for me to obey them, and I suppose I do. But not because I want to, but rather, a sense of dullness washes over me, dimming my senses, making my body stiff as I travel to another place, another time, one trapped in my head.

"No, Daddy! No!" He stands beside a man in a white coat, holding a very large knife in the air. "What are you..." My question fades as my body sleeps, compelled by the needle the man shoved into my arm moments ago. He warned me this would happen, but I didn't understand why.

Amid my mind's dreamlike escape, with only my fighting huffs as backdrop, a roar echoes through the space, causing the four men to freeze as a body barrels into all of us, causing their hold to loosen enough that they release me.

Instinct takes over and I right myself so my feet land on the ground first. Without caring which direction that I head in, I lunge to the side, throwing myself at the nearest building to make sense of what's happening and how I got free.

Rafael, out of nowhere, faces the line of four men, his teeth bared. The lighting of the building at my back catches on him at precisely the right angle, allowing me to notice the sharp blade gripped in his hand.

Without a word, he charges again, his arm slicing into the stomach of the nearest man. He drops with a scream that ends with a gurgle, maybe still alive. I pay him no attention for the three others turn and take off, but Rafael's right there, his hand snatching the shoulder of a second.

Yanking the man to the ground, his arm repositions his blade so the man's stumbling form lands right on the knife, his scream getting cut off. Rafael rips his weapon out of the man's heart, and takes off after the other two, leaving me with two dead bodies.

Holy shit, they're dead. I back into the building's shadows, unable to look away from the horror playing out. This isn't real anymore. This is...*something.* Something I can't name as Rafael, his shirt sprayed in the men's blood, shoots farther down the block, toward the two others. His role is so clear now. Being a mafia leader is more than running a sex club and babysitting an employee's daughter.

It's this.

The fight. The blood. The screams.

Of the two escaping, Rafael easily catches up to one. The man whirls right away, his hand jamming toward Rafael's side. Rafael staggers out of the way, but the way he stumbles has me rushing from the shadows, needing to see for myself he's all right.

He doesn't seem injured as he throws his body onto the man, his fist slamming into the guy's face. With a leg on either side of him, he pins him down, moving the blade to the man's neck, ending his fight.

Rafael shoves his fist into the man's face again, which increases my pace, because I could get there and very well find him dead. With the blade at his throat, Rafael looks completely unhinged as he leans over the man.

"Who the fuck are you and who sent you after her?"

The man chuckles, earning a nick from Rafael's blade. "You have no fucking idea, do you? You're rats chasing their tails. You'll never be ahead, so stop—" His rambles end on a scream as Rafael shifts the blade to the man's shoulder and jams it in, yanking it out with a cruel squelch.

The sound, scent, and trace of blood fill the area, and I gag, walking around the two other fallen bodies, stopping three feet away from Rafael and his captive. From my distance, the man with his tattooed bald head, mean eyes glaring at Rafael isn't someone I recognize, as he pants through his pain.

"Answers. Now. Or this will find its way into your throat."

"Go ahead. It's your plan anyway. I'm not getting out of here alive."

"At least you've accepted your death." Rafael places his blade against the man's throat again. "One more time, fucker. Who. Are. You?"

"A dead man."

"You tried to *touch* her. Harm her. Did De Falco send you?"

De Falco. That name again. The same one Nico mentioned in his text message.

The guy chuckles, rolling his neck until the blade rests against an artery, designing his own death. "Who I am doesn't matter, but who she is does. That little whore owes her life and—"

His cruel words cut off into a gurgle, Rafael dragging the blade against the man's throat without mercy. The guy slumps quickly, his head falling to the side, dead.

Another man dead.

Rafael looks to the left, down the street, but the fourth man has long disappeared. He curses as he stands, his movements slower than I've ever seen him make before. I don't budge, watching and waiting to see what's next. I hope he's not planning on chasing after the man because then I'm here alone with three dead bodies, a fear I can't quite name, and he doesn't look capable of running, given how he stumbles his next step.

Rafael bends and starts patting down the man at his feet. He lifts the guy's arms, pushing his sleeves up, seemingly searching for something, and only dropping the limbs when he's satisfied with finding the man's cell.

Rafael reaches into his back pocket and retrieves his own

phone. He dials a number, also lifting the phone to his ear. "Hey. Come to my condo. We need a bit of help half a block down." He hangs up and pockets the cell before moving away from the corpses and toward me.

He passes me, not even looking. He walks with a slight limp and his hand goes to his side, where I saw the last man hit. Rafael repeats the same with the other two guys. Checking their arms and then stealing their technology. Only then does he focus on me.

The crazed look in his eyes makes him unrecognizable. Still present, even after the men have been killed. Even after *he* killed *my* attackers. For everything that happened earlier in the condo, Rafael saved me from the men who've come to steal me away— for whatever reason.

He approaches, his face drawn in pain. With every step, he flinches, but his movements are so subtle, it's difficult to tell. No doubt, training has him able to mask pain until he's able to rest.

Rafael reaches my side and his hands come up, cupping my face. No words—just actions of a fevered man as he yanks me to him, claiming my lips in a challenging, rough kiss. A dare lines his action. A dare to take off again.

Something wet strokes over my skin, and Rafael notices the same time I feel it. He jerks away, wiping his hand on his shirt, cursing. "Fuck. No. Their blood does not deserve to grace your skin."

He's talking, which means there's some sense of his humanity back, I'm certain.

"Y-you killed them."

"They wanted to harm you."

He thinks I'm freaked out about the death? I mean, I should be, but somehow, seeing Rafael like this, *for* me, wipes that terror away.

"N-no. I mean, you killed them. Without a thought. *For* me. To save me."

His brows lace together. "*Ma belle*...yes."

Simple words. Impacting, nonetheless.

My reply is cut off by a black car pulling up to the curb. I stiffen, scanning the dead bodies decorating the cement in front of us, wondering how we'll explain this. My fingers grip his shirt, anxious. I don't want him to go after innocents, but there is no rational way to defend this scene.

His hands come over mine, stroking my knuckles. "It's okay. They're with me." Unhooking my hand from his clothing, he doesn't release me as he turns to the approaching men.

Both menacing in their own ways but couldn't look more opposite from one another if they tried. One's tall and lean, towering over his partner. He's so skinny, I wonder how he fights at all. While his partner is shorter, packed with muscle and an equally angry snarl beneath facial hair.

"Lumes. Cogs. Thanks for coming."

"Capo," the tall one greets, nodding his head. His gaze flicks to me quickly before scanning the murder scene. "Nice job."

"Well, that's what they fucking get," Rafael responds. "Deal with them. I'm taking Isabelle home."

He doesn't wait around to watch them work before pulling me down the block, toward his building. Everything from earlier is momentarily forgotten. My escape no longer important as the truth weighs my steps down.

I *was* in danger. While there's so much I get the feeling Rafael is keeping from me, he was telling one truth: people are after me.

People who admittingly took my father down.

Rafael's steps begin slowing, and I study him as a streetlight catches his expression. His face is drawn, his eyes pinching, his tongue bit between his teeth. One of his hands holds his side, and I hadn't noticed how much he *is* in pain.

"Oh, my god." I flit to his other side, my hands hovering over the spot he's holding. "You're hurt."

"I'm fine. Let's get inside."

I glance behind me, toward the two soldiers who could help him better than I certainly can, but they're busy gathering the bodies so I'd rather not interrupt them.

"Well, lean on me if you need to," I offer, only earning a small smirk from him as we approach his building, taking a side entrance with a direct path to his private elevator.

Inside the same space he had his mouth on me an hour ago, he slumps against the wall. The harsh lighting reveals how much he's been holding in.

I reach for his hand, nudging it away so I can inspect the injury. Blood is seeping through his dark shirt, and I peel the wet material away, gasping at the sight of a harsh slice over his ribs.

"Fuck, Rafael, you're—"

"Yep." He tips his head back to look at the climbing numbers. We're halfway there, but the trip seems too slow. "I'll be okay. I have medical supplies in the bathroom." He brushes my hand away, covering his injury again with his shirt.

By the time the elevator dings with its arrival, I'm an anxious mess. Fingers wringing together, I follow his slow walk to the bathroom, where he slumps onto the toilet seat cover, hissing and breathing through his pain.

"Beneath the sink. If you don't mind."

I should mind. I should mind very much that I'm stressing about the man who's knowingly lying to me. I should let him bleed out. So many shoulds, yet I retrieve the first-aid kit beneath the sink and start running water, warming it up as I also take a nearby folded-up facecloth to wet and wash the blood from his skin.

"If you give it to me, I can do it."

I shake my head, focusing on wringing the wet cloth simply so he can't see the emotions on my face. "You saved me. Least I can do. Remove your shirt."

"Next time you want me naked, Belle, all you have to do is ask. No need to go running into danger. In fact, I'd much prefer it if you didn't."

Folding my lips together, I hold back the giggle his words spark from me as he strips his shirt off. Muscles I ran my hands over earlier ripple beneath the bathroom's soft lighting. He spreads his legs and shifts his body, readjusting his angle for me.

Keeping my gaze low, I kneel between his legs, bringing the cloth to his side, stroking the warm fabric over the staggered, red mark, dabbing at the blood staining his surrounding skin.

He hisses between his teeth, his body instinctively jerking away from my touch.

"Hold still," I command firmly. "Besides, I thought you're trained in pain. You kept fighting with the injury."

"Still hurts," he counters, readjusting back to his old position, so I can continue wiping the blood. "Pain is pain, training aside. As for continuing to fight," he shrugs one shoulder, "adrenaline gets you through. I would have chased after the fourth, until I caught him."

"Why didn't you?" With the majority of the blood washed from his skin, I fold the cloth, and give it another final dab. It continues to bleed, but slower now.

Rafael looks at me with a weighted gaze. "Because you were there, and I didn't want to leave you alone."

27
RAFAEL

She doesn't respond to my last statement as she moves to the counter again, resting the bloodied cloth on the side, and unzips the first-aid kit. I'm ready to instruct her what to get, when she returns with a roll of bandages, gauze, and tape.

When she lowers herself between my knees, I imagine her there for a whole other reason. I could command her away and patch up my own injuries. It's not like I haven't done so time and time again, but her minor insistence is enjoyable. The last time someone cared for me like this was our family's private doctor, Dr. Shappo, and the aged man who helped birth me certainly doesn't make my dick jump to attention like Isabelle does.

Her fingers stroke the skin around the cut, making me grunt in pain. That fucker managed to get a hit on me out there, but at the time, I barely felt it. Killing him and his comrades was my entire focus, protecting Isabelle the drive. But now, as the adrenaline passes and I'm safe inside my house again, my body only feels agony.

Isabelle places the gauze over the cut, sparking another flinch. Her pressure is a bit rougher than she needs to be, but maybe it's her anger for earlier emerging.

"Hurts," I mumble.

"Hold still and it'll stop hurting."

"I wouldn't be hurting if you didn't run off. I told you, you're in danger and you chose not to believe me."

Angry eyes meet mine, narrowing as she reaches for the bandages on the counter. "If you weren't hiding things, I wouldn't have run away."

"Well, you shouldn't have read my cell phone," I counter. It's that damn message from Nico that destroyed tonight. We should be passed out by now, her in my arms after a sated night of fucking. An event that feels so long ago now.

Lifting higher on her knees, as though that gets her point across better, she yells, "Well, you should stop fucking lying to me."

For that, I have no response. Grumbling, I look away, hating that, ultimately, she's correct. If I told her the truth from the get-go, the message from Nico wouldn't have started this whole thing.

I take the tape from the counter and rip off strips, which I hand to her. After four, she lifts to her feet and returns to the sink to rinse the bloodied cloth. I follow her up, taking the cloth from her. She's done enough.

"Don't. It's fine. I'll deal with it in the morning." They'll go in the trash anyway. Reaching behind me, I grab a fresh cloth and run it beneath the hot water. "My turn," I murmur, shifting her body to face me. Brushing her hair off her shoulder, I wipe the cloth over the dried blood I stained her skin with.

After murdering the three assholes, I needed to hold her. To ensure she was safe. The fresh blood on my hands was secondary until I noticed it being smeared on her pale skin.

I clean her up, all with her heavy, watchful gaze on me, and when I'm finished, I drop it into the sink alongside mine and lead her into the bedroom. The moment we enter, she stops walking, even as I head for my closet to get out of these clothes.

"Rafael, what happened changes nothing. You're still lying to me."

I return to the bedroom with only a pair of shorts on and holding a shirt before returning to her side and removing her own clothing. She helps me a little, moving her limbs as I need, and surprisingly accepts my hand as I lead her toward the bed. I throw my shirt over her head, enjoying the look of her in my clothing.

"Rafael—"

"Tomorrow," I interrupt. "It's been a long day, and a longer night. Your body has gone through a lot." Nudging her into the bed, I force her down, in the spot I had her stretched out only an hour ago. I pull the blanket over her, before taking my spot on the bed again.

I don't ask when I slide closer to her and wrap my arm around her waist, pulling her against my chest. I stroke my hand over her hip, thinking this is how earlier should have gone. I would have cleaned her up and then slept the night before waking her with my tongue between her legs in the morning.

It's funny how a simple text can change so much.

"Tomorrow," she agrees, voice firm. "But you're not getting out of this."

"Tomorrow afternoon," I counter. "I have business, so I'll leave you at my family's mansion while I do so. We'll talk afterwards."

Her head whips up, her hair smacking me in the face. "This business. Is it something to do with me?"

Yes. Your old nanny, in fact. Keeping my voice low and murmured, I answer, "Tomorrow, Belle. I'll answer it all tomorrow. Sleep." Stroking my hand over her bare hip, I repeat, "Just forget about the past hour for me, and sleep. Let me hold you."

She doesn't respond, but nestles in deeper, which tells me I've won. Burying my head into her sweet hair, I pass out almost immediately.

～

What feels like much too early, I'm woken by an elbow in my side. Blinking my eyes, I expect to find hints of sunlight peeking in, telling me it's morning, but the room is still pitch dark.

In my arms, Isabelle twitches. Her hand thumps against the mattress at her side and her hips move, as though trying to push me away, but I only hold firmer.

"Isabelle."

"Daddy," she gasps, throwing her arm out into the air. "No...Daddy...no. Doctor, no. No needle..."

Her body slumps and a light snore fills the room as sleep takes her again.

It might have brought her back to dreamland, but for me, I'm more wide awake than ever. Stunned silent, I study the woman in my arms, her frazzled, sleep-filled words penetrating my mind again and again. Lodging there in a way that makes me murderous.

Daddy. Doctor. Needle.

What the fuck did you do to her, Maurice? What secrets are buried in this woman's head? What does she know that she doesn't even realize she does?

For the remainder of the night, my sleep is much lighter than it should be. Her words continue to replay in my head, and my need to ensure she doesn't have another episode too pressing.

It becomes yet another question I have for her ex-nanny.

I sabelle barely spares three words to me until I park in front of my family home. Her gaze takes in the massive house again, a slight shake to her head.

"Still can't believe there's people in this world who get to live like this."

"Believe it."

Taking her hand, I walk her up the front steps and into the, thankfully, empty foyer. I lead her down the hall, taking the first left toward the library.

"No brother this time?"

"Not for you." After leaving her at the library, I'll go see Nico.

"So where are you taking me?"

"Somewhere you'll love."

A room I've barely entered in all my years of living here, since books and I never were compatible. But this time, I feel excited to be going there and I know it's for only one reason—one person's reaction.

At the door, I drop her hand. "Close your eyes."

Instead, she rolls them, frowning. "Seriously?"

"Dead serious. Close your eyes. Believe me."

Huffing, she obeys me, lifting both hands over her eyes.

"No peeking," I tell her as I grasp her elbow and open the door, entering first, leading her in.

"Can I look now?"

"No. Stay here." I quickly circle the room, switching on every lamp—and my mother insisted on a lot in here—so she can get the full effect. Lastly, I yank on the golden rope by the window, using my weight to pull open the massive curtain covering the floor-to-ceiling window.

Returning to her side, I'm suddenly not only anxious, but nervous. A stupid emotion, but she's spoken so highly of books and reading and even about visiting this library that I can't wait to show her.

I step behind her and hold her wrists as I lower her hands back to her side, whispering in her ear, "Open your eyes."

Her gasp tells me she's obeyed. The way she immediately moves forward through the room, head rolling as she takes in every inch of the massive, vaulted ceiling room. I've never understood the power books can have over a person until seeing Isabelle standing in my family's library.

The wonder in her expression as she turns to me. The soft tone she uses to speak. "This is...holy shit. I might work in a library, but *this* is the real deal. The classic, home library."

Scanning the old shelves, I tell her, "I doubt there's anything in here you'd like."

"Doesn't matter." She wanders to the sitting area in the centre of the room. A U-shaped area with three separate leather couches and a lamp and table beside each one. "Still a dream. This place is beautiful."

"Good." I approach, needing to be closer. After yesterday, Isabelle is rightly wary of me, and last night might not have brought us to a good place. But she's so undeniably sexy right now and leaving without touching her would be a fucking crime. I tip her chin up, waiting until she stops studying the room to grant me an ounce of her attention. "Then you won't mind if I leave you here while I go conduct my business?"

"You're kidding, right?" She reaches into the small bag she's brought with her and retrieves her Kindle. "You've brought a reader into a home library with her Kindle and hundreds of books to entertain her. You could leave for a month, and I probably wouldn't notice."

"You wound me." I smirk, rubbing my hand down her back, pausing at her hip. "I'll have to leave you with something, so you *do* notice I've gone."

I nip her lips, urging her to kiss me back, granting her the control. She does, pressing hers to mine, her mouth softening as I take the kiss deeper, walking her backwards until I have her propped against the nearest couch.

Her arms wrap around my neck, her legs wind my waist. As much as I'd love to fuck her right here and now, and I vow to soon, I release her, backing away with heavy pants as she stares at me through calculatingly, light eyes.

"Maybe I'll notice you're gone after a few hours then." She shrugs playfully. "Only a few."

Rubbing a hand over my mouth, I back away in my search for answers before my dick commands me to finish what I started.

"I'll return in a few hours. Happy reading."

Then I escape the library in my search for answers about this compelling woman, aware that when I return, I'll be flipping her life upside down.

28

ISABELLE

I'm stuck in this weird limbo in which I want to read, but I also want to touch every single book in here. No doubt, there's a bunch of classics, but still. To say I'm in one of *these* kinds of libraries, just sitting, breathing in the air, is like a dream.

A strange dream. A dream in which the guy is keeping secrets about my own life from me, kills people, and still, I stupidly want a repeat of last night. It's the only reason I kissed him goodbye because even when I'm wary, Rafael makes it easy to forget the bigger picture.

My silly, confused heart. I suppose that's what sex does. Creates a connection between two people. I don't know how to go on from last night. My life isn't a joke and Rafael needs to stop treating me as such. Fucking him was probably a mistake. *Should* be a mistake...if my nerves weren't telling me otherwise.

If that kiss before he left didn't tell me otherwise.

Shaking my head of anything to do with Rafael, I push off the couch he perched me on and walk to one end of the library, curious to see what kinds of books are kept on these massive shelves. They stretch far above me, nearly to the ceiling, and I wonder if they have one of those rolling ladders somewhere to get up there.

For now, I only scan the lower shelves.

Shakespeare. Between high school English classes and my Bachelors, I've done so many essays on his plays.

Jane Austin. Classics for a reason.

Charlotte Brontë. *Wuthering Heights* is my secret love.

Steinbeck. Personally, not a fan.

Mary Shelley. A woman whose novel is probably the only non-romance book I've enjoyed.

Chaucer. Difficult poet but intriguing work.

Robert Frost. I like his poetry.

Elizabeth Barrett Browning. The history behind her name is interesting.

Then a whole lot of non-fiction books split into eras and countries—Ancient Greece, Ancient Egypt, prehistoric times, Victorian Era...the list goes on.

Once I'm satisfied in my study of the literature, I return to the sitting area, flopping on the couch, and retrieve my Kindle from where I tossed it. I unlock it, but instead of disappearing in the book, I scan the space again.

Dad was in this house, right near this room. I wonder if he was ever allowed inside the library. If he ever thought of me. What would he say knowing I was here? Happy for me to be immersed in such a lovely space or concerned that I ended up wrapped in the life he clearly tried to distance me from?

Dad, I miss you. But I don't know what to think anymore.

Shaking my head before the feelings get too heavy, I return to the fantasy world I abandoned earlier.

It feels like only five minutes pass when the door opens again.

"You're back already?" I ask, without looking away from the fight scene on my screen.

"Depends. Was I the one you were waiting on?"

That's not Rafael's voice, Blinking away from my Kindle, I look up to see two women wandering into the library. The first one I recognize. Della, Nico's wife. Who was in Nico's office and stood in the hallway with me when the brothers had to talk.

Behind her, a redhead trails. She shares many of the same features as Della, but her shoulders curve inwards, less confident than the woman I assume to be her sister.

"Rafael mentioned he left you in here."

"Did he leave?" He had said something about stopping by his brother's office.

"Yeah, a moment ago. He's estimating to be gone about two hours."

As they approach, I wonder how much they're aware of me, my life, and especially what Rafael's doing. Perhaps they can be useful in my search for answers. So, I inquire, "Did he say where he's going?"

Della pauses by the nearest couch, going still for a moment as her lips roll together. "No, no idea. It's all between him and my husband."

She's lying. But I won't probe the subject since she's not who my issue is with.

Della takes the seat directly across from me and the other woman lowers beside her, shooting me a small, tentative smile.

"Just figured we'd pop in to say hi. I don't know if you remember me, but I'm Della, Nico's—"

"Wife." I nod. "Yeah, hard to forget you."

She smirks. "This is my sister, Ariella."

Her sister, Ariella, smiles again and waves once but doesn't say anything.

"How have you...been? Without your—" Della's lips fold

together again, her eyes narrowing as she searches for the kindest words she can manage in her attempt to ask how I'm faring after my father's death.

"Fine," I respond.

Della nods slowly. "Well, we wanted to pop in and offer our company. We know all about grief and losing a parent." She shares a sad look with her sister. "So we know it can be hard being alone. Wanted to see if you needed an escape or anything. Rafael doesn't need to know we're stealing you away."

There's a lot to unpack in her words, and the most noticeable is they also lost a parent. I wonder which one, and how long ago. How long does it take for the pain to fade—or does it ever?

Pushing through to focus on the ending of her statement, I hold up my Kindle. "Believe me. He's doing me a favour by giving me a few hours of silence."

Ariella finally makes a small sound, an amused huff. She pokes her sister's arm, angling her head back to the door.

Della nods. "Got it. My mistake then. Sorry. We'll leave you be, but we're around if you want company."

"Thanks."

They're being kind, and while this interaction reminded me, once again, how shitty I am at talking to people, it also has me biting down on a smile. It'd be nice to spend time with other people...I think. Maybe. I'm not sure what I want anymore.

Ariella waves as she trails behind her sister toward the door. Della peeks back once before shutting it, a curious expression on her face, but I don't question it, because I don't really want to.

Rafael is enough. Not sure I can handle the influx of curious stares from his sister-in-law.

29
RAFAEL

The first time I met Isabelle, when I went to Maurice's house expecting to find a child, my gut was churning with the unfortunate tasks of being a capo.

This time, as I stand in front of the address Nico had given me, I'm met with a similar sensation but for different reasons. Marie Potts might know nothing useful, but she also might know a lot. For Isabelle, a child back then, it was easy to miss what was in front of her—her father's career. But a grown woman working for him would be more aware. Marie could provide answers.

My family's answer but Isabelle's horror.

Striding up the small pathway, I knock on the light blue door. Based on the car in the driveway, she's home.

Within a moment, I hear steps on the other side, so I remove my sunglasses, sliding them on top of my head. The door opens and an elderly, grey-haired woman fills the entrance-way. Her flowery blouse catches in the slight breeze.

"Hello," she politely greets.

"Marie Potts," I state, informing her I know exactly who she is. "My name is Rafael Corsetti. I'm hoping we can talk for a few minutes."

Gone is the kindness, immediately replaced by dread and she throws the door into my face. A quick arm out stops it as I step closer to the entranceway, willing to fight my way inside. Unlike Isabelle, who had to Google my name, it's clear Marie Potts did indeed know who Maurice worked for.

"I'm not asking." I plaster on my best cold grin to emphasize my words. "I have questions relating to Maurice Dupont and his daughter. You worked for them for a while."

Her hand falters on the door, her dark eyes widening a fraction more. "Is Isabelle okay?"

"She's..." I search for an appropriate word. "Alive."

Fear flickers in her gaze again. "And Maurice?"

"Not alive."

Her arm drops by her side, her gaze lowering. She's softening, which tells me I won't need to push my way in after a few more quick words.

"You obviously know who I am, who my family is, and what we can do. For the sake of Isabelle's safety, I need to ask you a few questions."

Resigned, her shoulders lower a fraction. She nods glumly and holds up a finger. "Fine. Yes, come in, but stay here for a second please." She gives me her back, shutting the door halfway as she calls through the house, "Kip, could you go upstairs and play for a bit?"

"But, Grandma, my show!"

"We'll rewatch it later. I have a guest and I need you to go upstairs for a few minutes please. Go, Kip."

Smaller steps tread through the room behind the door and eventually fade away. So there's a child here.

She returns a moment later, opening the door wider and gesturing me inside. "My grandson is visiting."

I move past her and into the living room that's decorated with way too much pink and lace. A boutique threw up in this room obviously.

"You can sit." She gestures to a flower-patterned couch, while she lowers herself into a matching recliner.

"Thanks," I say, but prop myself against the wall, staring at her from across the room instead. "I'll stand. I don't suspect this will take long. Isabelle told me you were her nanny for her entire life growing up."

"That's correct. Since she was four."

That magic age again. The age neither she nor Maurice existed before. "How did you end up working for them?"

She shrugs before reaching for a mug on the side table. After taking a small sip, she murmurs, "How does anyone get a job? I was a part-time nanny for another family and had an ad up for my services to get another family on my workload. Maurice reached out to me. Offered me four times the amount of money if I became his full-time worker—housekeeper and nanny. The other family was lovely but hard times, so I took the job."

"Why you, if you were already working elsewhere?"

Her eyes narrow over her mug. "What are you implying, Corsetti?"

"That it's odd to hire a woman who already has a job. Why you out of everyone?"

She shrugs one shoulder. "Resume speaks for itself. Not entirely sure why and I never asked."

Fair enough. "Well, you obviously know who I am."

"I make it my mission to be aware of the danger in this city. Maurice worked for you."

"Yes," I answer. "Right around the time he hired you. Around the time he moved to the city. When Isabelle was four. There's a lot of change in that short while."

Her brow arches. "Isn't that what accompanies moving? Change. New job, home, so on."

"Fair. What do you know of Maurice's past?"

Wariness flickers in her gaze again and she reclines back, pretending not to be affected by my question, but the lie is so plain on her face. "He was a good father. Always came home in the evening to his daughter. Isabelle and I had grown close over the years, and I still care for that girl very much. I stopped working for them when she turned eighteen and she started fighting against having someone constantly around."

"Did she already have her scars when you were hired?"

Marie bobs her head. "They looked really fresh when I first met Isabelle."

Fuck. Again, I wonder what Maurice was up to back then, recalling what she was crying about in her sleep last night.

"Did Maurice ever say anything about them?"

She shakes her head.

Going down my mental list of questions, I move onto my next topic. "Do you know why Maurice's past is unknown prior to seventeen years ago? I'm talking, federal police can't pull any records on him." I shove off the wall, slowly ambling toward the old woman. "Before then, neither he nor Isabelle had existed under their current names."

Marie stares into her mug.

Bingo. Poker player, she is not.

I stop in front of her. "Ms. Potts, you know, so skip the denial phase. The information you're holding *will* save her life."

Marie looks up at me, resignation making her sigh. "Is Isabelle safe?"

"Yes," I answer. "Only because she's under my protection. Maurice has information we believe our enemies silenced him for keeping, and now, they're targeting Isabelle. Anything we can find on the strange history of the Duponts could indicate what Maurice was hiding, which could help us unearth our enemies." I pause, lowering into a crouch, to her height. "Ms. Potts, everyone wins in this case."

"What would Maurice know that would be so crucial?"

I lift a shoulder. "I'm hoping you'd be able to tell me that."

Staring into my eyes, honesty rolls from her as she shakes her head once. "I don't know anything about his past. Only that he worked for your family, but not why or where he came from."

"Does the name Stefano De Falco sound familiar?"

She shakes her head.

Still progress. "You don't know why Maurice got inducted as a soldier in my family, or where he lived before here," I summarize, "but you do know *who* he was?"

Her next breath is no more than a shudder, followed by a nod. She takes a very large chug from her mug, as though it's much-needed liquor. "For Isabelle," she starts. "I was cleaning the house one day when I found something beneath Maurice's mattress. I was flipping it, you see, as I was washing the bedsheets. It was a birth certificate. I freaked out, because the names didn't match, and I was worried Isabelle was a kidnapped child. I confronted Maurice about it." She sucks in a burst of air, while I'm seconds away from shaking the truth from her. The need to know makes it difficult to sit still, shuffling from one foot to the other. "He didn't tell me where he came from, only that he was running from people who would harm Isabelle. Honestly, I figured that's where she had gotten the slices on her face."

Except it was "Daddy" she had yelled last night.

"He admitted to changing Isabelle's and his name, to ensure their protection. But I memorized the names on that birth certificate. All of them. Mother, father, and child. To this day, I can't forget them."

"What are they?" I demand, leaning forward.

"Isabelle's real name is Rose. Maurice is Lawrence Haynes. Isabelle's mother is Ivy Haynes."

Rose Haynes.

Belle's face fills my mind, trying to match her birthname to her. Rose. It doesn't fit. I can't picture *ma belle* as anything but Isabelle.

Marie reaches for me, a surprisingly strong grasp latching onto my wrist. "Mr. Corsetti, I think I helped raise a girl who was kidnapped by her father. I was terrified to investigate. So many times that first year, I almost went to the police to report them. But as the days, weeks, and months passed, Maurice hadn't done anything to harm her. She was a happy child. I homeschooled her, raised her, spent every single day with her. As the years passed, that birth certificate became a memory I was able to block out. Whoever Rose was, she's not Isabelle."

Except she should have been Rose. Rose with a different life.

"Had he ever said anything about her mother?"

"That she left them."

The same story he fed Belle.

"But I found it strange, if she left them, why change their names."

My sentiments exactly.

I lift to my feet, suddenly eager to leave, to call Nico. We have names to investigate. It shouldn't be long before the RCMP can pull them up and discover who the Haynes are, the entire story of Ivy, and why Isabelle isn't there anymore.

"This information is invaluable, Ms. Potts. Thank you."

She follows me up, trailing behind. "Mr. Corsetti, before you tell that girl, think of the life you're about to destroy."

That I'm about to tell her she's not even real.

"Believe me. It's all I've been thinking about."

I exit the house with a different sensation churning my stomach.

~

Nico hands me a glass of scotch, and then Rosen, where he sits in the seat beside me. My brother takes his seat at his desk, kicking back as the two of them wait for me to speak. To report on what I learned.

But, fuck...to even think it is a lot. To know the woman living in my house has a past I'm scared to learn myself.

Staring into the amber drink and not at either of the men—my brother nor my closest friend and ally—I push out, "Haynes. Rose Haynes is Isabelle's birth name. Her parents are Lawrence and Ivy."

Nico's glass thuds to his desk as he leans forward, jotting the names on a nearby notepad. "That explains why we can't find anything on Maurice and Isabelle prior to her being four. Maurice is obviously running from something and decided changing their names was the best way to hide."

"I'll reach out right away," Rosen says, already pulling out his phone. "It shouldn't take them long to dig up their pasts."

Both are so eager for the truth, when I'd rather shove it away and pretend to never have heard it.

"This is good, brother," Nico murmurs. "If we know where they're from, there might be a connection to De Falco we've missed." He lifts his own phone. "I'm texting the names to Flynn. Rozelyn's been tight-lipped against his torture but maybe this will loosen her mouth." Focusing on me, he adds, "You need to tell Isabelle, Raf. No hiding this. We still don't know for certain she isn't playing us. Look at what happened with Della. Women can be great fucking liars, and this could be a trap."

Clenching the glass, I remind myself to continue holding it before I heave it at my brother. "I'm not you, Nico. And Isabelle isn't Della. She's innocent."

"We don't know—"

"*I* know." I lift my eyes, staring at my brother with a challenge. "I can tell she doesn't know who she is. Trust me. She doesn't know where she got the scars. She knows *nothing* about her father."

There's a beat of silence in which Rosen and Nico glance at each other. Then, Rosen says, "Holy shit. You're falling for her."

"No," I counter quickly. I can't be. We all knew what her living with me would mean and it isn't romance. "I'm not. I just have some fucking empathy."

Nico smirks, folding his arms over his chest. "That so?"

Ignoring his jab, I pace backwards in my thoughts, returning to a fact my rant touched on. "Her scars. I think Maurice is behind them. We keep saying they look drawn, and I think that's exactly what happened. They're not done by accident."

"What makes you think so?" Rosen asks.

"She woke me with a nightmare last night. Mumbling something about her father, a doctor, and a knife."

Nico and Rosen both curse. Nico sighs, rubbing the back of his neck. "Her subconscious is aware of something at the very least. Maybe digging up her past will reveal what happened to her."

That's exactly what I fear.

30
ISABELLE

The next time the library door opens, I know it's Rafael. I could tell by the changing air. The stifling heat that ripples over my form, even as I pretend to ignore his advances and continue reading.

The fantasy book has gotten *hot*. So much so that my thighs have rubbed together a few times over the past hour.

Rafael's steps take him to the backside of the couch, where he trails his fingers until connecting with my neck. Brushing aside my hair, he bends, crouching behind me until his face is in my neck, tickling me with his breath.

I still pretend to ignore him, even as the words on my Kindle blur and become unfocused.

"So," he mumbles into my neck, flicking his tongue against my pulse, "have you missed me?"

"Who are you again?" I joke, turning my head into his, holding up my Kindle. "Told you. Reader. I've been occupied."

He hums into my skin. "I see that. I just read the first line, and I must say, I'm quite a fan."

I'm in the middle of a sex scene, so of course he would be.

"Read to me, Belle."

"Why?"

His fingers drift along my collarbone. "Because I asked nicely."

"I asked you to tell me what you're hiding," I counter, "and you still haven't." Turning my head, I catch his eye, lifting my expression in a *duh* expression. "We have bigger stuff to talk about."

"Ah, but you didn't ask nicely." With his hands, he straightens my head, forcing my eyes back onto my book. "We will talk, but I first want you to read to me. For me, Isabelle. Pause everything and let's just be for the moment before you hate me."

That's not exactly reassuring.

"Trust me, I'll ensure you enjoy it too."

I'm sure, I think wryly, before jumping back into the book, starting at the latest sentence.

"With his hand in my hair, he wraps the strands around his fist and holds me in a way that arches my back. He takes his hard cock into his free hand and taps it against my lips. 'Open up.'"

Rafael's fingers trail my collarbone to the centre of my chest before dipping lower, disappearing beneath the top of my sundress. His lips trace an invisible pattern against my neck and beneath my ear. My head tilts, allowing him better access, my body ensuring he doesn't stop what he's doing.

"He shoves his cock into my mouth, using my hair to keep me steady. He's rough, but I'm so fucking turned on, I love it. Love the feeling of him stretching my mouth, in my throat. He strokes my neck, feeling himself."

Rafael's hand comes up around my throat. "Right here," he whispers. "That's where he's touching. That's how deep down her throat he is. You'd look beautiful choking on my cock."

I want that. I'd love to see how much of Rafael I can swallow without choking.

When I return to reading, my mouth is a bit dryer, my words more spaced out.

"'You look lovely, little fae,' he murmurs, stroking my throat. 'Taking me so good.'

"His words make my thighs clench together and I moan against his length."

Rafael returns to his path down my top as his other hand goes to my thigh, inching my dress up. I don't fight my body as my legs spread.

Rafael hums again, licking a line up the side of my neck. "Keep reading. I want to see where this scene goes."

Is he serious? Not bothering to fight, because he'll win, I continue:

"His thrusts increase, his noises filling the room. My clit is throbbing, and I reach between my legs to stroke myself, needing my orgasm as much as I crave tasting his—"

Rafael's fingers shift toward my centre, his actions closely aligning that of the character, and I have to *really* concentrate on the words now.

"He growls and in the next movement, he's lifting me in his arms and lowering me on his cock. He's so big, my pussy stretches to accommodate him. The feeling making my body become his. His to claim. To mark. Bride. Captive. It doesn't matter."

Rafael's fingers lightly tug on my panties. "Remove these."

Setting down the Kindle, I do, kicking them off before picking up the book again, eager to return to where we were, for Rafael to continue his slow seduction.

"He growls in my ear. His thrusts are painfully impactful, and I'll feel them into tomorrow. Next week. Forever.

"'Feel how well you take me. You're fucking mine. You're done. Never leaving here.'"

Rafael circles my clit with his thumb, petting me with two fingers. My core is soaked from his touch and the book, and he slips them inside me as his teeth scrape my neck.

"Keep reading, *ma belle,* or I'll have to end this. Let's see if you can make it to the end of the scene."

"Rafael..." From his place behind me, he's at the perfect angle to hit the spot just right.

"Keep reading."

With every stroke of his fingers, words become more blurry.

"His words imprint into my skin, a promise. I don't want to leave. I want—"

I moan, Rafael's thrusts at the perfect pace. My hold on the Kindle gets weak, my muscles fighting to remain present. When Rafael makes his own growling noise, I'm compelled to continue reading.

"I only want this. And right now, I want to come. I want his claiming bite. To feel his cock everywhere. With the hold he still has on my hair, he arches me back, my nipples pointing to the night sky."

In response, Rafael pinches my nipples from where he's massaging my chest. I whimper, pushing my hips into his hand. I'm right there—seconds from orgasming.

"He takes one between his teeth, biting down as his cock pounds into me from below.

"'Right here,' he mumbles into my chest. 'This is where my mark is going. Right where you'll be forever reminded who owns your body. Your breasts. Your pussy. You.'

"'Yes.' It ends on a moan—"

"Yes!" My own moan fills the air as Rafael's onslaught takes my body to the edge. Makes me toss my Kindle to the side, my back arching off the couch, hips raising to keep the sensation going.

The door opens, my high stolen from me as the same tall

soldier from last night enters, his attention on his phone. "Hey, Capo—" He cuts off, his eyes bulging as he catches Rafael's fingers inside me. "O-oh, sorry." He takes a step backwards, but Rafael's command halts him.

"Stay." In my ear, he whispers, "Doesn't that sound nice, Belle? Letting my soldier watch me claim your little pussy."

I don't know. My thighs clench together around his hand, hiding myself from the stranger. It's one thing to watch but to *be* watched by someone Rafael works with every day, who'll leave here with these memories...

It's enticing but nerve-wracking.

Rafael's lips trail down my neck, shattering previous anxieties. He grips my hair and forces my head straight, so I'm facing the soldier who looks stuck somewhere between shock and lust. His hand, still holding his phone, lowers to his side and he shuts the door, ensuring no one else will interrupt. At least there's that.

"Let him watch you. Let him see your face." Rafael smiles into my skin, nipping and licking at my neck as his fingers return to that pace from earlier. "What do we let him see, Belle? How about you tug that little dress up and let him see your pussy."

I do slowly, questioning my sanity by allowing a stranger to watch me get finger-fucked. I fold the dress up on my lap and inch my legs farther apart. Apparently not enough because Rafael releases my hair to grab my thighs, forcing them farther apart.

The guy's eyes light up, focused on one place only—between my legs. I should want to close them, to hide from him, but I can't deny this is hot. This heats me in a way different than anything Rafael and I have done so far. The illicitness of it, the exhibitionism...

I moan, my head falling onto Rafael's shoulder, and this

time, he lets me. Rafael rises a fraction, his fingers changing their angle as he takes my mouth in a possessive, claiming kiss.

He's all I taste. All I know. All I feel.

And yet, as the soldier's gaze strokes over my bare skin, following the trajectory of Rafael's fingers sinking into my core, I know I'm not all Rafael's. Even for this moment, he's sharing me.

Rafael's tongue strokes over mine as his fingers push inside. He pulls them out for a second before adding a third, stretching me wider than I've been so far, making me whimper. I'm impossibly full; yet, it's not impossible, since he's making it happen.

Rafael releases my mouth, his heavy pants shared with my own. "I think you're making him turned on, *ma belle.* I want you to come now. I want you to be *mine* and show him what he's not having."

When he takes my mouth again, it's to swallow my orgasm. My moans, my whimpers, as my body convulses, hips rocking into his hand. My hands claw the couch beside me, body frenzied as I come.

"Leave."

I know his command isn't for me, and only when the door opens and shuts again does Rafael lift me from the couch, placing me on the back, where he had me earlier. Frenzied, he undoes his own pants, stroking his cock, once, twice, before reaching into his wallet and pulling out a condom. He slips it on quickly, lining up with my pussy, the couch giving us the perfect angle.

He glides right inside me, filling me, sparking my insides that have barely cooled from the two orgasms back-to-back.

"My men shouldn't be allowed to see everything," he comments, explaining why he sent the man away. "But you did so beautifully, Belle. Wherever the next chapter takes us, I need you in my club at least once. I *need* you in those rooms."

"Ye*s*." The word ends on a hiss, my nails curling into his skin as I ride his cock right into another orgasm. My own ripples into his, and with a low cry, he plunges into me a final time before removing himself.

I don't know the honesty behind my words, if I mean them, because I get the sense Rafael's about to wreck my life and being with him in Eden might be the least rational thing to do.

Rafael cups my hands, his heavy breaths the only sound in the room. "Why are you so addicting, Belle? You make it impossible not to tell you the truth."

"I feel the same," I admit. "I woke up this morning, hating you. Last night proved I might be in danger, but that's not the entire reason you've brought me into your life. Don't lie about that." I study the nakedness of his eyes. "You could have posted a dozen guards outside my house if it was simply being in jeopardy. There's another reason I'm in your life. That you're in mine. And yet, I'm the idiot who spreads her legs for you."

"They *are* very beautiful legs." He drags his fingers up my thigh. "I ever tell you I have a thing for legs?"

"No." I giggle, rubbing a hand down his shirt, amusement fading quickly, the conversation bringing reality back to the forefront of what matters. "I told myself I wouldn't do this with you again until you tell me everything. So, if that says something about how obsessed *I* am with you. Stupid, right."

"Well. I'm thankful for your stupid decisions, as you're referring to them being, because after today, you could very well hate me."

He helps me off the couch, keeping my hand in his, like he's too scared to let me go.

"Let's go home. If you want the truth, I want it to be where you can murder me without my family coming down on you."

I know he's joking, but a part of it sounds like the truth. As in, I'll *want* to after this. I'll want to kill him.

I'll hate him.

I should. Rafael Corsetti has brought nothing but pain to my life since the moment he entered it, and yet, he's also made me happier than I've ever been.

And I'm not ready for that to end.

31
RAFAEL

The elevator to my condo dinging and opening are the worst sounds I've heard all day. Even when I drove slower than usual from the mansion to home, I couldn't completely avoid coming here.

Belle was a means to an end, and while we're still not there yet, I feel like we're closer. As if the conversation I'm about to have with her will be it—the end.

She walks straight into the living room and drops onto the same couch she occupied the first evening we stayed here. When I first had her read to me, and essentially, imagined the outcome being similar to what we did an hour ago.

Gone is the girl from the library. The one who bandaged my side last night. The one I've spent the days with. Returned is the version from yesterday morning. Angry, cold, expression drawn as she stares at me, waiting for the truths she deserves.

"The games need to end, Rafael," she starts as I take the adjacent couch. "Is protecting me the entire reason I'm here?"

"No."

"Then why am I?"

Throughout the car ride, I debated how much or how little to tell her. My decision: all of it.

"My sister-in-law, Della, was sent to us on orders from her stepfather, the leader of a rival mafia. She was meant to lure and trap Nico. We later learned that his vengeance is the cumulation of years of anger. A deal was struck and broken between him and his first wife, and my family. After we learned who Della was, her stepfather, Stefano De Falco, went into hiding." I pause, looking up from my hands. "Does that name sound familiar?"

"Not at all."

I didn't think so, so it's a last-ditch effort. "De Falco has two daughters. One drugged my sister recently. She's now in our basement."

"What's she doing there?"

I give her a pointed look. "Do you really want me to explain?"

She doesn't speak, but her lips form a silent word: *Oh*.

"Right after my sister woke up from her drug-induced coma, your father asked for a meeting."

Belle leans forward, her expression softening at the mention of him. It shoots a pain through my chest I force away.

"He was scared, Belle. Mumbling about you. In all his years of service, we hadn't known he had a daughter. He was killed before he could tell us anything."

She blinks, her eyes beginning to fill with tears, which reminds me once again, I'm speaking of her father's death so easily. When death is common in life, it's simpler to speak about. But for Isabelle...

I move to the couch she's occupying and lean closer, but she angles herself out of my reach. She's shying away, but while I still have parts of her, I reach again, stealing her hand and locking it between mine. My thumb strokes over her pulse. She sneers, tries to pull away, but gives up very quickly.

"We assumed a child, which is why when I showed up on your doorstep that day, I presumed you were the babysitter. I wasn't expecting—"

"Me. So Dad was begging you to protect me."

"He was so worried about you. He demanded I protect you. If it helps, know that the last minutes of his life, his thoughts were only on you."

She looks away, her throat moving with her swallow. "So I'm here because you made a deal with my father?"

"Partially," I admit. "The other part of it being, he was killed before he could tell us what he wanted to. We were wondering if you were privy to your father's secrets."

Her hand stiffens and she tries to yank it away, but I hold tighter. She doesn't win the fight, but her chilling tone freezes my insides. "So that's it," she breathes through her realization. "That's why I'm here. You couldn't care less about keeping me safe from my father's killers. You want revenge on your enemy, and hoped I had the answers my father apparently did."

Yes. And no. I slide off the couch, onto my knees in front of her, showing her more vulnerability than I'm normally comfortable with. I release her hand to grasp her face, forcing her gaze onto mine. "Couldn't care less?" I repeat her ridiculous claim. "*Ma belle,* I chased after you last night. I killed three men to keep you safe. I care very fucking much about you and your safety if you haven't noticed."

Her lips part, and for a long second, she doesn't counter my comment. Whispering, she points out, "After the fact. After we...When you first showed up at Dad's door, your reasoning wasn't to protect me."

I wince, reminding myself of my own agreement not to lie

anymore, even when I want to save her from these emotions. "Yeah."

"I don't know anything. Like, literally nothing. I mean," she scoffs, her tone rising to higher levels, "I thought he worked for a damn security company. Finding out he was in the mob was a surprise."

"I determined that the moment I met you. Realized you couldn't give me answers."

"And yet," she gestures to the house, "I'm here."

Bracing myself for the next blowback, I admit, "Della once put on a good show for my brother. We couldn't be certain, not one hundred percent, you weren't lying. That you were pretending to not know."

Fury casts Isabelle's face into darkness. Her previous heartbreak secondary to the betrayal etched there. This time, she yanks her face away from my hands, lifting to her feet and pacing away, her finger rising in warning for me to remain back. Too bad I don't listen to her orders.

Trailing slowly toward her, I continue, "That's the entire truth. Of part one."

In an almost horror-movie manner, her gaze slowly lifts to me, her back stiffening as she repeats, "Part one."

"That's the truth as to what you're doing here. My job was to learn about you and see what you knew. You wondered why I was curious about your scars? Because they look drawn, and I thought they could mean something"—*and they may still*—"In the club the other day, I asked your nanny's name. Those kind of things."

"Wow." Tampering down her emotions with a pinched expression, she faces away from me again, turning until she's looking into the late afternoon Montreal skyline through the massive windows. "I can't, Rafael. I literally *can't* respond to that right now. Not rationally, anyway. Not with words that make sense."

Using the reflection of her in the glass, I approach. "We have connections to the RCMP. We had them investigate you and your father. This is part two, Belle, and only what I learned yesterday. I swear."

She scoffs.

"Look at me," I demand. "Look me in the eye and you can watch me vow on my oaths to my family I mean what I've said and what I've yet to tell you."

In the reflection, she bites down on her lip, debating to listen to me or not, but after a few seconds, she turns, positioning her back against the glass. With her attention, I rest my hand over my heart.

"You've seen the tattoo here. It's the one I got when I was sworn in. I vow on my family, on my oaths to them, my word as a Made Man, what I say is the absolute fucking truth. No more lies." I lower my hand. "The report from the federal police only returned yesterday. They found nothing on you or your father. That's what the text message from Nico was referring to."

Anger slips from her expression. Her nerves untensing. "What?"

"Nothing on Isabelle and Maurice Dupont is dated before you were four-years-old. Around the time you said you got those scars." I list everything, wanting her to piece it together too. "There is *nothing* on you two before then which tells us you...aren't you." I approach, my hands reaching for her, needing to touch her. "Belle, your father was running from something. He *took* you away from something."

She stills in my gaze. "That's impossible."

"It isn't. When I left you in the mansion today, I went to visit your old nanny."

"Marie." Her brows lace together. "She's okay?"

I shake my head. "I didn't hurt her, if that's what you're asking. She didn't know where you and your father came from, but many years prior, she found your birth certificate." I pause, letting her comprehend the weight to my words. "Your *real* birth certificate."

"No. That's impossible," she repeats, her tone more broken now. "No. She's lying. My name is Isabelle Dupont." But her eyes shift away, the tiniest fraction of doubt slipping in.

"It wasn't always." Stroking my fingers over her face right by her scars, I wish I could spare her from this pain, but we're too far into it now. "From the moment I met you, I was struck with how beautiful you are, Isabelle. Belle. *Ma belle.* So your birth name is more appropriate than either of us realized." *Still not right, though.* "Rose Haynes. Your parents are Lawrence and Ivy Haynes."

Her eyes get misty, covered with an indescribable confusion. Her jaw slackens as her head lightly shakes. The expression of a woman in firm denial.

"That's not my name," she counters, shoving out of my hold. I reach for her again, but she jumps out of the way, walking backwards, past the couch, her head continuing to shake in denial. "She's lying. I don't know why she said that but she's lying. My mother abandoned Dad and me. Dad's name is Maurice. Mine is Isabelle. Rose doesn't exist."

With every step I take, she tosses out another denial.

"That's impossible. That's..." Her voice falters, her deep breath filling the silence instead. "That's..." And again. "That's...no. Dad didn't..." Her eyes drop to my feet, her gaze lost. Confused. Her brows lower as tears spill out again. "No, you're fucking insane. Let me go, Rafael. Just let me go. You and your family only bring pain. Find my father and let us go!"

Grief. Those finicky five stages. When I met her, she immediately found herself denying his death as I reported it, and she's returned to that stage. To denying her father's death, to believing I can find him and bring him back.

"No," she repeats, her voice shuddering, her fight quickly disappearing as quivers wrack her form. "No...no!" Her back slides against the wall until she lands on the floor, still shaking her head, repeating her denial over and over. "You're all lying to me! Dad—no!"

I let her. With every "no" I take a step closer. It's not long before I'm crouching in front of her. My movement snaps something inside her and she kicks her leg, pushing me away.

"No!" Using the wall at her back, she shoves into me, kicking and throwing hit after hit at me. None of which actually hit me, but her attempt is there.

And here's the anger stage.

"No!" she screams, lifting first to her knees than her feet. "Fuck off, Corsetti. No!"

I'm a wall against her hits. A place for her frustration. A means for her emotions to fly out of her body. She'll have this, and then she'll sit down so I can finish what I need to tell her.

"Belle—"

"It's *Isabelle*," she screeches, her hands coming up as though that'll be enough to keep me back.

"Belle," I repeat again, not taking the bait of her name, as I reach for her wrists to pin them together and end her hits. She throws her body into me, trying to wrench herself free, but I hold firm. "You're still Isabelle. You're still here with me. You're who *you* want to be."

"No!" She counters my words, but I think her mind is so far gone she doesn't realize what she's fighting anymore. "*No, Rafael. This can't happen. This can't...*" Then, as though a switch was flipped, she slumps against me, her face in my chest, her weight only held up by my arms. I release her wrists, knowing she's done fighting, and instead hold her close to my body.

Sadness. Another stage.

Into my chest, she mumbles, "This can't be real. If I'm Rose, if Dad is Lawrence, that means my entire life...that means —Mom."

It means your mother might not have abandoned you. It means your life should have been different.

All I know, is everything with De Falco is secondary now. This woman officially has changed my priorities and learning why Maurice altered their life; what her life should have been, is now my focus.

"No," she says again, a whisper now. Sobs build, explode, her hands coming up to cover her face. "Impossible. Because that means Dad's been lying to me this entire time and...no. He can't be. He's dead and I miss him, but he loved me. He's not a liar. He wasn't hiding me from anything. Anyone."

Her rambles continue, the grief of what I've told her mixing with the grief of her father's death, resulting in a jumble of emotions and statements she's convincing herself of.

I reach for her legs and lift her in my arms, carrying her bridal-style toward the nearest couch, lowering us both into it. Her head is still buried in my chest as she sobs into my shirt and that's how we sit for a long time. With her shaking, quivering, crying.

"If Dad isn't Maurice, who've I been crying over?"

"Your father. He's still your father. This is why I held off trying to tell you until I had more information. That's why I visited Marie."

"So if you didn't learn my real name today, I still would be in the dark." It's a statement.

I hesitate. Probably. At some point I would have had to tell her before Nico did it himself, but I'd rather give all the truth to her, like this, than spoon-feed her pieces.

What *I* know is my gut feeling was correct. This reaction isn't fake. She truly wasn't aware of her past.

"Rose," she murmurs into my chest. "You know, that's my favourite flower."

"It's fate then."

"But why would Dad do this?" Another sob. "*Why*, Rafael?" Her tone picks up again, the anger, the heartbreak returning quickly. "I don't know what to think about this—how to feel about *him* anymore. What...why would he do this to me?"

"We're looking into it. I have the RCMP running checks on your real name, seeing what they come back with. I'll tell you as soon as we know."

"Will you?" she checks, skeptical, which is nothing less than I deserve.

But the ploy's up. What's next is determining why De Falco targeted her father, and something tells me it has to do with their real names. Something in their past must connect the two dots. It's the *only* thing that makes sense at this point.

"Unless you don't want to know, yeah, I will."

"Whatever," she mumbles, an offhanded statement, which defends her true emotions. "I fucking hate you." Even as she says it though, her hands curl into my shirt, ensuring I don't move. Actions and words that contradict one another.

"Hate me, Belle. I'm not going anywhere."

"At the beginning, I thought how you were nothing like the mafia characters I read about, but I was wrong. So damn wrong. You're exactly like them. Conniving asshole liars."

"Born and bred."

"Go die."

With the pain continuously flashing over her expression, the hateful waves rolling from her, I feel like I already am.

~

She falls asleep in my arms, crying. Eventually, I bring her to the bed, and strip all her clothes off and dress her in one of my shirts. She wakes for this part but doesn't fight me, her gaze so filled with sleep and tears, I'm not certain she was mentally present at all.

Once she's tucked into bed, I undress and do the same, claiming my side of the bed. I barely have my eyes shut before I feel her get out of the bed and exit the bedroom.

Smirking into the dark room, I give her exactly five minutes, staring at my phone as every second passes. Five minutes is enough time for her to think she's free.

I find her curled up on the couch, facing away.

"No," she denies sleepily, shoving her hand against my chest when I lift her back into my arms and immediately stalk down the hallway, to return her to bed. "No, I don't want to sleep with you. I hate you."

"You think that matters, *ma belle*? A bit of hate is a thrill, not a deterrent. Try again."

"Stop touching me."

"Besides," I continue, as though she hadn't said anything else, "it's not me you hate. It's your father."

3²
ISABELLE

Sometimes people talk about waking up on the right or wrong side of the bed.

Sometimes it's talk of making the day a "good day" —whether that be productive, fun, or some other goal they have.

Sometimes it's a New Year's resolution. To leave the outgoing year in the past and make the new better. A "new me" is how people often refer to it.

Without planning or making any such goals, I have a new me. A fresh life.

A life of a stranger.

The life of Rose Haynes. Daughter to two complete strangers.

Why, Dad? What happened back then?

I wake on the very edge of the bed, where I rolled to after Rafael returned me to the bedroom last night. Fucking determined asshole made me stay in his room. He claims I don't hate him, but the thing is, I do. I fucking do. Before Rafael Corsetti came into my life, I was happy. Fine, at the very least. I had a father, a job, my own apartment. My own life. A quiet, unexciting life, but it was mine.

And since he's entered my world, I've learned my father is dead. The same father who apparently stole me away from my home, from my mother, and gave us both new lives. *I* don't exist. Everything I am, everything Isabelle Dupont is, is false. A lie. Deception in its worst form because it deceived the very person it was also protecting. And somehow, almost worse than all that, Rafael gave me himself. Parts of him that make my heart a confused, rattled mess, unable to navigate the maze it's trapped inside.

Where am I supposed to go from here? No matter what Rafael learns about my past, it doesn't change the fact that I have one. I have a past and a present, which conflict with one another.

Which one do I choose?

A past with a mother. Dad always said she abandoned us, but then spoke fondly of her too. It's confused me, but now, I think I get it. In my gut, Mom didn't leave us. *We* left *her*.

Which means, somewhere in this world, my mother—the woman I've never spent more than a moment thinking about, opting not to waste that energy on a person who didn't want me—might be out there, *missing* me. Does she know where I've gone, who I've become? Or is she as lost and as puzzled as I am over Dad's actions?

I've never felt more at a loss.

With a sigh that really does nothing to ease me, I roll from the bed, scanning the empty room. No Rafael. Maybe he's officially given up on me. After all, he's finished with me, right? I have no useful information. He kept me around to learn what my father knows, which is a dead end. At this point, the sooner he gets out of my life, the better. He's brought too much misery to ever forget him.

I don't bother dressing in my own clothes and instead wander down the hall, still in his shirt. Rafael stands at the counter, slicing fruit, dressed in only a pair of grey jogging pants. Such a domestic activity after destroying my life. I suppose, that's a pattern of his type.

"Morning," he greets without looking up. "Hungry?"

"No." I drop onto the nearest couch, making a point to maintain my distance.

Rafael doesn't comment, still not glancing at me. He scoops sliced strawberries into a waiting bowl, grabs a fork, and marches over, shoving the bowl in my hand.

"Eat."

Holding it limply, I glare at him as he returns to the kitchen. "Commanding me doesn't exactly encourage me to obey."

"I'll force feed you if I must. Don't test me."

Scowling, I stand, taking the bowl with me to slide it across the counter, back toward him. "Who the fuck are you right now, asshole?"

His palms slam into the granite counter. His muscles ripple on his chest, his arms look larger than usual. "I'm a Corsetti. You seem to have forgotten that, Belle, but this is who I really am. When my family is at question, I become what I'm trained to be."

"So the fun guy I've met is a farce."

"Not at all. That's who I chose to be. But this," he gestures to himself, and I fight to not look at his chest, "this is who I *need* to be right now."

"Wow, sorry to inconvenience your life so much." Turning away, I mean to head back to the living room to get away from him. I only make it three steps before feeling him at my back, his heat, his very being trying to control me.

"Belle—"

"Isabelle," I correct. "Or is it Rose now?"

"Belle," he repeats, firmly ignoring me, "you act like I wanted this. There's a reason I didn't tell you right away."

I don't sit because then he'll be standing over me, and I can't handle that show of power right now. "Answer me one fucking thing, Corsetti: was fucking me part of the plan?"

If I thought I saw him ever turn angry, I was wrong. *This* is angry. This is cold death as he peers down at me, his nostrils flaring with his tight breath, his mouth a flatline as the green of his eyes ignite into a molten jade.

No one moves. Not him. Not me. Both of us in a stare down, each willing the other to break first.

And then he does, and he's so fast, his training seeping out yet again when he grasps me by my thighs and lifts me into his arms, immediately turning back toward the kitchen, where he drops me on the counter, stepping between my legs.

"Your turn," he growls, "did it feel like I was playing you when I had you spread out like a goddamn meal in my bed? When you became my every desire standing in a voyeur room of my club?" Due to the counter height, it places him right in line with my pussy, the material of his pants rubbing against my core. "When we were at the park and *you* kissed me, and I pulled away. You believed it had to do with your innocence." He scoffs, shoving his shirt up my thighs, his thumbs reaching between my legs where he lightly brushes over my core, his touch contradicting the rigidity of his words. "Not even fucking close, Belle. I would have *happily* taken you right there in that park. I pulled back because of guilt. *Guilt.*" With his emphasized word, he dips a finger inside me, his lips curling at the edges when his digit slips in easily, my betraying core already wet from his show of dominance. "Guilty because I was using you, yes. Guilty because I felt like I was playing you. Not because I didn't want you. So, tell me, *ma belle*," he curls his finger inside me, finding the button that makes hating him more difficult, "did any of that feel like I was using you?"

"I don't know," I breathe, my focus shifting to the desire he's driving through my core. For that alone, I hate him too. For making me lose my sanity—again—when I should be crying in a corner about my fucked-up life.

Rafael tugs his sweatpants down, his hard cock bouncing free. He grasps himself, slapping his cock against my pussy, sparking pleasure through my core. My head rolls back, arms struggling to keep me upright through his onslaught. Somewhere in the fog we're filling the kitchen with, I hear the sound of ripping foil.

"Tell me, Belle, was I playing you when I fucked you in my bed?"

With his question, he thrusts into me. A single plunge that takes him deep inside my core—deeper than I ever imagined he could be. A point I'll feel him for the rest of my life, and maybe that is his purpose.

I moan, rocking my hips into his movements, trying to spread my legs as wide as I can, craving him even deeper. Will there be a point I'm satisfied, where I don't need *more*?

"Tell me," he repeats. He grips my thighs, holding me still as he pounds roughly into me. So much harder than last night. Not painful—just perfect.

"I hate you," is all I manage, my statement tinged with a lie.

"Do you? Is this what your hate feels like?" He reaches between us, gathering some of my pleasure on the tip of his finger, lifting it to my face. "See how fucking wet you are? *Feel*," he thrusts forcefully, "how wet you are? If this is you hating me, I'll gladly take it."

Wrenching my face to his, he steals my mouth in a messy kiss. *We're* messy. Torn apart by my past and his lies. His exploitation of me. I was never anything to him.

"You never answered me. Was fucking me part of the plan?"

He growls, bending me over the counter and reaching past me, grabbing something out of view. "I think I answered it satisfactorily, but if it isn't a fucking enough for you, then no. No, Belle, it was *never* part of the plan. Awkward roommates for no longer than I needed you. Until I got the details of your life and could send you on your merry way. *That* was the plan." He brings a strawberry into my vision and taps my lip with it. "Open up."

In defiance, I clamp my lips together.

With a firm hold, he grips my face, squeezing my cheeks until my mouth opens into a small o, where he shoves the fruit inside. "Chew. I fucking told you you'd be eating breakfast. Before you decide to hate me for starving you, remember it was *you* who pushed away the fruit."

Despite my glare, I chew the fruit, and by the time I'm swallowing, his thrusts have become unforgiving, my back sliding against the granite countertop until my pussy grips him, not wanting to release him. He growls into my skin as he takes his final plunge, both of us falling off the edge together.

He almost instantly pulls out of me, removes the condom, and tucks himself away. With one arm around my waist, he removes me from the counter. Once I'm steady again, he hardly spares me a glance when he shoves the bowl of sliced strawberries in my hand with only a single command.

"Eat."

He turns away, heading for the garbage where he disposes of the condom, still not looking at me.

"What the fuck was that, Rafael?"

"That was me showing you that while you claim to hate me, your body says otherwise." Stopping by the sink, he washes his hands before returning to the fruit he's cutting, like we hadn't just fucked inches away from the food. "As I said last night, you're angry, and you're taking it out on me, but it's not me you should be mad at."

Slamming the bowl down, I gain his attention by nearly breaking it. "You know what, though? I am. I am because I'm only here as some convenience for you and your family."

"In case you haven't forgotten, you *are* being hunted. If the incident last night and at your house wasn't enough, by all means, leave." He waves at the windows behind us. "Leave. I'll follow you out. And we'll see how long round two takes before they find you again."

He makes me so fucking angry. How is this the same man I was laughing with the other day? The veil's dropped. I get to see Rafael Corsetti in all his assholeness.

I'm about to say something, or yell something. Either way, my mouth opens, but I'm interrupted by the buzzing of his phone, which rests on the other side of the sink. Rafael leans over to peek at the screen.

"Hm," he says after a moment. "You might want to call into work today. We have results about you and your father. About Rose and Lawrence, more specifically. We can head over right away." His bright eyes flick up, darkening as they land on the bowl in front of me. "Correction: we'll go as soon as you eat your breakfast. Wanna know your past? Eat."

"Bribery," I snarl, snatching the bowl and stomping away from the counter. "A whole new low for you."

"No. Low was being used as a punching bag last night, and then seconds after, a human Kleenex, and then reminded how much you despise me today. Before you take out the big guns, *ma belle*, remember who you're fighting."

If I could growl, I fucking would.

33
RAFAEL

So many truths. So many unveiled lies. All in the past twelve hours, but we're not done yet.

As I lead her down the hallway toward my brother's office, I'm struck with pleasurable memories of the last time we were here. When I fingered her in the library, in a place that brought her so much joy. Seeing her like that made *me* happy. I'd bring her here every single day if only to see her smile as brightly as she did in that moment.

This time, our walk is with dread. Nico didn't inform me exactly what today would involve, only that we're getting "answers," so I've assumed the RCMP has returned with updates.

Outside his office, I glance at Isabelle. So much of her life has changed since I entered it, exactly as she's claimed, but I'm merely the executioner to her peaceful world. No one's life gets to be that serene, and if they are, it's a farce. After today—after this—after *me*—Belle will need to create the new version of her life.

I open the office doors, stepping out of the way so she can

enter straight into the watchful stares of my family. Nico in his seat, Della at his right. Mother and Father on his left. To the right side of the room, Ariella, Aurora, and Rosen watch as we enter, Rosen tipping his head in a slight acknowledgement.

Everyone's here, which means this is bound to be interesting.

I lead Isabelle off to the opposite side of the room, stopping by the centre, so we're not immediately in my brother's line of sight. She stands closer to me than before, realizing that of everyone here, I'm the least of her worries.

Father lifts his nose in the air, glaring at the girl beside me. He still thinks she knows something. Today could prove otherwise. I move to her other side, blocking her from his intense gaze and based on the slight raise of his brows, he knows exactly why I've switched positions.

"We're here," I state the obvious. "Nico, you've heard something? Was it necessary for all this?" I nod my head at the fact that every single one of our immediate family is here.

Nico tosses his phone onto his desk before standing, and coming around the other side of the desk, where he leans, crossing his arms. "Believe me, yes, it does. Because all our lives have been affected by De Falco. Seems when throwing the Dupont's real name at Rozelyn, she's decided the game's up."

At that very second, before I have a chance to process his statement, the door opens again and Flynn stalks into the office. His leather cut and blood and dirt-stained jeans contrast the suits the Corsettis dress in, as everyday attire.

He scowls as he scans the room, his distaste for being around multiple people becoming obvious in his agitated steps. Our enforcer's trauma and abusive life before us has altered him in such a way that cruelty and gore is all he knows—all he *wants* to know.

Wrapped around his hand is a chain, and the other end,

another person trails along, her hateful glare focused on the front, toward Nico.

Still, Rozelyn De Falco marches through Nico's space looking more regal than a fallen princess should. Her long blonde hair is matted, there's blood and dirt smudges all over her skin. She's draped in a large shirt and I recognize it to be Flynn's.

Between the two of them, they look like they've been in quite the scrap.

At my side, Isabelle gasps, comprehending more details of the mob life I've only mentioned. Her skin brushes mine as she inches closer, and I wrap my arm around her waist, showing her Rozelyn is no threat. Between the chain around her neck and the number of people in this room, she's incapacitated.

Rozelyn's gaze goes to the right, toward Aurora, who she poisoned only a week prior with Fentanyl-laced marijuana edibles. My sister looks away, torn between the friend she believed and hoped she made at the community garden and the enemy she knows she has.

Lastly, Della and Ariella both take a subtle step toward their ex-stepsister, as though compelled. Nico texted the other day and said they'd been down to visit her but gave no details of that conversation.

Rozelyn barely looks at either of them, her gaze returning to Nico, who shoves off the desk, walking toward the duo and meeting them halfway. I recognize my brother's gait. The cocky, sly smirk on his face. Nico has multiple modes—and his retaliating, leader guise comes out occasionally, when needed.

"You've decided now to talk," he starts. "But the thing is, we've gotten the information needed from our sources. When learning who the Duponts really are, it only took a few hours before gaining their backgrounds. What city they're from. And I've pieced together why your father is so invested in the status of their life. Because where they're from, he is too, isn't he? So why do I need you?"

I stare at my brother, wondering why he hadn't mentioned that to me. As I guessed earlier, the RCMP did return with results, based on his statements, but seems he's wanting to see how many details Rozelyn will hand over nonetheless.

Rozelyn doesn't back down from his cold stare, which slightly impresses me. The little I know of De Falco's daughters always had me thinking of simpering princesses, but clearly, she's strong enough to withstand Flynn's torture and come out unscathed enough to battle my brother.

"Maybe. But do you know why my father chose Montreal as his base? Why your soldier's life and death were so important to him? You claim to know what city they're from, but do you know what's there?"

Nico's jaw shifts; the only signal that he wants the information she is holding.

Flynn shoves into her back before jerking the chain roughly, causing her to stumble into his chest and break the attitude. He growls something in her ear. Something that has her eyes widening a fraction.

"You came in here wanting to disclose information, so get talking."

At my side, Isabelle makes a small noise. I stroke the back of her hand with my finger, trying my best to ease her. She doesn't need to be here, but clearly, my brother's playing at something.

Nico steps closer, so close, she tips her head to look at him. "You have two minutes to talk before I stick a gun to your head, and we decide breathing isn't in your future."

Flynn jerks her chain again, emphasizing his boss's words, to which she only glares over her shoulder toward him.

"What do you know, so I can just fill in the gaps?"

"No," Nico responds. "Because then you'll edit the truth. All or nothing, Rozelyn. Tick tok."

This is how we're telling Isabelle where she's from? He's letting Rozelyn be the one. For fuck's sake...I glance down, wanting to hold her through the next part, but needing her to stand on her own. Not sure why this compulsion takes me over, but it does.

Rozelyn huffs once. "You know better than anyone else, truth isn't free. I want to strike a deal."

Nico laughs once, humourlessly. "In case you haven't noticed, you're nowhere near being able to strike deals."

She continues as though my brother hasn't spoken. "My sister. Or you kill me, and you'll only have half the answers."

"The half that matters," Nico counters.

"Is it?" Rozelyn's cocky look does exactly as she hoped for—makes Nico falter. "I have nothing left, Nico." She spreads her hands to the side, gesturing to herself. "In case *you* haven't noticed," she spits his own words back at him, "I'm stuck. Captured. I know very well any one of you will stick a gun to my head and end me instantly."

Behind her, Flynn makes a grunting noise. Likely wanting him to be the one.

"I have nothing left," she continues. "Nothing but my humanity, which I plead to you with." Peeking toward Della, she resumes talking. "Clearly, you fell for my stepsister, despite her operating under my father's commands. Why? Because you thought her to be strong, admired her drive to protect her family, right?"

She guesses correctly. I think back to when Della was chained in the basement for what she did. When we *all* despised her for her actions. But Nico was stuck between doing what was right and what he wanted to do, and ultimately, gave Della the option, freeing her from her transgressions.

Mafia. Family and loyalty are themes amongst us. Making deals for one's family might seem risky, but they're our best weapon when against an enemy. Our best and worst. They reveal our weaknesses, but family becomes the unspoken code amongst all of us. After all, it's all anyone would do—protect who we love.

When Nico doesn't respond, Rozelyn takes that as a green light. "All I want is my sister's safety."

Della takes another step, injecting herself into the conversation. Lowly, she asks, "Where's Yasmine?"

"With our father. *She's* his favourite. She's his only blood-related daughter, after all."

Because Rozelyn De Falco is the illegitimate daughter of Stefano's first wife. Birthed before her marriage to Stefano, because this life brings with it all sorts of lies and falsities, and her family couldn't let Stefano know his wife wasn't a virgin. But after the marriage, according to my own parents anyway, she told her new husband of her precious child and the two made a deal with Mother and Father to help locate the child, who is Rozelyn. The deal being marriage to Hawke, but after everything went down with him, the deal was broken. Shortly before then, Rozelyn's mother died, sending Stefano off the deep end.

Something flickers in Rozelyn's gaze; a small sign of being affected by her father's decisions. "Regardless, my deal is for her life. We're both products of our father's choices." Her stare slides back to Della, and then toward Ariella for the first time. "We're *all* products of that life. We're *all* on the same side."

Nico's eyes flick to me so quickly, no one would notice unless they were watching us. We share the same thought: there's something deeper in her words if she's trying to convey to her old stepsisters they're the "same." Knowing what Della has gone through makes me wonder what he did to the daughters he cared for and raised.

As though responding to my silent curiosity, Rozelyn continues, "You might have had it bad, Della. But I had it bad in other ways. Remember when you first came into our life, how kind he was to you? How much conditioning he forced upon you? Picture that, but for nearly one's entire life. Then come back to me and you'll be allowed to bitch."

This time, Nico glances at me for longer, again sharing my sentiments.

Fuck.

"What do you want?" Nico finally asks.

"When you go for him, keep her out of it. *I* was my father's soldier, not her. She's innocent. I want her here with me, safe."

Nico's jaw ticks again, but this time, it's less subtle. He peeks back at our father, our Boss, who ultimately allows Nico to control most of the decision-making now, then toward his wife.

"Fucking sake. This agreement feels awfully familiar."

He made one with Della, to ensure Ariella didn't pay the price of her transgressions after the truth came out.

"Deal." Nico's bold statement echoes through the room, into all of us, the weight of that word. The deal he's just made for De Falco.

The two of them end in a small stare down, occurring for about two minutes before Rozelyn accepts the arrangement with the tip of her head.

"White Rock, British Columbia."

That's all she starts with, but it's enough for me to look at Isabelle, wondering if that's the connection. When I focus on the trio in the centre of the room again, Nico's eyes slide to me, nodding once.

British Columbia. The farthest end of Western Canada is

where Maurice was running from. Where Isabelle, back when she was Rose, is from. Where her mother might still reside.

"There's an institution there," Rozelyn continues. "An academy. You guys are the mafia. You might rule the crime, the underground dark spots of this place, but they control the *country*. They're inside every level of government. They manipulate everything you could ever imagine. They're huge."

"Name?" Nico demands, his voice harder than earlier, edged with anxiety with learning about an enemy we've never known about.

"The Seven. I'm telling you the truth when I say I know little about them, only that they exist. Only that they're seven leaders scattered around the country, and my father works beneath one of them."

"Why BC then if they're all over the country?"

She lifts one shoulder. "Where do you think they're trained? Again, I don't know much about these details, but from what my father told me, there's an academy. It's where the richest of the rich kids all over the country attend university. It's where the kids of the Seven are raised, trained to one day take their fathers' spots. Fed under the umbrella of a degree, they're spoiled, rich...dangerous. Go through their own trials before taking their places hidden in society."

Across the way, Rosen meets my gaze. He inches closer to my sister, the mere mention of possible danger enough to raise his protective instincts.

"My father attended. Got close to one of the Seven. After graduation, he was given a single task: take down the crime lords in Montreal." She shoots a meaningful stare toward my father.

In the corner of my eye, I catch my parents sharing a look before Father takes a step nearer. For the first time since we've arrived, he speaks, demanding, "If this place controls the country, what does us owning the province matter? As you've said, they're manipulating things higher up."

Her head tilts a fraction, lazily staring at Father. "That's the thing. They're so tightly wound into the entire legal, political side of the country, they've let other things slip. And in that time, in the past few decades, their hold on Quebec's underground crime has gone unmanaged, leaving room for Corsettis to slip in."

Fuck. No other word comes to mind. No other word can come to mind as I stand there, dumbfounded, trying to keep up with everything she's telling us. By my side, Isabelle shifts, and I don't blame her if she's completely confused.

"You really never wondered why it all went down how it did?" She smirks. "How my father is Boss of his family, but where's the rest of them?" She scans everyone in the room, meaningfully pointing out, "His father, his mother, siblings, cousins. He wed my mother for the connection to the Costa family because he needed that alliance for strength." She focuses on my parents again. "The deal between Hawke and me for marriage—another ploy. He was all too eager to capitalize on my mother's request. Pretty sure she had no idea about the snake she got into bed with, but," Rozelyn shrugs a shoulder, "here we are. When she died, grief hit him hard, but worse—she was the *in* to you guys. *I* was his in. It's why he was sent here. The Seven knew it might be a multi-generational takedown, but in the end, they want to control you. My father was simply laying the groundwork for it to happen."

Mother steps closer, pausing beside my father, her hand coming up to cover her mouth. "How did we not see any of that?"

"Because he flashed my mother's fancy family name in front of you," Rozelyn answers for my father, smirking. "You were distracted by the alliance. When the engagement was broken off, you assumed he was upset for losing the union. It was more that he lost his link to you, and he was frustrated."

"Is that why he married our mother?" Della cuts in, sharing a sharp look with her sister.

Rozelyn smiles cruelly. "Told you, we're all the same. Pawns in my father's elaborate plan. Actually, no, because he too is a pawn in the Seven's plan. When I say they control everything, I mean *everything*. Yes, that's why, Della. His plan fell through with me, so he wed a woman with two teenage daughters. It wasn't random you two were chosen. Struggling family, no father in the picture, it was easy. He was able to be your mother's saviour, a father to you two. You'd fall for his charms. And then your mother died." She pauses, looking down, a break in her attitude.

The small break allows Nico to glance at me again, a worried question in his eyes. He reaches for Della's hand. A few weeks ago, when Nico learned of her deception and who she is, he had me and Rosen investigate her mother's accident, but I still can't find any proof of what we suspect.

This could be where Rozelyn reveals it. Instead, she looks up, her brows lowering as she scans her stepsisters before continuing, taking an altered path, even her tone changing.

"After your mother's death, my father went to work on his plan. There was some deviation," she glances toward Ariella, "but in the end, one of you managed to get in here under the belief he simply wanted Corsetti power."

"How do you know all this?" Father asks. "How do we know *you're* not lying?"

She shrugs again, pursing her lips. "You don't. That's up to you to figure out. I can't do everything for you." Focusing on Nico again, she continues, "It gets better. Seventeen years ago, something very interesting happened when two Haynes disappeared."

She stares right at Isabelle, who clenches my hand, her gaze flying to me. Mine goes to Nico's, trying to decipher how Rozelyn not only knows all of this, but she knows exactly who Isabelle is.

Instead of shying away, Isabelle takes two steps forward, coming closer to the woman she hasn't known before a moment ago. "Me."

"My father never shared the details of your past, but all I know is you're from there. BC. I doubt you're one of the Seven or else they would have found you by now, but you were supposed to be in that life, one way or the other. Your father fled with you here and struck a deal with mine. That's how he ended up working for," she rolls her head back to Father, "you. My father helped Lawrence Haynes get new identities for him and his daughter, provided he manage to get inducted here."

Everyone's silent in the room. And yet, everything feels so fucking loud. My heart thumping in my chest. Nico's flaring breaths. Dad's calculating thoughts. Della's stepping toward her sister, taking her hand. Rosen stroking my sister's arms, his eyes narrowed on Rozelyn. Flynn's own heavy breathing as he stares off, past everyone.

And Isabelle's soft pants. The wobble in her legs that has me stepping forward, her back to my front so she has someone to lean on. Someone to use as she stands there, looking lost. In her head.

To learn there's so many lies around your life.

"What was the point in sending me in?" Della asks. "If he already had someone on the inside."

She rolls her eyes. "My dad was determined to do right by the Seven. Guarantees and insurance. He was setting up layers. Besides, Haynes was able to report back on the little details. You were able to get more *intimate* with the Corsettis. You think it was random the attacks on your clubs?" she asks, directing her question toward Nico. "Nothing's random in this world. You should know that."

Coincidences don't exist. It's something Father drilled into Nico and me growing up. Nothing happens by chance.

"Anything else?" Nico snaps.

Rozelyn shakes her head once, the chain rattling in her movement. "Only that I hope to see you keep your promise, Corsetti."

Nico doesn't comment, simply shifts his attention toward Flynn, to whom he flicks his fingers at. "Get her out of here. Put her where we've discussed."

Flynn nods once before lightly tugging on the chain, urging Rozelyn away. She follows instantly, taking the lead when Flynn points.

But then she pauses and talks again. "When escaping the city, my father went back to BC. He was driving there to get backup because he knows he's in over his head. If I said anything earlier, you'd go to him. Attack on the Seven's territory, and you'd all die. If he brings them here, and you fight on your territory, you'll have a better chance. That's why I waited. I want him gone as much as you all do, and I needed to ensure your plan works. So I made my own."

"Why would you want your father dead?" Della demands right away, voicing the question we all have.

She stares at the ground for a second, a seemingly sad smile turning down her lips until she finally responds with a single word. "Because." Then she turns back to the doorway.

They make it nearly out of the room before Isabelle wrenches from my arms, chasing after them. I lunge too, missing her clothing by a fraction. She stops by Rozelyn, inches from where Flynn makes a low noise, shifting his body in front of De Falco, keeping the two women apart.

Despite the scarred giant towering over her, Isabelle hardly looks fazed, her attention solely on the blonde woman behind Flynn. "Your father had mine killed, didn't he?"

For the first time since entering, Rozelyn looks almost regretful. "I think so."

"But why?"

She shrugs. "Insurance, if I had to guess. When he needed to escape and his plans didn't pan out how he wanted them to, you and your father are loose ends. Someone who'd been working beneath the Corsetti influence for decades and who knew everything. Your father left BC for a reason, and whatever it was, scared mine enough that he took him out."

Isabelle too, are her unspoken words. If De Falco had her father killed, then that's why Isabelle's being targeted. Whatever deal Lawrence struck with De Falco was up when Stefano had to escape.

Isabelle's gaze drops to the floor, and she stumbles back a step, indicating she's finished with her questioning. I move toward her at the same time Flynn shoves Rozelyn out the door, shutting it behind them. I hold Isabelle's hips, folding her into my arms, her face in my chest.

But amid her heavy breaths, of her mind grasping for anything rational, my brother's voice rises through the fog. "There's more, Isabelle."

34
ISABELLE

I'm numb.

So numb.

Cold.

Chilling fear wraps my every nerve, making it difficult to breathe, to move, to *think*. To understand what just happened. Who that woman was. The daughter of their enemy, I've assumed, based on some of the things she was saying.

I spent the entire time by Rafael's side, trying to figure out why I was included in this meeting. Until she mentioned my real last name. Until my life came crashing down around me.

Until breathing became difficult. And I was sucking in harsh breaths, my fingers winding their way into Rafael's shirt. I should have shoved him away, gotten him away from me—gotten away from *him*. Despite his family observing us, I didn't. I couldn't. He used me to determine what I knew, and now I'm using him. His strength, his empathy.

When his brother speaks, I question if I'll make it through more. If I *can* listen.

"There's more, Isabelle."

There can't be more. I won't be able to deal with it.

Rafael strokes a hand over my hair, his words low and only for me. "Whatever he has, you need to hear it. You wanted to know, Belle. We're doing this for you."

"I don't…I can't."

Feet come up behind me, but I don't see who. I can't tell. There are *so* many people here, observing my breakdown. So many strangers. Strangers my father worked for.

No—he didn't work for these people. He was *compelled* to work for these people, while he was connected to their enemy. Their enemy who was a part of some fucking society on the other side of the country.

Where *I'm* from. Where my mother is from…

Hands, much smaller than Rafael's, lightly touch my back, encouraging me to release Rafael. A pretty, blonde woman, Rafael's sister, I believe, is standing beside me. I noticed her earlier, against the far wall. She too looked scared for most of the conversation, her eyes wide and confused, and I felt myself relating to the stranger.

"Isabelle," she murmurs, "deep breath. Breathe with me."

Breathe? She wants me to *breathe?*

"Trust me. I get panic attacks, and you look like you're on the verge of one. It'll help move oxygen to your brain, to make things a bit clearer."

What if I don't want clearer? Clearer means I'm able to think, to process, when I'd rather go back to when things were simple.

Rafael strokes the back of my hands fisted in his shirt, silently giving me the strength to loosen my hold and turn, wordlessly accepting her help.

She smiles gently. "Breathe in and hold it."

I do, sucking in fresh air and not releasing as she holds up three fingers, lowering each one with every passing second.

When all three are folded down, she commands, "Breathe out."

I blow out the air, already feeling my brain lighten. As she said, things becoming clearer.

"Do it again. One more time."

She breathes with me again as she walks me through the motions, and I even feel Rafael's chest moving under my hold, following along with us.

After two, she checks, "Better?"

No. Kinda. "Yeah."

Rafael brushes his lips across my forehead as he wraps an arm around my waist and leads me toward his brother's desk, who, in the meantime, has retrieved a small stack of papers, throwing them on the desk in front of Rafael. He releases me to take the stack, but doesn't show me, nor flip through them.

"The RCMP returned with results. Within minutes of my message to you," he says to Rafael, "Flynn informed me Rozelyn was ready to talk." Sliding his attention to me, he breathes once, sharply, so opposite from what the woman and I just did. "What she said aligns with the information they discovered. You and your father, Rose and Lawrence Haynes, came from BC. There's no mention of why you left, or what was there, but, Rafael, second page."

He rifles through the couple sheets of paper, pulling out a printout of a news article. He holds it away, but I know he's reading it.

"I don't think your mother knew anything, Isabelle. Show her, Raf."

Rafael hands me the paper. The large block lettering of the headline too large to ignore—too impactful to erase from my mind.

MISSING CHILD AND FATHER FOUND: DEAD IN A CAR ACCIDENT.

What?

I reread the words again. And again. And again, until finally skimming the first paragraph, my eyes catching two names—Rose and Lawrence.

"Oh my god."

"He faked your death. Or someone had. Read the end."

My eyes skip down the paper, toward the bottom of the article, finding the last paragraph. The quotation from a person they interviewed, every word seeming unreal. Spoken by a stranger, recorded by another stranger, about *me*.

"Sometimes, I wake up and still hear her small feet as she paces around the house, eagerly running into our bedroom before jumping on me. I'll miss being woken up like that. I've always sympathized with the parents who'd lost a child; I never believed I'd be one of them. It's like the club no member wishes to be a part of."—Ivy Haynes.

"Mom." My finger strokes over the name. "She didn't..."

It explains why Dad always spoke fondly of her. It explains *so* much. It doesn't explain why he took me away from her though.

I'm numb again. The emotions in my body slither away until I'm a shell. Grieving Dad so far has been easy to ignore, to avoid until it became important. But now...how do I be sad about a person who was a lie? Who *made* my life a lie? Who took me away from my mother?

I reread the paragraph, wondering if she's known the entire time. Was the article a ploy from her and Dad, and her grief faked, or does she truly believe I'm dead?

"I can't say for certain," Nico speaks again, "but I wonder if that's why De Falco targeted your father. With De Falco on the run, it was easier to ensure your father was truly dead, to tie up loose ends." He pauses.

I drop the paper, unable to hold it a second longer. Rafael's still holding a stack and I jerk my chin toward them. "And those? What fresh hell will those bring?"

"Just email printouts," Rafael murmurs, handing them to me to flip through. They're emails between Nico and their contact, details of my name, and my last recorded location.

I laugh. I can't help it, but I fucking laugh. A bit deranged, under the weight and sympathy stares of Rafael's entire family. It's okay, though. Losing my mind is better than dealing with *it*.

"We done?" Rafael's voice pokes through, but I don't know who he's speaking to. The response must be wordless because Rafael takes the papers from my hands and tosses them back onto the desk. He then wraps an arm around my waist and leads me from the office.

"Come right back," Nico demands. "There's more. For your ears only."

I follow or am dragged. One or the other. I barely feel like I'm keeping up with him as he removes me from his brother's office and down the hallway. He doesn't speak, not until we get toward a staircase, where he pauses, momentarily studying me, before scooping me into his arms and ascending the stairs.

The house around me blurs. I pay it no attention, closing my eyes entirely until I feel something soft beneath my body, molding to my limbs.

A bed.

Above me, a black canopy. To my right, a large window covered with a black curtain. It's all I manage to make out though because Rafael consumes my vision again, shifting the duvet until he's able to pull it over me.

"*Ma belle*, I'm sorry."

Don't be.

I hate you.

Go away.

Let me go.

All responses that flit in my mind, but leave just as quickly, one not sticking, not granting him any reply.

His soft touch strokes my cheek, pushing hair away from my face. "I don't want to leave you, but I need to return to Nico."

"Go." Do I whisper it? Yell it? I can't tell anymore.

He leans over, brushing his lips over my forehead, but I'm so numb, even his electrifying touch does little to ease me. "I'd take away this pain, if I could, Belle."

You could have if you'd never come into my life.

"Where am I?" I manage, changing the topic entirely.

"My room. The room I keep for when I'm here."

Fantastic. More of Rafael to surround myself with.

"No one will bother you. Unless you'd like me to send someone up. Someone to sit with you."

My shoulders move in a shrugging motion. How can I think about people after what I just learned?

Rafael makes a pained noise before he moves away, his arm stretching to continue to touch me until his feet take him too far away and he has to release me. He goes toward the doorway and shuts the door behind him, leaving me alone.

35
RAFAEL

Every step back to Nico's office feels like a monumental journey and one I really don't want to take when every fibre of my being insists I turn around, head back to my room, and try to take Belle's pain away.

Fuck you, Maurice. Lawrence. Stefano. The whole lot. Belle's father got into bed with the devil and she's paying the price.

Inside Nico's office, I find only Rosen and Nico, everyone else having been since cleared out. Rosen's in the same spot he last stood but wanders closer to the desk as I approach.

"You might want to sit," Nico suggests, nodding toward his chairs.

"I'd rather stand." Energy is hardwired into my nerves; the need to do *something* that makes sitting impossible.

"Very well. How is she?"

"How do you think she is?" I snarl, glancing toward the door, imagining her somewhere beyond there, knowing she's tucked away in my bed, broken, possibly still staring at nothing. "We blew up her entire life."

"That blew everything up," Rosen comments, dropping into one of the chairs. "All these years, and we've never known about the Seven."

Nico drums his fingers against the desk for a beat before snatching the top sheet of paper from the stack I dropped there before getting Isabelle away from this room. He scans the top page. "Today has been full of surprises. Our parents are shaken. They're headed back to their home."

I grunt, not really caring about them right now. My parents might be decent leaders, but they've made their share of mistakes—Hawke and Aurora, to name two—and every single time, they twist it to make themselves seem like the good guys. This time, they fucked up by not looking deeper into De Falco's strange family situation.

"You wanted me back here," I state, keeping my voice flat and demanding.

Nico stares at me for a second, like he's deep in thought. His eyes narrow. "Yeah. We found more on the Haynes family, specifically about Lawrence. He has a brother. That'd be Isabelle's uncle."

"Okay. Purpose in telling me this?"

The corners of Nico's mouth curl up in the same manner he does when he wins. Leaning forward, his eyes drill into me, his next words emphasized. "Rafael, his brother is a doctor."

"No...Daddy...no. Doctor, no. No needle..."

When Isabelle was sleeping, she mumbled something about a doctor. A needle.

"Holy shit."

"Her father's a psychopath," Rosen echoes my sentiments.

Nico tilts his head in agreement before reaching into his desk drawer and pulling out another piece of paper. This one, a small yellow sticky note, which he tosses across the desk toward me.

"I bet he has more answers regarding why they left BC and perhaps about those interesting scars on her face. Here's the address. Figured you'd want to do with that what you may." He smirks because my brother knows me too well.

Toronto. "He's close." *Fucking perfect.* A quick flight, or a five-hour drive. I'll be there in no time.

Folding the note, I spin on my heel. The second I met Isabelle, I was struck with a need to avenge her for being harmed, and now, I was just handed the green light.

Feet quickly follow behind me, but I don't need to look back to know who it is. "This is mine, Rosen. Thanks, but I'm going alone. Isabelle's in my bed. Keep her safe. Don't tell her where I've gone. Not sure when I'll be back."

The address is for a clinic in downtown Toronto.

Dr. Haynes, Cosmetic Clinician, the window reads. A fucking plastic surgeon. The lights couldn't be shining any brighter.

I drove from Montreal to Toronto. Getting the jet ready would have been an hour of prep time for the pilot, and then I'd have to sit there for an hour, waiting until we land. Driving meant doing one-forty on the 401, knowing any cop I pass would run my plates and then let me go because regardless of what we've learned of the Seven's control, *my* name is still Corsetti, which means I still influence this side of the country. Driving meant weaving through traffic, blasting music to make my ears bleed, and planning every scream I'll yank from the doc's throat.

I park across the street and wait out the final hour of the work day, my drive consuming much of the afternoon. I wait until lights begin flicking off through the window before entering. After packing my pockets with a few select tools from my trunk, I slink across the street as a woman exits, waving as she shuts the door behind her.

In the hour I've been watching the building, I assume it's his receptionist, who's about to find herself without a job.

She doesn't lock the door behind her because someone's still inside, and it's that someone that has me opening the door.

Isabelle mentioned this morning about me being different than the person she's come to know. It's true. I'm not Rosen or my brother who lives and breathes the organization. I'm also not Hawke, who despises the crime life. I certainly don't hate it, but *this* part is fun. The adventure, the fight, the revenge.

But revenge is only useful when it's in the name of someone else. And with *ma belle*'s face in my mind, I step through the front entranceway, past the waiting room, the glass receptionist desk, and toward the slight noises in the backroom. Typing.

Doc's finishing up his paperwork for the night most likely.

Keeping my steps light, he doesn't hear me as I fill his doorway, reaching into my pocket to retrieve my favourite knife. His back is to me as he works at his desk, which is entirely too fucking perfect.

I could sneak up and slice his throat.

Or I can let him decide what comes next.

I clear my throat.

He jumps, spinning his chair around, coughing in surprise. "I'm sorry, sir, what are you doing in here? We're closed and you'll..." My blades register in his mind, my expression not one of a customer coming in for Botox. He wisely lifts to his feet and paces backwards, his hands held up. "Hey, man," he uses words unsuitable for his middle-aged self, making me hate him that much more, "I don't know who you are, but take what you need and get out. Please."

Words never sounded better. I smile, but it's nothing like

the one I give to Isabelle, or even my family. This is an expression promising death. His death, after a long, painful, torturous journey.

"What I need," I repeat, taking a single step inside, increasing the scent of this man's fear, "is your heart in my palm after I rip it from your chest."

Widened eyes fly to the door behind me, and then to his desk, where his cell phone rests beside his keyboard. He thinks he has a chance, and I'll let him believe it. After all, playing with prey is half the fun.

With one of my knives, I gesture to the device. "Go ahead. I won't stop you."

Stricken for his life, the idiot lunges for his desk, grasping his phone, eagerly swiping at the screen to unlock it. With his attention is split between me and trying to call the cops, his movements are clumsy.

"Y-you don't want to hurt me. I have connections."

I bark out a laugh. "Oh, doc, me too. Which reminds me, I haven't introduced myself yet." Another step into the room, to which he backs up against the wall, holding the phone, his attention now solely on me instead of escape, if he were to only dial those three numbers. "Name's Corsetti."

His phone drops from his hand at the same time his mouth does too. "C-Corsetti."

"Oh, you've heard of me. Good, good. Means you and your brother stayed in contact."

His face flashes white as he finally gets why I'm here. "Maurice—"

"No, no," I wave my knife, interrupting him, "use his real name. The name you grew up referring to him as. Lawrence, right?"

"What did you do to him?" he asks, fear unhidden in his tone. His eyes dive to the floor and back as I take another step, searching for the phone he dropped. But the time for escape has long passed.

"Nothing," I reply truthfully. "It's what was *done* to him that put him on our radar." With my knife, I gesture to the chair he was sitting in earlier. "Sit. We have a lot to talk about."

Under the threat of my blade, he does so, hardly blinking as he positions his body on the edge of the small chair.

"Nice listening. Your brother has quite the history. In fact," I shift the blade, so it's pointed at his face, "so do you. The Seven."

His eyes flash, finally a bit of defiance there. "How do you know that name? I won't tell you anything."

"Oh, but you will." Holding his gaze, I swing my hand down in a sharp arc, stabbing the knife right into his thigh, deep enough that it penetrates through every layer of skin and right into the chair beneath him, pinning him to it.

He releases an ungodly, inhuman scream that only makes me smile. Did Isabelle scream when she was held under a knife? Reaching into my holster, I yank out another one, holding up the blade.

"I have another one. And a trunk full of more." And all sorts of other, fun tools, should I need them. "I could pull this one out," I gesture to the knife in his leg, the wound he's breathing heavily through, "but then you'd bleed out and you and I have a *lot* to talk about so I can't have you dying yet."

As his hands cup the wound, trying to put pressure on the spot, through clenched teeth, he demands, "What the fuck do you want to know?"

"What are they?"

"I'll die before I tell you about them. You took oaths to your family, right," he nods his chin toward my chest, smirking at my slightly surprised look, "yeah, that's right. Lawrence and I stayed in communication even after you inducted him."

Learning about the Seven could be a beneficial bonus to my trip, but not the reason I'm here, so I'll come back to that.

"Why did he take his daughter away?"

"To save her."

Lies. All that bastard did was harm her. With the knife in hand, I poke it into his chest, right between the sternum, deep enough it digs through his clothing.

"Try again."

"It's...the truth. The Seven. They run a society. Rich, powerful, beyond anything you can imagine. But they have *practices* Lawrence didn't approve of. To ensure Rose wasn't apart of them, he took her. Ran away with her."

My hold on the blade falters a fraction, my hatred for Maurice/Lawrence dropping the slightest. He was trying to save her.

"What practices?" I need to know exactly what he was saving her from before I play judge and jury on his soul.

"Fucked-up marriages. Murder plots. Backdoor deals. Underground shit." He sucks in a sharp breath. For someone who claimed he wouldn't say anything, he's squealing easily. He probably thinks the truth will set him free, but I've already marked his death. Doc isn't leaving here alive.

"Did Ivy know?"

"No." He swallows roughly. "She was as confused as everyone else when he escaped. We hid it from her. She's a daughter of the Seven. She knew what was expected of her and her family, having been in Rose's place herself once. My brother, after learning about the society and what having a child with one of them would mean, he didn't want that for Rose. He and Ivy fought over it, but she didn't see how messed-up it all was, so he planned an escape and disappeared from his wife's life, taking their daughter with him."

Which means the quote in the article was her mother's true

grief, and now I need to decide if knowing this would be better or worse on Isabelle.

"The accident? Obviously faked."

His eyes widen a bit more, realizing I know a lot more than he assumed I did. "De Falco's plan."

Just as Nico guessed. Means De Falco needed to tie up loose ends.

Mentally, I go through the bit of information he gave me, checking off anything I could bring back to Nico and what else I could learn, but come up empty, my need for revenge becoming too strong to care about having an informant.

"Now." I smile again, crouching until I'm in line with his face. I want him to *see* his executioner as he marches his way to Hell. "So that's all about the Seven and why Lawrence left them. Tell me about his daughter."

"Rose."

"Isabelle," I correct, dragging the knife down his chest. He stalks it, halting his breathing, as though the slight rise and fall of his chest would save him.

"She's why you're here, isn't she? My brother took great measures in hiding her away from everyone to ensure the Seven wouldn't come for her, including keeping her from your family. So, if you know about her, and you've already indicated my brother's dead...Well, you have the same insane look in your eyes that my brother had when he married Ivy."

"She is why I'm here," I agree, skating the knife over his face, tracing the same lines that Isabelle has. "From the second I met her, her scars confused me. You see," my forehead forms a V, as though I'm being thoughtful, "they look drawn."

The scene of fear radiating off him tells me enough. I follow it, catching the dark spot on his crotch.

"She has no memory of it. Nothing more than her overly-protective father telling her the scars will keep her safe. Then, randomly the other night, in her sleep, she starts mumbling about a doctor, a needle, and calling for her father to stop. So tell me, *doc*, how does this look to you?"

I don't wait for his answer before my hand slips, dragging down his fleshy cheek, slicing a line. It swells with fresh blood instantly, to which he screams and tries to jerk away. My free hand shoots out, grasping his chin to hold him steady as I move my knife to his forehead, right where one of her scars begins.

"Start. Talking. Or I cut again."

"The society, they value beauty. My brother knew if he made her less attractive, it'd be a level of protection for—"

Without waiting for him to finish, I trace her scars over her uncle's face, digging deeper. He screams, trying to wrench free from the torment, but I don't release him. Not with her sweet face in my mind, controlling my movements. My need for this fucker's blood growing stronger with every delectable noise from his mouth.

"You said..." He breathes in and out harshly, his words staggered. "You wouldn't...do that."

"I lied. Keep talking before I rip the knife out of your leg and watch you bleed out."

"He was only—" *sharp inhale* "—trying to protect her! He loved his daughter more than *anything*. Everything...was for her. He was desperate. Brought her to me because he thought if he could ruin her face, they'd be less interested in her, if they were caught. He was trying to guarantee their safety. Was anxious when he escaped. I was still in med school at the time. Gave her a shot to knock her out, cut her skin deep enough they'd be permanent scars. That's...it." He lifts his hands, palms toward me, as though he thinks I'm done. As if admitting that fact will save his life. "Weeks later, he made the deal with Stefano De Falco."

"You marked her skin up," I summarize, speaking softer. "You scarred her. A child. You're fucked up."

With another quick movement, I angle his head the other way and trace another matching scar down his other cheek. He screams again, his body convulsing in the chair. But it's okay because I'm nearly done. I've gotten what I need.

"I'm...sorry."

I chuckle darkly. "Oh, doc, I'm not the one you should be apologizing to. God is because you're going to fucking Hell. You know what happens when someone makes an enemy of a Corsetti?" I swing my arm down, stabbing the knife right into his other thigh, but instead of leaving it in, I yank it out, a spurt of blood hitting my arm. His hands fly to his thigh, squealing through the pain, trying to cover the injury. I'll only have a few more minutes of his life. "You die."

"Fuck...*you.*"

"No," I croon, stroking my thumb down the side of his face, over one of the freshly cut lines. He hisses as I wipe the blood, tracing it over his skin. "No, fuck *you*, doc. Corsetti enemies die but when you dare *harm* someone we care about, you die slowly."

Releasing his face with a hard jerk, I yank the other knife out from his thigh, watching in complete pleasure as blood pours from that wound too.

"Slowly, bleeding out, alone. A message to the Seven, if you must. Not to fuck with the Corsettis because there's no fucking way they're taking our territory. But first," I lift both blades, one in each hand, into his quickly fading gaze, "one more scar will do."

In a quick lunge, I place both blades against his throat in an X and jerk them apart, slicing each one in the opposite way. Twin slices fill with blood, and he gurgles, his body slumping against the chair, death taking him much too soon.

I meant to drag that out for longer, but I can't regret it now. He's dead and it appeals to my need for vengeance. That the person who dared harm Isabelle isn't here any longer.

Taking out my phone, I snap a few pictures of the scene to send to Nico, then text Rosen, asking him to pull the camera footage of this place. Lastly, I steal the doctor's cell in case something useful can be taken from it.

Then I exit the building, pocketing my knives as I go, with one goal in mind: to hold Belle.

36
ISABELLE

Time no longer matters. Lying here in a near-stranger's bed does, though. Pretending to be okay every time a knock came to the door. Eventually, even those went away when people gave up on me.

Until I feel him slide into bed and pull me to his chest. I should force him away, rather than roll into him, but I crave his comfort. Need to feel normal again, like I had before my life blew up.

He smells like soap and rubbing my palm against his chest finds his skin damp. Sliding my hand to the back of his neck, I play with his wet strands of hair.

"What time is it?"

"About four in the morning. Go back to sleep."

"You just get in?"

"Yes."

"You showered. Where were you?"

"*Ma belle*," he purrs in that voice demanding I drop it, "go back to sleep. I'm here."

"I still hate you." I *should* anyway. Do I? That's another question even I don't have the response for.

"That's fine. Doesn't stop me from holding you."

I guess. Nestling into his chest, but before sleep comes again, I ask the one thing that's been plaguing my mind all evening. "Is my father a good guy or a bad guy?"

For a long moment, he doesn't respond. I know he's still awake because his fingers dance over my back, up and down my spine. "He's whatever you want him to be. Things aren't always black and white. People don't fall into categories of good and evil. We're all capable of doing good things, bad things, selfish things."

Like him. Him and his family. The institution he's a part of is bad. Criminals. The mob. I'm only with him because he used me to get ahead. All that suggests him being evil. But then, he's also the guy who beat up someone to ensure they wouldn't go near me again, killed three men, who took me to a park simply because I said I rarely got the chance to as a child, who's held me every moment of the past twenty-four hours as my life got destroyed and I gained a new identity. Those aren't actions of an evil person.

Dad loved me, there's no denying that. He did what he thought was right, for whatever the reason. He raised me, protected me, gave me a fine enough life. Signs of a good man. But he also kept me away from living normally, from my mother and the world I should have been in—whether for a good reason or otherwise—hid beneath the Corsetti name, fooling even them. So he's bad?

Rafael makes a noise and pets my hair, holding me tighter to his chest. "Sleep, *ma belle.* I can hear your mind racing and nothing you do now will change anything or determine your feelings. Just rest." His lips trace delicate kisses over my forehead, and it's like that, I fall asleep.

"When am I free?" are the first words I demand of him the second Rafael opens his eyes.

I've been waiting an hour for him to wake up, too terrified to leave this room, but nearly bored out of my mind.

He groans, rubbing a hand over his face as he blinks into the bright morning sun, shining through the window from where I yanked open the curtain earlier. "What?"

"You got what you needed from me." *Technically nothing.* "And better yet, you know where your enemy is, which means I'm free to go home. That was the deal."

He sits up, still rubbing sleep from his face as he rapidly blinks himself awake. "Do you not remember being attacked the other night?"

"You killed them. Three of them."

"Out of four. And we don't know how many others are after you."

Thankfully, I've been up longer and have thought of a plan to counter his every point. "So? You and your family are going after your enemy soon, right, which means this problem will go away."

Rafael slides off the bed, shaking his head and stalks his way to the connected bathroom. I turn, watching him go, inspecting his backside.

"Maybe," he calls out, shutting the bathroom door. "No guarantee."

I slide from the bed, yelling through the bathroom door. "When's the end date? That could be tomorrow. Could be next year. Rafael, you need to let me go!"

The door swings open, Rafael filling the doorway. His massive size seems so much larger as he looms over me, his eyes narrowing until he spits out one single word: "No," before pushing by me.

Sputtering, I spin. "I'll leave."

"I dare you."

"I'm not your captive. That's not what all this is. If you feel I'm still in danger, stick a guard on me."

He turns back to me, easily answering, "Okay." He continues walking, not pausing even as we stand toe to toe, as I press my back to the wall and he crowds me, ensuring I have nowhere to escape to. "*I'll* be your guard."

His eyes are a bit crazed, but sexy. The past few days fill my head, mingling with the past twenty-four hours. Every moment with Rafael before yesterday has been a dream come true. A fictional time I hadn't expected to find, but he and I run at different paces. He's the mafia. I'm not meant for this life, if last night proved anything.

I can't do this—whatever *this* is. Whatever he wants from me. Right now, I don't even know who *I* am.

He takes my silence as agreement and lifts me into his arms, using the wall at my back as leverage as he claims my mouth in a kiss full of heat and pressure, of unspoken promises, of feelings neither of us wish to admit.

I can't. It's too fast. I'm so fucking confused.

Through the kiss, I stop kissing him back, shaking my head so he understands my unspoken statement. *No.* Emotion pricks at my eye, but I blink it away, not willing him to see through my tough façade.

He releases my mouth, pressing his forehead against mine. "Why do I feel sick with the thought of you out there on your own?"

"Because you've gotten used to me being around. That's all this is, Rafael. We've gotten so used to each other's company; it's consumed us."

He mistakes my words, his expression slipping. "Do you regret anything we did?"

"No." It's an easy answer and one I don't have to at all think about. I don't. I gave him my virginity willingly. Willing and wanting it to be *him*, to make something of this experience.

But we still need to stop before I also lose my heart in the process.

Cupping his cheek, I aim to make him realize that. "Yesterday was a lot, but I woke up with one vow: my father gave me a new life. Whatever his reasoning, I shouldn't throw that away. The past is the past. My mother thinks I'm dead, so why dredge it up again?"

It was the rational decision. Despite everything I've learned about myself, it seems like nothing's certain. Nothing but my own experiences of living with Dad, whose shown me only love. Whatever Dad's reason for stealing me away, it must have been a good one and I'd dishonour his memory by chasing a past he fought to get me away from.

Rafael opens his mouth to reply, but then goes quiet again. Opened. Closed.

Finally, a resigned sigh leaves him and he lowers me back to my feet. "Fine. You win, Belle. I only have two requests."

"What are they?" I ask carefully, mind racing with every possible way this smooth talker will somehow walk away the winner.

"Whether you like it or not, I'm sticking a bodyguard on you. He can watch you from a distance, and you won't even know he's there. But until this is dealt with, you will be protected."

I guess that's acceptable. "Not you."

"Not me," he agrees.

"And the second request?"

"One day. One final day with me. We pretend the past

twenty-four hours haven't happened and go back to the beginning. We make it a day of our choosing."

That sounds like a risky idea, but I owe Rafael that much. I owe *myself* that much.

"Okay."

The look on Rafael's face becomes everything and I know I've responded correctly.

37
RAFAEL

The library isn't where I imagined our final day being spent, but I can't complain that much. It feels like it's been a while since coming here, and I've come to realize I've missed it. I've missed watching that fucker, Gage, glare at me every chance he can, and watching Isabelle work. As she talks with the few parents who come through during the daytime, shelves all the previous day's returns, and organizes and catalogues any new books that were ordered.

Besides, this is good, because while we're here, I have staff ensuring everything for tonight goes off without a hitch.

One final day isn't enough. It doesn't *feel* nearly enough, and I've spent half of Isabelle's shift trying to figure out when exactly my heart changed. When it became less about her past and what she could know and more about *her*.

Not wanting to let her go. It feels too soon because after yesterday's discoveries and murder, to close the book on her history now, seems wrong. But I can respect why she wants to.

After a quick debrief with Nico, Father, and Rosen this morning, collectively, they agreed with Belle. She's no longer useful to them, so they don't understand my drive to keep her around. Nico kept smirking, so I think he knows where my head is.

Her agreeing to one final day was less of an option than she realizes, but I'm pleased she said yes. To drop her off at home and never see her again is a kick to the balls I really don't want. Isabelle's lived a sheltered life, and before she returns to creating a new version of that, I crave giving her a few final positive memories.

She emerges from an aisle and finds me instantly, her smile so fucking wide, natural, and beautiful, it makes my heart hurt. I've never thought of women as more than bodies to fuck, good times to be had, but turns out, all I needed was Belle's quiet demeanor.

When she disappears down another aisle, that cute sundress showcasing her legs makes me groan, knowing what's beneath it. I follow behind, the need to sate one forbidden craving driving me forward. No one's down here on this level, no one except Gage, but his presence is simply an added bonus. And before another mother arrives and gets an eyeful—

At the end of the aisle, she's moving around books. I've seen a lot of this task, but not quite sure of the reasoning behind it. I'd ask, but I have a different focus now.

She must hear me but doesn't comment until I step behind her, wrapping my arm around her waist and burying my head into her neck. She giggles, angling herself away.

"Rafael, I'm working."

"And? I'm hungry."

She glances down the aisle, searching for anyone listening. Harshly, she whispers, "We're in public."

"Isn't that the point?" Smiling, I turn her around, removing the books from her hands, and methodically position them on the shelves at her side.

"Gage."

"Again, isn't that the point?" Lowering myself to my knees, I look up the length of her form, into her heated eyes as the very idea of this consumes her. "You can't tell me this doesn't excite you. Just like the Corsetti library, only more public."

Lifting her dress, I trail my hand up her thigh, right toward her heat, covered by her panties. Shifting them aside with my thumb, I drag a single finger through her core, a noise coming from the back of her throat.

"Just as I thought." I take her leg and hook it over my shoulder. The quick change in stance makes her gasp and hold onto the metal shelving tighter. "Now, careful how much noise you make, *ma belle*."

I dip my finger inside her, stroking gently before adding another, pumping in and out of her, making her whimper, her teeth biting down on her lip as she fights to conceal her noises.

Then I put my mouth on her, flicking my tongue rapidly against her clit. Her bud is swollen and sensitive and it won't take long for her to come. Which is good because time may be limited. I'd rather not traumatize a visiting child.

She slaps the metal shelf, making it clang. Her hips rock into my touch, my finger gaining another fraction inside her, while I suck her clit between my lips, adding the right amount of pressure I know she needs.

"Hey, Isabelle—"

She gasps, but it's not because Gage stumbled upon us, kind of how I was hoping he would. As much as I'd prefer he not be a voyeur to this experience, it'll make my point.

I feel her orgasm approaching. She's wetter, her moans building, less restrained now that the person we're hiding from is observing. Her pussy flutters around my fingers, a warning of what's about to come.

Pumping my fingers, I increase the pressure until her moans

turn into one long continuous stream and her pussy constricts around my fingers. I continue to suck her, slowly pulling my fingers out as her orgasm subsides, her breath slowly evening out.

Standing, I lick her from my fingers beneath her watchful, heated gaze. Then, making my final point, I hold the sides of her face and place the deepest kiss I can, one packed with possessive meaning before releasing her.

"Told you," I whisper, a smile in my voice. "Now, every time you're here, you'll have something to remember me by."

At the end of the aisle, I shove by Gage, who's still staring dumbfoundedly at her.

"Mine," I growl, pushing him away. "If you know what's best, you'll find somewhere else to be."

He scowls and drifts to the other side, around the corner and thankfully out of sight. This might be our final day, but I'll still stake my claim to ensure he doesn't think twice about her again.

Even if it's a short-lived claim.

The remainder of her shift went by quickly. Every time she spotted me in the corner, her cheeks got red, and I've decided it's my next favourite colour on her. Second only to the pale-yellow dress Della leant her this morning. The moment she dressed at the Corsetti mansion, my instructions for tonight became even more specific.

Still, it couldn't end fast enough because driving to the park becomes our next destination. When I pull up into the same spot as last time, she makes a noise.

"Here again."

"Holds good memories. First kiss and all."

Her cheeks get red again, and I fucking love it.

Instead of heading for the swings, I lead her toward the grassy part in the far corner of the park. To the single, freshly planted tree I had put there this morning alongside the small plaque on a wooden post.

She thinks nothing of it, likely believing it to simply be one more piece of nature around us, until I halt her steps. Her eyes immediately find the plaque, curious, and the second she reads the entire inscription, her expression falters, tears beading in the corner of her eyes.

In honour of Maurice Dupont. Loving father. Loyal soldier.

Loyal might have been a stretch, but this is for her, not me. Until recently, we believed him to be loyal.

Isabelle drops to the grass, her hands reaching for the small wooden pellets surrounding the freshly planted tree; something for her to physically grasp onto.

"When did you do this?"

"While you were working." I crouch beside her, laying my hand over hers. "For everything that's happened, this is for you and him. I'm sorry we never found his body, but I want you to have somewhere you can come to and visit. Somewhere you can *feel* him. A park for you and him to visit frequently."

With a pinched expression and lips pressed together, she nods, peering up at the sky, into the late afternoon sun, using the rays to burn away her tears, but that won't do.

"Cry, *ma belle*. It's okay. It's normal to be sad over losing a parent."

"I'm sad and happy at the same time," she admits with an amused huff. "Thank you, Rafael. I don't know how often I'll get to visit but thank you for doing this."

I could have had it planted somewhere in the city closer to her, but truth is, I've become selfish where she's concerned. This is a short drive away from the Corsetti mansion. It's a three-bus trip for her otherwise. Plus, with the affluent neigh-bourhood we're in, I know it won't be vandalized.

"Reach out whenever you want. I'll drive you here myself."

She rolls her eyes, smirking through her grief. "Why do I think you did this on purpose?"

Because I did.

"Does it matter?"

For a long moment, she's silent, her finger stroking the plaque over and over. A solid few minutes pass before she whispers, "No. It doesn't."

Her voice gets swallowed by the gentle breeze, coasting into the world.

Exactly where she will be soon.

38

ISABELLE

When Rafael requested one more day, he meant one more day of pure bliss. Because if the day already wasn't amazing after being eaten out at work and then getting a memorial place for Dad, it certainly becomes so when Rafael leads me to his bedroom in his condo.

His bedroom, where the most beautiful dress is stretched out on his bed.

"Holy..." Going forward, I pause at the end of the bed, too scared to touch the ornate dress that looks like it easily cost as much as my rent. It's very similar to the simple mid-thigh sundress Della leant me for the day, but a deeper shade of yellow. Almost a gold. Mid-thigh like the one I'm wearing, with a sweetheart neckline giving the dress an elegant yet simplistic appearance. "This is..."

"Yours."

"Excuse me."

"We're going out on a date because if I get one final day with you, then I'm ensuring you remember it."

Like I could forget anything about this day.

"But this dress…" My hand floats over the sparkling material. "It's—"

Rafael comes up behind me, cupping my shoulders. "Yours," he repeats. "Take your time getting ready. I'll be in the living room. Come out when you're done."

A date. Like a normal woman. A normal couple. Rafael and I are the opposite of normal.

I turn in his arms, about to tell him this is silly. That we can order pizza again and I can even read to him, if he wants. Anything but a public activity. But when I see his expression, the hopefulness, I can't rob him of it.

Which means, when I speak, my mouth forms the word, "Okay."

Rafael drops a kiss to my forehead, and I'm struck with how much I'll miss those forehead kisses after tomorrow. When he leaves his room, I somehow feel more alone than ever.

One hour later, I've realized I don't know how to *do* this. To dress up and be fancy and do my hair and makeup in a way that'll suit being on the arm of Rafael Corsetti. I'm a joke.

I stand in his walk-in closet, ready and biding my breath before I make my way to the living room, where he is waiting. I've showered and done my makeup in the most minimal manner—how I feel most comfortable with it being—and my hair in an updo. I wanted to show off the dress, but it leaves my scars visible. I've never concerned myself with them in the past because I've never had a reason to but being on the arm of a Corsetti is *more*. How many people will stare at us, wondering what he's doing with the plain, scarred woman?

The dress and I certainly don't match. It's elegant. I'd

almost rather put on the one I wore all day again. Based on the clothing he's gotten for me, I get the sense that where we're going demands something nicer than the sundress.

The hallway has never felt so long. Every stride in my shoes is weighted, making my steps louder than I'd prefer, but finally, I make it to the end of the hallway, where Rafael is perched on the edge of a couch, scrolling on his phone.

He looks up at my entrance, his mouth falling open in an almost-comedic manner, making me appreciate him even more. "Holy fuck."

Clutching the delicate dress, I swirl it around my thighs. "Too much?"

"Too much?" he repeats, his tone spiking in disbelief. He stands, pocketing his phone as he slowly approaches, his hungry gaze devouring every inch of me. "No, *ma belle,* not too much. I'm fucking stunned speechless. You are every dream I've ever had come true."

Oh. Well, I guess that's better. I manage a small smile, unable to completely meet his gaze. Instead, I study him. His fresh suit, a deep blue tie. His hair is brushed, and a fresh scent of mint wafts from him.

He follows my attention. "I showered when you were dressing. Got the outfit when you were showering. Now, come on," he reaches for my hand, tugging me to his side, "we should go, before I cancel tonight so I can keep you in my bed."

That idea also doesn't seem too bad, but now that I'm dressed and by Rafael's side, him gazing at me with eyes packed with emotion, I'm no longer anxious.

I'm excited.

～

The restaurant we pull up in front of looks as expensive as this dress. The cursive writing on the windows, the fairy lights lining the short pathway to the front door, and a valet that immediately steps forward when Rafael parks.

"Rafael—"

"Relax," he tells me, countering the anxiety that creeped into my tone, "it's Corsetti owned. Like I would take you somewhere I knew wasn't completely safe." Playfully, he rolls his eyes before getting out and handing his keys to the valet. He comes around to my side of the car and opens the door, reaching his hand inside for me to take.

I do, and he helps me to my feet. He smiles before leading me to the front door and opening it, gesturing for me to go ahead.

The restaurant I step into sweeps me into another world. One with clinking crystal China, servers who speak in hushed tones, and the scent of money that fills the air. That's what I imagine this place looking like normally anyway, based on the expensive décor. But right now, it's empty.

As in, most of the circular tables have been moved to the far side of the room, with only a singular table in the middle, two chairs on either side.

"Rafael." I turn as he comes up behind me, his arm winding around my waist. "This is too much. You shut the place down for the night."

"And?" He pulls out the nearest chair for me to sit. I do, despite the anxiety coursing up and down my spine, making me stiff in the seat. "You seem to think I care about other people's dining experiences when I'm working to make this one your best."

My only one. I scan the space—the very intimate space. Restaurants have diners eating, servers flitting from table to table, bartenders preparing drinks, but this one is completely empty.

"The staff."

"There's a few here. Everyone else got a paid day off."

"At least they're paid."

"Of course." He narrows his eyes.

I laugh, only stopping when a server approaches. She chuckles too, matching my energy as she smooths her apron, gesturing first to Rafael. "Mr. Corsetti, having a good night, I hope? Do you need the menus?"

"Just one." He motions to me. Because, of course, he's memorized the menu items.

"Oh, no," I lean forward, gaining the server's attention, "please. Anything chicken-based is fine. Pick something for me —whatever's good."

The server looks thoughtful for a moment before nodding. "You got it. I'll have the chef make his favourite. And you, Mr. Corsetti?"

"The same. And two waters, two cabernet sauvignons. Whatever you recommend."

"Got it." She moves away to go fulfill our order, leaving me to continue freaking out at Rafael's lavish experience. This isn't something regular people do.

"This is insanity."

"This is a final night."

But how am I supposed to move on from this after today?

After a delicious meal, tasty wine, and casual conversation in which it feels like I did most of the talking, the server returns to take our plates away, right as a soft tune fills the space.

Rafael stands, rebuttoning his jacket and reaches for me, not giving me an option as he pulls me to my feet, leading me away from the table.

"What are you doing?" I whisper, though we're the only ones here.

He swings me in a small circle, his hand enclosing mine, his other going to my hip and he twirls us around, stepping in exact pace to the music.

"We're dancing," I answer for him.

"Always the observant one."

As he turns again, I don't move my feet fast enough and end up bumping into him, feeling my chest and face heat.

"Don't be nervous. Just let me lead."

"You know how to dance?"

He crooks a smile. "Mother forced my brothers and me into mandatory lessons."

"Nico and you."

"And Hawke."

He spins us again, this time taking my arms and placing then lazily over his shoulders, his steps becoming slower and less calculated, but somehow more intimate.

"I am sorry, Belle. For what we did to you."

I force a half-baked smile, the truth of my emotions seeping into my next words. "After learning everything, I guess it wasn't your fault. You didn't kill him, or get him killed. He made his own decisions. As for everything else..." No statement suits because I have no idea what to think and I won't for a long time. "It is what it is."

His lips press together, almost angrily, but he doesn't push the topic. "I'm still able to be sorry. I feel like we dragged you out of your little hole and dropped hell on you."

Pretty much. Stroking my fingers over the back of his neck, I playfully shrug, "It wasn't *all* bad. Got to make a non-reader appreciate books."

He chuckles. "Now that I know what's inside them, I might need to take up the hobby."

"Do it! I'll give you a list of recommendations. Actually," I fake debate, "don't. Because then we'll never leave. I'll be so busy listing out titles."

"That doesn't sound like a bad idea," he says huskily, pulling me tighter against him, no space between our bodies. I feel him everywhere. We're not really dancing anymore. Just swaying. His head bends closer, his lips brushing over mine, making my heart skip a beat.

"Thank you, Rafael. For everything. Today especially. I must say, this is quite the date."

He smiles gently, his hand sweeping over my face, stroking my scars. "These weren't your fault, *ma belle*, and never let them hold you back. They're a part of you, which makes them beautiful."

I swear, I made Rafael up. Like one day, I'll open my eyes and be back in my apartment and Dad will be there for our scheduled dinners, but everything with Rafael will have been a dream. In some ways, a nightmare, but in so many others, the best dream my cruel mind could have created.

The look in Rafael's eyes is one I don't want to name. A look he certainly shouldn't be having, and I shouldn't be feeling in return. A look that has me questioning *everything* about my decision.

Why *can't* I be with him?

Whoa—stop. I can't be with him because nothing's been labelled. Because frequent fucking and his family's battle have thrown us into an emotional tailspin. Neither of us feels anything past a slight admiration for one another, driven by our body's physical needs.

What a lie.

It'll fade. This will fade.

I lift higher on my toes and bring him down to me, his lips meeting mine halfway. His arms reclaim my waist, and he lifts me completely off my feet, spinning me in a circle.

"Rafael, can I ask for one more thing for tonight?"

"Anything."

"Can we visit Eden?"

His hands trail up my side, igniting flames up my spine, where his hands grasp the expensive dress as though he's about to yank it off right here.

"Fuck yes."

Returning to the same room we watched the duo and trio use when I fingered her for the first time is purely for sentimental reasons. On the wall, I tap all the necessary buttons to make this an exhibitionism room before turning back to her.

She's staring straight at the glass, her hands folded together in front of her. Still in that fucking gorgeous dress, she looks too regal for a den of sin. Too rich, amidst a club of people who'd either enjoy making her a slave or *being* her slave. Too delicate, too able to be broken.

For this final night, she's *mine*. Mine and only theirs to watch.

I sidle closer, trailing my fingers up and down her arms, over the fresh goosebumps that form there, trying to ease her. Stuck halfway between wanting to slowly peel that dress from her form and cherish it forever as a reminder of tonight and wanting to rip it from her in my urgency to get her naked and beneath me.

"Still want to do this?"

"Has there been any indication I've changed my mind?" She rubs her palms up my chest. "But I'm nervous."

"We don't have to be wat—"

"No," she cuts in, fervently shaking her head. "I want to. Doesn't remove the nerves though."

"Once we start, I'll get you so wrapped up into it, you won't have a chance to think about anything else." With a finger, I tap the side of her head, her temple, making my point before my hand shifts to the back of her neck and I bring her to my body, stealing her lips in a heady kiss.

With that kiss, I back her onto the bed, continuing until she's reclining, arching her back to meet my touch. Her hands slide down my body, hooking on my pants, her fingers winding through the loops before working at the button.

I let her, hoping undressing me will give her the kind of confidence she needs. I would have much preferred to already have her naked, but tonight's about chances, and this is the final time she and I will be together, so she's in more control than she might realize.

She undoes my pants but doesn't reach inside, instead untucking my shirt, her hands sliding back up my body, trying to shrug off my jacket. I do it for her, tossing it to the side and unbuttoning my shirt too.

"Rafael." Her teeth scrape over her bottom lip, uncertainty moving her attention away from my face and into the far corner of the room. She doesn't speak for another moment, but reaches for me, her hands returning to my waist. "Can you—I want—can you teach me how to...I want to use my mouth on you the same way you did for me."

Working halfway through my shirt's buttons, I pause, mentally replaying what she asked. Every desire comes to life in that second and my shirt feels too constricting.

I glance at the window across from us. No one's here yet—

the room will ding informing us when there are—but this might not be the best idea for one of her firsts.

"No." She shakes her head, catching where my attention is. "Leave it. I want..."

To let other people see me teach you.

Could she be any more perfect than she is in this very second?

Backing away, I remove the remainder of my clothes until I'm standing there bare, and she's perched on the edge of the bed, still donning that sexy dress.

"Come, Belle."

She lifts to her feet, her heels making her wobble a second before she regains her footing. Those heels are staying on all fucking night if I have my way.

"On your knees."

Grasping the edges of her dress, she adjusts as she lowers to her knees, her eyes remaining on me. Cupping her face, I rub my thumb over her cheek, just beneath her smoky eyeshadow, memorizing this vision. By the end of the night, her hair will be taken down from their pins and mussed, her makeup smudged.

"Touch me, Belle. In whatever way you feel comfortable."

She releases the hold she has on her clothing to tentatively reach for me. Her small hands wrap around the base of my cock, while her other keeps her steady, holding onto my thigh. Just seeing her like this already has my cock hardening.

"You won't hurt me," I encourage. "Stroke me however you feel comfortable until I get hard."

She does, her eyes intent on her job, almost hyper-focused. But it's cute.

A soft ding echoes through the room and I grin. "We're no longer alone."

She lets out a small gasp and peeks behind her, toward the glass we can't see through. Biting her lip, her speed increases as she focuses on me again, and when I'm fully erect, she stops, her fingers lightly dancing along the my skin as she seeks direction.

Taking her hand, I move it to my base, pumping for her as silent direction before releasing. She understands my instructions and doesn't end her movements.

"Whenever you're ready, take me in your mouth. Careful with your teeth. Do whatever feels natural."

"But I want you tell me what *you* like."

I bite back a groan. "I will but get comfortable first."

She shuffles closer, hesitating only for a second before her tongue flicks against my head. Just the tip, but it feels so good, like she's already taken me down her pretty, little throat. She does it again, before opening her lips and swallowing me. She keeps them tight, suctioning my head, and I groan, reaching out to stroke a hand over her hair.

"You're doing great, Belle. And in front of strangers. Wonder who's behind the glass."

She sucks me an inch deeper, my words seemingly spurring her on.

"Think it's a couple, like we were? A guy standing behind her, his fingers buried in her cunt? Or maybe his partner is on their knees, replicating your actions, using you as a guide."

She makes a noise over my length that I feel to the base of my spine. My fingers flex in her hair as she takes another inch of me, pausing for a second as she adjusts. I ache to shove down her throat, even though it's the last thing I'd do.

She swallows as much as she can before I hit the back of her throat, and she jerks back quickly, but doesn't release me.

"Breathe through your nose," I instruct, waiting until I feel her breath against my body before also telling her, "If you need to stop, you stop, Isabelle. You're not forced into anything." The use of her full name, one I so infrequently use now, conveys my seriousness.

Her eyes flick up as she drags her mouth away from my cock, her tongue the last to touch me. Big, round, dark eyes meet mine and the corners of her mouth curl before she drags her mouth over me again, moving slowly, watching me as I watch her.

"Fuck," I curse when I reach the back of her throat again. My hands tighten in her hair, the need growing so strong. Somehow, she knows what she's doing. It's hard to believe the shy, virginal girl I met is now sucking my cock like a fucking porn star. "You have no idea how gorgeous you look with my dick in your throat." I stroke the base of her throat.

She releases me to mumble, "It's those books. You'd be amazed how good of instruction manuals they are when you're inexperienced."

A breathy chuckle bursts from my chest. I'll buy her every goddamn library in the world after this.

She swallows me again, this time creating a slow pace as her lips drag up and down my length. I wrap my hand over hers, the one holding my cock, reminding her to pump at the same time.

"Use your tongue too," I instruct after a moment, when I feel she's gotten the hang of it. "My underside can be sensitive."

She releases me with a pop, grinning as she whispers, "You mean right here?" Her tongue flicks the very spot between my head and my shaft and my hips flex, pushing back into her mouth.

"Holy fuck, Belle, I'm sorry." With my hand in her hair, I try to pull her off me, to let her be in control again, but her nails dig into my thighs.

She takes me deeper, her tongue now doing wicked things, and I realize how bad of an idea standing is. How weak my legs feel, the heat flashing through my body. My hand relaxes on her head, simply letting her control my plea-sure. My eyes lock on the window across from us, the awareness that every second of this is being watched by strangers exciting me.

Her hand lifts, coming on top of mine, where she pushes on it meaningfully. My insides heat in hunger, but with her, I can't do this like *that*.

"Belle—"

She removes my cock from her mouth, glaring up the length of my body. "Stop treating me gently and use me how you want to."

"That was the wrong thing to say," is the only warning I give before my hand tightens around her hair, fisting it. My other cups her neck, locking her in my hold. "Tap the back of my leg if you need me to stop."

I hit the back of her throat, and this time, I don't let up, thrusting her mouth over my cock relentlessly, my speed no match for her suction.

"You're being watched," I remind her. "Just on the other side of that wall, people are watching you take my cock like the good girl you are. Dressed how you are, all dolled up, your makeup getting messy."

She moans, unpeeling yet another layer of her. A little degradation goes a long way with this one.

"God, you're hot," I breathe, my hold on her relentless. My hips jerk into her at the same time my hand propels her over me. When I feel her nails drag up and down my thighs, I prepare to end this, but instead, her hands trail over my skin, between my legs, where she cups my tight balls. "Fuck, Belle. Keep doing that."

Beneath my encouragement, she massages the skin there. The pressure building in the base of my stomach, the weakness in my legs—I will come soon.

I'd love to drench her throat with my cum, but I'm not ready for this night to end. Not for a long time.

With my grip in her hair, I peel her mouth off me, tipping her head back. Drool drips from the side of her mouth, her eyes watering, and her breath comes out shallow, but still, she smiles at me.

I lift her to her feet, taking that mouth, licking up the mess I've created. She nips at me, her hands fusing themselves to my arms as I begin working the back of her dress.

She tries to help, reaching behind her, but I gently smack her hands away, shaking my head. "Turn around."

Grinning, she obeys, facing the glass, exactly how I wanted her to be. Through the reflection, I study her expression, seeking any sense of previous anxieties, but among the cloud of lust filling the room, she's seemed to have overcome all that.

"They're watching you," I murmur, dragging my lips over her neck. I'll never get tired of the taste or the scent of her skin. "Watching and waiting for what we'll show them next. I think it's time for them to see your pussy, don't you?"

"Yes," she hisses, watching me in the reflection as I continue working the zipper at her back, trying to figure out how she dressed herself in the first place.

Every bit I drag it down, another inch of her skin is revealed. My fingers follow the path, right to the curve of her ass before I take the drop sleeves of the dress and pull them down her arms. She lifts them, helping me, baring her chest to the observers on the other side, in only a basic, strapless black bra.

Hooking my fingers into the side of the dress, I tug it over her hips, and it pools at her feet. Tapping the back of her legs, she understands my silent command and lifts each foot, still wearing heels, so I can remove the dress, being certain not to let it hook on the delicate material before I toss it with my clothes.

I trail my hands up the inside of her thighs, staring at her perfect ass encased in lace panties. Where the fuck did she get this lingerie from? All I know is I owe a raise to whoever bought it.

"You're sexy, Belle."

"You make me feel like that." In the reflection, I catch her hands lifting to her face, lightly touching her scars. "From the beginning, you've barely paid them any attention."

"Because I was so intrigued by the rest of you," I say, removing her panties too. As sexy as they are, they're in my way. "Your attitude. Your tenacity." Slipping my hand between her legs, I pet her, watching as she instantly responds, her legs inching apart. "You never backed down from anything. Even as life changed around you."

"Blew up is more like it." She chuckles, quickly shifting into a moan as I sink a single finger inside her wet core.

"*Ma belle* enjoyed sucking my dick, clearly." I slip another finger into her from behind, where I'm still crouched.

"Yes."

"Which means it's my turn to thank this pussy of yours. How many times do you believe you can come for our audience?"

"I don't know." She shuffles her legs farther apart.

"Why don't we find out then?" Leaning forward and ducking, I lick her from behind as my fingers continue to move inside her. My free hand comes up around her hip, splaying on her stomach to keep her steady.

"Rafael!" she cries. "Fuck."

I'll have her cursing many more times before the night is up. Something about this woman's taste drives me absolutely fucking insane. As my fingers pump inside her, my tongue drags over her core toward her backside, pausing at the tight ring of muscle.

She gasps, her legs going stiff, but I reassure her, "You'll enjoy it. I'm not going in, don't worry."

My statement seems to ease her, and her leg muscles contract. Her weight leans onto my hand, her legs continuing to spread, trying to ease that ache inside her.

"Remove your bra," I instruct. "Show our audience your perfect breasts. Play with yourself."

A second later, I hear her bra hitting the ground. I don't pull away to check if she's obeying me because I know she is. She wants this too much to deny me.

My fingers work at her, my tongue at her back entrance, her cries building and building until I feel her legs quivering, threatening to give way. Based on her pants, she's second away from—

Even my thoughts get interrupted as her orgasm is a long moan, her core tightening around my fingers as she all but falls forward, only my hand holding her up.

I wait until it's passed before lifting to my feet, turning her around. Sleepy, lust-filled eyes blink slowly up at me, a grin slowly expanding on her face.

"Why was that so hot?"

Because you were made to be mine.

40

ISABELLE

Rafael doesn't respond to my question; he simply backs me toward the bed. I glance at the window, wondering who's on the other side. How many people? Are they watching or are they preoccupied with their own pleasures? It's invigorating to have their attention on us, to think Rafael and I are the ones controlling their desires.

"Nervous?" he whispers, mistaking my attention.

I shake my head. Not anymore. Not with him staring at me how he is.

Rafael lowers me to the bed, putting my face more in line with his hard cock. I reach for him, stroking my hand up and down his shaft, recalling earlier when he was fucking my face. Now *that* was hot.

"Lie back," he orders gently.

I do, knowing everything he tells me is for one reason and one reason only.

"Look toward them, Belle. Let them see your face."

Again, I do, imagining the people on the other side staring at us, waiting as I am.

"I ever tell you how addicted I am to your taste?" is the only warning I get before he dives between my legs, his tongue sinking into my core, his mouth eating the rest of me. His hands cup my breasts, thumb and finger pinching my nipples, using my body as his hold to keep me steady.

My head tosses back into the pillow, my insides sensitive from the orgasm minutes ago. His tongue went places I never thought I'd enjoy, but it was pleasurable.

Rafael *eats*, using only his mouth and nothing else. Facial scruff roughly rubs at my core, but it increases the sensitivity. My hands come over top of his, feeling his fingers mold around my breasts.

"Rafael." Because I have no other words to tell him how much I love this. How much I don't want this to end. How I'll imagine this moment for the rest of my life.

It hits suddenly, but somewhere between the pass of sadness and the increase in pleasure, I feel the orgasm slam into me as Rafael sucks my clit between his teeth, drinking everything I give him before diving right back in, giving me barely a second to recover. His tongue takes the place of his cock, which I can't wait to feel inside me.

"Come for them," he commands.

"Come for you," I counter, breathing hard.

"No. You come for *them*. You *ruin* me."

Oh. I smile, flicking my eyes toward the glass again, wishing we could watch them too. Something about sharing pleasure in that way is rousing.

It's the final thought I have as his tongue feels like it licks the deepest parts of me, curling and twisting as much as the limited length can. It's enough, though. Enough that beneath his control, a wave slams into me again, wiping me away to the endless sea.

Not endless, I remind myself. It will end. In the morning, when we reach the shore and depart in opposite directions. Or when we crash and burn together.

"I don't think..." Reaching down, I tap his head, until he looks up at me, grinning through wet lips. Wet with *me* and the sight does something to my fragile heart.

"Don't dare me like that," he says nonetheless, but climbs up my body, licking his way up. His teeth lay claiming bites to my hip, my stomach, and each of my breasts, before finding my neck.

"Think they're jealous?" he mumbles into my throat.

"Of me? Maybe. After all, I have the Corsetti capo's attention."

He chuckles darkly. "I'd say they're jealous of me. After witnessing a fucking goddess orgasm, how does one go back from that?"

Compliments, he is proficient at. I giggle, stroking my hand over his hair. "You're sweet."

He lifts his head to show me the honesty reflecting in his gaze as he flicks stray strands of my hair aside. "Not sweet. Candid. You really have no idea how you look right now. Flip over. There's another position I've been dying to get you into."

I think I know what he's about to do, but still, I flip onto my hands and knees, watching him expectantly. He walks around the bed to the opposite side, turning me with him, until I'm facing the window.

He moves away, to the other side of the room, and when the tell-tale sound of foil rips through the silent space, I smile.

A finger strokes through my very wet core before I feel the head of his cock replace his fingers. He gives me no warning before thrusting inside me in one, swift movement, my back arching with my low scream, my fingers pushing into the bed beneath me.

"This is...this..." Is deeper than anything I've felt before. Somehow, even more than when I was on top of him.

"Yes," he agrees to my directionless statement. He reaches forward and takes my hair, now a complete mess and nothing like the updo I created earlier in the evening, and gently yanks on the strands, tipping my head back until I'm forced to look straight at the window again. "Let them see you, *ma belle*. That's why they're here, after all. Those strangers want to see you taking my cock."

"Yes."

With my hands and knees, I try to push back into his thrusts, but his speed makes it a challenge, leaving me completely in his control as he roughly takes me. He's more unrestrained than earlier, but I love it. Like the knowledge I'm leaving tomorrow, and he'll probably never see me again, has him more animalistic, but I love it so much. The ripples he's causing inside me are like a domino effect.

Will I ever find this again? Will my tormented, soul be able to find a shred of happiness like this in the future? Will someone ever appeal to me as much as Rafael Corsetti does?

"Give me everything you have, *ma belle*. Show them how good you come on my cock. How fucking great you are at taking me."

I want to hold off and come with him, but he's making it impossible. I stare ahead, my vision blurring as pleasure wracks my form, my screams are loud, unabashed, and *free*.

He makes me free.

This whole time in my life has been freeing—open. Nothing I'll forget, even as I work through next steps.

He growls, his fingers digging roughly into my hip. I love when he forgets to be gentle, unable to stop himself from claiming in the best possible ways.

"I can't—I can't hold back any longer, Belle. I don't want this night to end."

Because once he comes and we leave Eden, it's a countdown until morning.

But I need this—need him. Need to feel him fill me again.

I lean back on my knees, silently begging him to finish. He listens to my request and thrusts into me a final time. The condom prevents his warmth from coating my insides, and while rationality says the protection is wise, I find myself *wanting* his cum.

His low groan coats every corner of the room; a sound imprinting on my soul. I'll never forget this.

As his pants subside, his hands loosen their hold, and his softening erection slips out of my sated core. He reaches down, petting me gently.

"Think we gave a good enough show?"

"I think so. Feels like it anyway."

He leans over me and presses a single kiss to my sweaty back, lingering there for a second before moving away from the bed and heading to the tablet on the far corner. He taps a button and then explains, "They're not privy to the next part."

Next part? There's more? I'm not sure my knees can handle more, so I flop to my side as he returns, lying beside me.

"Greatest day ever," I tell him honestly.

He grins, taking my hand and rests it over his slowing heart. He doesn't explain why, but there's a sense of purpose in the gesture I don't want to think about.

"Greatest everything, Belle. In case you haven't noticed, I strive to make every experience better than the last."

"You exceeded." I laugh, before peeking around the room, our surroundings prompting me to wonder, "Will we be going back to your bed?"

With his responding sigh, his eyes glide closed. "We will. I just want to stay here for a couple of minutes."

With my hand over his heart and *this* feeling so right, even in the middle of a world that makes no sense, I shut my eyes, letting my body lull to the sound of his breathing.

~

I'm only woken when I feel his arms coming around me. He lifts me with one hand before retrieving my dress, which he balls on my lap, and his coat, which he covers me with. Through the reflection of the glass, right before he exits the room, I notice him dressed in his pants again.

"Sleep," he murmurs, "I'm getting us back home."

Home. Not my home, but the concept feels pretty fucking inviting.

Sighing, I curl my head into his neck, letting myself drift to the sounds of him walking through Eden, into his private elevator, and right up to his apartment, where he only stops when we're in the bedroom.

He stops long enough to deposit our clothing in a messy pile on the floor before turning back around, entering the bathroom.

"What are we—"

My question is answered when he steps into the shower, switching on the water, waiting for it to heat before he immerses me. He places me on my feet, but maintains such a hold on me, he has most of my weight.

"I'm going wash you with my soap, Belle."

And then he does, managing to maintain a decent hold on me. I don't sleep, just gaze up at him as he cares for me, only releasing me once he's done to quickly wash himself.

The second he's finished, he's wrapping a warm, fluffy

towel around my body and lifting me back into his arms, carrying me straight to the bed where he lays me in the centre and removes the towel, tossing it to the side.

Silently, he climbs in beside me and takes me in his arms. No need for pillow walls anymore.

"I'm sorry, *ma belle*."

I pretend not to hear him, to already be asleep.

Truth is, I remain awake half the night.

And I know he does too.

41
RAFAEL

Around ten in the morning, after a long sleep-in, I feel her pull from my arms, but pretend not to be aware as she exits the bed. I listen, hoping she's merely taking a bathroom break, but also knowing in my gut, this isn't the case.

She's leaving.

Worse, she's trying to sneak out without me knowing.

I should be angry she's taking the coward's way, but I instead force myself still, allowing her to do what she needs to. So much of her life was controlled by others, and she's making this decision for her, whether I like it or not.

There's some shuffling as she dresses, and then I hear her exit the bedroom, rifling around in the bathroom. When she returns, I assume it's with her items. She drops them in her suitcase and the zip the bag makes is so loud, it echoes through the room and right into my sanity.

Every fibre of my being demands I block her from going. To keep her here. To not let her go.

What's the saying? When you care for someone, you'll allow them the space they need? Caring for someone is to let them go. Those kinds of sentiments anyway.

Which is why, when her steps bring her to my side of the bed, I don't react. I don't show her I'm awake or that I've already claimed her mind and pussy, and my final step is her heart.

Her soft touch paints over my lips. It's this sensation, her scent—her very being—I'll remember after she goes. There's no returning after this. No normality I can live through where I won't imagine her lying beside me, sitting on the couch reading, or finding her in one of Eden's rooms.

"Goodbye," she whispers, believing me still be to be asleep. "I..." With her unfinished sentence, her fingers slip from my skin, landing on the bed beside my hand. She strokes the back of my hand before her energy, her warmth exits, backing up.

Me too, ma belle. Me too.

So many unspoken words. I want to wake up, to tell her now, but she'll see it as a method to keep her here and if Belle wants to go, there's nothing I can do shy of locking her inside the Corsetti mansion.

Tempting. But I won't do it because she deserves to fly free.

Her steps move slowly to the doorway, where they pause. Through the tiniest slits, I watch her look back. Pure longing and emotion consume her expression, but flipping a switch, she turns it off and exits the bedroom.

I sit up, listening to her journey down the hallway, imagining her staring at the living room where she read, where we laughed, where she first broke down with the truth.

I imagine her pausing in the same spot she had yesterday when she entered the living room after getting ready for our date.

I imagine her studying the kitchen, recalling the first day, and then when I roughly fucked her on the counter.

Maybe she's not doing any of that. Maybe I'm being hopeful and she's already at the elevator.

All I know is that when the elevator dings with its arrival, I slide from the bed, getting to my feet and finding my pants from last night, which I discarded on my side of the bed.

My side. There's a my side and a her side. I scoff, trailing to my doorway, pausing there as I stare down the long hallway, toward the end where, around the corner, she's getting into the elevator.

When I hear the doors shut, I leave the bedroom, slowly treading to the living room, counting the length of time it'll take her to exit the building entirely. I wonder if she's standing in the elevator, remembering the first time she rode my mouth.

Or is this simply more of my stupid emotions getting entangled?

The windows from this height don't give me a great view of the base of the building, but eventually, I see her poke out as she drags her suitcase along behind her, her head roving the morning downtown streets.

I watch her until she's out of view. And then I stare at the spot she disappeared in for a long time afterwards. A *long* time.

Too long.

My cell phone rings. I don't know how long it's been—the sun's higher in the sky now, shining through my apartment and lighting it up—but I finally remember I need to get a soldier on her. Cogs will be suitable. He won't go near her.

Returning to the bedroom feels like a knife to the stomach

because it seems so empty. Without her suitcase in the corner, or her in the bed, there's no reason to be here. I snatch the phone and bring up my text thread with Cogs.

But instead of typing out the message I should, I open my contacts list and click a name I need to speak with instead. Call it brotherly advice.

"Rafael," Hawke greets right away.

"I should be lucky you programmed my number into your phone," I comment dryly, thinking back to when he handed me his number right before leaving Montreal.

"Yeah, so I can field your calls."

"Asshole. If that was true, you wouldn't have answered." While joking with Hawke loosens the tightness in my chest a fraction, it doesn't at all unfasten the knots formed there.

"Maybe I was curious why you're calling me at noon on a weekday."

Noon. It's already that time? I've completely lost hours staring out a window, toward a woman who's probably already forgotten about me. I tread slowly into the kitchen, every step feeling heavy as I head for the coffee machine.

It's where I stop but end up reaching into the cupboard for a glass rather than a mug and a bottle of liquor rather than a coffee pod.

"Rafael?" Hawke prompts.

"Yeah," is all I mumble, unscrewing the bottle with one hand.

"Are you drinking?"

"Water."

"Liar." There's some shuffling on the other side of the call and then a door shutting. "Raf, what's going on?"

"I don't know. How did you know?"

"Know what?"

"That you loved Willow. Was it before or after you killed someone for her?"

There's a beat of silence, and then he probes, "What are you really asking?"

"Exactly what I said." With my glass poured, I skip recorking the bottle, since I suspect I'll need it again, and swipe the glass, heading for the couch. "You killed for Willow. Brutally, I might add. Haven't seen a head smashed in like that before. Did you do that because you cared for her, or another reason?"

"Because I loved her," he responds carefully. "That bastard broke out of jail when I should have had him executed right away. He kidnapped her from my friend's wedding. The moment I realized she was gone; it was game over. Everything I spent years running from—being a killer—"

"A Corsetti," I interject. "Be honest, Hawke. You avoided becoming us."

"Exactly. But my own wants didn't matter when it came to her. Once I found them, there was this primal, guttural requirement inside me that demanded for me to ensure her safety. Which meant taking him out."

Like when I saw those four fuckers trying to kidnap her that night. I went into pure protection mode, only thinking about saving her and ensuring they'd never come near her again.

"If there was someone from her past that harmed her, and you found them, would they be breathing?"

"No. There were...others...from her past. Others who—" Hawke leaves me to fill in the gaps, which I get the sense of what he's telling me. "She's asked I don't go searching, and if I'm honest, I wouldn't know where to start. But if I ever stumbled upon one of them, then yes, I would return to that dark place, to wipe them from the earth." He pauses, weighted and dragged out. "Raf, gonna tell me what this is about? You didn't only call to ask these questions."

No. I didn't. I down the alcohol in one swallow and then drop the glass on the table in front of me, returning to the kitchen to retrieve the bottle. Should have just taken it in the first place.

Once I'm seated again, I mumble, "I killed for her. Four people. I'd do it again and again if I could."

"Who's 'her?'"

"*Ma belle.* Belle," I correct, using a more typical nickname. "Isabelle."

Just the sound of her name on my lips has me lifting the bottle to my lips.

Hawke curses. "Raf, put the bottle down. When did all this transpire? Because I was there, like, a week ago. And you didn't have anyone with—"

"A week ago," I interject. "The day Aurora woke up, Rosen and I met with one of our soldiers. He knew something about De Falco. But then went on about protecting his daughter. Well, Isabelle is his daughter."

"Ah. I'm still not drawing lines here."

Another chug. "Nico thought maybe she'd know what her father did, and since he was in my regiment, I had to deliver the news anyway. That night, I found someone slinking outside her house. Oh...I guess that's five deaths in her name. Anyway, it ended up where she moved in with me, and once she was here, I guess we became friends."

Hawke makes an appreciative noise. "Well. You've guaranteed I will always answer your calls, because if future ones are this interesting...I hadn't told any of the family this, but that's how I fell for Willow. We skipped past friendship though, but I had her moved in with me after we saved her from the fucker's torture chamber. It's funny what being in close proximity can do." He pauses. "This all sounds great, but it doesn't explain why you're drinking."

Which reminds me to take another chug. I do, flopping back against the couch. "I'm drinking because she's gone, and I don't know what do to. I'm drinking because after fucking everything, so many truths of her past were revealed. The ploy with De Falco, yeah, a lot more fucked up than any of us thought. Let's leave it at this, Hawke: secret society shit. After everything, she was pissed I was basically using her, and now the truth is out, there's nothing I need from her."

"But?"

"But I *need* her." Realization, irrational thoughts, and depression. Everything mixes into that statement. "I don't even know when it happened, but it did."

"You love her."

"No. I *care* for her."

He grunts, amused. "All right. You *care* for her. You think drinking is really the wisest thing?"

"I mean, I called you. Brotherly advice and all. Got any for me?"

"Yeah, put the bottle down."

"Try again."

"Call her."

Both options are not doable.

"Try again."

"Call our brother or I will."

"Don't." Nico doesn't need to see this. I'll sleep off the alcohol and will be back at work by tomorrow. Belle can return to life as she knows it with a bodyguard protecting from afar. Everyone's happy and she'll become another woman of my past. A fun time and nothing more. "I'm fine. 'Kay, I have to go, Hawke. Thanks."

I hang up before he can counter with more bullshit claims.

Love.

Right. What even is love?

Love doesn't exist in this life. Maybe for Hawke, it does. For Nico, but his scenario was unique. For Father, because he took what he wanted.

But Belle isn't of this life. It doesn't work the same way.

Lifting the bottle to my mouth again, I chug until I black out.

42

ISABELLE

With my suitcase heaving on my arm, I stalk my way through downtown until I get to the nearest bus stop, where I catch the next one right to work. Maybe it's a bad idea to go directly there, but it'll give me a much-needed reprieve from thinking. Keep me focused on something normal, which is why I never called in.

Because that's all I can do for the entirety of the bus ride. The entirety of the short walk from where it drops me off to the library.

I arrive minutes after my shift's start, and let myself in the side entrance, dropping my large suitcase in the small staffroom before heading to the counter to begin work.

For the next hour, my gaze continues to find the corner. Even when little kids and mothers come in and are occupying my day, helping it to go by quicker, I continue to peek in that corner, picturing Rafael standing there, smirking every time I pass by.

It gets worse when I pass *the* aisle. When the memory of him on his knees hits. The illicitness of being eaten out in a library. And then it reminds me of last night, when I was on my knees for him, being taught how to swallow his cock in front of those strangers.

Needless to say, there's been a few instances of crying in the bathroom today.

And it's only noon.

Right after lunch, Gage swaggers in, jerking his chin in greeting. Another reason to miss Rafael's presence because Gage wouldn't have done that if he was here.

He swings around the counter, where I'm reading on my Kindle, which reminds me of a time before Rafael bombarded into my life. Gage leans beside me, crossing his arms. The bruises on his face have yellowed in the past few days, which make them look worse.

"Where's your boyfriend?"

Breathe. It's the only way to not snap at him.

"Don't got one of those," I mumble, continuing to pretend to read. In truth, the cute romance on my screen isn't doing it for me right now.

He makes an appreciative noise and bends closer, smirking. I gag with the scent of cigarette smoke wafting from him. "No? Then who was the one between your legs yesterday, sucking on your cunt?"

I don't respond, instead shoving my Kindle beneath the counter and stalking past him. I have no tasks to keep me busy but escaping him is key. Gage trails close behind, his massive size allowing him to see over my shoulder.

"I didn't realize that's what you're into, Isabelle. I can certainly accommodate that."

Like I'd ever— My teeth smash together, the burst of anger spinning me around, where I shove my hands into his chest, pushing him an inch back. Only an inch because his sheer size is more than my strength can manage.

"Fuck off, Gage. Weren't you warned away from me?"

He barely looks fazed, instantly coming back into my space. "Ah, but that's the beauty of it. He's not here anymore, is he? You finally scared him off."

The growl coming from me would make Rafael proud. As does the shove into Gage's chest, this time throwing my entire body into it. I channel the rage Rafael had when he killed those three men, picturing the animalistic way he charged them and replicating it.

"Leave me alone, Gage. I fucking mean it, or I'll talk to my supervisor about you and then we'll see how well your community service goes."

His eyes narrow, but he backs away, his palms up. "Whatever. I was only joking around, Isabelle. I'm sorry it didn't work out between you and Corsetti." He walks away, his shoulders a fraction lower, but I don't fall for the dejected behaviour.

Fuck you, I think, twisting the opposite way.

～

Gage sticks to the agreement, for lack of a better word, that Rafael once forced on him and he doesn't pay me any more attention until the end of the shift.

He trails behind me as I exit the staff door, waving to a few of the other librarians, ones who work in the adult section. I head in the direction for the bus stop, while he stops at the edge of the staff parking lot, thumbing toward his truck.

"Hey, I'm sorry for acting like a dick earlier. Can I give you a ride home to make up for it?"

With the heavy suitcase, a ride home would be more pleasant than travelling on a bus, but every instinct has me shaking my head, managing a polite, "It's fine, but thanks for the offer."

"As you wish." He turns for his truck.

At least *that* interaction was pleasant.

There's a slight incline from the library to the bus stop, causing my bag to tug on my arm to the point of pain. It's extra effort to pull it up the slope, and a sweat breaks out over my neck. The slight afternoon breeze is a small relief.

As I pass the slim alley between two buildings, I hear a scuffle. Like the kicking of a rock. My steps increase and I glance over my shoulder. I'm only half a block away from the bus stop and already my nerves have me believing there's something worse slinking in the shadows.

That's what I get for being shoved into mob life.

So busy looking behind me, I miss the person approaching until I walk right into what feels like a wall. Large hands come out to steady me, a kind face peering down.

"Hey, sorry there. I think I was too busy on my phone."

With my attention on the stranger, I don't hear the steps behind me until too late. Until the man's eyes flick up, recognition lighting them as their constructed plan works.

A hand covers my mouth while another rips my suitcase from me, tossing it to the side.

From behind me, an arm loops around my throat and that's when the alarms in my head flash. When fight or flight kicks in and I shove my legs off the ground and into the one man in front of me. The grip around my neck constricts, squeezing the sides until white and black spots take over my vision.

I claw at them both, kicking and punching until I get my sight back. But it's too quick.

Black, white, and then nothing.

～

My head feels like bricks landed on it. My body slumps against whatever I'm sitting on. My neck aches as awareness begins returning. I try to move but find myself hindered by something tight around my wrists and ankles.

The room around me is dark, lit only by dim, low hanging lights, but I make out enough—the stone walls, the metal beams. A warehouse.

"What the...?" My voice sounds thick, like I was drugged, but I don't think I was since my mind seems to be clearing. Maybe. I don't know.

"Oh, good, you're awake."

That voice...it's familiar.

A figure steps into my line of sight, calling my attention to the few others who shift in the background. Too many to count, but at least a dozen. A small army, plus the one approaching in front, who tugs down his hood, revealing the face otherwise hidden to me.

The black, greasy hair and large form. The eyes that slither over my body. The yellow bruises around his eyes.

Gage grins, meeting my glare as he advances, bending until his face is lined up with mine. "Hi, Isabelle. Don't take it personally, but this is what we were paid to do. I must say, you were especially hard to take down. Your father, easy. But you? The girl who barely left her house. Worse when Corsetti got involved."

Gage? I'm still trying to wrap my mind around that fact when one of the other figures in the dim light approaches, positioning a tripod a few feet away.

"Hope you don't mind. We borrowed your phone. It'll have more impact this way."

"What will?" Horrified, I glance between Gage and the man

setting up my phone on the tripod, sleep still making me foggy and unable to think straight. "Gage—"

"Illegal hunting." He rolls his eyes. "A small fib. Hunting. Yeah, that is my speciality, but not animals." He grins wolfishly, understanding of the meaning behind his statement crashing down on me. "My court papers were faked for the library. It was never community service I was there for, but you."

"You work for De Falco," I piece together. After everything I've learned, it's the only thing that makes sense.

His mouth purses in an appreciative manner. "You know the name. Yeah, hired mercenaries. He wanted to keep his own men away from the action, knowing they could be traced back to him as he was escaping. But us? We're a separate entity, known for our *specialized* work. You and your father were in his way. You don't find it convenient I only appeared in your life days before your father's death?"

I *never* would have made that connection, so no.

The guy behind Gage unlocks my phone and opens the video chatting app, and that's when it hits.

"You're going to kill me."

"Not while you're still useful. Our orders might be to take you out, but Corsetti pissed me off, so this is *my* revenge. You and I are going to make a bit of a movie." He whistles, and steps behind me for a second, returning quickly with a gun poised in his hand.

Holy fuck! I try to jerk free, my heart flying to my throat, but every attempt is made impossible by the zip ties around my wrists and ankles.

"Relax," he croons, rubbing the barrel of the gun against my neck. It's cold, like death, and I twist my neck, trying to escape its unwanted touch. "Like I said, you're not dying yet. Not while you're still useful." To the man across the way, he commands, "Call Corsetti."

43
RAFAEL

At some point, I've passed out. At another, I waken to a setting sun, an empty bottle in my hand, and a massive pounding headache, only made worse by the two fuckers sitting across from me.

Rosen barely looks up from his phone, but Nico immediately explains, "Hawke called. Big bro was worried about you. Isn't that what you always wanted from him?"

I hate you, Hawke. Groaning, I nudge the bottle off my body, and gripping the back of the couch, right myself into a sitting position. My head thumps, my body's energy in the negatives due to the nearly-full bottle I chugged.

Slumping against the couch, I rub my hand over my face, mumbling, "You've confirmed I'm alive, so you can leave now."

Nico sighs heavily, propping a leg on the opposite knee. "Oh, if it was only that easy. What say you, Rosen?"

He tosses his phone aside, focusing on me with a smirk. "I say little Raf here is in love. Based on Hawke's reports of your ramblings."

Eyeing the empty bottle beside me, I either need it full again to deal with their asses, or to lob it at them. "I'm going to deny that until the day I die." And if it's anything how I feel at this second, that day will be soon. As in, today. "I'm going to piss. When I return, be gone."

Standing requires momentous energy, but with every staggered step, my senses clear. The haze over my vision lifts, as does the one over my heart. Belle's gone, and I can't live life passed out drunk with my older brother and friend hovering over me all the time.

In the bathroom, I down a few pills to alleviate the headache before walking back to the main room, praying I find it empty of other Made Men.

It's not.

"Did I not tell you two—"

The ringing of my cell phone fills the air, cutting me off. Nico leans forward, glancing at the screen from where it rests on the centre table.

"Um. Isabelle's calling."

Despite my claims two minutes ago, I can't get across the room fast enough, holding the phone up to face height and answering the video call.

Only it's not Isabelle's face I see. Well, I do, but not in the manner I should.

Instead, it's a living, breathing nightmare.

The camera's held from afar, but it doesn't matter because *ma belle*'s frightened expression will haunt me until the day I die. She shakes, tears streaming down her face, her lips pressed together, attempting to keep her cries as silent as she can. Her legs are tied to a metal chair and judging by the way her arms are angled behind her, I assume they are too.

But the most sickening aspect of my viewpoint: the gun held to the side of her head.

My own legs feel weak. Weak, but invigorated. Shot up with

adrenaline. With the immediate, compelling determination to find her and rip out the spines of whoever the fuck has her.

I failed. I didn't get someone on her quick enough. The *moment* I wasn't by her side, the wolves hunted.

"Ah, Corsetti." A figure walks into the space between her and the camera, blocking my view. I *need* to have eyes on her always and my frustration grows immediately, nothing else mattering but memorizing her face, her fear, so I can imagine it when I slaughter whoever this fucker is.

At the sound of my name, Nico and Rosen stand, both about to come to my side, but I gesture for them to remain where they are. Whoever this asshole is has Isabelle, which means it's personal. They targeted her for a reason and are now calling me with *her* phone to gloat. If it wasn't personal, she'd be dead already.

They bend their legs, putting themselves into sight of the camera. The same snarky grin in place, the same one he had before I shoved a fist into his face.

Gage.

The phone becomes extremely delicate in my hand, an urge to *destroy* expanding inside me. Logic—the *tiny* shred my sanity clings to—is what prevents me from slamming my phone through the windows behind me. I can't break my phone, not now, not yet, while it's my only means to figuring out where she is.

"What the fuck do you want with her?"

"She's bait. I want you."

"Done," I reply without a thought. *Anything.* "Let her go and you'll have me."

He chuckles darkly. "Oh, you know that's not how it goes. She's my insurance you're not going anywhere."

My reply is halfway up my throat when it's ripped away by a sound more chilling than the feeling that courses through me.

A sound that makes every one of my senses numb. A sound that'll echo in my nightmares for years to come.

"No, Rafael, he's not! He's going to ki—"

Whatever goes on behind Gage muffles her yell, and my arms begin shaking, the requirement to know what is happening growing to the point of pain for every second she's not in my sight. Gage smiles cruelly before giving me his back, blocking the entire stream.

I shake the phone, almost growling, although I know it won't do anything, but seeking control anyway I can get it. This is all in his hands, and while I know I have to be patient, I fucking can't.

Gage finally steps aside, forcing me to witness as he approaches her side and places a knife against her throat. My brave girl whimpers, tilting her head, trying to lean away from the sharp edge.

Blood fills my vision. *His* blood when I find him. The phone begins shaking again, the person on the other end no longer holding it steady. Or is it me who's shaking?

A knife at her throat. A gun at her head.

Is this what Nico felt like when he saw De Falco's man holding Della with a knife at her throat?

Helpless. Stuck. Unable to make sense of the world around him, except for one thing: revenge.

To her, Gage croons, "Tell him how much you want him, Isabelle. Let's see what your life is worth." He lifts strands of her hair between two fingers, rubbing his dirty fingers along the soft, chocolate strands. Hair that is only *mine* to hold.

"Rafael," she gasps, trying to twist her head to look at the phone, but the knife by her throat prevents her from turning all the way. "Rafael, don't—"

Again, she can't finish. Gage's hand flies toward her face, backhanding her hard enough I spot the red filling her cheeks even from this distance. The way she flinches away from him again as he lowers his hand by his side.

Red. Deep red. Every motherfucking shade of red.

A growl rips through me—the demand to find her but stuck on this call, forced to witness the abuse. Her life in someone else's hands, while being aware it's all my fucking fault.

"You're dead. You're fucking *dead* when I find you."

"You won't have to look far. Corsetti, I'd jot this down if I were you." As quick as his warning, he recites an address.

Rosen holds up his phone, showing me he's recording the entire call, and Nico's already typing in the address. *A warehouse,* he mouths.

"Better hurry, Corsetti, before I find myself bored and decide to add another scar to her pretty, little face. No soldiers. No family. Just you. I see anyone else, she's dead."

The call ends, returning my phone's screen to the app's main menu page. A fucking taunt was what that was.

"Rafael—" My brother starts but throwing my hand in his direction shuts him up immediately.

"Neither of you follow me."

Rosen rushes in front of me, his hands coming up to block my advance toward the elevator. "You can't storm that place alone and both of you make it out alive."

I shove him away, slapping the elevator button. "Only one of us needs to get out alive. Her. She's all that matters."

His mouth slips in an O, his eyes sliding to my brother. "You really do fucking love her."

"Yes." It's a weird admittance but one that lifts the weight off my heart. The drive to find her, to be able to tell her myself, is what will keep me going. "Which is why you guys can't come with me. He'll kill her if the three of us pull up."

Nico blocks the elevator doors. "Raf, I think his plan is to kill her either way. You'll require backup."

"Then follow behind me. *Far* behind me. Don't fuck this up, Nico. One of you, text me the address."

"And when war breaks out?"

I understand the underlying question in his words. "Get her out. She lives no matter what. Come back for me later."

I slap the button again at the same time Nico's hands fall away from the door, and they slide closed, shutting my comrades up. I stare at the declining numbers as the elevator travels to the parking garage, each floor another slice to my nerves, could be another injury they're giving Belle.

Just fucking be okay.

I never believed I'd find myself in love. I knew marriage would eventually be in my future as an alliance my family would force me into and I was indifferent to the concept. Nothing I concerned myself with until it was actually happening.

Growing up, I've witnessed my parents' love for one another. I saw how love made my brother soften from the callous underboss into someone gentler, and yet, even more deadly when it came to her life. How love made a loyal friend and solider defiant to the very people he took vows for.

I understand now. The agonizing demand to make another person happy—alive, in our case.

The doors finally creak open, and I throw myself from them and toward my parked sports car in the underground garage. It's still stocked with weapons from my trip to Toronto, so I grab two guns and two knives from the trunk, strapping them to myself, so I have something immediately upon arrival.

Nico's text comes in and I copy the warehouse's address into the maps app, letting the robotic voice direct me out of the city. Downtown traffic has me nearly ready to fucking explode, but thankfully, with the time of evening, it moves quickly, and soon, I'm on the highway, headed for a northern part of the city.

Every street passed seems like I'm still too far away. No speed is fast enough. I run numerous lights, get honked at every single one of them, but I fucking *dare* the cops to pull me over. I won't hesitate to slaughter anyone who tries to slow my journey down; Nico and Father can deal with the consequences later.

After twenty minutes, I pull off onto a run-down road, passing a few abandoned warehouses. Each one, I take a quick scan of, certain Gage could have lookouts posted at any of them. If he was smart, anyway.

The last one in the row matches the address provided and my car is barely stopped before I leap out, heading for the single, metal door on the side. I don't hesitate, yanking it open and ignoring decades of training, which demand I scope the scene out first. The door's rusted creak echoes right through to my bones.

As long as she's fucking here...

What if she's not? What if this is some ploy?

The moment I'm immersed into the dim warehouse, I have two men on me, each grasping at my arm, trying to yank me down. One rips at my shirt, the other throwing a punch into my stomach.

I lower into a crouch, feigning that they've succeeded, as my hands reach into my holsters and grab each gun's handle. Standing upright again, I shove the barrels into their stomachs and pull the trigger, making them drop instantly.

Two down.

"Nice show," the voice from my nightmares calls out. "But if I see you create one more corpse, it'll be my turn." He gestures the same knife from earlier toward Belle.

Training deems me to study every corner of the room. To

catalogue the people, the weapons they have, any possible exits, to understand my surroundings before I go charging in. Every ounce of that training instantly leaves me when I spot her. I don't study my surroundings, don't pay the numerous people in the shadows any attention; my vision tunnels only toward her.

She's no longer secured to the chair, but rather standing, Gage's disgusting firm grasp on her upper arm. Her arms are zip-tied in front of her, and a dirty cloth is shoved in her mouth, knotted behind her head.

The fear in her gaze will haunt me long after my death. I crave to ease her, to tell her it'll be okay. But it won't be. Not until every single one of these fuckers meets the same fate as the two I just shot.

"Lose the weapons, Corsetti."

Again, going against everything Father taught me, I open my hands, dropping the guns to the ground with a clang and my steps don't falter, walking as close to her as he'll allow me. Without my guns, my chances of survival drop exponentially, but for now, I'll play by Gage's rules to ensure Belle's safety.

I still have my knives and my fists. Hand-to-hand combat might be how this goes down, and I'm okay with that. It'll make Gage's death more thrilling. My arms stay up, my palms open in submission, feigning as though losing my guns means I'm helpless.

Gage studies me, his brows lifting. "You didn't come here with only two guns."

"Maybe I did."

"Check him."

Instantly, two more men swarm me, patting down my legs, my chest, pausing on my pockets, where they reach inside.

"Careful now, I'm taken."

They each pull out a knife, pocketing them, leaving me officially weaponless and then grasp my arms, keeping me steady.

I could fight them, and it'll be two less against the handful I'm spotting in the shadows. But the killing spree must wait until she's away from them. Until she's safe and out of harm's way.

Gage smiles cruelly and with his hand around her arm, tugs her closer to his side. His nose skirts up the side of her neck— *my* neck—and I add it to the transgressions he'll pay for.

"Ah, Corsetti, she truly is beautiful. I could do without the scars, mind you, and the innocent, virginial thing, but based on what I witnessed yesterday, that's been taken care of. So thank you for that."

His tongue flicks out and he licks a line up her neck, which she flinches away from, her eyes tightening in disgust. Every passing second, my earlier promise to ensure she's away from him before the killing kicks off becomes less vital as the urge to slaughter him grows.

Throwing both elbows out, I slam them into the men's stomachs. They cough, and one releases his hold, curling on himself, but the other remains steady, his hand coming down on my shoulder, shoving weight onto me. The other quickly rejoins his partner and the two manage to get me to my knees.

"Yes, I like that better," Gage comments, staring from over Isabelle's shoulder. "A Corsetti finally on his knees."

I try to hold her gaze, to tell her it'll be okay, but in truth, I don't know anymore. If Nico and Rosen are on their way, I might need them soon, if only to get her away from here. There are too many people for me to win against. Not that I won't fucking try, of course.

"I'm here now. Let her go."

"That's not how this works. You owe me for a few things, Corsetti." In a flash, he has a knife against Isabelle's arm, inches from where he grips her. Without warning, the blade sinks into her skin. She screeches, and despite the cloth making it muffled, I hear it clear as fucking day in my head. "Count with me."

I growl, watching as blood immediately fills the cut on her skin.

My skin.

She is me and every mark on her is an injury, one I'll return the favour on.

I shift my feet a fraction, getting into a better position to lunge and throw the fuckers off me, to fight Gage for her, to *end* this, but the moment I move, a third is on me, his weight dropping on my back and the guy angling the gun toward Isabelle moves its trajectory, aiming at me.

"One more time, Corsetti. You move, he'll shoot. And then you and I won't get to play our game. Now," he drags his thumb over the fresh wound, sparking a muffled gasp from Isabelle, a sound I *will* rip from his throat, "count with me. This one was a test to see how her skin fares. How lovely it looks bleeding."

Isabelle turns her glare toward him, jerking her shoulders, trying to get free, but he only shoves his finger into a nerve on her shoulder, stopping her with a pained cry that awakens the feral beast inside me.

"One, jumping me the other night. Not very kind of you." *Slice.*

Another pained cry rips up her throat, and I fucking curse myself for not looking into Gage further. I gained his address by the library's files, and that was as far as I went. I truly thought he was simply a douche who freaked her out. Not a leader of whatever gang he's erected here.

I wish I hit harder. I wish I fucking killed him that night.

"Two, killing my men when this one," he pokes Belle with the handle of his knife, "was out alone the other night." *Slice.*

I huff. Of fucking course it was him.

"You work with De Falco, I assume."

He pauses, his blade resting an inch lower from the most recent slice on her arm. "We do. When De Falco had to flee, he needed some old loose ends tied up. First, her father, and then her."

"Guessing there is no community service then."

Keeping him talking prevents more injuries to her. Ensures not another fucking tear slides down that face of hers I'm trying to focus on.

"All made up to get me near her. She's difficult to get to, you see, only exiting her house at certain times. Getting close to her meant learning her schedule. As a hunter, I enjoy taunting my prey. That's all it was. Fun." Eyes flash to me, his mouth pulling into a snarl. "*You* made that difficult. Which brings me to number three: stealing my fun."

Isabelle jerks through that one, her eyes squeezing shut. How I fucking wish she could close all of this out, drift to a better place. But that's not how this will go.

"Belle, look at me."

She obeys instantly, and I want to tell her it'll be okay. I want to tell her I'll get us both out of here alive. At the very least, she'll be safe.

I want to tell her I love her in a way more clearer than beneath the anxiety clouding my gaze.

Instead, I nod, mouthing, *I'll save you.*

Gage makes a gagging noise. "God, you two make me sick. I knew it was only a matter of time before you fucked up and she was alone. *You* did this, Corsetti." With the blunt side of the knife, he taps her arm. "She's only here because you let her out of your sight." To Isabelle, he lowers his voice into a loud whisper, "How's it feel knowing you're about to die and it was all the prince's fault? If only he cared for you more."

The growl working through my chest is because as much as I despise the asshole, he's correct.

"Get to the fucking point," I demand, jerking against my holders again, seeking any break in their grip. "I'm here, as you said, on my knees. You don't need her anymore."

"That's the thing." He trails the knife up her arm, not piercing the skin, but making her flinch regardless. Her eyes remain on mine, the plea there making Gage's slow, vile discussion more aggravating. "I do. Because I don't get the second half of my payday until I have proof of her dead body."

Solves the question of what happened to Maurice's body.

"But you're a bonus, Corsetti. You pissed me off, that's all. I figure, have fun with it. I could have killed her quickly, from afar, or drag it out and make you watch. What do you say? Her skin really does bleed in the most lovely shade." Gage steps behind her and repositions the blade by her face. "I could add a few more scars to her cheeks, a final one around her neck. Watch her bleed out slowly, dragging her death on for every torturous minute you're forced to observe, helpless to save her."

She whimpers, jerking in his firm hold again, a noise he ignores.

"Or," he skates his nose up the side of her neck, breathing in her scent—*my* scent, "after being teased for weeks and denied at every single turn, I can finally *take* her."

The gun pointed my way—no matter. The men pinning me to my knees—useless. The explosion of rage that exits me, that makes my muscles tighten with frenzy, is my entire focus. Getting freed from the men holding me. Slicing her skin earns Gage a slow death, but if I see him touch her in *that* way, there will be no mercy on his soul.

More men join the fray, shoving me to the ground. I'm one against a crowd.

Click!

The gun steps closer, lining up with my forehead. The man attached to it lifts his brows, silently daring me to continue fighting. My own expression reflects their pending deaths.

"Hm," Gage murmurs into Isabelle's neck, his free hand cupping her stomach, pinning her back to his front. "Seems your boyfriend doesn't enjoy the idea of sharing. That's too bad."

Isabelle's eyes squeeze shut, trying to hide herself away.

"No matter," he continues, "we should hurry this up before your family comes for you." The corner of his mouth lifts in a cocky smirk. "Because that's what's happening, isn't it? No Corsetti fights alone."

I don't respond.

Gage shrugs, unbothered by my lack of a response and pulls the tie from around Isabelle's face. He tosses it to the side as she sucks in a large gasp of breath.

"Gage, you fucking ass—"

His hand whips out, backhanding her again, exactly how he did during the video call. His strength causes her to stumble, and when he releases her with the hit, she ends up crouching near where I'm pinned down.

"Silence from you, Isabelle. It's your turn to play the game." He reaches down, wrenching her from her crouch, his hand grabbing her right over the bleeding cuts he gave her. Her eyes get tight, and I'm sure it hurts, but she makes no noise. "I'm a hunter. There's a reason I got into the mercenary business. Hunting people is the greatest sport alive."

No...

Her eyes flash to me, understanding hitting us both in the same instance.

"Run, Isabelle. Run so I can hunt you down and reunite your corpse with dear ol' dad."

Belle hesitates, and it's in that hesitation, her glare moving from Gage to me, the chocolate of her eyes melting, that I see her love. She looks like she's about to say something, and my throat is tight. Tight with fear because unless I can get these men off me, I'm about to witness her death.

A new emotion begins growing inside me. Mounting. Disturbing. Not dread, not adrenaline, but death. The utter anguish of losing my lucidity, should I witness her murder. No one will be safe then.

Fuck, brother, time for you to show up.

"Go, Isabelle. *Now.*"

She's still looking at me, as though seeking direction. But for the first time in my life, I'm wordless. Stunned and incapable of speech as fresh terrors play out in my head. I can't watch this. I can't watch her run and be taken down by him.

But I can't have her here any longer. She needs a chance.

In the half-second more time we have, I stare at her. Study the shape of her hair, the smoothness of her skin, her deep eyes, that face. I memorize it all, so I have something to take with me into the darkness.

"Go," I whisper, jerking my head to the side. Every beat of my action tears at my heart—it feels so fucking wrong, but beneath the weight of five men, I'm useless. Weaponless.

Unable to help her.

There is no worst pain.

With her hands still strapped together in front of her, her initial steps are awkward. She stumbles a few times before managing to properly run, her strides taking her across the warehouse.

Softly, not so loud that Isabelle will hear, but loud enough that the order implants itself into my brain, Gage commands, "Shoot her."

44
ISABELLE

All those times I laughed at myself for thinking my life had become a fictional novel... Yeah. Complete with the bad guy kidnapping me at the end, using me to lure the hero out.

I've never been more upset and more happy in my life than when Rafael strode through the door. Instantly taking out the two guys who went for him, I was hopeful that he'd be my saviour and we'd already be driving away from this hellhole by now.

Instead, he lost all his weapons and ended up pinned on the ground. His gaze spoke volumes though. The apology in their depths when he was unable to rescue me how he planned.

Every second being in Gage's grip was a second more my abhorrence and dread grew. The future is unknown. Gage already said he's planning on killing us both, but it can't end like this.

It *can't*.

Books end happy. So why can't my life be the same?

The moment Rafael whispers, "Go," I push to my feet and obey him. There doesn't seem to be a better way out of this. Staying equals a quick death. Running gives me a shot, but based on the sly grin Gage has been sporting the entire time, I don't think the chance is very high.

My wrists cry in agony, still tied in front of me, which makes my first few steps awkward. But they're driven forward by a racing heartbeat and shallow breaths, and the determination behind Rafael's pleading gaze, but I wobble more than once, trying to get my footing on the cement as my balance is constantly altered by not being able to use my arms.

There's a door on the far wall, and I head for that, jerking a fraction to the right, trying to ensure I'm not running in a straight line from Gage.

When I'm about twenty feet away, I hear Rafael yell; a sound that imbeds itself into my soul. The fear in it doesn't make me hesitate, and I obey him immediately.

"Belle, get down!"

Down. Trying my best to cushion my fall, I throw myself onto the cement, aiming for my side. Fucking useless hands. The cement is solid, but the numbness locking my every sense since Gage kidnapped me ensures I barely feel it.

There's a beat of silence as I try to roll around to see what's happening when another, louder sound comes from across the warehouse. A sound heard in movies and TV shows, and I never believed I'd be so happy for it now.

Gun shots.

Multiple of them.

Two men push through the same door Rafael had entered earlier, shots immediately flying through the room and right into the heads of the men pinning Rafael down. I recognize Nico, and the other soldier from Nico's office.

Chaos breaks out. The two continuously shoot the surrounding crowd while Rafael, now unhindered by his captors, breaks free, his fist flying to the nearest man's face

From afar, I go still, stuck halfway between escape, needing to ensure Rafael will remain alive, and not wanting to draw attention to myself while Gage and his men are occupied.

As though remembering me in that instant, Gage whirls around, narrowly avoiding a flying bullet and focuses his gaze straight on me, stalking across the cement.

"Shit!" I crabwalk backwards, while my tied arms attempt to shove myself upright. The entire thing becomes an awkward mess, but death barreling down on me makes it entirely worth it.

"We're not done playing," Gage coos, his arm coming up with every step closer he takes, and that's when I see what's in his hand.

A gun.

"Shit!"

Gage's finger flexes on the trigger, and there's no speed, no path I can take that gets me away from his shot. I'm going to die and—

Bang!

The same instance as the gun shot, a body flies into Gage, knocking them both to the ground and causing Gage's bullet to miss. Rafael throws fist after fist into Gage's face, swiping his hand against Gage's, unhooking the gun from his grip.

"You're finished, you bastard!"

Punch.

"For daring to touch her."

Punch.

"For taking her from me."

Punch.

"For every single mark you left on her skin."

Punch. Punch. Punch. Punch.

Gage's fight becomes weaker, his arms unable to block more and more hits from Rafael. Rafael then reaches above them and grasps Gage's gun, angling it right at his chest.

"Oh, how I'd love to make this painful for you, but you're done, fucker."

Bang! Even from here, I catch the shiver coursing up and down Rafael's arm as he pulls the trigger right into Gage's chest. His body slumps once before his head rolls to the side, his arms defeated on the ground, life instantly gone from his eyes.

Everything is silent for a beat. The fight has finished. Nico and the other soldier head toward Rafael; their footsteps over the warehouse's cement ground the only noise. Rafael remains perched on top of Gage's corpse, his shoulders rising and falling with every heavy breath he takes.

Then he turns, spotting me across the way, but before I can decipher his emotion, he slumps, rolling off Gage's corpse and onto the cement with a low groan.

"Rafael!" I manage to scramble to my knees, trying to get all the way up when Rafael's soldier is right there, sliding a blade through the zip ties and releasing my binds. I don't thank him or even consider how pleasant it is to have free motion in my wrists when my entire focus is Rafael.

I'm by his side quickly, dropping to my knees, the hard ground shooting ignorable pains up my legs.

Rafael's hazy gaze finds me instantly, but I finally spot what has him down. What I hadn't noticed at first. What he continued to *fight* through.

Beneath his hand, holding his side, red is quickly seeping between his fingers.

The shot. When Rafael leaped in front of Gage's bullet, it went somewhere. Inside him.

"Rafael! No!" Nudging his hand away, I press mine there, one on top the other, trying to pin in the blood. His life.

"Ma...belle..." His hand twitches, his gaze wildly searching.

Nico drops on the other side of Rafael's body and shoves my hands away, pressing a large cloth to the injury. It's then I realize he's now without a shirt, having used his to sop up Rafael's blood.

Everything's a flurry of emotion as Nico takes over, two fingers going to his brother's pulse. He curses. "Rosen, we got to get him out of here. He's fading fast."

Fading fast. Two words that have never sounded worse. Is this what Rafael felt like earlier when he watched me through the video stream? Helpless. Unable to do anything but sit and stare mutely until *something* makes more sense.

"Don't die on me."

Regardless of Nico's attempt to quell the blood, his shirt quickly becomes soaked, Rafael's gaze becoming more distant with every passing second. I lean over, grasping his face and brush my lips over his. I aim for gentle, to not hurt him, but instead it's broken. My lips coated with the tears I hadn't realized I'm crying and now painting his with them.

"Don't die. I fucking love you, Rafael. I'm sorry for leaving. I'm *so* sorry."

My heart skips a beat when he shows no sign of hearing me. That I've already lost him, but Nico hasn't indicated anything. Either out of respect for the moment or horror of what's already happened.

But then Rafael let's out a smtall cough, his lips curling up at the edges, and his lashes flutter, a confused gaze trying to focus. "F-finally...*Je t'aime aussi, ma belle.*"

His eyes shut, a sigh his last breath. His body stills beneath mine.

And my heart shatters.

It's been a day. One full day and he hasn't woken up yet.

One full day where I've sat beside him on the bed, unmoving, gripping his limp hand in mine as I hold onto hope that in every single second passing, a finger will twitch, or he'll squeeze back, or *something*.

Has there been a moment when I've looked away from him? Can't be certain. The Corsetti's family doctor who was called immediately yesterday confirmed Rafael will live. The injury was a flesh wound so after sleep and rest, he'll be fine.

That single statement is what I've clung to. Knowing he'll be *okay* is what keeps me by his side. I must be with him when he awakens; must see those bright eyes open for myself.

I won't lose him.

I've already lost one man who was my entire life, my past. I refuse to lose the one who's my present, my future. Losing Rafael would kill me—if the guilt doesn't do it first. Guilt that he was only shot saving me.

Guilt that every single person cycling through Rafael's bedroom has reassured me of. I haven't mentioned my feelings, but I guess it's been clear for them to read.

Sitting on the bed beside him is all I've done, except for the two minutes the Corsetti's doctor tugged me away to clean my injuries. I'm fine because of Rafael, so he deserves all the focus. Not me, therefore the check-up only lasted moments before I was pushing my way back to Rafael's side.

The only other person to remain in the room the entire time has been Nico, who's spent most of the day leaning against the window, circulating between staring outside, on his phone with their parents, and watching Rafael. He's only spoken a handful of words to me, mainly reassurances of Rafael's life, but I've hardly heard them.

Rosen—I finally learned his name—has switched between sitting in here with us and the living room where Della and Aurora wait this out. They've also visited often, but less for Rafael's well-being and more my own.

Like I've called them, their steps come up beside the bed. Della rests a knee on it, leaning close enough her face blocks my view to Rafael. It's like I'm not seeing her, staring through her to Rafael.

"It's been nearly twenty-four hours, Isabelle. He wouldn't want this for you. You need to eat, to wash the blood off your skin. To rest. You won't be any good to him like this."

"No."

Like clockwork, Aurora cuts in with the next leg of their typical argument. It's the same conversation every few hours with these two. They're trying to get me to leave but I won't. Not again.

"He's okay, but you're not. You're in shock. You're grieving."

Grieving. It's all I've done since Rafael's come into my life. All I know how to do now. Seems suitable I continue.

"No."

They sigh and move away from the bed.

Their next visit, they bring food with them. I don't eat it. Don't even look at the tray; don't know what they're trying to feed me.

Their next, they insist on a shower and sleep.

Their next is for Aurora and Rosen to say goodbye for the night before they head downstairs to their apartment. Della sleeps on one of the couches in the living room. Nico remains in the bedroom, seated on the ground, his head tipped against the window pane as he dozes.

Eventually, when night falls and my eyes are drooping, I do

what they suggest and lay down beside him. But I don't sleep. I don't close my eyes.

I won't miss a moment of the pain which gives me the adrenaline to remain awake. It's this pain that fuels me. I won't leave his side, not again.

"I love you, Rafael. I'm here, waiting for you."

45

RAFAEL

I've been beaten, kicked, tied up, starved, abandoned in complete darkness all in the name of training.

I've been cut and shot, bones broken during fights. And yet, something about this time hurts so much more.

The room is bright, but I've never been more happy to see my bedroom ceiling rather than the black walls of death that creeped over my vision moments ago. Or, what feels like moments ago.

A figure moves beside me, getting off the bed and into my vision, his cocky grin so irritating it forces me upright, my side screeching in agony as I push into a sitting position.

"Stay down," Nico commands, nudging my shoulder. "Doctor's orders."

Past him, Rosen kicks off the wall from where he was leaning and strides closer. No one else is in here.

"There's no doctor here, so I don't have to listen."

Agony flits through me again. My teeth smash together, trying to bite back the cry of pain. On my side, a bandage about the size of my hand is taped to my skin, inches from the slice gained on my ribs the other day when I fought them on the street.

"What the fuck happened?"

The moment I ask it, flashes of memory dart through my mind. Of a warehouse, of Belle tied to a chair, a gun at her head, and then her running and Gage lifting his gun in her direction. Things got fuzzy after that.

Rubbing my head, I groan, willing it to remember everything clearly. "Tell me he's dead."

"They all are. But yes, your fists did most of the work," Nico answers, crossing his arms. "The gun to the chest finished him."

"I...don't remember that." Everything after the gun pointing toward Isabelle is gone, blurred between the red coating my eyes—the need to slaughter his ass.

"Don't die. I fucking love you, Rafael. I'm sorry for leaving. I'm so sorry."

Words of an angel, right before I was dragged to my death. Of *my* angel. I may have blocked out murdering Gage—too bad because I could do with that memory—but I seemed to have clicked back in for the exact second that really mattered.

"Amazing what adrenaline can do to a brain," Rosen comments, positioning his hands on my footboard and leaning toward me. "Doc said you'll be fine in a couple of days. Bullet missed anything vital, so he cleared you to be here rather than a hospital. We got you back here in time, so just some blood loss and a deep sleep."

My knowledge of how bad a minor injury can be compels me to wonder, "How many days has it been?"

"Two," Nico answers, jerking his head toward the dark outdoors peeking through my black curtains. "I suppose, we're headed into day three. It's minutes from being midnight."

"Fantastic." Now that I have that information, sitting in

bed is the last thing I need to be doing. Positioning my hands onto the mattress, I push myself up, my intestines bitching at me, making my breathing shallow and difficult.

This time, Nico doesn't stop me. One brow arches and he even steps out of the way, watching as I limp past him and Rosen, toward my walk-in closet for pants to throw over my boxers.

"You really should stay in bed."

"Where is she?" I demand instead, pulling on grey joggers. Injuries aside, Belle is my entire focus. I make it to the doorway before Nico speaks again.

"Before you go ambling your injured ass down there, I need you to slow the fuck down."

What is his problem? "What?" I bark.

Nico follows me to the door, where he sends a gentle brotherly whack to my back. "I told you that for your own well-being, Raf. That girl sat by your bedside for the past two days and refused to eat or sleep until she saw you awake. Della and Aurora have taken turns trying to get her to properly rest and they *finally* convinced her."

"And when he says 'finally,' Nico means, as in, like, two hours ago," Rosen interjects, pacing toward me as well.

"Yeah, so if you wake her up, my wife will castrate you. Believe me." He gives me a warning look, gesturing down the hallway, toward the living room, a smirk in place of the memory quickly taking over. "That girl *will* happily hand you over to your enemy, should she feel the urge to. She and Aurora have taken quite a liking to Isabelle, so don't fuck it up. Hear me?" He presses a bit of weight into my shoulder. "Remember once when I said Della would be leaving, and you stood in the doorway and called me an idiot?"

I shoulder him off. "Actually, 'You're a fucking moron, brother' were my exact words."

"Precisely. Same advice back to you now. I won't even pretend to understand how all this went down, but the girl who stayed by your side, who wept over your dying body, isn't the one who walked away from you. The one who pained you so much, Rosen and I came to check up on your sorry, drunk ass."

"That's the thing, brother," I slap his arm, ending this conversation with a step away, "I'm not you. I only make mistakes once before learning my lesson."

They trail behind me as I eagerly stride toward the living room, my gaze immediately landing on the farthest couch, where Belle's stretched out, a dark blanket over her. The living room lights are dim, and Aurora and Della each occupy one of the other couches, glancing up simultaneously with my entrance.

Aurora leaps from the couch and bounds over toward me, throwing herself in my arms as she whisper-yells, "Jesus fuck, never do shit like that again. I just gained a family. I'm not ready to lose them."

I stroke a hand over my sister's blonde curls, briefly hugging her back. "You forget, I'm the cool brother," I say, referencing an old conversation we once had regarding me being more understanding than Nico after she first returned to the family. "I can't die. Someone needs to keep our grump of a brother in check."

Della stands too, joining Nico. "Glad you're awake," she whispers. "Isabelle will be so happy too, but she finally recently left your side. Girl is exhausted."

"I got it." I understand and maybe even appreciate their concern for her, but it doesn't change the fact that I need to be near her. Even if I don't get to see her beautiful eyes yet, I need to be close by her.

Of the crowd, thankfully one of them seems to understand. Rosen, with my sister's hand in his—still a strange sight—steps around me. "Since you're awake and breathing again, we'll leave you two be."

Aurora waves as she passes, and Della trails behind with a parting smile. Nico takes up the rear, pausing to say, "Text if you need anything. Heal fast because we have shit to deal with."

"Of course, Nico. I'll be sure to inform my guts they need to 'heal fast' that way *you* can put me to work." Chuckling, I shake my head, shoving him toward his wife. The movement pulls on my bandage, making me wince. Okay, I see why he wants me healed because I'm useless in this manner.

Once the four of them are gone into the elevator, leaving Isabelle and me alone, I head immediately for her side, dropping to my knees on the floor. The impact makes my side sting, but it's nothing compared to the pain of nearly losing her.

She's only been asleep for a couple hours, but my selfish ass can't stop my hand stretching toward her, stroking a patch of skin on her cheek, right over her scar. She moves at my touch but doesn't awaken.

I really should let her sleep longer, but I also want to inspect her and the injuries I was forced to watch her receive. When the urge becomes overwhelming, I tug the blanket down her shoulder, revealing every mark left on her arm, each one making me murderous again. I wish I could have made his death longer and more painful, sliced him up as payback. Dr. Shappo obviously cleaned her up since they already look partially healed. They're not deep so shouldn't scar either.

I back away, heading for one of the other free couches, spotting my cell phone in the centre of the coffee table. Nico or someone must have returned it and my car then, since my car is the last place my phone was.

On it, a dozen work emails I swipe away, a few text messages from soldiers wishing me well or reporting on other business, a couple from my parents demanding a call the second I wake up

—not happening; Nico can inform them—and a particular few texts I do click on.

HAWKE

Nico called. Told me what happened. Let me know when you're awake. Offered me to come visit but said it wasn't life threatening, and I'm knee-deep in cases right now, being backlogged from the wedding and the stuff with Aurora, so no offense, but I can't.

Also, don't let her get away again.

Every word he's written causes me to chuckle, which I taper down as to not disrupt Belle's sleep.

ME

I have words for you.

I stare at the screen, knowing with the current time, he might be asleep, so feeling a bit surprised when the message's receipt switches from delivered to read.

HAWKE

That so?

ME

You reached out to Nico.

HAWKE

Dude, you drunk called me rambling about a girl. YOU.

ME

Yeah, well…I guess I should thank you. I'd be dead had he not been here when I got the call.

HAWKE

I'll take that as a thank you.

How'd you manage? Nico told me what happened. When you got the call.

I glance at Belle's sleeping form again, the vision of her tied to that chair, terrified, telling me not to come to her.

ME

Like something I never wish to feel again. I get why you did what you did that day. It's different when it's her on the line. Nearly being kidnapped on the street was one thing, but it wasn't as bad. I don't think I loved her then. Then being able to slaughter a man who harmed her in the past was purely for my satisfaction. But SEEING her tied up, scared for her life, guns and knives directed at her...I can't do that again.

HAWKE

Why do you think I was so hesitant to even visit with Willow? What if the wedding was attacked and it was Willow who was kidnapped? After the first time, I wouldn't survive that hell again.

ME

Still happy you came. After all, if you didn't, I wouldn't have your number, and who else would have gotten my drunken ramblings?

HAWKE

I'm still questioning why I gave you my number.

But same. I'm happy I came too.

Now, get off the phone. Go be with your girl.

ME

You and Nico have more in common than you think you do. Goodnight.

Tossing the phone on the table, I aim to make the sound

echo loud enough it'll wake Belle up. When it doesn't, I return to her side, reaching out to touch her. She should sleep longer, but the restless animal inside me must see her eyes open too.

It's okay. That's what beasts do, after all. We're untamed, brutish, and greedy. And I'll make sure Belle knows it too.

46

ISABELLE

Something warm strokes over my neck and I move into the touch. It's pleasant, if not a bit relaxing. After forcing myself awake for two days, Aurora and Della were unfortunately correct, my body requires sleep, and now that I am, it feels like nothing will wake me from this deep slumber.

"Ma belle."

Even in my dreams, Rafael's voice is poetic. I could sleep forever with him whispering in my ear.

The touch comes again, this time trailing over my arm, stopping right above where I was cut. A finger hooks into the blanket Della laid over me, removing it inch-by-inch, the room's warm air brushing against my bare skin.

"Ma belle, I need you."

Wait.

My eyes fly open, staring at the back of the couch, exactly where I fell asleep. The soft touch continues down my arm, toward my wrist, electrifying every inch he passes over.

I push myself into a sitting position, immediately throwing

myself into his arms. The previous fears only go away when his strong arms wrap around my waist from where he kneels beside the couch.

"Oh my god, you're okay. Even when your brother and the doctor and everyone said you'd wake up fine, I couldn't believe it until I saw you for myself."

He tightens his hold, his hand on my hip stroking the bare skin between my leggings and tank. "I'm okay, Belle."

"When did you wake up? I was so determined to be there for you."

He makes a shushing sound as he leans back, releasing me enough I can see him. "Only ten minutes ago. I know you were by my side the entire time. Everyone told me. Multiple times. Seems you've gained quite the fanbase with my family."

I shouldn't. They should all hate me. The *only* reason Rafael was put into that position was because of me. If I wasn't at work alone, Gage wouldn't have captured me. And I wouldn't have been at work alone if I faced my feelings for Rafael instead of running away from them.

"Whoa, Belle, no." His thumbs stroke over my cheek, showing me the dabs of tears making his tips shiny. I hadn't even realized I was crying. "Unacceptable."

"You should hate me," I say more as a sob than anything. "Your family should hate me. If I never left here—"

"Belle—"

"No." I shove my hand over his mouth, blocking his speech, dropping it when I feel he won't interrupt again. "No, stop, Rafael, and let me talk. I shouldn't have left that day, especially not when you were asleep. I took the coward's way out."

"And I was the moron who let you walk away." He mindlessly drags strands of my hair away from my face, tucking them around my ear, smiling sadly. "I was awake the moment you got out of bed. I let you take the reins that day because it's what you needed. But we don't have to talk about this right now."

"I want to," I insist. "*Have* to. I was scared, Rafael." Resting my hand over his heart, I use every steady beat as a reminder he's okay, as strength to push through my speech. "Everything happened *so* quickly. You arrived in my life with news of my father, who we later learned everything I knew of the man isn't even real. Our entire life had been a lie. *I'm* a lie. A lie with another name and a life I should have had. A mother. Grand-parents. Maybe more of a family. It just...it got to be so much. And you have your life. You're a mafia capo, for fuck's sake. We barely know each other. I hardly know anything about your past. I fell hard and fast for you and it scared me." Staring at my lap makes the next part feel easier to admit. "It terrified me, Rafael, because I don't know how to be what you need me to be."

He tips my head back up. "A few things to address then. It all happened quickly, and I know you got freaked out. You hated me for ripping you from the life you had, and it's why I let you go. There's that saying, if you love someone, you're able to let them go." His arms tug me closer, until my ass is barely perched on the edge of the couch, our souls pressing right against each other until I can feel every beat of his heart, every breath he takes. "I've learned how fucking wrong that expres-sion is. I can't let you go, no matter how much I love you. I did, I tried, and look where that got us." He smirks. "That's twice, I should remind you. Have you learned yet, it's not wise for us to be apart? You get in trouble; I go on a murderous rampage." He shrugs playfully. "Shit gets real."

"Very real," I agree, cupping his face.

He rests his palm over mine, ensuring my touch goes nowhere. "Lastly, we will get to know one another in time. My brother and sister-in-law got engaged a week after meeting one another, because in this life, uncertainty is so prevalent. You either take what you want when you find it, or you lose them before ever having a chance. I won't lose that chance, Belle, not again." His lips brush over mine, imprinting me with those final words.

"Good," I tell him. "I'm sorry."

"You need to stop saying that." He crooks a smirk, which I feel beneath my hand. "As for your final point about not knowing what I need you to be." He pauses, searching my eyes. "You don't have to know everything, *ma belle*, because you're already everything I need."

Am I crying again? I feel like I am. Only good tears this time. Tears that I watch drop onto his hand, staining his skin. Marking him as mine.

My attention trails down his bare chest, to where the gunshot hit him. The place that nearly took him from me. I reach for it, lightly brushing the bandage that I've seen placed and replaced over the two days of his healing.

"You literally jumped in front of a bullet for me."

"Exactly. If that doesn't say love, I don't know what does, Belle."

His parting words echo through my head with his mention of love. "Do you remember right before you passed out, what you said to me?"

"Je t'aime aussi, ma belle," he correctly recites. "I love you too, my beautiful. In response to what you said when you were pleading for me to stay alive."

"And it worked. You remember?"

"I'll put it like this: I remember that gun angling toward you, and I remember you telling me you love me. Everything else was lost in a blur of rage, adrenaline, and agony."

"Agony from the shot?"

"No," he whispers, moving his head to press a kiss to the

centre of my palm. "The agony of almost losing you again. The second he found you across the room, I knew he wouldn't hesitate."

"Thank you for coming for me."

"Always, *ma belle*. Always and for fucking ever." His voice his thick, lined with emotion. "You know what that means, right?"

"Hm?"

His hand comes down over the one I have covering his heart. "The life I lead, the life your father joined, the life you've seen, it's dark. I have duties and responsibilities. I lead a regiment of men, help Nico manage the clubs and bars, while my focus is Eden. One of the legal fronts we have for some of the underground businesses that we manage. There might be times I don't come home until late. There might be times Nico calls me away. Shit's about to go down, Belle. War is coming once we retrieve the bastard. You heard what we're up against, and it's not going to be pretty. My brother has Della. Rosen has my sister. If you're with me, that'll be your life too. I'll help you every step of the way, and so will my mother. Believe it or not, Aurora and Della are also still learning." He pauses. "And I *will* tell you all the gritty details of the family. I won't shadow you away and hide any of the darkness from you unless you ask me to. Della's in a lot of Nico's meetings, and that was a choice she made. To stay in the light. You'll have the same. While you continue your Masters degree and working at the library. That will remain if you wish to do those things. Also...marriage."

I know his reality. Hell, Rafael and I even spoke about it in the park one night, that he'll eventually need to wed for an alliance. I wonder how his parents would take me, knowing I am everything opposite of an alliance. The daughter of a traitor.

"It doesn't have to be right away, but my family will expect it. This life demands it, because if not to you, they'll try to ship me off for an alliance."

"So I'm your protection?" I joke, making light of the topic.

"You're the only thing that can hurt me," he responds, his voice deep and serious. "You're it for me, Belle. And one day, I *will* call you my wife. Belle Corsetti has a nice ring to it."

It does. "Rafael, from the moment I met you, you've been a walking mafia romance novel. I know marriage is a huge deal in your life, and I agree." My smile expands with every word. "Rose Haynes is a stranger. Isabelle Dupont is a timid woman with a whole lot of heartbreak. But Belle Corsetti sounds like a future to claim."

Rafael's eyes fill with emotion. "I need one more thing from you." Without waiting for me to ask what, he continues, "Tell me again. This time while I'm one hundred and fifty-percent awake."

"Just that?" I tease, wrinkling my nose. "I only tell people I love them when they're two-hundred-percent awake."

"Belle." He growls, rising on his knees, bending my body back into the couch. "One-fifty, two-hundred, two-thousand, a fucking million. Believe me, there's no one been more awake than I am this very instance."

Dramatic. "You're weird."

"Belle," he repeats, in that growly tone I love so much.

"I love you, Rafael."

"Je t'aime aussi." He lifts to his feet, taking me with him, claiming my mouth as he walks me away from the living room. He grunts, shuffling me in his arms, reminding me about his injury again.

"Rafael, you're still hurt! I think your family's doctor will kill me for letting you do this."

"Which is why we're headed to the bedroom," he explains, cocking his head in the direction we're walking. "If I wasn't so sore, I'd be fucking you against the living room windows for the entire city to observe."

Oh. That sounds appealing too. Wiggling my legs, I insist, "I can walk so you don't hurt yourself."

"Deal with it." He turns into his bedroom, heading straight for the bed. "Told you, I'm not letting you go and we're starting that this instance. Besides, I'm fucking you in a way that won't harm me."

He deposits me on the bed, his lips trailing down my neck as his hands go for my tank. As he pulls away from me, he takes the shirt too, tossing it behind him in an action way too sexy to be ignored.

With a bit of shuffling, he has my leggings off too, but instead of giving further instruction, he merely stands there, staring between my legs, a pensive expression on his face.

"You always make me so hungry."

He climbs onto the bed beside me, lying on his back before reaching for me, bringing one thigh over his leg, until I'm nearly sitting on him, my core inches from his waiting mouth.

"I'm a starved man."

"Well, you've been injured and passed out for days. I think food and water is in order."

He blows on my core, making me jolt. "I only need you, Belle. Only ever you. Now sit." His hands wrap around my thighs, giving me little choice in the matter, and I sink down onto his waiting tongue, riding the bliss he provides.

The bliss he *always* provides.

47
RAFAEL

Late in the morning, I'm awoken by the shrill of my cell phone. I don't even bother looking at the screen to know it's my annoying older brother, who only got worse when Father made him underboss. Suddenly, he's the damn leader and is quite demanding.

"What?" I growl, without opening my eyes. Against my body, Belle curls in deeper, her nails scraping at my abs, as though trying to cling to me even in her sleep. "I was sleeping."

"I know," he replies drily. "It's nearly noon and I've texted you with no response back. You seem to forget; I know your schedule. You rarely sleep this late."

"Get shot and then come talk to me."

Once I had Belle, I continued to wake her up throughout the night with my mouth between her legs, unable to get enough of her taste. I know I should sleep, and I know her body certainly requires it, since getting a few hours' sleep after being awake multiple days isn't healthy, but when it comes to her, I'm a selfish fucker.

"Isabelle still there?"

361

"Of course." I glance down, stroking a hand over her hair, noting how desperately we both require showers.

"Everything between you two is good then?"

"Everything except the date of our wedding picked out."

"Wedding?' His voice spikes. "Hm, there goes my plans for you."

"That's the point. What do you want, Nic?"

"For you to come to work."

I huff laughter. "Wasn't it just yesterday you were telling me to heal? Now I have to get out of bed?"

"Dude, I saw you practically sprint down a hallway to get to Isabelle, and then you sleep till noon and she's still there. Doesn't take much to draw a line here. If you have the energy to fuck her, you have the energy to come to work."

"Fucking and war are two very different things," I point out, my hand trailing down her spine, toward the curve of her ass. She wakes slowly, blinking up at me as I dip my fingers between her legs, petting her contented pussy. She glances to my cell for a moment before shooting a devious grin and flips over on me, one leg on either side of my hip. Her cunt drags over my cock, which almost immediately is awakened by her heat.

"It's not De Falco," my brother says gravely. "A bit more immediate than that. We have another problem on our hands. Flynn."

Last I saw Flynn, he was leading Rozelyn from Nico's office before everything with Gage went down. I'm trying like hell to focus on this conversation while Belle grinds against my cock, but she makes it impossible.

"What'd he do?"

"Disobeyed my direct order to stay away from Rozelyn and lost his shit on the man who found him in there with her. Just get here. We're ending this today."

"Will do." I hang up and toss the phone onto the other side

of the bed, reaching for her hips. "I gotta go, *ma belle*. But you started this, minx, so now you have to finish it."

"Obviously." She grins. "Gotta show you what I read in a book the other day."

I now have a larger appreciation for novels.

After three days of hell and endings, of chaos and death, it's over and I'm able to focus on Belle again. More so, the conversation we had last night.

"I think I'm ready to go to my father's house again. It needs to be cleaned out. Sold. All his estate stuff dealt with."

I've already had a death certificate put together and his finances being managed, to make it easier on her, but the house has remained untouched ever since my men finished scouring for truths and came up empty.

"There's no rush," I tell her.

"I'm ready."

Pulling up in front of his house, it feels like we've come full circle. The first time I came here was to inform Maurice's daughter of his death, and now I return with her as mine. The moment I put the car in park, she finally makes the first noise she has since leaving home.

"Belle, we don't have to do this today. We've made it this far."

"I want to."

She's either lying to me or herself because her expression claims otherwise. I reach for her hand, just as she pulls away and slips from the car. I make it to her side quickly, blocking her path.

"Once we go in there, it might be hard to leave. If you're not one hundred percent ready, we try another day."

She shoulders me away and steps by, reaching into the back pocket of her jeans for the lanyard she has tucked in there. Once home to her apartment keys as well, but those were handed in yesterday when she officially moved in with me, so now her father's house key hangs alone.

She strides up the path, her steps conveying no hesitation. The key slips into the lock and she twists until the door clicks open. She takes the key back, pushes open the door, but doesn't step inside.

I come up behind her, about to repeat my comment about trying again another time, when she manages a deep but shallow breath, locks her shoulders, and steps inside. I follow, closing the door behind us.

She makes it three steps before stopping, her gaze flitting through the space. Over the couch, the entertainment system. She doesn't look sad, but rather surprised.

"Belle?"

"I'm okay," she whispers after a beat. "A lot of memories in here. Thinking about all the times I sat on that couch, watched cartoons with Marie, and waited for him to come home from work." Her brows meld together, a slight shudder running through her. "From work with your family. That'll never get less weird."

She walks forward, toward the kitchen, and I trail behind her. I've seen her hold it together in the daytime, only to break down at night time, but this is different. This is like the moment Mother finally allowed me to enter Hawke's childhood bedroom, an entire year after he left us. I think that was when they realized he meant what he said, and he wasn't coming home. Despite months of me begging to enter, to reconnect with the only part of my brother I still had in my life, I made it as far as the doorway before I cried and Nico dragged me away. Took me another two months to go inside.

She pauses and turns, facing me again, studying the living room. Her lips move, press together, and flatten. Her tongue dabs her bottom lip, and then again. Her hands curl into fists at her side and water fills her eyes. She's trying so hard, and it kills me to not say anything, but now that we're in here, I'll let her decide how far she wants to take this.

"This kitchen," she murmurs, "is where he cooked breakfast for me on the weekends. Pancakes were his favourite to make, and I loved his batter recipe." She meets my eyes, smiling through her pain. "I thought about him that first morning with you, when I heard you cooking breakfast. It reminded me of him, even before I saw you. Took me a lot to leave the room that morning."

"But you did it."

"Put away the pain to focus on living." She smiles bitterly, and while it might be selfish of me to think, I'm glad she did.

"He was really good at making lasagna too," she muses. "I loved it so much that he'd cook it for every one of my birthdays. He'd work and I'd sit right there," she gestures to the couch behind me, "watching a show while going through the pile of DVDs we used to own. With dinner, we'd watch a movie of my choosing. Then—" She cuts off, her deep breath more of a shudder. She stares at her feet, pressing her lips together again.

I don't stay still this time and head for her side, taking her in my arms, tucking her beneath my chin.

"This hurts, Rafael."

"I know. We can leave if you want."

She shakes her head, burying deeper in my chest. "I think I need this. Has there really been a moment where I've relived everything Dad meant to me?" It's a question, but I'm not sure if it's for me. "There's a lot of positive memories here, but then I think about why we were even here in the first place, and I get confused."

"Confusion is okay. It's natural. Focus on what you decided that morning you woke in my family's mansion."

She pulls from my arms and wipes tears away from her eyes. "I know. I'm trying. He did what he had to for his own reasons."

She moves away so I let her. She enters the kitchen, her gaze locked outside to the backyard. I'm taken back to when I spotted her staring out this window, when I was stalking her from the outside and made my first kill in her name.

"Marie and I spent a lot of time outside in the warm months because Dad wasn't a fan of the outdoors. He often came home tired." She faces me again, her gaze more distracted than earlier. "Talked about being sore, but as a kid, you don't question these things, you know? It all makes sense now, I guess."

I nod, giving her the mental space to go where she needs to.

She stares over my shoulder, back into the living room. I'm starting to get they spent a lot of time in there together.

"That was where I first learned to read," she murmurs. "It's where Dad handed me my first book. Where Marie and I did my school work. If I wasn't alone in my bedroom, I was right there, on that couch."

Tears form in her eyes again and she shakes her head but says nothing. Twice, she tries, and I'm seconds away from ripping her away from this painful place when she finally talks.

"I can't do this, Rafael. Not today...I can't."

"That's fine." I stretch my hand for her to take. "You don't have to."

I expect her to fight the offer, like she has any other time, but she takes my hand. I begin walking to the door, and she follows, but her gaze remains behind her.

"Belle?"

She tips her head to the side and leads me to the couch. She sits, pulling me down with her.

Just stares at the floor.

Tears build in her eyes again.

And she cries.

She cries out what she's spent so many days and weeks, holding inside her. Her grief emerges like a wave, and I sit there silently, holding her hand as she grips the life from me.

After nearly an hour, she wipes her face, stands, and leads me from the house.

She's silent as we get back into my car, although I'm watching her, waiting for it to hit again. It never does.

"You know, in some weird way, I'd think Dad would be happy how this turned out. He gave me you."

The man who was protective of his daughter might not approve of her getting with a mobster, but she could also be right. There's no one in this world that will protect her better than I will.

"I love you too, Belle."

48
RAFAEL

Nico rests the black, velvet ring box on my desk, still open. The engagement ring instantly brings a smile to my face. I had it custom-designed and picked it up earlier today. A single princess-cut diamond, surrounded by smaller citrine gems, one on either side, shines in my office's lighting.

"Still can't fucking believe it," my brother says, chuckling. "I definitely thought I would have had to drug your ass to get you to the end of an aisle."

Shutting the ring box, I place it in my desk drawer, to keep it safe until I'm ready to give it to *ma belle*. "You probably would have if it was anyone other than Isabelle."

"All your bitching about doing your duties, and turns out, this is the one time it definitely paid off."

My gaze drifts to the drawer again. "That it did."

"When are you giving it to her? Considering she's already agreed to marry you."

I rock back in the chair. "She did but I'm waiting a few more weeks until I think she's ready. She's still processing everything and there's been so much change in her life in such a short time, I don't want to rush her."

My brother grins, knowing the feelings swirling inside me, even without me stating them. "You're nervous."

My shrug is to downplay the truth, but he sees right through it and laughs.

"Maybe," I grunt. "But you can't tell me you weren't either when you gave Della a ring." And I know for a fact, like Isabelle and me, they agreed to be engaged before he officially proposed.

That wipes the humour from his sly expression. "Fuck you. Ever think you're not giving her enough credit?"

I level Nico with a glare, amusement coming at me slowly until I laugh. "Damn, brother, you approve of her, don't you?"

"Maybe I just approve of how happy you are with her." His phone buzzes, cutting through the air. He glances at it and turns for my office's door. "You look at her how I look at Della, so that's how I know she's right for you. And speaking of Della," he shakes his phone and opens my door, "I'm meeting with her. Bye, Raf."

The moment the door's shut behind him and I'm laughing off the interaction, I return to the paperwork all over my desk that I was working through before Nico randomly dropped by Eden. He knew I was picking up the ring today, so I think in his strange brotherly fashion, he was using a random drop-in to check it out.

My phone rings just as I pick up my pen.

BELLE

Come find me in Room 4.

Not thinking twice about her offer, I abandon my work again and exit my office, passing the various couples already here in the main lounge area. We've recently opened for the night, so the club is still winding up.

Room four is simple to find, considering it's the one I caught her in the very first time, when she watched the couple, and then we observed the threesome together. When everything between us took off.

I enter, switching the door to the locked position, immersing myself in the darkness. She's not there, but the light is on in the room beside it, and somehow, I know what I'll find before I do.

She's sprawled on that same bed I fucked her on when we were having our "final" night, observed by others. Her legs are spread, her breasts arched to the sky, and two fingers deep in her pussy.

"Rafael." Her moan comes through the connected speakers. She's obviously turned everything on for this moment. "When I fuck myself, it's your cock I imagine."

Pressing my hands against the glass, I lean into the vision, willing myself to break through the window to get to her. It'd be easy to exit the room and go next door, but she directed me to this one for a reason, so I'll stick it out.

For now.

Her lips curl deviously as she peers over, spotting me. Her hips rock, her thighs falling open wider, her moans building with every stroke of her fingers.

"It's not enough. I crave you, Rafael. I have to show you what you do to me."

I head for my tablet, flicking on the connecting speakers, which will allow me to reply. "*Ma belle*, you're teasing me."

"I am. I was just reading a sex scene." Then she lifts something from the bed I hadn't noticed before.

Her fucking Kindle.

"Describe the scene," I demand, hands forming fists over the glass, determination to be near her growing.

"I'll read it to you later."

"Belle." I growl, eyes unable to look anywhere else but her core taking her slim fingers. I long to remove her hand and fuck her the way she deserves. "Belle, you're playing with fire."

"So come to me."

My hands can't push me off the glass fast enough as I back out of the room, shoving by a couple stumbling down the hall, until I reach the next door, throwing it open immediately.

She pulls her fingers from her core, the room's light catching on her juices as she grins.

"Ah, there's my beast."

"Et voilà ma beauté." And there's my beauty.

And what do you know? The beast really fucking loves to devour his beauty.

Thank you for reading! Continue the series with The Freedom in Captivity (Fractured Ever Afters #4), a Rapunzal inspired second-chance romance between Rozelyn & Flynn.

Shop signed books by scanning the code below:

ALSO BY M.L. PHILPITT

Fractured Ever Afters

A 6-book (& 2 novellas) mafia romance series of interconnected standalones based on fairytales, featuring the Montreal mafia and the New York Famiglia.

The Desire in Deception (Prequel Novella)

The Hunt in Elusion

The Craving in Slumber

The Beauty in Scars

The Freedom in Captivity

The Sound in Silencea

The Obscurity in Wishing

The Bonds in Christmas (Epilogue Novella)

The Bratva's Elite

A 4-book mafia series of interconnected standalones featuring the Russian Bratva.

Merciless Queen

Deadly Knight

Defensive Rook

Violent Pawn

Captive Writings

A new adult suspenseful romance series that progressively gets darker with each book

Ruthless Letters

Obsessive Messages

Vicious Texts

Burning Notes

Twisted Holidays

A series of dark romance holiday novellas

Silent Night

Egg Hunt

Fright Night

Be Mine

Midnight Kiss

Lucky Clover

Black Magick

A 5-book paranormal romance series of interconnected standalones
featuring witches, vampires, shifters, mortals, and demons.

Dark Flame

Dark Mist

Dark Storm

Standalones

A Vampire for Christmas

Audiobooks

Silent Night

ACKNOWLEDGMENTS

First and foremost, thank you to YOU - my readers.

To my betas: Megan, Colleen, & Lee Jacquot - Thank you!

Thank you to my editor Rebecca Barney from Fairest Reviews Editing Services. Another book down!

To Megan, my PA, who keeps me on track.

Thank you to The Next Step PR. Colleen, Megan, Anna, and of course, Kiki - you're all amazing. Thank you for everything you do. You're the best team to have!

Thank you to Cat Imb of TRC Designs for creating this premade cover which I snatched up instantly knowing it was ideal for the Beauty and the Beast mafia romance idea I once had. Who knew it'd turn into a series and end up becoming the cover to the 3rd book?

Thank you to Karina (@id_rather.be.the.moon) for double checking my French.

Thank you to all the bloggers, booktokers, and bookstagrammers who helped with the release of this book. Your help doesn't go unnoticed!

ABOUT THE AUTHOR

USA Today Bestselling author M.L. Philpitt writes both dark romance and paranormal romance. When she's not writing made-up realities, she's reading them. She lives in Canada with her four pets and survives life with coffee and an obsession with fictional characters, especially the morally grey kind. By day, she masks as a therapist.

WARNINGS

- Explicit sexual content
- Death
- Parental death
- Murder
- Physical violence
- Depictions of grief
- Kidnapping (not by main characters)
- Exhibitionism
- Voyeurism